BRIARHILL TO BROOKLYN

BRIARHILL

TO

BROOKLYN

AN IRISH FAMILY'S JOURNEY
TO FREEDOM AND OPPORTUNITY

JACK BODKIN

JOHN S. BODKIN, JR.
www.BriarhilltoBrooklyn.com

Library of Congress Cataloging-in-Publication data is available.

ISBN (paperback): 978-1-7363787-0-0
ISBN (hardcover): 978-1-7363787-2-4
ISBN (ebook): 978-1-7363787-1-7

Book design and production by Domini Dragoone
Cover painting: "Opportunity" © Rodney Charman

Images in the text: Maps © Alan Gilliland, "Below Deck" © Rodney Charman,
"Galway Girl" © Sally Plemich, "Georgie" and "Briarhill Cottage" © Dan Buchwach,
O'Donnell portrait courtesy of Diocese of Galway Kilmacduagh & Kilfenora.
All other images are in the public domain, or from the author's extended
family's personal collection.

This is a work of creative nonfiction. Some parts have been fictionalized in
varying degrees, for various reasons, and for various purposes. Many of the
characters in *Briarhill to Brooklyn* are fictitious. They bear no basis in the reality
which may, or may not, have existed in the nineteenth century. The individual
names of those fictitious characters may be similar to the names of people the
author has known throughout his life. Some of those people are living and
several are deceased. In a few cases, the characters and the role associated
with a name may bear certain consistencies of a profession, or a personality,
to an actual person with that particular name. Any similarities are intended
to be complimentary. The scenes, events, and conversations depicted in
Briarhill to Brooklyn are the product of the author's imagination.

For my granddaughter, Sally
... live, learn, and remember.

CONTENTS

Bodkin

THE FAMILY

DA: John Bodkin (c. 1798–1848) 50

MAM: Eleanor O'Donnell Bodkin (c. 1800–1848) 48

The Children:

MARY: Mary Bodkin Duval (1825–1878) 53
MARY'S SPOUSE: Daniel Duval

CATE: Catherine Bodkin (1827–1912) 85

BIDDY: Adelia Bodkin Flanagan (1831–1881) 50
BIDDY'S SPOUSE: Michael Flanagan

DOMINIC: Dominic George Bodkin, M.D. (1834–1902) 68

MARTIN: Martin R. Bodkin (1835–1912) 77
MARTIN'S SPOUSE: Pamela Eliza Densmer (1839–1917) 78

LAWRENCE: Lawrence P. Bodkin (1838–1896) 58
LAWRENCE'S SPOUSE: Maggie

JOHN: John "Angel" Stanley Bodkin (1839–1894) 55
JOHN'S SPOUSE: Catherine "Kate" McGivney

NELLIE: Eleanor Bodkin (1839–c. 1880) 41

THE BISHOP: Laurence O'Donnell (1777–1855) 78

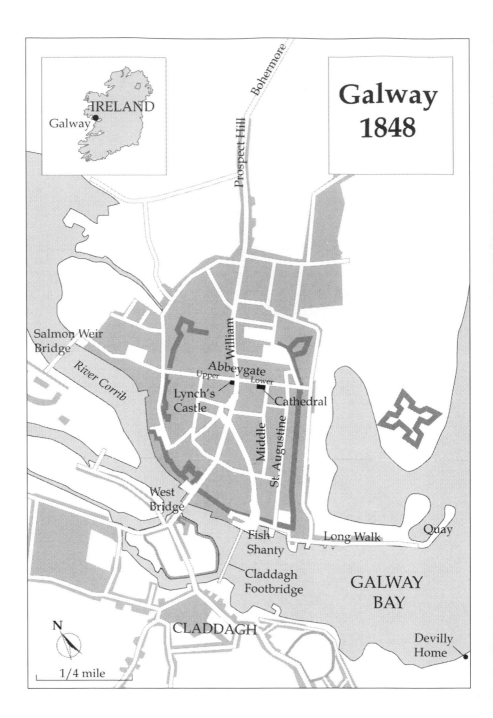

PROLOGUE

8:23 AM: *It was January 23, 1902, and as I stood in the cold vestibule of our decaying cathedral—waiting for the pallbearers to receive their instructions from the undertaker—me thoughts wandered through a lifetime gone by. At the age of sixty-plus-six years, many of the memories of me life as a young lad in County Galway had faded. Me old brain held paintings of people, places, or events, and all of the colors on the canvasses were similar, but different shades of grey. One event, which I clearly remembered, took place in our cottage in Briarhill. It happened more than fifty years ago. February of 1848, it was ...*

"John, do todhchaí ár bpáistí, ní mór dúinn dul go Meiriceá," me mam said, looking straight into Da's eyes. Her words, etched in me brain forever, startled me. "John, for the future of our children, we must go to America."

Nine of us crowded around the table, and as usual, Mam had boiled a potful of lumpers with turnips and butter from a neighbor's cow. "We might not starve to death, John, but the fever will surely get us." The finality in her voice tore at me. Me brothers and sisters, those who were old enough to comprehend her words, looked stunned. I knew Mam was right. She usually was.

Later that night, Da said that he wanted me to walk to Galway City with him in the morning to see Uncle Laurence. Uncle was the Catholic bishop of Galway, and Da said he needed to talk to him before we could go to America. Was Da going to ask for his approval for the family to leave Ireland? Was he just going to tell him we were leaving for America? I wasn't sure, but I was over the moon that Da had asked me to walk with him. He had chosen me instead of Dominic.

The morning was cold, but fortunately no rain fell. I was still a young lad—twelve—and the six-mile walk from our cottage to Galway was easy. Me and Da talked as we walked. He went on and on about the problems the people of Galway were facing. He said everyone claimed America was a land of opportunity, and young people like me, and me brothers and sisters, would have a far better future in America than we would ever have in Ireland. At the young age I was, it was a surprising conversation for Da to be having with me. Was he practicing what he would say to Uncle Laurence? Me head spun with the excitement of going to America.

The hills on the path to Galway were no bother to me, but Da was breathing heavy when we got to the top of the big road called the Bohermore. From there we could see to the bottom of the hill toward the city. The small, attached, white cottages lining both sides of Prospect Hill had smoke billowing out of their chimneys; peat fires would burn all day at this time of year. Our path was downhill now. We couldn't see Galway Bay yet, but the smell of the sea filled me imagination with visions of a voyage to a new world. A seagull soared in the distance.

At the bottom of the Bohermore, we walked through a muddy parcel of land. It was all that remained of Galway's ancient city gates. Peasants overflowed the space, large families like our own crowding around small fires. We entered Galway City and passed hundreds more peasants of all generations, waiting in a soup line which wound along the grey cobblestones of William Street. Families waiting for hours to get a cup of watery soup made with some meat and vegetables—and if they were fortunate, they collected a small sack of cornmeal to be boiled into some liquid mush.

Da put his big hand on me shoulder, and mine was around his hip, as we walked past a family huddled in front of a shop. The mother and father wept over the body of their son. His young brothers and sisters held each other, standing silently by their parents. I didn't want to look—but I did—and found the face of the dead boy. He might have been the same age as me, but it was hard to tell. His sunken cheeks, spindly limbs, and swollen belly made reckoning his years difficult. The lad's dark eyes were frightening, as was the soft downy hair that had grown on his face while he starved.

"Don't look, Martin," Da almost whispered as he guided me away.

The front of the soup line was at old Lynch's Castle on Upper Abbeygate Street, where three elderly nuns—Sisters of Mercy, Da said—ladled soup from a steaming cauldron into tin cups. A fat British overseer barked at one of the sisters, "Remember, papist! Only one cup per person!" Someone should have driven a stake through the son-of-a-bitch's heart—to this day I wish I had. The Sassenach hated us. We all knew. Da told us whole families would have to stand in the soup line all day. If a young cailín or an old granny was to get a cup of soup, she stood in the line.

As we walked farther, I saw more starving children shuffling along next to their parents. Many wore no shoes on the cold cobblestones. Their heads were down, blank eyes staring at the ground.

We turned left at the castle and walked along to Lower Abbeygate, where the old cathedral stood. Me father's face showed concern. Was it fear?

Uncle Laurence's rectory was next to the cathedral. Da banged the shiny, brass door knocker against a well-worn spot on the rectory's oak door, and a woman with a pretty face appeared and welcomed us into the parlor. She and Da seemed to know each other. He greeted her and said, "Kitty, this is my son Martin—Martin Bodkin." He beamed with pride. She smiled at me and told Da to go ahead into the bishop's study. Kitty motioned for me to have a seat in a chair in the parlor. I sat and waited nervously, recalling what I'd seen since we entered Galway City. The image of the dead boy's face was frozen in my mind. Finally, after nearly an hour, the door to the bishop's study creaked as it swung open, and Da walked over ...

1

A DOCTOR'S DAY IS
NEVER OVER

December 19, 1894

THE SHIP'S STEWARD, CHARLES TILTON, WAS ORGANIZ-
ing the service stand in the corner of the dining room on the SS
Gallia. It was the third week of December 1894, and the *Gallia* was
bound for New York from Liverpool, England. Its elegant dining
room was comparable to the ballroom of a first-class New York
City hotel. The elite passengers expected high ceilings, polished
hardwood floors, linen tablecloths and napkins, fine china, crystal stemware, and a Tiffany silver service during their voyage. A
string quartet played softly in the corner.

Tonight had been the last dinner before the arrival in New
York. Dinner was now over, and Charles was setting places for
tomorrow's morning meal. The cabin passengers were always
early for the breakfast service on the day they arrived in New
York Harbor, and Charles would have everything in order. The
morning would bring a sense of relief that the trip was over, and
the sight of the ever-growing city skyline would bring a feeling of
excitement and anticipation.

For a little more than a decade, the Statue of Liberty welcomed ships arriving at New York Harbor, and everyone wanted to see "the Lady." It didn't matter if it was a person's first time to see her or the fifth. It was always exciting. Before daybreak, as the *Gallia* approached land, every passenger—the cabin passengers as well as steerage—would be allowed on deck; they would press against the ship's railings to see the majestic statue as she welcomed everyone at the entrance of New York Harbor.

Dr. Dominic George Bodkin

After dinner, as Charles set up for breakfast, there were only a handful of passengers left in the dining room, and he offered the last cups of coffee from a silver pot.

Charles Tilton had been doing his job as a steward—and doing it well—for nearly twenty years. He was nineteen years old when Abraham Lincoln emancipated the American slaves.

"More coffee, Dr. Bodkin?"

The doctor nodded, but knew he shouldn't. "Yes, please. Just a little more."

Dr. Dominic George Bodkin knew he should stop drinking coffee. It was burning a hole in his stomach. He didn't smoke or drink alcohol, but he did love his coffee. He drank it black. The first cup of coffee he ever drank was on a different ship—a Civil War troop transport, USS *Catawba*, heading to New Orleans from New York City. In 1865, near the end of the United States' Civil

War, Dominic had been assigned to the Union Army's hospital at Fort Gaines—outside of Mobile, Alabama.

Bodkin looked into his coffee cup and tugged at his long, bushy, grey beard. He was tired. After all, he was an old man now. But fortunately, this voyage across the Atlantic had been comfortable. The *Gallia* was a transatlantic steamer ship, and in 1894, the crossing only took eight days. Navigating the cold, windy, and stormy North Atlantic was significantly easier than it had been on his first trip to America nearly half a century ago. He was a first-class passenger now. He wasn't in steerage as he had been with his family on the first trip. In March and April of 1848, Dominic, his da and mam, his three brothers, three of his four sisters, and two of his cousins had been in the belly of a packet ship, the *Cushlamachree*, under sail out of Galway, Ireland. That voyage took thirty-six days to cross the Atlantic. Dominic was just a boy. He was three weeks short of his fourteenth birthday when he first stepped down the *Cushlamachree's* gangway onto the lower east side of Manhattan Island.

In December 1894, however, traveling first-class on the voyage meant porters, maids, and waiters for Dominic. On the *Gallia*, the crew attempted to heat his cabin, and there was fresh water to drink. The food was well preserved and expertly prepared. Meals always ended with interesting political or economic discussions with his fellow passengers as they sipped their glasses of brandy or port and smoked expensive cigars in the saloon. But now, Dominic could imagine the end of his life more vividly than he could remember his days as a boy.

Charles Tilton placed a folded piece of notepaper on Dominic's table. "Dr. Bodkin, sir, there is a message for you from Mr. Kantor."

"Thank you, Charles." Dominic opened the note.

Dr. Bodkin,
Robert and Stuart are smoking cigars with me in the saloon
and we would be pleased to share your company after you
have finished your supper. Another of our fellow passengers,
the Englishman named Wilson, is currently experiencing some
discomfort in his belly and would appreciate your professional
opinion. Please join us.

—David Kantor

"Charles, would you be so kind as to bring another cup of coffee to me in the saloon? I'm going to join Mr. Kantor and the other gentlemen for a while before I retire for the evening."

"Yes, sir, Dr. Bodkin. I'll bring it right in."

⬦⬦⬦ ⬦⬦⬦ ⬦⬦⬦

The buttons on Wilson's waistcoat were stretching to the point that they looked as though they would burst open any minute. A coughing fit nearly caused him to spill his snifter of brandy.

"What seems to be the problem, Wilson?" Dominic asked the fifty-year-old Englishman.

Wilson laid his cigar in an ashtray and put his brandy on the table. "I've got a pain in my belly, Dr. Bodkin," he answered with a grimace. Dominic watched as Wilson placed his hand on the upper-right section of his abdomen. "The cramping started just after dinner."

"It could be some gas, Wilson. Or, in the worst case, you've got some stones in your gallbladder. I suggest you call it a night and try to get some rest. I think it's just gas. But please, sir, if you still have pain in the morning, find me, and I'll get you to a hospital in New York." Wilson's face showed relief. Dominic looked at the portly Wilson, his burning cigar, and the snifter of brandy. He continued, "Sir, I believe that controlling the intake of food and complete abstinence from alcohol is the key to good health. I suggest you consider that in the future."

Wilson looked askance at Dominic and said, "Thank you, Bodkin." He picked up his cigar and turned his attention to the steward who had just entered the saloon.

"Your coffee, Dr. Bodkin, and a message from Captain Boehmcke that a pregnant woman in steerage requires your attention."

"Thank you, Charles. Good night, gentlemen." Dominic took a swallow of his coffee and rushed out of the room.

Dominic knew some patients were not pleased with his advice. But the very experienced, internationally well-known, and respected Dominic George Bodkin, M.D., of Brooklyn, New York, wasn't fazed by that anymore, and he had earned the right—*no, he had an obligation*—to tell them what he thought. Between meals, card games, and the occasional afternoon nap on the *Gallia*, the doctor frequently found time to render aid to the pregnant, sick, and sometimes dying passengers traveling in the *Gallia*'s steerage compartment. Fortunately, deaths on board weren't as common now as they were in the 1840s and '50s. The Irish Coffin Ships, as the packet ships were known back in those days, frequently reported the loss of thirty percent of their steerage passengers. Burial was at sea.

Dr. Bodkin's excellent medical reputation and leadership skills required him to cross the Atlantic several times to represent

New York medical societies at international conferences. He had traveled to meetings in London, Paris, Berlin, and Moscow. In years past, Dominic had sailed with his brother John, and they would take detours to the place where they were born—a County Galway townland called Briarhill.

Tonight was the end of the doctor's third trip to Europe in the last twenty years. This trip wasn't business or pleasure, though. John wasn't with him this time. This trip was to say farewell to Ireland and goodbye to Nellie.

Well beyond midnight—after delivering a baby girl in steerage—Dominic was finally able to attempt sleep in his first-cabin bunk, but rest didn't come easily. Memories of Nellie, his youngest sister, haunted him.

As he returned to New York for the last time, he couldn't escape the grainy images his sixty-year-old mind held of sweet little Nellie: Nellie riding in the back of the cart the day the family left Briarhill; Nellie frightened and weeping on the Galway quay; Nellie lonely and depressed as a teenager in Brooklyn. These were images that made his heart ache, made him question his intelligence, and made him doubt his compassion. He took some solace in knowing that Nellie eventually led the life she wanted in the tiny stone cottage in Briarhill, but the memory of the recurring nightmare still persisted.

He thought about their lives as children in Galway and the unusual things he had experienced in his life, starting with the day they left Briarhill in 1848.

Brooklyn, New York, and Briarhill, Ireland, were different worlds, and his family's first journey to Brooklyn began many decades ago.

INIS MÓR

July 1834

ON A CLOUDY NIGHT ON THE ISLAND OF INIS MÓR, IT could be so dark Séamus might not see his hand, even if he held it right in front of his face. As he prepared for sleep, he thought, *Tonight is one of those nights.* Séamus was only twenty-six years old, with a face already bright red and weathered from being in the elements, in the wind. His missing teeth had fallen out in a pattern that left him with the ability to eat, but his smile made him look like a madman. He anticipated he would die within five to ten years. The elements killed most men on Inis Mór before the age of forty. If he died in five years, his daughter would only be eight years old and destined to live her life alone in their cottage on Inis Mór. As he drifted off to sleep on this particularly cloudy night, however, Séamus' thoughts about what he planned to do tomorrow morning led him to imagine he might live to be forty. When he was forty, he knew his daughter would be seventeen, and by then, she should be able to care for herself. Tonight, he decided that tomorrow morning they would leave for the mainland.

The largest of the three Aran Islands, Inis Mór, was twelve square miles of limestone, which separated from the mainland of Ireland hundreds of millions of years ago. Grasses, plants, and shrubs of all kinds survived on the island, but hardly anything as tall as a tree. Séamus built his cottage on a southern point, on the east coast of the island. It stood on a slight plateau, which was about seventy-five feet above the beach. From the back window of his one-room cottage, he watched the sunrise every morning. After the sun was up, he could clearly see Inis Mór's neighboring island, Inis Meán, and looking much farther off into the sunrise, he could see the Irish coast, but, of course, the farthest he had ever sailed in his curragh was Inis Meán. He had never been to the mainland. The body of water connecting the North Atlantic Ocean to Galway Bay was usually choppy and foreboding—called the North Sound, it separated Inis Mór from the mainland. The westerly winds and the strong currents in the North Sound were unpredictable. Frequently, the currents pushed and pulled vessels toward Galway Bay while the wind ripped the white tops off the ocean's waves in the same direction.

From time to time over the years, Séamus had heard of a few men who left from the beach in a large curragh. Sometimes, he would hear of a husband and wife sailing off in a smaller boat. They were all trying to make it to the mainland. But no one ever came back, so their neighbors on Inis Mór never knew whether they made it to the Irish coast, or if the North Sound's currents had dragged them in the opposite direction—to a horrible death out in the stormy North Atlantic. The men and women who sailed away from Inis Mór were chasing the fantasy of a better life, perhaps at the risk of death. The stories handed from generation to generation fantasized about mainlanders earning money by working in the bogs—cutting peat for the turf fires that heated cottages, castles, and shops all over Ireland. Mainlanders, Séamus had been told, could travel safely by land to places like Dublin or Sligo.

Until today, Séamus had never had the nerve to try to get to the mainland in his small curragh, but he believed that if its single sail caught the westerly wind, the currents in the North Sound would pull him east, toward the mainland of Ireland. The sixteen-foot curragh had been his father's boat and his grandfather's, before that. A few years ago, Séamus had replaced the animal hide stretched over the original wooden framework, and he had rigged the mast and replaced the sail several times. *On a clear day, I can see the mainland for God's sake*, Séamus thought, as his brain entered the peace of sleep. On a good day, his plan could work. For his daughter's sake, it would have to work.

If his plan failed, maybe people would assume it was a suicide; perhaps they would think it was a suicide and a murder. He wasn't sure. Maybe no one would know. What people said didn't matter to him anymore.

His wife left him five months ago. On Inis Mór there was no place to go, and when a man said his wife "left him," he meant she died. He buried Siobhán on the plateau between the cottage and the water. He saw her grave every time he looked to the sea and every morning as he watched the sunrise. Séamus covered the place where he buried her with stones he gathered from around the property. The grave marker was six feet long and two feet tall. Siobhán had been a tall woman, but the six-foot grave marker made her even taller in his memory. She would be on Inis Mór forever. Séamus made sure her marker would be there forever, too.

Séamus and Siobhán's only child had her third birthday on the day Siobhán died.

When Séamus awoke from his restless sleep, he went outside to measure the wind as it buffeted the northeast corner of his cottage. He thought the wind seemed right. He went back inside to rouse his little girl from her sleep.

"*Dúisigh, mo stór. Tá sé ina mhaidin.*" Wake up, my treasure. It is morning. Séamus whispered as he brushed strands of red hair from his sleeping daughter's forehead.

"*Dúisigh, Honora beag.*" Wake up, little Honora. "*Tá sé am chun dul, mo stór.*" It's time to go, my dear.

Honora's eyes blinked awake, and the first thing she saw was her father's face.

"*Maidin mhaith, Dhaidí. An lá an taistil atá inniu ann?*" Good morning, Daddy. Is today the day of our voyage?

"*Sea, mo stór. Is é inniu an lá.*" Yes, my treasure. Today is the day.

Séamus and Honora closed the cottage door as they left their home.

Father and daughter stopped behind the cottage, at Siobhán's grave, to say a final prayer and goodbye. Over the past weeks, Séamus frequently found himself standing at Siobhán's grave, asking for her help with his decision. But today, the die was cast. His silent plea to Siobhán was for help with the winds and the currents—he prayed she would keep a watchful eye on Honora.

Honora reached for her father's hand, and they walked together to the water's edge, where Séamus helped her over the curragh's square stern. He had her sit on the bench closest to where he would sit as he rowed. He pushed the curragh from the water's edge and guided it into the small waves that were lapping onto the sandy shore.

Séamus climbed into the curragh, set the oars, and started to row.

STRÓC! STRÓC! STRÓC! STRÓC! STRÓC!

With each stroke, he watched his little girl. For a while, he could see Siobhán's grave marker, too, but it grew smaller and smaller until finally Siobhán was gone forever.

After an hour of rowing against the incoming waves, his muscles screamed and his heart pounded. He was far enough from the island that he could finally feel the wind on his face.

He stood up, balanced himself, and set the sail up to the top of the mast.

As the sail began to catch the full breeze, he sat back down at the stern of his boat with his little girl. From his seat, he could manage the tiller. He made sure Honora was as secure as a three-year-old could be, out in the open water in a sixteen-foot curragh. He let the westerly wind carry the curragh away from Inis Mór and maneuvered the rudder as he sailed toward the mainland of Ireland and their future.

Thirty-six hours later, a small crowd of fishermen gathered at the shoreline in the small seaside village of An Spideál, on the western coast of Ireland.

On the last day of their 1834 summer holiday from their diocesan responsibilities, two Catholic priests were celebrating with a pint of ale and a sunset view of Galway Bay.

As they walked onto the beach at An Spideál, they saw the crowd of fishermen. Something out of the ordinary was taking place at the water's edge. The fishermen had gathered around a small curragh, which had beached on the rocky shore. A gash was evident in the curragh's animal-hide hull, and her sail was torn from its mast and draped over the side of the small vessel—half in the boat and half in the water. The closer the two priests got to the curragh, the more obvious the tragic scene became.

The unconscious body of the sailor was slumped near the stern, his hand still grasping the tiller.

A young child, cold and shivering, huddled at the sailor's feet.

"He must be her father," a fisherman said. "Get the child out of the boat and away from the man's body."

"Get her a blanket!" someone shouted.

"Go find a woman to care for her."

"What is your name, child?"

"Where have you come from?"

"She needs water!"

"How old are you, little girl?"

The fishermen were all shouting questions and yelling commands at the same time, and no one received any answer from the little girl, whose long red hair had been matted against her face by the salty spray from the white-capped waves.

They looked at one another, and no one knew what to do next.

The older of the two priests stepped closer to the crowd of fishermen and said, "Allow me to try."

"*Cad is ainm duit, a cailín óg?*" The man in black smiled as he asked the little girl what her name was.

"Haaw…" The child seemed to hesitate. "Haaw," she repeated before timidly finishing her answer to the priest's question. "Haaw—nohraa." The girl finally looked up at the man, her blue eyes tired and frightened.

"*Bhuel anois. Tá sé iontach bualadh le cailín chomh deas leatsa, a Nora bheag.*" Well, now. It's nice to meet a girl as nice as you, little Nora.

"*Cad as a tháinig do bhád, a Nora?*" The priest asked her where the boat came from.

She offered no words but pointed out into the water, toward Inis Mór, and the priest nodded.

"*Cén aois atá tú, a Nora?*" The priest thought the girl looked to be around four or five years old.

"*Tá mé trí bliana d'aois!*" The three-year-old replied with a strong voice, as she smiled proudly at the man.

One of the fishermen examined the sailor more closely, as he released the man's grip from the tiller. "He might as well have gone to Jones' locker, lads. He's as dead as Davy Jones can be."

"Alrighty then, three-year-old Nora Jones from Inis Mór," the priest said to the little girl. "I know someone who will take good care of you."

LEAVING BRIARHILL

March 17, 1848
The Journey Begins

THE YOUNG, RED-HAIRED PASTOR'S VOICE REVERBER-
ated through the small church. *"In nomine Patris, et Filii, et Spiritus
Sancti. Amen."*

His right hand touched his right shoulder with a flourish to
complete the sign of the cross, as he turned to look straight at the
Bodkin family. *"Ite, missa est,"* he instructed his congregation. The
thirty parishioners replied, *"Deo gratias,"* and the Mass at Saint
Columba's was over. It was March 17, 1848, and John and Eleanor
Bodkin knew their family would "go forth," after a small gathering to wish the family well on their trip to America.

Daniel Duval's father was a contractor who lived in Galway City,
and Dan was trying to carry on the family business in the townlands. He had a cart and two horses that he used most days to
haul beams, stone, and the thatching he layered on the roofs of

homes he was building. Unfortunately, construction jobs were scarce this year, so the business could spare Dan, the cart, and his horses for the few days it would take to transport the Bodkins to Galway, visit with his parents, and return home. Daniel was married to Mary, the Bodkins' eldest daughter. Today, her da would drive the two-horse team, and the Bodkin family would spend the first night of their trip at the Duvals' home, in sight of the quays at Galway Harbor.

Mary and her sister Cate sat with Daniel and Da on the front bench of the cart. The driver's seat was only wide enough for three of them, but they would squeeze together. "How long of a ride will it be, Daniel?" Mary asked. The young couple had been married the previous year and lived in Castlegar, halfway between Galway and Briarhill. Mary was holding their infant son, Lucas, bundled in blankets, to shield him from the cold March air. "We should arrive long before dark, *a stór.*"

The men and boys all wore woolen caps and bulky overcoats to protect them from the cold wind. Mam and the girls had blankets wrapped around long dresses, and woolen scarves covered their heads. Da held a pipe in his teeth, and his beard helped to warm his face as he encouraged the horses to keep moving with their heavy load. The Bodkins had two trunks and two cloth bags that held everything they owned.

The trip to Galway would be very uncomfortable for Daniel Duval. He would be driving back home to Castlegar, alone with his wife and baby, and Mary would be crying, not knowing if she would ever see her family again. It would not be pleasant. Sitting on the outside seat of the front bench of the cart, Daniel had his left arm around Mary's shoulders to support and warm his family.

It would be a gut-wrenching trip for the rest of the Bodkins, too. Different emotions pulled at them. They talked with excitement about the new path the family was taking, the opportunities, and the freedom they were seeking. They had nothing left to lose, yet they voiced fears about the trip and their separation from Mary, as well as every other friend they had. It would be painful.

Mary had been lucky to meet and fall in love with Dan. He was a young man with a good head on his shoulders. He had a business and a plan for his life, an unusual combination around County Galway in 1848. There were many good young men in Galway, but not many had a future. As long as Dan's business worked out, Mary could have a sweet life with him in Castlegar, or Moycullen, or even in Briarhill. Wherever they decided, Daniel would build a house, and together they would make it a home and raise their family.

When Mam and Da Bodkin decided to sell what little they had and leave their beloved Ireland, they knew the moment would come when they would have to say goodbye to twenty-three-year-old Mary. Mam and Da saw no hope in Briarhill for their other children—life was hard in western Ireland in 1848; the couple had no hope for themselves either. Too many friends, neighbors, and relatives had died. Families they knew were separated, forever, at the gates of the Galway workhouse. "Adults this way, children that way," the workhouse keeper would yell. In County Galway, young orphan children were starving to death, dying alone, in homes where their parents had died months before. A decision was required, and John and Eleanor Bodkin made it. The risk of contracting typhus, known as "the fever," or cholera, was too great. They were going to America.

The cottage they rented in Briarhill belonged to Mam's brother, Laurence O'Donnell. Years ago, the cottage's builder used flat limestones, collected from the surrounding land, to construct the walls. Its steeply angled roof was covered with thatch, to protect from the rain and the infrequent snows. The Bodkins warmed the cottage by burning blocks of peat in the

Briarhill Cottage

fireplace. The family sliced peat each day during the spring, summer, and fall, at a nearby bog.

The cottage was the Bodkin family's salvation. Living in a place owned by Uncle Laurence meant John Bodkin did not pay rent to a hateful and unscrupulous landlord; he did not have the threat of eviction hanging over his head. The meager wages John earned provided necessities, and he occasionally saved a few shillings in a jar. The mysterious blights in 1845 and 1846 killed only a small percentage of the family's lumpers, and the family joked that their potato patch was "blessed" by Uncle Laurence. The family did not have as much as they wanted, but they had enough potatoes to live on—and even enough to share with neighbors. They were not overwhelmed by the fear of starvation, and they did not fear a landlord. They considered themselves to be the luckiest "poor" family in County Galway.

The Bodkin children called Laurence Uncle—but everyone else knew him as Bishop Laurence O'Donnell. He was consecrated as the second bishop of the Catholic Diocese of Galway only four years earlier, in 1844. Before becoming a bishop, his parish was only a few kilometers away from Briarhill, in Castlegar. In the early 1800s, he held his Masses, funerals, weddings, and baptisms in secrecy—in barns, homes, and open fields. As the British had loosened their grip on the Irish, and the Penal Laws had slowly been dismantled, his church eventually became an actual physical structure. The church, Saint Columba's, was initially built in 1828 by Father Andrew Martyn. It was in that church where Father O'Donnell and Father Martyn had baptized the youngest of the Bodkin children. The children's godparents included several O'Donnell cousins as well as friends and neighbors—Michael Diskin, Patt and Bernard Flatly, Peter and Mary Kirwan, and Ann Joyce—who were all from around Briarhill and Castlegar.

While he was the pastor at Castlegar, Uncle Laurence spent many afternoons at the Bodkins' cottage in Briarhill. He worked with the children on the Three R's—Reading, wRiting, and aRithmetic. The well-educated priest taught the children in both Irish and English. Mam could not read or write, so she would sit with the children and learn along with them. Da was always working, and thus he never joined in the lessons. Like most of the families in County Galway in the middle of the nineteenth century, the Bodkin household spoke both Irish and English. The British had discouraged and suppressed the use of the native Irish language for two hundred years, with their aim being to eliminate its existence, and, throughout most of Ireland, they were accomplishing the goal. The island country's Atlantic coast—from Dingle to Connemara—was proving to be a stubborn exception, however, with many of the townlands and villages being Gaeltacht.

Mam and Da spoke mostly Irish to one another and in private conversations with friends and neighbors. Mam spoke mainly English to the children, but she reverted to Irish when she was agitated and had to get their attention or to make a disciplinary point. The children spoke almost entirely English among themselves. The boys could have gone to an English-speaking school if the family had lived closer to Galway and if they weren't Catholic. But they did not live close enough to Galway, and *they were Catholic*. School wasn't an option for the girls in any situation. Girls in Ireland—especially Catholic girls—were thought to be better off learning to cook a passable meal and keep the house clean.

Along with teaching them all to read and write in both languages, sometimes the children's amazing Uncle Laurence would expand the lessons into history, geography, science, and mathematics. He taught with stories about kings, emperors, and wars. His lessons were about the pyramids and the oceans and the bones in the body. The children learned about stars and planets. "The captain of a sailing ship uses the stars to navigate," Laurence informed them one day. "He always knows he is going in the right direction if he can find the polar star. Sometimes the polar star is called the 'north star,' because, when sailing toward it, a captain is always heading north." He taught his lessons with books, maps, and charts he had collected over many years. He taught the children how to add and subtract, how to count money, and how to make change.

Dominic was his uncle's favorite.

Uncle Laurence had moved to Galway when Dominic was about four, and Laurence had it in his mind that one of the Bodkin boys should become a priest. Dominic was always interested in the stories his uncle would tell about the different places in Ireland where he had lived while he studied in school and in the seminary—cities and towns like Belfast and Dublin, Waterford, Oughterard, Maynooth, and Shannon. He had even been across the Irish Sea to Liverpool.

Dominic listened to it all, and he asked questions.

"Why, Uncle Laurence?"

"How, Uncle Laurence?"

Laurence loved questions. So, Dominic became Laurence's prime candidate for the priesthood from the Bodkin family. Over the years, as part of Dominic's unofficial priesthood apprenticeship, Uncle Laurence would tutor young Dominic and had begun to teach him Latin and Greek. After all, every Catholic priest needed to know Latin, and many bright people knew Greek, and Dominic Bodkin was a bright, young, Irish Catholic boy who might, someday, become an excellent priest. But now his apprentice Dominic was moving to America.

Uncle Laurence came to Briarhill several days before the family's departure to help Eleanor and John in any way he could. He helped his sister while at the same time entertaining her children.

"Dominic," he called one afternoon, "find Cate and Biddy. It's time for us to go down to the patch to see if we can find some suitable lumpers still buried in your da's pit. Martin, come with us, please, and collect some scallions along the stream. Your mam wants to get the cooking pot boiling. Let's help her fill it to the top for today's meal. Your da will be home soon, children, so let's hurry along." Uncle Laurence watched as Martin led his siblings in a race over the rolling meadow behind the cottage, toward the pit Da dug to store the potatoes after they harvested. Martin continued past the pit, toward a stream that divided their property from a neighbor's, in his search for the fragrant spring onions. Uncle Laurence had helped the Bodkins financially with the trip to America, and he wanted to make sure their departure went smoothly. The priest said Mass, he heard confessions, he blessed meals, and he made the children laugh with his stories. *"Fadó,"*

Laurence would begin. "A long time ago …" And he would tell a story about growing up with Mam, in Oldchapel, just a small group of cottages—a *clachán*—on Lough Corrib, in Oughterard, a few miles north of Galway.

When the family had left the cottage on Saint Patrick's Day morning, it had been very sad. Everyone cried. At almost fourteen, Dominic was nearly a man, practically a man anyway, but he cried. And so did his da.

Their cottage was a quarter of a mile down a little boreen, which intersected with the only road in Briarhill. The nearest neighbors lived out along that road, and some of them—Jamie and Carmel Flynn, and Mickey Bellew—had come to see them off as the sun rose on another cold March morning. Jamie Flynn had been friends with Da since they met as young boys, right after the Bodkin family first moved to County Galway, forty years earlier. The friends had all shared more than a few pints at a pub called the Tigh Ó Moráin over the years, and this morning they all expressed the belief they would never see each other again.

Tears ran down Flynn's face.

The neighbors stood with Uncle Laurence and waved goodbye as the cart headed west through the morning mist, away from the rising sun, bumping its way along the narrow, stone-walled path, toward the only road in Briarhill.

Uncle Laurence made the sign of the cross, and the cart disappeared from his sight over the hill.

TROUBLE ALREADY

January 23, 1902
Saint James Cathedral, Brooklyn

8:27 AM: *The last time I stood in the vestibule of this old cathedral was six years ago. Dominic was embarrassed because he was laughing, and— like a fookin' schoolboy—he couldn't stop. After all, it was our brother Lawrence's funeral, and we should have been more respectful. But, while we waited for the undertakers to get organized, me and Dominic started reminiscing about us being in the back of Dan's old cart the day we left for America. Dominic remembered I was sitting next to Lawrence and recalled how our nine-year-old brother squealed when I poked him in his ribs right after we left Briarhill. Standing next to Dominic, in a corner of the vestibule, I mimicked Lawrence's high-pitched voice, "OUCH! MARTIN. THAT HURTS!" That's when Dominic started laughing. Jesus, I did love to torment Lawrence. I loved him, but the little sap was so skinny and timid.*

Dominic tried to stop laughing, but he couldn't. It was good to see him laugh like that. He had worked hard during his life, and he had so many responsibilities. I should have made him laugh more. Now it was too late.

Me own memory of the rest of the story was better than Dominic's ...

Mam shook her finger and swore she was going to crawl across the cart and smack me in the head if I didn't stop teasing Lawrence. But I knew—no matter what she said—she wouldn't do it. At least I hoped she wouldn't. With a sharp pitch in her voice, she told me to move away from Lawrence. "Say you're sorry and go sit with Dominic," she demanded. "Behave, or you'll have to sit next to me and little Nellie." Only fifteen minutes into our trip to America, and I was in trouble already.

The apology I made for poking Lawrence came with a sly smile. It was a way of telling him "Don't worry, I'll be back." But Mam saw me smile. The serious edge to her words, when she told me to behave, should have tipped me off that she was pissed. But it didn't, and as I crawled past Lawrence to move next to Dominic, I squeezed hard on Lawrence's leg—right above his knee. The grip caused him to emit a timid little yelp.

Mam called to Da, "Stop na capaill, John!" Me mother spoke Irish when she was mad. Da quickly brought the horses to a halt.

"Your son needs to change his seat," she explained as she grabbed me ear and dragged me next to Nellie. Nellie quickly moved over to make room.

I was in trouble a lot as a lad.

"Yes, Mam. I'm sorry, Mam. I'm sorry, Lawrence." This time with a little more sincerity.

Lawrence smiled at his victory. He leaned over to Dominic and whispered something about waiting to see if Nellie would introduce me to her "friend." We all knew Nellie had a fairy friend. Her relationship with the fairies—na daoine maithe, the good people—always amused me. She certainly believed her fairy was real. Nellie's fairy talked with her; she sang with her; she helped Nellie draw the images she saw. Me and the brothers had listened to Nellie talk to the fairy, and we knew her name was Sadhbh.

Our youngest brother, John, was only eleven months older than Nellie—Irish twins, they were—but he was sure fairies did not exist. He must have overheard what Lawrence said to Dominic and boldly told Lawrence not to make fun of Nellie. John used a quiet voice he hoped Mam wouldn't hear. He told Lawrence that Mam said Nellie was allowed to have as many "friends" as she wanted. Mam heard everything, of course, but feigned to have her attention still focused on me in the new seat next to Nellie.

Da turned in his seat and asked Mam if everything was all right in the back of the cart. The look in Father's eyes convinced me it was time to behave. Mam nodded her assurance, and Da clicked the horses with his whip. "Coinne ort, a chapall!" Da encouraged the horses, and the cart lunged ahead.

It was time for me to behave for a while. The trip from Briarhill to Galway City would take all of the afternoon, and into the evening ...

5

DA

John Bodkin

JOHN STANLEY BODKIN WAS FORTY-NINE YEARS OLD as he drove the two-horse team from Briarhill to Galway on March 17, 1848. Da had worked hard for most of his life.

When he was twelve years old, he carried marble in a Connemara quarry. At sixteen, he unloaded ships docked in Galway Harbor. When he was eighteen, he was a laborer working on the outskirts of Galway. He was doing the hard work—carrying stone, setting beams, mixing mortar. For the last ten years, good work, even the work that was hard and dirty, was challenging to find. Work that would feed his growing family of six, seven, and now eight children was almost nonexistent. He worked for house builders when he could find one who needed a laborer. They paid a fair wage. But fewer houses were being built in and around Galway, and the younger men could do more in a day than John could. So, to keep from having idle hands and to earn whatever meager wage he could, he cleared rocks and stones from the land, and he worked on building "the walls."

Many of the stone walls in western Ireland had been there for hundreds, if not thousands, of years. Stories of the Aran

Islands—twenty-five miles off the coast of Galway—recounted some of the walls on those ancient islands being built well before the time of Christ. On the mainland, when the potato crops failed, the new walls had become known as the "Famine Walls." The Famine Walls—mile after mile, stone after stone, day after day. In the rain, in the cold, in the wind, John piled stone on top of stone. The wind never stopped. Large stones on the bottom. Smaller stones on top. Four to five feet tall. Three to four feet wide. A quarter of a mile across a field. A half-mile back to the road. Up one side of a hill, down the other side. To the creek. Along the creek. Maybe the walls were designating property lines, but perhaps they were just walls separating nothing from nothing. Separating not much from not much else.

John's wage was only a pittance to work on the walls, but it kept his family out of the workhouse. It kept his family together. But the work had taken its toll. A ten-pound stone felt like ten pounds in the morning, but by afternoon it seemed more like twenty to him. The exhaustion made sleep come easy, but everything hurt now—his back, his knees, his legs, and his shoulders. His hands were large and strong, but his fingers were all gnarled—snapped by a wayward stone now and then. The weather had made its impact as well. John had chills and fevers now. He was afraid he would not be able to provide for his family much longer. He had to give them another chance, lead them in a new direction. America was that chance. America was that direction.

In 1824, when John was a young man of twenty-six and living in Moycullen, times were a little better, but even then his work was hard and dirty. He was young, with a square jaw and all of his hair. He was healthy and as strong as an ox. He and his friend Jamie Flynn were building the road from Galway to Oughterard. For about a year, John and Jamie lived in the Gaeltacht townland of Moycullen—about halfway to Oughterard from Galway. They shared a room in the foreman's house as the construction of the new road progressed through the area. Jamie was John's best friend and had been for years, but he could be trouble. Flynn always wanted to stay out late. John wrestled with the pressure of having to be up early to be on the job, but Flynn had different priorities. Flynn loved every woman he met. Sometimes he did not come back to the room all night.

To build a road in 1824 required immense manpower. Stones had to be carried from the fields and placed on the route the road would follow. There was no shortage of stones. Some of the men wielded sledgehammers and smashed the limestone into pieces small enough so that the wooden wheels of a cart could roll along without getting stuck in a rut, and horses and mules would be able to walk without the risk of breaking a leg. Almost every night after work, John and Jamie would have a pint or two of their favorite ale or a cup of *poitín*—illicit whiskey—at either the Forge or the Venue, the two pubs in Moycullen. The Forge and the Venue were next to each other at the intersection of Clifden Road and a smaller road named Páirc Na gCaor. The front door of the Forge was on Clifden, which was going to be part of the new Galway-Oughterard Road as it passed through the small village. Brian and Carmel Naughton owned the Forge. The Naughtons were a couple of years older than John and Jamie.

Late one cold, rainy night—after the last of the pub's customers left—Brian Naughton finished his cup of *poitín*, locked up, and headed to his home on the opposite side of Clifden Road. While he walked on a muddy path along the road construction site, he slipped and fell into a trench that workers dug that day. He landed on his head, and at daybreak, they found him. Brian was dead. Brian Naughton's cousin was a young woman named Eleanor O'Donnell, who was from Oldchapel. Several months after Brian's death, Eleanor moved to Moycullen and worked, side by side, with his widow, Carmel, at the Forge.

Shortly after that, John and Jamie found themselves at the Forge having conversation and pints of ale with Eleanor and Carmel. Everyone said Eleanor was beautiful. John thought Eleanor was wonderful. She was a little younger than John but already a woman—and a lady. Her brown hair was so dark it was almost black. Her big blue eyes were so blue they were almost violet. She was petite. After a while, Flynn figured out why John never wanted to go to the Venue anymore.

John and Eleanor O'Donnell Bodkin named their first child Mary. She was born the year after the young couple married. The sponsors at Mary's baptism were Jamie Flynn and Carmel Naughton. A few years later, Flynn made an honest woman of the widow Naughton, and the newlyweds remained friends with the growing Bodkin family.

⁂

Twenty-four years later, bumping along the road from Briarhill to Galway, John and Eleanor's second daughter, Cate, sat between Mary and her father on the driver's bench of the horse-drawn cart. Cate tried to share a blanket with her da, covering his legs to shield him from the wind. She knew her job was to help her father, help him deal with the pressure of moving his family from their beloved Ireland.

Da surely felt the pressure, but he was ready for the challenge, and he was excited for his family's new hope and for the opportunity he and Uncle Laurence were giving them. The pains in his legs, though, were being made worse each hour by the seemingly endless ride.

"Thank you, *cailín*." He smiled at her as he pushed the blanket back. "Keep yourself covered. I'm plenty warm, Cate."

Keep the horses moving, John, he said to himself. *Just keep them moving,* he thought, as he bit down on his pipe to keep his teeth from chattering. *This is only the beginning.*

6

MAM

Eleanor O'Donnell

ELEANOR O'DONNELL WAS BORN IN 1800 AND SPENT most of her early life around Oldchapel and Oughterard—about fifteen miles from Galway. She had a brother and a sister, the oldest of whom was Catherine and next was Laurence. Catherine was more than twenty years older than Eleanor, and they barely knew one another. Before Eleanor was born, Catherine had already married Peadar Hickey and moved with him from Oughterard to a fishing village on the coast of County Galway. Laurence entered the seminary at Maynooth in the months after Eleanor's birth.

After Eleanor married John Bodkin in Moycullen in 1824, the newlyweds moved to Mayor's Park in Rahoon Parish, where they lived for several years. Their daughters, Mary and Cate, were born in Mayor's Park, and the Bodkins' other children were all born in Briarhill. Eleanor was known as Mam after Mary arrived. In total, they had eight children—four boys and four girls—and at the age of forty, Eleanor told John that the new baby, Nellie, would be the last.

John and Eleanor had lived together for more than twenty years, and they were always poor. Somehow their poverty was perpetual yet never seemed to be impacted one way or the other by the addition of another child. If they needed more food, they shared. If they needed more space, they squeezed.

⁂

It was windy on the Friday morning when the family left Briarhill. The road wasn't bad, but the weather was cold for a morning in March, and Mam hoped for a day without rain. She was in the back of the cart, right behind Mary and Dan. Seven-year-old Nellie was to her left, leaning on her Mam's arm. Next to Nellie was Martin. Then Biddy on the end. The other boys—Dominic, Lawrence, and John—were huddled on the opposite side of the cart, sharing a couple of extra blankets and being as comfortable as possible. Their eyes were closed, not with sleep but with boredom—as boys often do. Mam was watching the boys because she loved watching them, and on this trip, she wanted to remember every detail of her boys' last days in Ireland.

In recent months Martin had grown to tease Lawrence incessantly, but Mam knew it was Martin's way of trying to toughen his rather meek little brother. She knew Martin would never really hurt him. Lawrence was a slight boy, to the point of looking sickly, and even though Lawrence was nine, John, at seven, was almost as tall and weighed as much. Lawrence was quiet and shy with pale skin and freckles. His hair color was light, almost red, but not bright red. Everyone in the family took care of Lawrence to be sure he wasn't last, he wasn't left out, he had something to eat.

Martin had his father's looks: a square jaw, a longer face, broad shoulders, and the same hairline Da had as a young man. *Hopefully*, Mam thought as she looked at Martin, *he will keep his hair longer than his father did.* Martin was nearly two years younger than Dominic, but he was already a good bit bigger. Dominic, a gangly boy, wasn't a very big teenager, and Martin was large for a twelve-year-old. Martin had always been a robust child who never backed down from his older brother. Now any confrontation would be a complete mismatch—so it never happened.

Mam thought John had a chance to be as tall as Martin. John looked a lot like his father also, and while mothers probably shouldn't pick favorites, John was her favorite. In part, her preference was because John was her youngest son but also because he was so well-behaved. John always did what his mother and father told him to do and never had to be asked twice. He knew his parents liked to hear "Yes, Mam," and "I will, Da," as responses to their requests.

Mam was thrilled when John made his first Holy Communion just weeks before they left Briarhill. The new pastor at Saint Columba's, Father Kevin McCann, was a nice young priest who had bright red hair and a friendly way about himself. He gave John his first Communion and had grown to know him during the months of preparation for the Sacrament of the Eucharist. After his first Communion, Father Kevin joined the family in the church's garden for some biscuits and a stirabout with turnips. In an attempt to encourage his new communicant, he put his hand on John's shoulder and announced to the family that John looked "angelic" as he received his first host. John's brothers immediately gave John a new nickname, "Angel." John liked it. Not everyone had a nickname.

They were all good boys, and Mam was proud of each of them.

⟨⟨⟨⟩⟩⟩ ⟨⟨⟨⟩⟩⟩ ⟨⟨⟨⟩⟩⟩

As the cart rattled along toward Galway in the late afternoon, Mam noticed the air had chilled a little more, even though the midday sun was shining. Dark clouds filled the western sky as they continued on the first leg of the trip to America.

7

THE STORYTELLER

BISHOP LAURENCE O'DONNELL WAS A STORYTELLER and a teacher. Like most men of the cloth, he would tell a story to his congregation—or to his nieces and nephews—to make a point, to teach a lesson.

As Mam's children were growing up, and Uncle Laurence was still a parish priest, he instructed and entertained them with several significant stories that were more than just fables. They were history lessons, and he thought it was important for children to know and to learn from their own family's history. The Bodkin children loved Uncle Laurence's storytelling.

Laurence was an O'Donnell—not a Bodkin—but he knew all of the stories about the Bodkins of Galway. Everyone in his generation who lived around Galway knew these stories and understood that one story, in particular, explained why very few families of Bodkins remained in Galway.

One warm summer day, Laurence had all of the children gathered around him as they sat in the shade of a magnificently large tree in the meadow behind the Bodkins' cottage.

"Tell us a story today, Uncle. Please, Uncle," Lawrence begged.

"Maybe ..." He paused for a moment. "Maybe the FitzGeralds?"

he proposed to the children. "That's it! Today I'll tell you about the FitzGeralds and the Bodkins."

The children gathered closer to their teacher.

"A long time ago ... the Bodkins were named FitzGerald," he began.

"Do you mean our name wasn't always Bodkin?" Biddy interrupted her uncle with disbelief.

"Many years ago, Biddy, you *were* FitzGeralds. It was a long time ago, but yes, you were all FitzGeralds. The FitzGeralds were the Norman invaders who descended from Strongbow— I've told you the story of Strongbow and his Irish princess bride,

Bishop Laurence O'Donnell

Aoife. You remember the story of Aoife, don't you, Biddy? Anyhow, one of the young FitzGerald men was quite a warrior who brought honor to himself when he won a battle over a famous Irish knight. '*Crom a Boo!*' he yelled for everyone to hear as he slew the Irishman by using a new type of weapon—a short, sharp-pointed spear called a 'baudekin.'"

"What does '*Crom a Boo!*' mean, Uncle Laurence?" Dominic asked.

"Well, Dominic, five hundred years ago—way back in the 1300s—the FitzGeralds' home was a beautiful castle, known far and wide as Crom Castle. The warrior FitzGeralds swore allegiance to each other and their home. They pledged to protect the castle, and each other, as they went into battle, with the war cry 'Crom a Boo!' which to them meant, 'Our Castle Forever.'

"The young FitzGerald who used the baudekin to slay the Irish knight earned himself a sobriquet that day. From that day forward, he was called 'Baudekin'—B-a-u-d-e-k-i-n—by everyone who knew him. Over hundreds of years, and generations of his relatives, 'B-a-u-d-e-k-i-n' changed slowly into 'B-o-d-k-i-n.' The Bodkin family has always retained 'Crom a Boo!' on its coat of arms, but it's no longer a war cry. Now it is your family motto, with the meaning, 'Our Family Forever.'"

Martin, the most aggressive and fun-loving of the children, grabbed a small branch that had fallen from the tree, held it in his right hand, and thrust it in the air. He swung the branch around over his head and challenged his siblings, "Follow me, Bodkins!" He yelled, "Crom a Boo! Brothers! Crom a Boo! Sisters!" They all raced across the meadow to do battle with imaginary invaders.

Another lesson Laurence taught the children was the story of the Tribes of Galway. He told it something like this ...

> In Galway, going back many hundreds of years, the Bodkin family was one of the fourteen families who controlled all of Galway. For the most part, these families—primarily twelfth-century invaders from England and Wales—were merchants and landowners. They worked together to ensure each family got its fair "opportunity" in the Galway business world, and maybe more importantly, they worked to ensure a fifteenth family would never claim another piece of Galway's economic pie. To this end, no son or daughter of one of the fourteen families ever married an outsider. These families became known as the "Fourteen Tribes of Galway."

"Tribes" was intended to be a derogatory designation given to the fourteen families by the native Gaelic Irish Galwegians, but being one of the Tribes of Galway also carried status, power, and accrued benefits for its fourteen members. In addition to the Bodkins, the other thirteen families who constituted the Tribes were: Athy, Bláke, Browne, D'Arcy, Déane, Font, French, Joyce, Kirwan, Lynch, Mártin, Morris, and Skerritt.

Other than the Kirwans and the D'Arcys, who were actually native Gaelic Irish themselves, all of the other twelve families were of Anglo-Norman descent, not native Irish—at least not within the last five hundred to one thousand years. All of these families, including somehow the Kirwans and D'Arcys, considered themselves superior to the native Gaelic Irish and never associated with them, except when all Irish Catholics had to work together to try to stem the growing oppression of their shared Catholic faith by the British. The multiple invasions of the British, and the rule of Cromwell, were ultimately successful in deflating the level of control the Tribes had in Galway—at least in part because the Gaelic Irish would not support the Tribes in their militant resistance effort against Cromwell. Over the years, the power of the Tribes disappeared.

Laurence hoped the children understood how heavy a price the Tribes paid for thinking they were better than someone else. But why, on the other hand, were there still a large number of families from the other Tribes still living in Galway? The names Athy, Bláke, Joyce, and Lynch were still common among Galwegians.

Uncle Laurence also loved to tell the story of the "Bodkin Murders." He had to be careful when the younger children were around because the details of these gruesome days in the 1740s could be frightening to a child, but telling this terrible story helped to explain why so few Bodkin families remained in Galway.

Different versions of the Bodkin Murders story had slightly different endings. The version Laurence liked to tell did not end with answers. It ended with a question. Laurence told the story of the Bodkin Murders something like this ...

About a hundred years ago, there were three brothers, Oliver, John, and Dominick Bodkin, who lived just outside of Galway City.

The first of the three brothers, Oliver, lived at Carrowbaun House and had two sons by different women. His first son was John, whose mother died. Oliver's second son, by his second wife, was named Ollie.

The second brother, John, also had two sons, another named John and a boy named Patrick. He owned Carrowbeg House, which was about a mile from Carrowbaun, though they did not live there.

The third brother, Dominick, who was also known as "Blind Dominick," lived at Carrowbeg House and was the caretaker. Blind Dominick was a notorious character, blind in one eye with an ugly, pockmarked face and a reputation for trouble.

Oliver's second wife naturally loved her biological son, Ollie, more than her stepson, John. John understood the situation and became concerned that Ollie, his three-year-old half-brother, had also earned their father's favor. John convinced himself that his father would disinherit him, and in a fit of anger with his step-mother, he moved out of Carrowbaun and took up quarters in Carrowbeg House with Blind Dominick.

John was engaged to be married to the beautiful and seductive Catherine Atheny, and disinheritance would put all of the riches he had promised her in jeopardy. Catherine was an adventurous woman and frequently, under cover of darkness, would sneak into John's new quarters at Carrowbeg, where she would drink wine and express her love to her fiancé until dawn.

Patrick, the second brother's son, who was about thirty years old, came to visit his cousin for a fortnight at Carrowbeg and was imme-diately attracted to Catherine's beauty and determined to pursue a relationship with her as he became aware of her nocturnal adven-tures. One night during Patrick's visit, while John was tending to his horse in the stable, Patrick lured the beautiful Catherine to his room and vigorously attempted to entice her into a dalliance of their own.

In the morning, Blind Dominick found Patrick's body in the visitor's bedroom and reported his sudden and unexpected death to the authorities. The authorities proclaimed it was "death by natural causes" and delivered Patrick's body to his father at Car-rowbaun House for burial.

Several months after Patrick's death, the soon-to-be-disinherited John decided his best option to save his inheritance—and his engagement to Catherine—was to kill his younger half-brother, Ollie. Blind Dominick and two of his nefarious friends agreed to help John commit the murder. They decided to carry out the awful deed that same night.

Here Uncle Laurence would vary his versions of the story depending on which children were in his audience.

By the end of that terrible night, John Bodkin (Oliver's son), Blind Dominick, and their villainous band had murdered young Ollie. They had also killed young Ollie's father, Ollie's mother, another man who was an overnight houseguest, as well as six employees of Carrowbaun House, and three dogs. Within two days, Blind Dom-inick and his two friends were captured, arrested, convicted of the murders, and sentenced. John Bodkin, however, was not accused of the killings of the ten people and three dogs.

Standing on the gallows, with the noose around his neck, Blind Dominick admitted to the murders. But in his final act, he pointed into the crowd of onlookers—his shaking finger aimed directly at John—and yelled, "Several months ago, John Bodkin murdered his cousin Patrick as he slept at Carrowbeg!" After the hanging of the three murderers was complete, they were drawn, quartered, and dragged through the streets of Galway. As was the custom, the severed heads of the three criminals were impaled on the end of tall spikes and displayed in Galway's Eyre Square for thirty days as a warning from the British authorities to other would-be Irish criminals.

The investigation into Blind Dominick's accusation against John Bodkin commenced. His arrest for the crime and his trial for the murder of Patrick took nearly a year. At its conclusion, John Bodkin was convicted of Patrick's murder and suffered the same fate as his co-conspirators, though he never confessed. The now lonely, but still beautiful and seductive, Catherine Atheny and her mother successfully petitioned the British authorities to retrieve his head from its spike after only a few days, so his head could be buried with the other parts of his corpse.

John Bodkin never told who killed Patrick. But did he know?

Uncle Laurence was sure he had taught the Bodkin children why their family was now the last Bodkin family in Galway.

⊂⊃⊂⊃ ⊂⊃⊂⊃ ⊂⊃⊂⊃

The Catholic Church was a big business, spanning Europe, from Rome to Galway, and as the bishop of Galway, Laurence was a powerful and influential man. He tried to use his power and influence, as well as his talents of persuasion and financial acumen, to help those who needed the most help.

Laurence was also a community leader and a successful businessman. He knew that poverty caused the problems he dealt with every day. In Galway, businesses could not sell their goods because consumers did not have jobs and, therefore, did not have any money. Each business failure resulted in a cycle of shops shutting down, employing fewer people—thus increasing the number of Galwegians living in poverty. They were dying in poverty.

Over the past several centuries, the British Penal Laws had systematically stolen the homesteads and farmland from Irish Catholics, forcing them into servitude on their own property. The Penal Laws impoverished and debased the Irish. The British landlords allowed the Irish to pay rent to farm on what had been their own land—land on which only potatoes would grow.

The prospect of eviction loomed over every tenant farmer's head. Eviction from a man's own property, for being in arrears with the rent; eviction from his own property, for crossing the landlord; eviction from his own property, because of the landlord's fancy. Many landlords were cruel and heartless. It was not uncommon for a British landlord to take the virginity of his tenant's maiden daughter on her wedding night. "Additional rent is due!" the treacherous landlord might laugh at his tenant as he dragged the bride away from her father and her groom, greedily heading toward his manor house for hours of debauchery, as he claimed the lord's "right of the first night."

The day he was installed as bishop, O'Donnell knew he had an impoverished congregation, and in the four years since becoming a bishop, the forces of nature had decimated his flock.

Most of the Irish Catholics in County Galway lived only on the potatoes they grew. A man working the fields, or laboring on the public roadworks, might consume five to ten pounds of potatoes in a day. Every day. Meal after meal, the magical "pratties," or "lumpers," provided nearly complete nourishment for most of the dispossessed families in the rural townlands, boiled with some butter made from the milk of a neighbor's cow, and occasionally mashed with a turnip. The women of the family made a kettle full of pratties seem like a feast.

In 1845 and 1846, the Irish potato crop failed, however, when more than half of County Galway's potato crop turned to a black, rotten-smelling mush in a matter of hours. A blight—of unknown origin—killed the pratties. The disease spread across Galway's potato patches and storage pits as quickly as a fog might roll in off Galway Bay and blanket the mainland. Significant famines had plagued Ireland before, but this period became known as An Gorta Mór, the Great Famine. The starvation of the Irish people that ensued during An Gorta Mór was as much the result of the political strife which had existed for centuries between Great Britain and its subjects on the island nation of Ireland as it was the result of the potato crop failures.

A brutal winter in 1847 yielded a reprieve from the food shortage when months of frigid temperatures temporarily killed the blight and allowed a few seed potatoes from the previous fall to survive through the spring and summer harvest. But the harsh winter became known as Black '47 because the freezing temperatures and unusually heavy snows killed many of the already starving Galwegians. All around County Galway, families who had sold their blankets and coats for food during the 1845 and 1846 potato crop failures froze to death in the winter of 1847. They died huddled in cottages, on the roads, and snowy fields, trying to get to a soup line or a workhouse in the city. There were no burials for thousands who died during Black '47—the ground was frozen. For the rest, the term "survivor" would be a stretch, as the immune systems of hundreds of thousands of Irish peasants had been weakened by the ravages of malnutrition and the weather, to the point that the county became a breeding ground for several devastating diseases. The spread of usually fatal diseases like typhus and cholera struck fear in the hearts of peasants and noblemen alike. Even the wealthy landlords and noblemen were fleeing Ireland for the relatively disease-free safety of England, France, or Spain.

Bishop O'Donnell had to help his people. He worked with the Galway town commissioners, and together they sought funds from everyone they could. The British government representatives in Galway had endless resources, and many wealthy families lived in Galway. The wealthy families were not Catholic, but O'Donnell's approach to them all was simple. The bishop would say to them, "Our community is being ruined. People, mostly Catholic people, are dying on Galway's streets. Children are dying on our doorsteps. Give me money, and I might be able to save our community." He implored the wealthy Protestant families—mostly Anglicans and Episcopalians—to give him money to get these Catholics off the streets of Galway.

The response to his request was the opposite of what he wanted. Some members in the British Parliament believed the potato blight was nature's way of cleaning up what they saw as the inferior, inbred population that existed in this small island country, and expressed their hope to have no Irish left in Ireland. The government stopped funding work crews to build roads, and it halted the sale of grain and Indian corn from America. The unloaded grain and corn rotted on clipper ships in Galway Harbor while Ireland starved. Protestant landlords continued to demand rent from Irish Catholic tenants who had no money, evicting those who did not pay. Magistrates sentenced O'Donnell's parishioners to hard labor and years of exile in the penal colony in Australia for crimes as minor as stealing a loaf of bread. Protestant religious sects organized soup lines for the starving Galwegians but then offered soup to only those who would denounce their Catholic faith.

Laurence O'Donnell did what he could in the face of all of this adversity. He worked with the Sisters of Mercy and the Dominican nuns to distribute soup and to care for the sick. He visited with prisoners in the squalid conditions of Galway Gaol. He tended to peasants in ramshackle huts in the alleys of Galway City or the *clacháns* in rural townlands. He fed the poor. He increased the number of people the diocese employed in building the Famine Walls. He worked to find British and Protestant money to buy tickets on the packet ships to encourage the immigration of the Catholic Irish to America, getting them off the streets of Galway and giving them a new chance at life in New York, Boston, Virginia, or Chicago—wherever they wound up.

Bishop O'Donnell used his own money to buy the tickets to America for his family. He bought the tickets for Eleanor and John Bodkin and all of their children. He purchased tickets for Patrick O'Donnell and Nora Jones, because they were family, too.

8

GALWAY CITY

March 17, 1848
Late Afternoon

THE RIDE ON THE CART FROM BRIARHILL TO GALWAY
on Saint Patrick's Day morning was full of excitement, fear, and
questions for Dominic. The Bodkins' trip to America had begun.
Except for Castlegar, there were no towns between Briarhill and
Galway City. Occasionally, Dominic saw what he knew were the
remains of a *clachán*.

"That's the third one, Dominic. Was it the *Sassenach* did this?"
John asked his brother. Dominic nodded his sad agreement.
This scene had been repeated several times between Briarhill
and Galway. The cart would pass through a *clachán* of about
seven or eight cottages along the side of the road. What the
Bodkins encountered was a part of Irish life they had thankfully never experienced. Half the cottages in the *clachán* were
tumbled into nothing more than a pile of stone and mortar by
a sheriff, enforcing the wishes of a Protestant landlord to evict
his tenant by making the cottage uninhabitable. Cottages still
standing had thatched roofs that had been burned or ripped off,

doors and windows torn from their hinges—destruction caused by the same officials, for the same purpose. The remaining residents of the *clachán* huddled around a few open fires in front of their destroyed cottages. The emaciated families were dirty, starving, and freezing. They lived outside, dressed only in rags during the cold winter.

At one fire, Dominic saw two boys he guessed to be around his age. They were cooking a small animal—about the size of a jackrabbit—skewered on a stick over an open fire. They watched the Bodkins' cart as it rattled along past the *clachán*. The boys could tell the family was on its way to America.

One boy said, *"Go n-eirí leat i Meiriceá,"* sarcastically to the other. Good luck in America.

"Agus go n-eirí linn, mo dheartháir. Go sabhála Dia ár dteaghlach." And good luck to us, my brother, the other boy replied. May God save our family.

Why them and not us? Dominic thought. He could see the despair in the eyes of the two boys. *Why are we the lucky ones and not them?*

⬤⬤⬤

Stone walls were everywhere. Properties seemed to be divided by walls. The roads had the same three-or-four-foot-high-and-wide walls that delineated property lines for as far as the eye could see. Occasionally Da would stop the cart, allowing a few sheep, goats, or a pig to pass along the road. As they bounced along the narrow and winding road of crushed stones, Dominic talked with his brothers about the sailing ship they would be living on for more than a month as they crossed the Atlantic. "She's called *Cushlamachree,*" Dominic told his brothers. John wondered out loud, "Will steerage be as bad as they say?"

They talked about America and New York City and Brooklyn. The Bodkins were going to live in Brooklyn. Dominic asked, "Will America be as wonderful as we hear?"

"Maybe Mary and Daniel will come across to visit us in a year," John said. "Or maybe two years?" Dominic tried to make his brothers' expectations more reasonable.

"Maybe Mary will have more children when they come to visit us in Brooklyn," Biddy chimed in, knowing more about mothers and making babies than her younger brothers. Dominic looked up at Dan and Mary on the driver's bench, and he hoped they would visit soon. He saw Da had his pipe clenched firmly in his teeth and a stern look on his face. Dominic worried about his father's health.

"Are you doing all right, Da?" Dominic called out. His father smiled and nodded, and then he raised his pipe in a salute. *"Táimse ag déanamh go maith."* I'm doing well, Dominic. He didn't turn around. "We are almost to Galway."

It had been a long day, and the sun was getting lower in the sky in front of them. In two hours they would be at Dan's family home, and Da could get out of the cart and stretch his aching legs.

⬥⬥⬥ ⬥⬥⬥ ⬥⬥⬥

Dan Duval had an air of sophistication about himself that the Bodkins did not have. Dominic did not understand certain things about Dan. First, he had his own business. Everyone else Dominic knew worked for someone else, if they worked at all. Next, when Mary first brought Dan around to meet the family, he was living in a cottage by himself. He didn't share a home or a room with a brother or a cousin or a friend. He lived in a house by himself! Finally, and most surprising, Dan owned his cottage. He didn't rent it; he owned it. The only other person Dominic knew who owned a house was Uncle Laurence, and he had five. He owned the cottage where the Bodkins lived in Briarhill, one in Galway City, one in Moycullen, another in Oughterard, and still another in Maynooth.

The Duval family's house was near the Claddagh, on the bank of the River Corrib, where the river's rapids emptied into Galway Bay. It was not far from the Dominican priory, where Bishop O'Donnell frequently said Mass and preached his Sunday sermons. The bishop liked to preach from the elevated pulpit at the Dominican priory. His cathedral was on the other side of the River Corrib, on Middle Street, just down Abbeygate from Lynch's Castle—the heart of Galway. But the cathedral was dilapidated and dirty, and he thought it was no place for a bishop to be saying Sunday Mass.

The Bodkins arrived at Dan's parents' house in the early evening, as the sun was beginning to set behind the house. *This is the house where Dan grew up!* Dominic said to himself in amazement. As they approached the house, Dominic realized that now he knew three people who owned houses, and this was a big one. It had both a downstairs and an upstairs. Three steps led to the front door, which was actually two doors side by side. A barn and a shed stood beside the house, and there was a shiny black carriage parked in front. Da drove the cart around the drive to the front steps, and Dan's parents immediately came out of the house to greet the Bodkins with smiles and hugs all around. "HAPPY SAINT PATRICK'S DAY"—"*LÁ FHÉILE PÁDRAIG FAOI SHONA!*"

Dan's parents, James and Ailis Duval, were a little older than Da and Mam. Mrs. Duval was wearing what Dominic thought was a fancy dress, and Mr. Duval wore a suit of clothes that looked like the suits Dominic had seen the bankers and solicitors in Galway wearing when he had been to visit Bishop Laurence at the chancery. The senior Duvals ushered everyone into the house, where a huge Saint Patrick's Day feast was set at a banquet table. A roaring wood fire spread much-needed warmth through the dining room.

"Sit down, please sit down," Ailis encouraged everyone. A seafood dinner of cod, herring, and lobster from the day's catch that had been brought in by the Claddagh's fishermen awaited the hungry Bodkin family. "Eleanor, we are so blessed to be able to buy fresh seafood every day. It's wonderful! The fishmongers' little shanties are on the other bank of the river, near the Spanish Arch."

Everyone found a seat, and Mam and Da thanked the Duvals, and they thanked the Lord that the two families were together again. They all praised the Lord, again, for the meal before them. The Bodkins had not eaten since after Mass, and the feast created a silence in the room that assured Ailis Duval it was a good meal.

After dinner, and many stories of Saint Patrick, the Bodkins were exhausted. Ailis led everyone to the second floor of the house, where there were three bedrooms for the Bodkins and still another bedroom for Dan, Mary, and little Lucas. Each room had a small turf fireplace. Mam and Da would spend the night in the first room, and the girls in the second. Dominic, Martin, Lawrence, and John took the third. The beds stood two feet off the floor and there was one for every person, with plenty of blankets. At home in Briarhill, the Bodkin cottage had two rooms, and Mam and Da slept in the smaller room, at the back of the cottage, with little Nellie. All the boys and their older sisters slept in the main room. The main room, the kitchen, had a fireplace for heat and cooking, as well as the table for eating. In the cottage in Briarhill, they all slept on the floor on mattresses made from straw.

John, the Angel, was tired but still excited to be sharing a room with only his older brothers. Just the Bodkin boys. John listened to his brothers talk about the trip and what they imagined about the days ahead. He did not say much—Dominic and Martin were the talkers. Lawrence listened, too. The boys talked about how the family was going to get bigger tomorrow.

Tomorrow, in Moycullen, they would be picking up Patrick O'Donnell and Nora Jones.

Patrick and Nora would travel to America with the Bodkins on the *Cushlamachree*, and they would live with relatives of their father, in a place in New York called Harrison. Patrick and Nora were both seventeen years old, and somehow, not twins. The boys would have plenty of time to figure out how they were cousins, but Dominic said he hoped Nora was pretty. Martin agreed, but the young boys, John and Lawrence, didn't understand what difference that would make.

Mam and Da told the children that Patrick, Nora, and their parents had moved to Moycullen from An Spideál years ago. Mam explained that their cousins were the adopted children of Mam's older sister, Catherine, and her husband, Peader Hickey. Patrick and Nora were not born as brother and sister, but both were orphaned when they were young. Mam had never talked about her sister, and Dominic did not think Mam had even seen her more than a couple of times in her entire life, certainly not since Dominic was born. Dominic was confused by all of this, but he knew that by the end of the day, when they left Moycullen, Patrick O'Donnell and Nora Jones would be with them and become part of the family.

That night, Mary and Dan were alone with baby Lucas in their bedroom. "Your parents' home is beautiful, Daniel, and I can't wait to see the sun rising over Galway Bay in the morning. I must confess, my family is somewhat overwhelmed. Your parents were so welcoming, and they provided such an excellent meal, and now, getting to sleep in real beds is a new experience for my family. I heard my father say, 'Mam, did we ever sleep in our own room before?' Mam said she didn't believe so."

"Thank you, my dear. Galway was a wonderful place to grow up. The bay is beautiful. When I was young, my father, of course, had a couple of Galway hookers. I remember his first one; she was a great boat with crimson sails. I learned to sail and fish with her. We were very fortunate." Dan explained to his wife that the Duvals had lived closer to Dublin when he was a young child, and his father's construction business was, for many years, the primary builder for a brewery in Dublin. The brewery had grown to be the largest in all of Ireland, and each time the brewery expanded its storehouse, his father's wealth increased.

"Why is it, Daniel, your family was allowed all of their wealth, while most of the other Irish Catholics we know live in poverty, and so many, like my family, are fleeing to America or Canada?"

"It's only a matter of timing, Mary. My family fled, too, but it was years ago. Actually, it was only my grandfather who left for Newfoundland in 1780. As a young man, he left his parents to sail from Dublin to Newfoundland. Even then, Newfoundland had a large Irish community. He learned the fishing business. Cod fishing it was. Over the years, he became financially successful, and forty years later, in the 1820s, he returned to Dublin." Dan had not revealed his family's history very often, and he had to dig deep into his memory to remember the details.

"My grandfather was able to return to Dublin, with my grandmother and their child. The child was my father, of course. By then, the British relaxed the Penal Laws, somewhat, and allowed him to keep his fortune and own some land. My grandfather prospered even further with his businesses in Dublin, and years later, so did my father when he started the construction business. The fortuitous timing, my dear, was that my grandfather came back to Ireland when his new fortune was already in place. In contrast, your family, like so many others, had their property confiscated by the Crown many years ago and had no chance to recover."

Mary had only met Dan's parents once, at their wedding, and did not know any of this. With the prospect of losing her family in two days breaking her heart, she was wistful. "Maybe my family will return someday, too."

As usual, in the morning, everyone was up before dawn, and Mary got to see the sun rising over Galway Bay.

James and Ailis had a big breakfast of eggs, sausage, potatoes, tomatoes, bread, and milk all set for them. The meal was nothing like the breakfast they had yesterday. Or maybe ever. After breakfast, Dan hitched two fresh horses to the cart, and Da, Cate, the Angel, and Dominic headed out for Moycullen.

PÁIRC NA GCAOR

March 18, 1848
Maigh Cuilinn

THE ROAD FROM GALWAY NORTHWEST TOWARD MOY-
cullen was less hilly and not as rocky as the route to the Duvals'
home had been the day before. Moycullen was known as "Maigh
Cuilinn" to the people who lived in the Gaeltacht village, where
everyone spoke Irish. The street address Bishop O'Donnell had
given for Catherine and Peadar Hickey was "sixth house on Páirc
Na gCaor."

"Páirc Na gCaor is not too much wider than the boreen in front
of our cottage," Da said as he encouraged the horses to move
along. His mood was lighter today as he drove the team of horses
through the towns along Clifden Road. "Jamie Flynn and I lived
here in Ballycuirke, when we were working on the road." Cate
elbowed Dominic and rolled her eyes. They knew this story well.
"We would work all day," Da continued, "and then go to Moycullen in the evening for a little taste of *poitín*."

"At the Forge and the Venue, Da?" Cate tried to hurry the story
along. "And you met our mam at the Forge. Is that right, Da?"

"Jamie and I went to those pubs every night, Cate. We spent too many shillings there, we did!" Da chuckled and smiled over at her. Da entertained everyone—again—with his tales about the years when he and Flynn had lived in Ballycuirke, and unusual excitement filled his voice as he reminisced and laughed some more about his friends Jamie and Carmel. "They're Mary's god-parents, you know. Carmel was a widow, and it took Jamie a couple of years to make an honest woman of her. Did I ever tell you about how her first husband died?"

Cate stuck her elbow into Dominic again. "Yes, Da. He had too much *poitín* one night and fell in a ditch on his way home." Cate knew her da would miss the Flynns. She also knew this was the first time in a long while she had heard her father laugh. The last three years had taken a toll on him. He was a hard-working father who labored from morning until night to feed his family. He was the love of her mother's life. He was the quiet man who was loyal to his friends. He had lived through a lot in his forty-nine years. Some years were good—lately, most were terrible—but the good always outweighed the bad.

The decision to move to America had been difficult and pain-ful, but with the decision made and the Bodkins' trip underway, Cate saw that perhaps a significant burden had been lifted, at least temporarily, from her father. "Were you and Mam married near here, Da?" Cate encouraged her father's good spirits with a question she knew he would love to answer.

"Not too far from here, *cailín*. No churches were allowed in those days, so Uncle Laurence came and married your mam and me on a hillside overlooking Lough Corrib. They were magical times back then. Not like these times, Cate. Wonderful years, back then." He tapped the horses with his whip. "Come on, horses!" The reminiscing was over.

The Hickeys' stone house was directly on Páirc Na gCaor. It was attached to three seemingly identical two-story homes. Da pulled the cart close to the door to try to keep from blocking the narrow path, and they all climbed out. Before they had a chance to knock, Patrick filled the doorway. His smile was almost as big as he was.

"*Dia dhuit! Dia dhuit!*" Hello! Hello! "*Tar isteach.*" Come in. "*Tar isteach.*" Come inside. Patrick ushered them all directly into the parlor.

Inside, Cate performed the introductions for the Bodkins, and Patrick introduced himself. "I'm Patrick O'Donnell, but call me Patt." His father, Peadar Hickey, stood up from his chair and greeted the group, which had just made the small parlor very crowded.

Uncle Peadar was much older than Da and had lived most of his life seven miles from Moycullen in a town called An Spideál. He was one of the few men in the small seaside village who was not a fisherman. Peadar and his younger brother, Eamon, had learned the boatbuilding trade from their father, and, in County Galway's most prosperous fishing village, their expertise was valuable. They made the boats fishermen wanted. The most popular boats they built were the smaller Galway hookers, the *púcán* and the *gleoiteog*. The larger hookers they sold—the *bád mórs*—were primarily used for hauling peat and limestone between the mainland and the Aran Islands. The Hickey brothers prospered.

In 1800 Peadar married Catherine O'Donnell, and they lived a comfortable life, enjoying everything An Spideál offered. But, by 1840, Eamon had left An Spideál for America, and Peadar's health was failing, so Peadar and Catherine abandoned the boat-building business and moved inland to a home in Moycullen that was owned by Catherine's brother, Laurence O'Donnell.

Moycullen itself was small, but it gave the impression of a city with several attached houses, whereas, at home in Briarhill, the Bodkins could not see the nearest neighbor's cottage. The Hickeys' house on Páirc Na gCaor was bigger than the Bodkins' house in Briarhill, and it was different. The first floor of the house had two rooms. The parlor was attached to a narrow hallway at the front door. The hall led back to the kitchen, which was also the room for eating meals. Upstairs there were two rooms for sleeping.

Nora Jones and her mother entered the parlor and broke a moment of uncomfortable silence. Cate noticed immediately that her aunt Catherine was much older than her mam.

Aunt Catherine and Nora were cooking a fish stew and baking bread, which was filling the house with wonderful aromas. Moycullen was close to the coastal villages of An Spideál and Barna. The sea provided the citizens of Moycullen with abundant nourishment.

As they sat in the parlor and got to know each other before lunch, Aunt Catherine and Nora asked and answered most of the questions for their family, and Cate did most of the talking for the Bodkins.

"My mam always said I was named for you, Aunt Catherine, though I've always been called Cate."

"It was so kind of your mam to do that, Cate. Your mam and I haven't seen each other for so many years, and when I heard she had named you Catherine, I cried. Not being able to bear children for Peader had been so difficult for us. We could never have a daughter of our own, to name Catherine. But Patt and Nora have been sent from God to create our little family. The children happened so suddenly. It was like a miracle. Maybe it was a miracle. Do you know the story of Patt and Nora?" Aunt Catherine said to the young Bodkins.

Cate looked at her brothers before speaking up. "We do not, Aunt Catherine, only that they are cousins."

"Well, it all happened within a week. Patt arrived first, and Nora next." Aunt Catherine paused and then continued to relay her family's history. "It starts with Laurence, of course. He was only a priest back then, but I think he is a saint—he might be canonized someday! It all happened almost fifteen years ago."

Peadar corrected her, "Fourteen, Catherine. Fourteen years ago."

"Very well, Peadar, fourteen years ago. As I was saying, he was just a priest then—Laurence, that is—and he was the chaplain at Galway Gaol. A horrible place. Laurence always said the gaolers mistreated the inmates. He was about to come to visit us for a week-long holiday with another young priest. Father Fitzpatrick was his name. We were living out on the coast at An Spideál at the time.

"Well, the night before they were to travel to An Spideál, two prisoners, a man and his wife, were sentenced to the penal colony in Australia. They begged Laurence for help and said they had a son. A three-year-old named Patrick. 'Find him a good home, and a good mother to raise him,' the wife begged Laurence.

"So, Laurence went out, around midnight, to find the boy. As he told the story, it was a stormy night, but he made his way across the Salmon Weir Bridge, past the courthouse, down Saint Anthony's Place, up along Woodquay Street to an alley off Saint Brendan's. In the alley, he found the door to a shack that was the prisoners' residence—right where they told him to look.

"The boy was inside, cowering in a corner. He was dirty, crying, and hungry. Laurence wrapped the small child in his cloak and started carrying him back toward the priory. That's where Laurence was living—at the priory with the other priests. He made it across the bridge and was passing by the gaol when a guard called out, 'Halt now, priest! Where are you going with a child at this late hour?'"

Catherine paused for a few seconds, as she caught the anxious look in the eyes of all of the Bodkins.

She continued, "Laurence thought quickly, and he showed the dirty, crying little boy to the guard, and said, 'Have no fears, Sergeant; this is my brother's son, three-year-old Patrick. Patrick O'Donnell is his name. He was feared lost by his parents, and now I have found him in the slums on the other side of the River Corrib. I'm taking him to my home for the night.'

"'Very well, priest,' the guard replied. 'Carry on and use care, being out so late at night in this area. As you well know, murderers and robbers loiter around a gaol. See that you go straight to the priory.' The next day Laurence and Fitzpatrick came to An Spideál with the little boy. We called him O'Donnell, Patrick O'Donnell. The house was so festive that week. We had a child! Peadar and I finally had a child. Laurence and Father Fitzpatrick had a holiday, and we all had fun together."

She went on. "Then, on their final afternoon in An Spideál, the two priests walked down to the shore with a pint to drink, as they did most afternoons."

"'Tell the truth, Catherine! Tell the truth!' Peadar protested rather loudly. "Truth be told," he continued, "they went for a pint many mornings also. Fitzpatrick liked his ale, you know, John." Peadar looked directly at Da. "He was not much of a good influence on Laurence. Was he, Catherine?"

"That's right, Peadar. A nice fellow he was, but we did not believe he was a good influence on Laurence. How he ever became a priest, I'll never know. Anyway," Catherine went on, "they came back from having a pint faster than usual, and this time they had a little girl walking along, hand in hand with themselves. It was our Nora."

Catherine went on to tell the Bodkins the story of the small *curragh*, the dead father, and Laurence's first conversation with Nora. "The fishermen on the beach had not gotten a single word from her, but Laurence did. He found that she was three, and her name was Nora," Catherine bragged about her brother. "We didn't know her last name since her father was deceased, but a fisherman had said something about Davy Jones' Locker. So, Laurence called her Jones. Little Nora Jones."

Now, both seventeen years old, Patt and Nora looked very much as though they could be brother and sister, although they were not. He was a good-looking, tall, and muscular young man, and she was tall, slender, and pretty.

Aunt Catherine, Nora, and Cate served lunch. Catherine sat next to Peadar so she could help him with his soup. Da understood the Hickeys' decision to send the children to America. Catherine and Peadar were well into their sixties, and Laurence had already discussed with Mam that their health was failing. As difficult as the decision must have been, Da knew it was the right decision. Aunt Catherine explained that Peadar had family in America, his brother and sister-in-law—Eamon and Gabriela Hickey. She seemed sad but thankful for Uncle Laurence's generosity. Patt and Nora would go to live with Eamon and Gabriela in Harrison, New York.

After lunch, the tearful goodbyes created a tragic scene, and Cate thought the decisions parents in Ireland had to make were cruel. They were decisions that should not be necessary.

The "new" and larger Bodkin family headed back to Galway. Tomorrow would find them all on the quays in Galway, and the real journey would begin.

10

BON VOYAGE

The Night Before

IT WAS STILL DAYLIGHT AS DA DROVE THE CART BACK across the Salmon Weir Bridge. Patt and Nora had their first view of Galway. In the distance, they could see smoke from the fires peasants built in the alleys to ward off the cold. The spring rains in western Ireland's northern counties had the rapids of the River Corrib pounding violently under the bridge as the river snaked through Galway City toward the Claddagh and Galway Bay. At the western end of the bridge was the old Galway Gaol. Next to it was a large, flat, undeveloped area that Bishop O'Donnell had identified as being the site he was considering for a new Galway cathedral. He had said it would be years before Rome approved the construction of a cathedral for the "barbarians from the western coast of Ireland."

Da drove the cart along the west bank of the river until they arrived at the Duval home and the "new" Bodkin family was greeted at the front door of the house by the "old" Bodkin family.

"John!" James Duval greeted Da with a cup of *poitín* in each hand. "How was your trip, my friend? It's a long ride to Moycullen and back again, all in one day. Come, walk down to the water and have a cup with me before the sun sets. I've been waiting all day to show you my boats." Da accepted the whiskey from James, and they laughed together as they walked to the water's edge to admire James' hookers. They were small hookers, *púcáns*.

The parlor in the Duval house was large enough for Mam, Ailis, and all of the children to find a place to sit. The chairs were lined against the walls and around a large oval-shaped table. From where she was seated, Mam observed how the boys were melding nicely with their new cousin. Patt had taken a seat between Lawrence and Martin. There was a difference in age and size between Martin and Patt, but the two largest boys seemed to be getting along well. They were talking about the upcoming voyage.

Mam watched as her oldest girls were getting involved and making friends with Nora. Mary, Biddy, and Cate seemed to have gained some understanding of the unusual family group from Moycullen, and they were getting comfortable with it. Nellie was curious about her new cousin from the Aran Islands.

"Do you remember anything about living on Inis Mór?" Nellie asked Nora.

"Not very much, Nellie. I was only three when my father and I left. But I do remember his name was Séamus, and my mother was Siobhán. I could see the sea from our cottage, and Inis Mór was always cold and windy, Nellie. It was always cold." Nora smiled at Nellie with a twinkle in her eye as she talked. Nellie had a new friend.

"You must be brave, Sadhbh … I mean Nora," Nellie said to her cousin. Nellie looked around and hoped no one noticed that slip! She had never told anyone her fairy friend's name was Sadhbh, although she had a suspicion that the boys knew. Little Nellie had done an excellent job of hiding her fear of the upcoming voyage to America from her sisters. But, as tomorrow approached, her anxiety was building, and she had been talking with Sadhbh every night and had gained strength and encouragement when Sadhbh assured her she would be on the voyage, and that she, too, was looking forward to being in Brooklyn.

Nellie smiled, proud she had asked Nora a question in front of her sisters, *and* Nora had answered her. Nora talked to Nellie as though she was a person—and not just the baby of the family.

The tall, beautiful, and well-dressed Nora had the looks and confidence of a city girl. Her high cheekbones, long auburn hair, fair skin, and green eyes gave her a totally different appearance than any of Mam's girls. Mam's girls were beautiful in their own right. They were girls from County Galway. None were tall, and, except for Nellie, all had black hair and azure blue eyes. Mam watched the girls develop a sisterly friendship—the trip was going to be long enough without any conflicts.

Years ago, when Mam learned her sister was raising a child, a girl from Inis Mór, she did not know what to expect. To Irish mainlanders—including Mam—the Aran Islands were the home to real barbarians who, unfortunately, were also Irish. Mam was only a poor, pipe-smoking, unsophisticated Irishwoman who had conceived, given birth to, and raised eight children in a two-room cottage. But tonight, she was sorry she had not gone to Moycullen this morning to see Catherine and Peadar, and now she was proud they had raised such a nice daughter.

Ailis Duval prepared another feast. The Duvals wanted to send everyone off with full stomachs, and they succeeded. A few toasts were raised at dinner as the senior Duvals and Mam and Da wished each other "Goodbye for now!" … "*Slán go fóill!*" … and "Health!" … "*Sláinte!*"

After dinner on that Saturday night, all of the Bodkins bathed and repacked their few possessions for the voyage. Before they left Briarhill, Da had entrusted all of the prepaid tickets for the

Cushlamachree to Cate. He didn't want to be in charge of them and was afraid Mam would lose them. Additionally, Da had given Cate the responsibility of being the Bodkins' banker. The "bank" consisted of a small purse that contained all of the thirty pounds that Mam and Da had saved from selling their possessions, plus two gold coins Bishop O'Donnell gave them before they left Briarhill. The money had to last. In total they started with forty pounds, enough money for fresh straw for bedding on the *Cushlamachree*, and a little for extra food for the voyage. Some money had to be left over to show the authorities in New York that they were not arriving in America as vagrants.

Before going to sleep, Cate made sure she had everything secure.

THE QUAY

March 19, 1848

AFTER SUNDAY MASS AT THE DOMINICAN PRIORY, James and Ailis climbed into their carriage and led the Bodkins' cart across the river to a path known as the Long Walk. This route brought them to the quays and kept them well away from the soup lines that were in and around the city square, but not from the misery and disease that were everywhere in Galway City. Families crowded in an alley around a small fire; filthy brothers and sisters looked like skeletons with swollen bellies; a mother dressed in rags hugged her daughter with the blank stare of death in her eyes. The images of death and dying were everywhere.

Dominic again asked himself, *Why do we have the good fortune of going to America and not this person or that family?*

At the end of the Long Walk, James Duval quickly found the *Cushlamachree*'s berth. The *Cushlamachree* was not the largest of the packet ships transporting the Irish to America in 1848; it was one of the smallest. Because of the ship's size, the trip across the ocean would be more difficult, but since it was smaller than most sea-worthy vessels, it could depart from the relatively shallow Galway Harbor. She would sail with one hundred and twenty-five steerage passengers, and only one first-cabin family. To cross the Atlantic on one of the larger ships, the Bodkins would have had to travel east across Ireland by cart to Dublin, take the ferry across the Irish Sea to Liverpool, England, and then depart for America. It would have added at least a week to the trip.

As they approached the quay, the family looked at each other in amazement. A large crowd of people was already there. More than a hundred were waiting to get on board. Hundreds more—well-wishers, family, friends, and the curious from the surrounding streets of Galway—had come to see the ship's departure for America. Half a dozen redcoats, with their tall black hats and shiny swords at the ready, patrolled the quay. Street vendors were hawking anything a passenger would need on a voyage across the Atlantic that might last the better part of two months. Vendors sold straw for bedding, coats, hats, blankets, mittens, pots, pans, food, tobacco, ale, jugs of *poitín*, wine, cheese, water, candles, knives. The family's confidence in their ability to endure the voyage was quickly evaporating.

James and Da drove the horses through the steerage crowd toward the *Cushlamachree*, which was no small task considering how many people were on the quay. Several of the dirty steerage crowd initially were outraged that a family was driving a carriage and a cart to the front of the throng of passengers waiting to board. One man yelled out to Da, "Hey, you! Go no farther with that cart." But, when the man saw James Duval driving the carriage and leading the cart, he touched his cap and called out, "Pardon me, good sir." Everyone in Galway City knew James Duval. To the rest of the crowd, the man yelled, "Make way for Mr. James Duval! Follow me, sir. Make room, everyone. Allow them to pass."

James and Da finally brought the horses to a halt next to a family who looked like they had to be the first-cabin passengers. The Bodkins looked around—they didn't belong with either group waiting to board. Standing behind the first-cabin passengers, Da knew the Bodkins did not belong with them, and he hoped they did not belong with the "other" group. Reality quickly set in. They were going to spend the voyage with the "other" group. Steerage would be an experience for them, and it would not be a good one. The family was suddenly huddling together. They had their blankets and the bags with their few possessions. The younger children were in the middle of them all.

"Mama! Mama!" Sweet Nellie pleaded with her mother. All of her sisters and brothers called their mother Mam, but little Nellie had not advanced beyond "Mama."

"Nellie, please do not weep, my little girl," Mam said to her seven-year-old. "All will be well, *mo stór*." All will be well, my treasure. "You will be with me, and with your da. We will keep you close, and you, *a stór*, will be safe."

Nellie trembled with fear as quiet tears ran from her brown and amber eyes down her cheeks, which framed the tiny features of her beautiful face. "I'm so afraid, Mama. The boat is scary. It looks old, and the people are smelly, Mama." The appearance of the crowd on the quay, loud voices, bad odors, and size of the boat all combined to overwhelm the senses of the youngest Bodkin.

The shouts and pleas of a young boy being dragged away from the steerage crowd by two redcoats caught everyone's attention and struck fear in every mother's heart. Mam hugged Nellie close to herself, trying to bring some calm to her frightened daughter. She wiped her tears and gently brushed the child's long, honey-colored hair from her face to a position of momentary security behind Nellie's ears.

"There there, my little Nell. Stop your shivering." Nellie was comforted by her mother's warmth, her strength, and the assurance in her voice. She stopped weeping as control came back to her emotions. Her trembling subsided.

The seven-year-old noticed that Biddy was sitting quietly with John and Lawrence, and she saw that Cate, who was old enough to be her mother, had left the small group to turn in the family's tickets for the *Cushlamachree.*

Why can't I be strong like my sisters? Nellie's mind asked her friend, Sadhbh.

Mam interrupted Nellie's thoughts when she produced a prize for the little girl from her bag. "I was saving these for the voyage, Nell, but now seems like a good time to give them to you."

Galway Girl

Mam handed Nellie several new sheets of white paper she had folded up in a bag and some charcoals. Even at her young age, Nellie loved to draw, and Mam believed she was quite advanced as an artist.

"Thank you, Mama. Thank you," Nellie said enthusiastically with a smile coming to her tiny lips.

Nellie spread a piece of the paper out on the quay. Mam's little girl looked at her surroundings, and Sadhbh appeared—as she always did—wearing a flowing gown of white and gold silk. She floated among Nellie's family as they sat, huddled on the quay. Only Nellie heard Sadhbh say, "Let me help you with that, *a stór,*" and Sadhbh helped Nellie as she began to draw a young girl who was sitting among the steerage passengers. "Look at how her frightened eyes tell a story, *mo stór.*" She guided Nellie's hands as the child moved the charcoal over the white paper. All of Nellie's

fears vanished. The sights, sounds, and smells of her surroundings, which had frightened her, now challenged and inspired her.

Da squeezed Mam's shoulder, and he gave her a wink and a
nod to acknowledge her success with Nellie.

The family passed the minutes waiting for Cate to return by
watching and listening to the crowd on the quay while Nellie and
Sadhbh finished her drawing.

"Here, Mama! Is this good, Mama?"

"Beautiful, Nell! This is wonderful, Nell. There are schools in
America, my little girl. Schools for artists. Even young girls are
allowed to go to these schools, and I will get you there, Nell. I
will get you there." Mam kissed her daughter's cheek, and she
hugged her to her bosom. Nellie smiled with the knowledge that
her mother loved her.

Sadhbh smiled, too.

Cate returned from the ticket office and reported that steerage
passengers would board thirty minutes before departure. Along
with Dominic and Martin, she made her way to the vendors to
see about buying straw and to calculate how much some extra
food might cost. The family would have to be on constant guard
against physical attacks and thievery. They ran the risk of being
tricked out of their possessions by cunning and untrustworthy
people. Precious little food would be on board, so they would
have to covet it as though it was gold.

The family decided to do their best to keep to themselves.
They agreed to minimize conversations with strangers. Not to be
rude to other passengers but to be guarded in communications.
Cate said it would be best if they would all refer to themselves
as "the Bodkins." Patt and Nora were fine with this, reducing the

chance they would have to explain their somewhat unique family upbringing to total strangers.

Da did not show his fear, but he had as much apprehension as any of them. He would have to keep the family together and safe on the voyage. He had a strong family, though, and the addition of the mature Patt and Nora increased that strength. They would all be looking out for the younger ones—Nellie, John, and Lawrence—and the men would have to watch out for the women. Uncle Laurence had also told them to be aware of vile and unsavory men on board.

The family devised a system which provided for two adults to be awake at all times, to protect their belongings, staying in their bunks even when the steerage passengers were allowed to the main deck for fresh air.

❧❧❧ ❧❧❧ ❧❧❧

The first-cabin family was well-dressed and clean. The mother carried a parasol and was wearing a dress with a big skirt and a colorful bonnet. The man wore a suit of clothes, like the ones James Duval wore, with a grey stovepipe hat. He carried a cane with a fancy handle that he did not appear to need. The children, a son and a daughter, were dressed as miniatures of their parents. A young nanny attended them.

This family had large trunks that were being moved along the quay by men who were porters. The first-cabin family seemed pleased to have a clean, well-behaved family of steerage passengers near them, and the father had his porter move the trunks to make more room for the Bodkin family. The nanny was an Irish girl who looked to be about sixteen, maybe a little older. Patt noticed her—she was very pretty, with nice red hair and freckles. She had a beautiful smile and was thin, like so many Irish girls. He began to talk to her, and they introduced themselves. Patt, being a gentleman, introduced her to the rest of the family in line. Her name was Maria Teresa Jones, and she was from Edgeworthstown, in County Longford. According to the agreement the Bodkin family made, Patt did not tell Maria that Nora was also named Jones. He knew they could not be related.

Mr. and Mistress Stephen Massey hired Maria the day before to be the nanny for their children on the trip to New York. Maria told Patt she was afraid of both Mr. and Mistress Massey, and she was happy that she would have her own separate sleeping space.

"I'm afraid of what the voyage will be like, Patt. But I'm lucky to have been selected by the Masseys. Free passage to America is quite a prize! There were four other girls they interviewed yesterday, and I was the youngest." *And I'll bet you were the prettiest too,* Patt thought.

Maria told Patt that when she arrived in New York, her employment would end because she would head off on her own to find some of her Jones family from County Longford. They lived in a village called Port Jervis. All Maria knew about Port Jervis was that it was north of New York City. Maria didn't know how she would get to Port Jervis, but she anticipated long days of walking. No one was going to meet her since there was no way to predict how long the voyage would take. Fortunately, she had only one small bag of possessions to carry, and whatever was in the bag did not weigh much.

The steerage passengers were only allowed on deck for an hour each day, and only if weather permitted. Patt and Maria agreed to look for each other, but they understood her work schedule would not often coordinate with the Bodkins' time on deck.

Mr. Steven Massey introduced his family. He explained that he was a textile merchant who was traveling home to New York after meeting with customers on Oxford Street in London. The

Masseys had departed England at Liverpool and then crossed through Ireland from Dublin to Galway.

Cate, Martin, and Dominic returned with the fresh bedding for everyone. Cate bought some very basic cooking utensils: a pot, a pan, some forks, spoons, and a knife. She was proud of herself that she had bargained with the street vendors and had spent only a little more than three pounds in total. They bought some cheese that would keep for a while and a couple of loaves of bread they would eat the first night or the next. Cate also spent some of their money on a bag of candies, called Berwick cockles, that they would use to surprise the children after a few days on the voyage. Patt introduced his cousins to Maria and the Masseys.

"Mistress," Cate whispered to Mistress Massey, "your children are beautiful and so well-behaved." She tousled the young boy's hair. "We don't have many, but we have a few Berwick cockles to share on the voyage, if the children would be allowed?" Mistress Massey smiled at Cate. "That's very kind, my dear. Thank you."

Cate resumed her role as the leader and told the family, "We have just a few minutes left before boarding."

Mam, Cate, and Mary rushed to each other, and they sobbed. The others were overwhelmed by the finality of the moment and began to hug Mary, Dan, and Lucas. It would only be "a year or two at the most," and Mary and her family would come to Brooklyn for a long visit, maybe to live there. They all said it could happen. Da hugged Mary. They both cried. He knew it was likely they would never be together again. He knew he would never see his grandson grow into a man. Dan's parents hugged everyone, and they said their goodbyes.

The Masseys would be first on the gangway, to be followed by the steerage passengers.

A man from the shipping company stood on the top of the gangway and yelled:

"THE *CUSHLAMACHREE* IS SAILING TO AMERICA! TIME TO GET ON BOARD FOR NEW YORK."

Everyone started to move toward the *Cushlamachree*, and they pushed closer to the rope lines, which kept the passengers from falling into the water.

Mr. Massey straightened his hat and said, "Let me take your arm on the way aboard, Precious." He called his wife Precious. "The lovely Miss Jones will help the children." Maria clutched her bag securely, with its strap over her shoulder and the bag itself between her body and her arm while still holding the two children by the hand. The Masseys, in a calm and orderly fashion, all moved ahead toward and then up the gangway.

Dominic was pleased with how things went at the ticket office and with shopping at the street vendors. He knew that after Mam and Da, it was Cate who was in charge, but his responsibilities as the second-in-command were growing, and he was doing well with his new role. He knew that over the next few months, there would be more than Cate would be able to handle alone. The voyage would be difficult for all of them, but especially for Mam and Da. They weren't old yet, but they weren't young either. Cate would focus her attention on the younger children, and Dominic would need to help Mam and Da. Security and safety on board were going to be an issue, but Patt and Martin could handle

Opportunity

that. Martin was only twelve, but he was strong and sturdy, and, together with Patt, they would keep them all safe.

The first-cabin Masseys made their way to the top of the gangway, and now the Bodkins were the first steerage passengers to follow.

There was pushing and jostling on the way up, but the Bodkin family held its position. Patt was at the lead. Dominic called out to the others, "Follow Patt. Stay close together!" He hoped by being first up the gangway they had improved the chances of getting better bunk space in the belly of the ship.

In total, there would be around forty bunks for the steerage passengers, on a deck of the *Cushlamachree* below the waterline, called 'tween-decks. The best bunks on the 'tween-deck were amidships because they minimized the ship's pitching and rolling motion. The Bodkins were allotted three bunks for the family of eleven to share. The family would have no privacy … not from each other or strangers. The bunks were two levels high and arranged so passengers would sleep head to toe. No decision had been made as to whether the family wanted to try to claim three bunks on the top row or three on the bottom or how to mix them up. Three bunks in a row would allow them to protect the younger children better by keeping them in the middle. But, still, bottom or top?

It would be a race to get below and stake claims over these temporary quarters.

BIDDY

BIDDY MADE HER DECISION ON THE GANGWAY. IT WAS time. She was sixteen years old, after all, and she did not want to be grouped with the children anymore. She loved the younger ones, but she was older and wanted to be an adult, like Cate. Biddy thought Cate had too many responsibilities. Mary was left behind now, and the family needed another young woman to help. Biddy was determined to be that woman. She was a mature sixteen and could hold her own in an arm-wrestling match with Martin. She was taller and heavier—more muscular—than Cate, and her well-developed body made her older sisters envious. Biddy kept her straight black hair cropped short, almost as short as the boys'. Her round face and short hair made her almond-shaped, azure eyes stand out and they were unforgettably beautiful.

Halfway up the gangway, she said, "Dominic, the family moves too slowly. Everyone will pass us before we get below. Let's break ahead together and run for it. If we can be the first ones to the ladder, we can select the bunks we want and hold them until everyone else arrives."

Dominic grabbed Biddy's hand, and they took off, ahead of the family at a sprint, up the remainder of the fairly steep gangway.

"Run, Dominic!" Biddy yelled.

Patt saw what Biddy and Dominic were doing, and he decided to use the rest of the Bodkin group to clog all the other steerage passengers on the gangway. The crush of passengers would give his two sprinting cousins a few more seconds to get across the main deck to the bulkhead, where the hatch for the ladder went down into steerage. At the top of the gangway, Dominic hesitated for some reason—maybe he stumbled a little—which allowed another teenage boy to push past him. The other boy was short but muscular. Biddy noticed a strange and menacing look in the boy's eyes.

Biddy took off by herself, with a determination she had never displayed before. The other boy was next to her, but not ahead of her. They were elbow-to-elbow as they raced for the hatch. It was only about ten strides across the *Cushlamachree*'s white oak deck. Biddy got to the hatch at the same time as the new boy. She thought, *No búachaill is going to beat me.* No boy was ever going to beat her. They were moving at full speed when she shoved him with all her might, right into the bulkhead.

"Owwww," the boy screamed as he smashed into the bulkhead, hitting both his shoulder and his head before collapsing onto the deck. Biddy bolted past him and down the ladder. Dominic, still on the deck, was now several steps back, but right behind her. He leaped over the injured boy, and he headed down the ladder. They made it quickly to the bottom. The siblings were the first ones into steerage and had their choice of the bunks. They both surveyed the area and, at the same time, came to the identical decision to choose three bunks in a row across the bottom.

"Take these, Dominic!" Biddy yelled to her brother, pointing to a row of bunks that was near the ladder and, hopefully, would provide a little more ventilation from above.

Below Deck

Dominic dove into one bunk and Biddy into another, laying their feet across the bunk between them to claim it for the family. They faced each other and realized their success.

"We did it, Biddy. We were first, and we got the best!" They grinned at each other for a few seconds before they looked around.

Within moments a few dozen other passengers were scurrying around like rats in a maze, carrying bags and bedding, shouting back and forth.

"Come here. Let's take this bunk."

"No, let's take these."

"Do we get two bunks or just one?"

"Let's get as far away from the toilet pots as possible."

There was complete chaos.

The rest of the Bodkins had not come through the hatch. The ladder was steep and narrow, and Da was not doing well getting down. He was slowing the rest of the family.

As Biddy sat on the bunk, she was proud of herself. She made the right decision at the right moment. And she had knocked that *búachaill* out of the way and right to the deck. Nobody was going to beat her. Not ever. But she hoped the boy was not injured too badly. Dominic looked at his older sister and smiled.

The family made its way down the ladder, and the rest of the steerage passengers followed, quickly claiming the remaining bunks. Every bunk had three or four people. The shouting and chaos continued for a while until everyone claimed a place. It seemed that every steerage passenger sat on a bunk, or on the deck of the *Cushlamachree,* to look around at the rough, dark, damp, and dirty surroundings they would call home for the foreseeable future. The new neighbors became quiet for a while

The crew might have cleaned the 'tween-decks since the boat's last arrival in port, but the strong odor created by many previous passengers' vomit, feces, and urine remained. Only in the case of an emergency would the crew come to 'tween-decks at all because of the stench.

The Bodkins were in shock at the surroundings and shocked again by the people around them. The odor in 'tween-decks was made worse by the inherent dampness of being so close to the water and waste left over from previous passengers on long voyages. It was evident that the bodies of most of the one hundred and fourteen fellow steerage passengers had not had the luxury of bathing yesterday at the Duvals'.

Biddy saw that the boy she had beaten to the hatch on the main deck eventually made his way down the ladder and did not seem to have been injured too severely, although he had a red welt above his right eye. She was embarrassed his bunk was close to theirs, and she knew she would have to apologize to him. *Oh God,* she thought, *I knocked that búachaill to the ground!*

Biddy learned his name was Damen Goldyn. He was Irish, from Dublin, and traveling alone.

Steerage was damp and cramped. The 'tween-deck area was at least partly below the water level, which explained both the dampness and the darkness. The only light came from the hatch being open at the top of the ladder. From the deck of steerage to the deck overhead, it was only about seven feet. Bunks lined the bulkheads on both the port and starboard side of the *Cush-lamachree*'s hull, and the open area across the middle was little more than six feet wide. The bunks themselves were nothing more than rough wooden posts connected to flat boards that served as the beds. The adults were barely able to sit in either the top or the bottom bunk without hitting their heads.

Dominic, Martin, and Patt spread fresh straw around the three bunks, and the girls used some of the blankets to cover the straw. Looking around at the other passengers, it was clear to all the family that the security of their possessions and themselves would be an issue they could not ignore, not even for a moment, for the entire duration of the voyage.

Two primitive toilets—basically buckets—were on either end of this deck for the steerage passengers to use. A line had already formed at both. For some passengers, the line was already too long. They didn't bother to wait and relieved themselves on the deck. The passengers would clean the entire deck themselves, including the toilet areas. Most of the steerage families didn't look like they were bothered by the mess, and the family decided that no one would go to the toilet pot alone. There would be a minimum of two Bodkins at a time in the line to use the toilet, and always at least one adult.

Biddy was suddenly considered one of the adults.

SAILING FOR AMERICA!

DOMINIC HEARD THE CALL, AS ONE OF THE SAILORS moved throughout the *Cushlamachree* shouting on every deck, from the bow to the stern so that everyone would hear:

"ALL ASHORE THAT'S GOING ASHORE."

When the sailor's warnings were complete, the rest of the preparations began for the vessel to cast off from her berth. The lines wrapped around the short iron cleats on the quay were untied and thrown back onto the ship. Dockhands removed the gangway, and sailors scurried around the decks. They climbed into the rigging and to the top of the masts. They straddled the booms to untie the sails. A team of men on the quay held long poles with big pads wrapped around the ends. The men pushed the boat away from its berth and out into the channel that connected Galway Harbor with the River Corrib.

"HEAVE," the men with the poles groaned in unison. "HEAVE." And with tremendous effort and strength, they pushed and pushed, again and again.

HEAVE! HEAVE! HEAVE! HEAVE!

HEAVE! HEAVE! HEAVE!

When they pushed the boat far enough for it to be out of reach, the men stood on the quay and watched. They joined the cheering crowd as the old sailing ship started to move, ever so slowly, making headway on her own, out into the current being caused by the ebbing tide of Galway Bay. The men in the riggings set the sails, which began to flutter, then billow as the canvas caught the breeze coming out of the east.

Sunday afternoon—the nineteenth of March 1848—was a beautiful day, and all of the passengers were allowed on deck. They stood by the rails to wave goodbye, and to receive cheers from those who had come to watch the canvas sails carry the compact floating craft and its one hundred and thirty passengers.

A mooring line was left dangling from the stern of the ship, and three young men—who were not part of the ship's manifest—jumped into the water and swam to the line trying to get aboard. The crew pulled the line away and back on deck. The trio's desperate attempt at freedom would have to wait for another day.

From where they stood on the main deck, the Bodkins saw Mary and Dan standing on the quay and waving with Dan's parents. "Mary! Mary!" they called. "Farewell, Mary!"

As the *Cushlamachree* left Galway Harbor, Da gathered his clan around him, and they all stood with arms around the waist or shoulder of their brother, sister, cousin, or Mam, or Da, whoever was next to them. Da saw tears, and again he had his own. They were tears of both fear and joy.

After the *Cushlamachree* left the harbor, she would pass Mutton Island, sail through the channel by An Spideál, and then continue south-southwest, away from Galway Bay toward the Aran Islands in the North Atlantic. Dominic knew he would soon see the smallest of the Aran Islands, Inis Oirr, off the starboard side, and then Doolin and the Cliffs of Moher to the port side of the *Cushlamachree*. Tomorrow, at the last sight of land, some would imagine they could see Great Blasket Island—An Blascaod Mór—at the western tip of the island country. For most of the passengers, it would be the last time they would ever see their homeland.

Dominic had paid attention in Uncle Laurence's geography classes, and he knew the next land they might see would be the Azores as they sailed southwest. Over the next several days and nights, Captain John Thomas would navigate the *Cushlamachree* to a point south of the Azores, where the ship's sails would catch the favorable, easterly trade winds as they headed northwest to New York.

⧉ ⧉ ⧉

After hours at full sail on the North Atlantic, the breeze turned into a stiff wind, and the ocean's swells became huge, rolling the *Cushlamachree* from side to side. Word came from Captain Thomas to the crowd on the deck that the steerage passengers had to get on the weekly food queue and then go back belowdecks. The fresh air and sunshine of the first day at sea were coming to an end.

Only one food distribution point was established on the main deck, and every one of the steerage passengers got on the queue for the first week's distribution. Earlier, a posting at the ticket office on the quay in Galway had stated: "Every steerage passenger will receive a weekly allotment of oatmeal, biscuits, rice, sugar, molasses, and tea." The ration of food was minimal. The above items would total seven pounds, per person, per week. Cate was happy they had bought the cheese and bread before boarding. The bread would be good tonight, and the cheese would be an excellent addition to their daily nutrition.

The Bodkins—even young Nellie—collected their weekly allowances of food, and once more retreated into the smelly and damp bowels of the boat. It was clear to Dominic that Mam and Da would not be making the trip up and down the ladder every time they were allowed up for fresh air. The ladder was too steep.

When it was time to cook the first supper, Mam, Cate, Nora, and Biddy had to wait in line to use the small, shared fire for cooking. Mealtime was a test for every woman. A fire aboard a wooden ship was dangerous, and the steerage passengers tried their best to limit how long it burned. It was, after all, their own lives at stake.

In the queue for the cooking fire, an argument broke out, resulting in a fight. Every woman wanted to be sure she was able to cook her family's meal before the fire went out, and some passengers were more patient than others. The steerage compartment became very smoky while the families were using the fire to prepare meals. The "meal" they were cooking was the same for everyone. Oatmeal mixed with water, sugar, rice, and some molasses. The passengers called it "mush." The grey, sloppy mush would be the only meal, as many times as they could stand it, for the entire voyage—which the family understood would last at least five weeks.

Even without a storm brewing, strong winds and rough seas led to the call: "BATTEN DOWN THE HATCHES!" For the steerage passengers, this meant no more light coming through the hatch and no air moving. The smoke from the embers of the cooking fire had nowhere to go. There was no ventilation for the terrible stench from previous voyages or from this voyage's passengers, many of whom were retching and vomiting in their bunks from their initial experience with seasickness. It was now dark, and with the first day of the voyage over for the Bodkins, it was time for sleep.

The Bodkin security rotation included everyone except Nellie, John, and Lawrence. Two of the others would stay awake and alert, in two-hour shifts. The family slept poorly on the first night. The fear, the rolling and pitching motion of the ship on the ocean, the stench, the noises from the other passengers, as well as the creaking sounds of the *Cushlamachree* herself made sleep almost impossible.

They would have time to get used to most of it.

By midnight the wind decreased, and the crew opened the hatches. A breeze sucked some of the smoky, stagnant air out of the steerage compartment.

The first frightening day on the voyage to America was over.

14

MARY

WHEN THE DOCKHANDS PULLED THE GANGWAY AWAY, Mary held her baby as she stood with Dan and his parents on Galway's quay. The Duval family found themselves in the middle of the crowd of Galwegian onlookers and well-wishers waving goodbye to family and friends bound for New York. They watched as burly dockhands muscled their long, padded poles to push the old sailing vessel away from its berth. "HEAVE!" Mary heard the men groan. "HEAVE!" she heard again as she saw them strain. "HEAVE!"

James and Ailis Duval stood next to their son and watched as the ship's sails caught some breeze, and the vessel moved through Galway Harbor.

Tears were running down Mary's cheeks, and the young mother's hand trembled as she tried to wipe them away. It was no use. She let them fall. Mary wanted to be leaving Ireland with her family, but Dan and Lucas were her family now. It was the strangest feeling she had ever had. Dan had his arm around his wife's shoulder and guided her away from the quay, back to the cart. She hung her head as she let Dan lead her.

Mary did not want to accept that her family was gone. "Let's spend the night here at your parents' home, Daniel. In case the ship has to return because of bad weather or something." Dan agreed. It was too late in the day to leave Galway anyway.

Mary sat in the cart and thought about her family. *Will they be safe?* Mary missed them already. *Is Da all right?* Mostly she missed Cate.

Cate was not only her younger sister but also her best friend. The two young women looked enough alike that there was no doubt they were sisters. Both had the very dark hair and the azure blue eyes that myth assigns to every girl from Galway. Cate's features were angular, like Da's. She was tall and thin, whereas Mary—like Mam—would be described as having a rounder face with a fuller figure. Both were beauties; Cate was twenty-one and Mary twenty-three. They had been together constantly for their whole lives. Mary and Dan's wedding night was the first night the girls had ever slept apart since Cate's birth. That night had been a crisis for both girls. Mary's earliest memories included Cate. They shared all of their thoughts, and the sisters kept no secrets from each other.

Now, Cate was gone, and Mary began making mental plans to go to America to visit. She doubted Dan could be away from his work for as long as it would take to visit Brooklyn. So she would go alone with little Lucas. Just the two of them. She was brave enough.

Mary snapped back to reality as they arrived at the Duvals' house.

Ailis suggested, "Let's stay out front so we can see the ship as it sails away from the harbor." They stood on the front steps of the house, and they could see the *Cushlamachree*—her sails stretched against the wind—as she headed out of the harbor and into the bay. The ship sailed south toward Mutton Island and then west into the North Atlantic. "Stay at our house tonight, and if the ship hasn't returned, leave in the morning to go back to Castlegar," James said. Everyone knew the *Cushlamachree* wasn't turning around, but Mary sat on the steps until the last sail disappeared over the horizon. Later she cried herself to sleep.

In the morning, at breakfast, Mary explained to the senior Duvals how devastated she was. "Oh, Máthair Ailis. Athair James." Mary confided to Dan's mother and father, "I so dread going back to Briarhill and Castlegar. I have such wonderful memories of my childhood—my mam and da—and growing up there with my brothers and sisters. The thoughts of the past will haunt me. I will miss them all so much. Oh, will you be safe, Cate?" The concept of being without her sister made her sob.

Ailis looked at James with a nod that told him, *Go ahead, James*.

James said, "Daniel, Mary, your mother and I have something we would like to talk to you about." James and Ailis went on to explain that at their age, the demands of James' everyday business were becoming too much for him, and they wanted Dan to take over management of the construction company. "The house is much too large for the two of us, Daniel," James continued. "We want you, Mary, and our grandson to live here in the house with us. Daniel, I need you to come home and work with me."

The younger Duvals were stunned but excited. It did not take long for Mary and Dan to accept his parents' invitation and begin to make plans.

In the morning they headed home to Castlegar. As Dan drove the cart over the Salmon Weir Bridge, Mary realized that not all of her family had left Galway. "We have to come back and go to the chancery to see Uncle Laurence as soon as we can, Daniel." Mary had to tell her uncle about their plans.

15

I THOUGHT YOU KILLED ME!

January 23, 1902
Saint James Cathedral, Brooklyn

8:29 AM: *I was surprised and disappointed in myself for allowing me mind to wander through memories a person shouldn't be having in a church—certainly not at his own brother's funeral. After recalling that I made Dominic laugh hysterically with my imitation of Lawrence's squeaky voice, thoughts of punching another boy now occupied me brain.*

I never told Cate, Dominic, or any of the others about the times in me life when I actually fought for what I thought was right. They all knew that forty years ago, I was willing to fight the Rebels in the South, but we never discussed any details of the months in New Orleans. None of me battles were like the one Dominic just went through, but there were fights.

Watching Cate quietly speak with some of the late-arriving mourners, I realized she didn't know much about me. She probably didn't know the real story about Damen Goldyn ...

We were only three days out of Galway Bay, and Biddy and Nora had drawn an afternoon security shift. They remained down in the bunks while the rest of the family enjoyed some fresh air. The girls were alone 'tween-decks, except for Damen Goldyn, who also stayed below. They knew the búachaill *Biddy smashed into the bulkhead was stealing glances at them, listening to their chatter as they lamented the squalid conditions in steerage.*

After their two-hour shift, me and Patt went belowdecks to relieve the girls so they could go topside with the others. They told us Goldyn had been watching them the whole time. He was pretending to sleep, they said, but he was awake and looking at them. Biddy, in particular, did not like the way Goldyn stared at Nora. "He scares me, Martin," Biddy whispered to me. "He keeps looking at us." Biddy's face reddened as she told me the boy had his hand down his trousers while he was watching Nora.

The girls went up the ladder to join the family. Me and Patt each took a bunk to settle back and begin our security shift. With Nora and Biddy no longer in their bunks, Goldyn had changed his position, so he now had his back to us.

Since the day we boarded the Cushlamachree, *I had been sizing Goldyn up and knew something wasn't right about the boy. He worried me. Evil was in his eyes. Maybe it was because Biddy knocked him to the ground when they raced across the deck, but that wasn't the full measure. She had embarrassed him, yes, but it was deeper than that. Some things were wicked about Damen Goldyn, and now with what Biddy told me, something had to be done.*

I told Patt that the arse needed a lesson. He agreed the girls shouldn't have to put up with some búachaill *staring at them, givin' hisself a hand shandy—or worse. Who knew what he'd try next? I got to me feet and told Patt to stay behind me. He looked surprised by the backbone I showed. I was nervous but moved quietly to the side of Goldyn's bunk.*

"On your feet, idiot!"

Goldyn was startled by the words. Without thinking, he jumped to his feet and was ready to fight. He was older and bigger than me, and

I remember sweat running from the back of me neck, trickling down the middle of me spine. The nervousness began to lessen as anger generated energy that made me feel bigger and stronger than I was.

Goldyn screamed at me with a threatening voice. He wanted to know what was wrong with me. Why did I wake him from his sleep?

I moved to within a foot of the muscular boy's pockmarked and scarred face and threatened to beat him, making sure he understood he had to stop leering at the girls. "Stop it now!"

His breathing was excited and his breath putrid. He called me a vile name and said he would do what he liked. If he wanted to squeeze the tall one's bum one day, he would, and she'd like it. He laughed at me. "They always like to get touched," he bragged. "You can't stop me, you fool." He laughed again as he turned his back to return to his bunk.

Suddenly, Goldyn wheeled back and swung at me with a dagger that he had hidden in his trousers. The tip of the blade missed me by inches. Off balance, and back on his heels, he tried to square himself in front of me to attempt another slash with his six-inch knife. Nervous energy took over, and I swung me right arm back, and then low and forward, as me fist drove up and into Goldyn. The punch landed hard, hitting the boy right below his chest, in the hollow space where the rib cage splits into its two sides. Instinctively, I drew the arm back again and landed a second blow—this time lower in his belly.

Goldyn looked stunned. His face turned white, and he made hollow, snorting sounds as he gasped for air. He dropped his knife, and he slumped to his knees. Patt kicked the knife away as I stood over Goldyn. The evil pile of sheep shit understood that if he wanted more, all he had to do was stand up. He stayed on the deck and struggled to get air back into his lungs, but in seconds his breath returned.

He tried to curse me, but he couldn't speak. He was defeated. "I thought you killed me!" he gasped. He was able to get on his knees and crawl into his bunk. Still wheezing, he curled up again with his back to us.

Patt retrieved Goldyn's knife and secreted it away. He put his hand on me shoulder, and his eyes showed surprise and pride. We settled back into our bunks and planned what I would tell Da—wondering how he would react. Would he be angry? Proud? Would I be in trouble?

Once the family came back below, and everyone was all secure in the bunk, I had a brief and private conversation with me father ...

16

ONCE, TWICE, THRICE.
SHOOT!

THE VOYAGE ACROSS THE ATLANTIC BROUGHT DAILY
and constant boredom. After weeks at sea, it was almost unbearable for Dominic.

Before the Bodkin family left their home in Briarhill, Uncle
Laurence gave Dominic two new science textbooks to read and
study on the trip. Both texts related to the human body's ability
to preserve good health. One was entitled *The Graham Journal of
Health and Longevity,* which included chapters about the human
body's bones, muscles, and organs. The other text was *Health
and Longevity,* written by Lionel John Peale, from which Dominic
learned that the author's secrets to good health included the min-
imization of the animal instincts to eat and drink to excess. After
two weeks on the *Cushlamachree,* Dominic had devoured both
books—several times—and he knew them by heart, understanding the human body and how it worked. Now, he needed more
books to read, but there were none.

The three younger children were close in age and played well
together—most of the time. They played a couple of simple games,
requiring only fingers, for hours at a time.

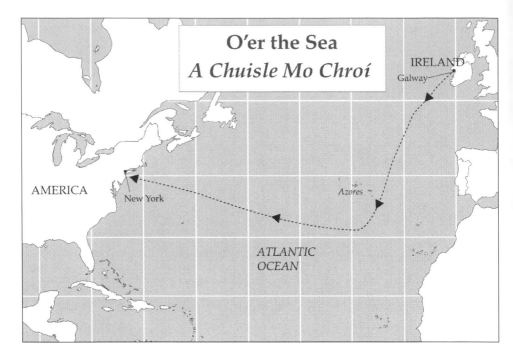

One game was "Once, Twice, Thrice. Shoot!" It was simple. Two children could play at a time. One child would choose "odds" and the other "evens." Each child would hold out a fist, and they would say, "Once." Then they would say, "Twice," as each child stuck out a fist again. Finally, another fist and they would say, "Thrice." Then they would all shout, "Shoot!" and each would decide whether to stick out one or two fingers.

If they both stuck out the same choice, the child who chose "evens" won, because the total fingers added up to two or four. But, if one child stuck out one finger and the other two, the total was an odd number, three, and the child who chose "odds" was the winner.

The loser would be replaced by another child for the next game.

They played game after game after game of "Once, Twice, Thrice. Shoot!"

"Rock, Paper, Scissors," was another popular game.

One afternoon, after a couple of weeks on the Atlantic, the children were getting bored. "Mama! Lawrence wins every time," sweet Nellie complained to her mother. "He beats me and John every game. No matter what fingers we shoot, he says he wins." John, the Angel, agreed with his sister. "Lawrence changes the rules every time we shoot, Mam. It doesn't seem fair."

"Lawrence, your brother and sister should win once in a while. Don't you think?" Mam admonished Lawrence and gave him a "stare," which commanded his attention. "Play nice, or you won't be allowed to play at all.

"Nell, why don't you ask Mary Niland to play for a while," Mam encouraged her little girl.

Mary Niland was a six-year-old, traveling with her father and three brothers. Her father was a widower, who had his hands full with four children and no woman to care for them. Mam had been working to foster a friendship between Nellie and Mary. Nellie, excited by her Mam's suggestion, went straight to Mary's bunk and began teaching her the rules of "Once, Twice, Thrice. Shoot!"

The bigger boys, Martin and Patt, spent hours together. They had started the voyage as big and strong boys—arm-wrestling to see who was stronger. But, like everyone else, they were losing weight. They tried doing push-ups and sit-ups for a while, but the lack of proper nutrition forced them to stop.

Cate, Biddy, and Nora were always together. Talking constantly about America—and their dreams about the future. Their dreams—and some fears—about American boys. They slept for hours and looked forward to when they were allowed to go up on deck. The fresh air was cold and invigorating. They learned the weather in March and April on the Atlantic was much like the weather around Galway. Rarely was it sunny and warm.

On a couple of trips to the deck, the family met Maria Teresa Jones again. She was doing well with Steven and Precious Massey.

The Masseys, as it turned out, were kind to Maria and they were very appreciative of how she cared for the children. Patt had a crush on Maria and talked to her as much as possible.

Mam and Da spent time with all of their children. Mam played "Rock, Paper, Scissors" or "Once, Twice, Thrice. Shoot!" with the young ones. Even some of the older Bodkin children joined in on the fun, once in a while. Sometimes, Mam would gather all of the girls and they sang songs and clapped in time for the beat. The girls teased each other as Mam told them stories about their childhood years.

Mam spent time with Dominic, too, allowing him to tell her all about the books Uncle Laurence had given him. He used the books to help Mam with her reading, and he used Da to demonstrate where different bones, muscles, and organs were.

"This is your tibia," Dominic would say. "And these horizontal bones, Da, are called clavicles." Dominic ran the fingers of both hands along the bones that were at the base of his father's neck— between the shoulders. "Your lungs, Mam, would be under here and, Da," Dominic explained to his father as he moved his hands from his father's chest toward his abdomen, "your solar plexus is here, where your rib cage begins, and down here is your pelvis." He could place his hands touching parts of Da that would be inappropriate on Mam.

Many of the passengers were sick, and Dominic wished he knew more so he could help them. It seemed as though someone in steerage died almost every other day, and when that happened, the other passengers would say some prayers, and several men would carry the deceased person's remains to the upper deck and throw them into the sea. Most of the dead had contracted typhus from the insects and rodents on board. Of the passengers with typhus, only the fortunate died quickly. Most lingered for a week or two with a piercing headache that announced another victim of the fever. Other passengers died of starvation, cholera, or dysentery, which caused significant diarrhea, vomiting, and intestinal pain. Some of the passengers were already starving when the *Cushlamachree* left Galway. Their condition was only exacerbated by dehydration and lack of nourishment during the voyage.

Mam and Da were among the oldest passengers on the ship, and they seemed to have aged noticeably in just a few weeks on the voyage. They always made sure all of the children ate the daily ration of mush first—often forgoing their own rations. The meals were horrific. The stench of rotting food added to the overall putrid smell in steerage.

The cheese the Bodkins bought from the vendors on Galway's quay was gone after two weeks, but the young children were always surprised when Mam found more of the tasty Berwick cockles. The minty flavor of the candy would stay on their tongues for hours.

Every day produced a fistfight among the steerage passengers. Men fought with men. Women fought with women. Women fought with children. The fights were almost always over the theft of someone's food or blanket, a father protecting the honor of his daughter, or two young men venting their boredom.

A break to the monotony was "bath day." Once a week, everyone was allowed to take a bath topside. A bath consisted of getting naked and having someone pour a bucket or two of ice-cold seawater over your head. When the women bathed, all of the clothed women waiting their turn crowded around the naked woman and held up blankets to try to provide some privacy. All of the women tried to be careful and very quick with a bath. The concept of standing in a crowd naked was still embarrassing for women the age of Biddy, Cate, and Nora. Especially since some boys stood in places where they hoped to get a glance.

Damen Goldyn—Biddy's *búachaill*—was one of those boys trying to catch a peek. "Bath day" was the only day he came up on deck.

Biddy's *búachaill* had no family onboard. He had no friends onboard. Goldyn was a teenage Irish boy, running from legal issues he had caused in Dublin. He was short, husky, and strong. And he was trouble. Goldyn's face showed scars from all the fights he had fought. The beating he took from Martin was just another lost fight to Goldyn. Martin had caused no new scars and had not drawn blood, so Goldyn had put it out of his memory.

His legal problems in Dublin were related to a young woman named Julia Mary Murphy. A month ago, at the end of his brief moment in the magistrate's courtroom in Dublin, he had been found guilty related to the attack on Julia Mary. He considered himself lucky the authorities allowed his family to pay his way to America, rather than being exiled to Australia. Australia would be a death sentence.

On the *Cushlamachree* he had to share a bunk with a family he did not know—the Rowleys, from County Leitrim. The family was unaware of his legal history. Billy and Kathleen Rowley, and their two sons, were escaping the same poverty, disease, and oppression in Ireland as were the Bodkins.

On Sunday morning, April 9, the *Cushlamachree* was beginning the fourth week of her voyage. As usual, Damen Goldyn was slumped in his bunk against the bulkhead, eyes closed, pretending to be asleep. Because of the proximity of their bunks, the Rowleys and Bodkins had become friends. And, on this particular morning, Mam and Kathleen were in a conversation. Goldyn overheard Mam.

"Today is bath day for me and my girls, Kathleen. Would you bring your blanket and join us? It should be another hour, and the sun will be high enough to warm the air a little."

Kathleen agreed.

Goldyn snuck out of his bunk almost immediately, and he climbed the ladder to the main deck. He knew the women bathed on the upper deck, between the captain's cabin and the starboard bulwark, and he had determined that his best place to hide and watch was on the forecastle—at the base of the foremast. The foremast was large enough in diameter that he could lean against the mast and not be seen, as long as no one was behind him.

He arrived at his position, and, as he expected, no one was around. He waited anxiously for the sun to get higher in the sky, but after an hour, his patience was wearing thin. Did they change their minds? Was it too cold? Were they going to wait until tomorrow? Finally, Goldyn saw the group of women, led by Nora and Biddy, as they appeared at the hatch at the top of the ladder from steerage.

The memory of Biddy's smashing him into the bulkhead—next to this same hatch—flashed in Goldyn's angry mind. *She deserves anything I do to her,* he thought. *But the tall one. The one they call Nora is mine today.* He watched with a trance-like intensity.

The women giggled and laughed as they prepared the buckets of ice-cold seawater.

"It's still cold!"

"You go first."

"I'm going last."

"Hurry up, hags," the pervert Goldyn whispered to himself as he quietly implored the women. He clutched as tightly as he could to the mast, so no one would see him. Goldyn was disappointed when Mam started to disrobe first. "Not the old one. Anyone but her," he mumbled to himself.

Then, without warning, a pain at the base of his neck shot into his eyes and his forehead. He thought he was going to lose consciousness but instead found himself being dragged by the neck to the bow of the ship. Someone was crushing his face and nose into the bulwark, with a force that made it difficult to breathe. He was bleeding from his nose and cried with pain, "Owww! Stop, stop."

"Can you swim, *búachaill*? Can you swim?" a strong voice asked.

"No, I cannot swim, sir."

Da pressed Goldyn's face harder into the bulwark and held it firm until all the women finished with their baths and went back down the ladder. Da released his hold on Goldyn and said, "If you torment these women or anyone else on this ship again, I will find out how fast you can learn to swim, boy. Or maybe my son will visit you in your bunk again. Do you understand?"

Goldyn was trembling. His face was bleeding, and he had soiled his trousers.

"I understand, sir. I understand, and I am sorry, sir."

The following Sunday was Palm Sunday, and everyone was allowed to gather on the main deck for a prayer service celebrating Jesus' triumphant entry into Jerusalem. Even onboard the *Cushlamachree,* today was the beginning of Holy Week.

The Bodkins and the Rowleys were standing together on deck, and after the prayer service, Billy Rowley said to Da, "John, do you see Damen Goldyn standing over there? Something has changed about him in the past few days."

"What do you mean, Billy?"

"Well, for the first three weeks of the voyage, the young man never said a word to me. Nor has he said a word to Kathleen or my sons. He was always pretending to be asleep. But the other day, his face was all bruised and bloody, as though he had been in a fight. A fight he lost. Since then, he has been talking to us. Not talking too much, but he's been saying, 'Good morning, sir,' and coming on the deck with us. He has even started sharing his food ration with me."

"Interesting, Billy, very interesting." Da looked at Goldyn and nodded, as he thought to himself that if he ever saw Laurence again, he would ask the bishop to pray for Goldyn's soul.

The Palm Sunday prayers were over, and Dominic lingered on deck for a little while, looking northwest to the horizon, trying to figure out how many more days it would be. The weather had been good, and the wind steady. They had been sailing for twenty-eight days.

It was just a week until Easter, and Dominic hoped they would see land soon. Uncle Laurence's lessons on geography taught them all that the first land they would see would be a part of New York called Long Island.

Dominic wondered if Long Island would look like Ireland.

TWO TRAVELERS
SHORTEN THE ROAD

December 20, 1894

EVERY MORNING ON THE SS *GALLIA*, DR. BODKIN wanted his eggs scrambled. A little loose. Not too dry. He liked his bacon crispy, a little butter on his toast. "Orange juice this morning, please." Dominic looked up from the menu. "Thank you, Charles." Tilton kept the coffee in Dominic's cup hot.

As was his routine, the *Gallia*'s captain joined the first-cabin passengers for their arrival breakfast. It was an honor to have the captain sit at your table, and on December 20, 1894, the captain was at Dominic's table. Seated at the round table, between Dominic and the captain, was a married couple Dominic had dined with several times on this voyage. The man, David Kantor, was a German-born merchant banker, and his wife, Coreen, was Scots-Irish. They lived in London and were traveling to New York on the vacation of a lifetime. David told Dominic that he planned to visit the New York Stock & Exchange Board on Wall Street.

Also at the table was Dominic's old friend Father Kevin McCann, the pastor at Saint Columba's Church in Briarhill. Father

Kevin was several years older than Dominic, and the priest was on his first holiday away from Ireland. He needed a break from Briarhill, and nearly a year ago, when Dominic first wrote to McCann to suggest the voyage to America, Kevin remembered the old Irish saying, *Giorraíonn beirt bóthar*—Two travelers shorten the road. Sailing to America—first-cabin—with an interesting man like Dominic Bodkin would make his crossing easy and fascinating.

The captain of the *Gallia* was an experienced seaman, who had earned his sea legs on many crossings. He was a tall, thin man with angular features and a receding hairline. Dominic had sailed on the *Gallia* before with Captain Bruce Boehmcke and considered him a good friend. The two spent many hours together at the dinner table. Except for Dominic's bushy beard, the two friends might have looked alike. However, Bodkin had noticed over the past couple of years that even though Boehmcke was only a few months older, his age was beginning to show. He had less and less hair, and his eyesight was failing. To read the dinner menu—or to look at a friendly note passed from one of the attractive spinsters in first cabin—Boehmcke had to hold the document close to his nose and contort his face, while squinting his eyes in an attempt to read the message. Dominic, who believed his own eyesight was still perfect, did not understand why the captain simply did not get a pair of spectacles, or at least a monocle. Thank God, Dominic thought, Boehmcke was able to see to the horizon from the bridge as the Gallia crashed through the fierce waves of the Atlantic Ocean.

Captain Boehmcke was originally from Bremerhaven, a busy North Sea shipping village on the eastern coast of Germany. He had been a captain on one ship or another for forty years. His life was on the water.

At breakfast, Dominic told Boehmcke the details of his travels around Ireland as he said farewell to his homeland—and goodbye to his sister Nellie.

"I haven't many years left, my friend. This might be our final voyage together."

⁂ ⁂ ⁂

As the sun rose, and the *Gallia* approached land, passengers' voices filled the ship with a murmur of anticipation. All of the ship's second cabin passengers, including those in steerage, were making their way to the ship's main deck to celebrate the end of the crossing and to view the sights on this cold December morning.

Most of the passengers did not know what the first sight of land would be, but, in the distance—looking north off the starboard side of the ship—was the southern shore of Long Island. Off the bow, an outline of the buildings in Brooklyn was becoming visible.

Father McCann and the Kantors could not contain their excitement. They excused themselves from the captain's breakfast table and went to the windows. An hour later, off the port side of the bow, the New Jersey coast was visible in the mist.

After Captain Boehmcke finished his breakfast, he also left the table and headed to the bridge to prepare for the *Gallia*'s passage through the Narrows, past the Statue of Liberty, and into New York Harbor. Dominic joined the Kantors and Father McCann at the windows, and he narrated the sights of New York and New Jersey over the next few hours.

"Father Kevin, what you are looking at now is Brooklyn— one of the fastest-growing cities in the world. That's where you and I are going." McCann would be staying at Dominic's Clinton Hill house during his visit to America. Dominic had been a busy and very successful physician since he returned from his service in the war with the South, almost thirty years ago. He had never married and now lived with his younger brother,

Lawrence, and Lawrence's wife, Maggie. Over the years, other family members had also lived at his house, but now it was just the three of them, plus a maidservant, Annie Corliss, and Dominic's coachman, John Alpers. The house had more than enough room for the priest from Briarhill.

18

MESSAGES

March 21, 1848

IN THE MIDDLE OF THE NINETEENTH CENTURY, THE
Catholic church had a robust communication system all across
Europe—including Ireland. With the increased number of Catholics emigrating from Europe to America, mail was also regularly
transported between the continents by the same packet ships that
carried the emigrant passengers. Pastors had to communicate
with other pastors, and churches had to communicate with their
diocese. Dioceses had to communicate with other dioceses, and
everyone had to communicate with Rome.

In Ireland, messengers on horseback traveled from church
to church, from rectory to rectory, from chancery to chancery—
delivering letters, notes, and documents. Frequently money
was being sent from a bishop to his pastors. On the quay in
Dublin, four messengers would meet each ship as it docked and
race to their destinations: Belfast, Cork, Sligo, and Galway City.
Inclement weather and the dark of night slowed the system, but
it never stopped.

On a Sunday afternoon in February 1848, Father Bernard
Joseph Fitzpatrick of Brooklyn wrote a letter to his friend in

Galway. The letter to Bishop Laurence O'Donnell traveled on a packet ship from New York City to Liverpool, and then by ferry from Liverpool to Dublin. On the evening of March 19, it was received by a messenger on the quay in Dublin. The messenger immediately left on his horse, starting his route west across Ireland. His final destination was the Catholic bishop's rectory in Galway City.

On the route to Galway, a horseman would ride from Dublin to Maynooth, through Milltownpass to Athlone, Ahascragh, and Briarhill, and finally Castlegar, on his way into Galway City. Horse and rider would make stops at several churches and rectories along the way, where mail was delivered and picked up. Riders would switch to new horses at some stops, and a fresh horseman would take over about halfway to Galway, at a church near Athlone.

When Bishop Laurence O'Donnell sat down for his Irish breakfast of eggs, sausage, black and white pudding, half a tomato, and leftover potatoes on Tuesday morning, March 21, he smiled as he opened the letter from his friend Bernard Fitzpatrick.

Saint Patrick's Church
Brooklyn, New York, USA
18 February 1848

Dear Laurence,
It has been too long since we have shared a pint, my friend. We have to make arrangements to get together.
I received your letter yesterday, and I am very excited to learn the Bodkin family will be arriving in New York soon.

I am not familiar with their vessel, Cushlamachree, *but one of my parishioners keeps me informed every day as to the new arrivals in the harbor. I will know when they are safely in the Narrows and what day they will dock at the pier in New York.*

Your estimate of a departure from Galway—15 to 20 March— should make for an arrival in the last week of April. Hopefully, before the 1st of May.

I will do my best to personally meet them on the wharf when they disembark the ship.

I do remember John and Eleanor Bodkin from our previous outings, and that will be helpful in my finding them. My parishioner will meet them on board for the customs inspection, and he will inform them that they should be searching for me on the pier.

I am looking forward to meeting your nieces and nephews again. I am also excited to meet the now grown-up Nora and her brother, Patrick.

With the help of my faithful parishioners, we will make the whole family comfortable when they arrive.

I pray for Saint Christopher's blessings, that the family enjoys an uneventful passage, with sunny skies and a crisp breeze to the Cushlamachree's *sails.*

If I plan to travel back to blessed Ireland in the near future, I will be sure to write to you in advance so that we will arrange a night in a pub somewhere. I wonder if McCabe's Pub in Maynooth still operates? Those were the days, my friend!

Or perhaps you might find time to visit me in America. I would take pleasure in showing you my church, Saint Patrick's, which has grown substantially in the past year with many new parishioners each week. Some weeks we have as many as fifty new faces from Ireland, or Germany, or Italy in the pews. Soon they will be standing in the aisles!

Our church, in the Wallabout section of Brooklyn, is a short walk from the Brooklyn Navy Yard. The Navy Yard provides the attraction of employment to many individuals.

Life here is not all work, however. Several of the wealthy spinster ladies in the parish have vacation homes on the beach here in Brooklyn, or farther east on Long Island. One of the ladies even spends summers in New Jersey, near the ocean shore. My trips with the spinsters usually involve being away from the rectory for at least a couple of nights. The value of which I am sure you remember.

As Always,
I am Yours in Christ.
B.J.

P.S. As you requested, I will get a message to Eamon Hickey in Harrison to make the necessary arrangements for Patrick and Nora.

Years ago, Fitzpatrick and O'Donnell had been classmates at the seminary in Maynooth. Laurence always called Fitzpatrick by his initials: B.J. Father Fitzpatrick left Ireland for America in 1843 and was quickly assigned to Saint Patrick's Church in Brooklyn. The newly opened Saint Patrick's was only the sixth Catholic church in New York.

Curiously, the next letter the bishop opened that morning was from James Duval. James' letter prepared Bishop O'Donnell for when his niece Mary and her husband, Daniel, walked into his study three weeks later.

Bishop O'Donnell had many friends.

The bishop and his staff were involved with the final preparations for Holy Week on the morning of Wednesday, April 12, when Kitty Carr welcomed Mary into the rectory's parlor.

"Hello, Mrs. Carr," Mary said to the bishop's housekeeper. "Is my uncle in?"

"He is, my dear. Hello, Daniel and little Lucas. He's an adorable one, don't you know, Mary!" Mrs. Carr smiled as she pinched the baby's cheek. "The bishop has been busy this morning, but I'm sure he wants to see you. Just go on in."

Mary opened the door to Bishop O'Donnell's study and peeked inside. "Uncle Laurence?"

"Come in, Mary. Please, come in. Hello, Daniel! Little Lucas! How he's grown!" Laurence welcomed the Duval family as they came through the door.

The bishop greeted his niece with a hug, and they all sat near the warm peat fire while Mrs. Carr brought them a pot of tea and some biscuits. They spent some time catching up about the things that had transpired over the last month and Mary told Uncle Laurence about the day of her family's departure on the *Cushlamachree*. Uncle Laurence relayed the details of his letter from Father Fitzpatrick and his friend's plan to meet the family when they arrived in New York.

"Will it be Father Fitzpatrick who will write to us when my family is safe in Brooklyn, Uncle? When will we know? How long will it take to receive a letter? I'm so worried about them. It's been three and a half weeks since they sailed. Do you think they are safe?" Mary began to cry, and Daniel put his arm around her shoulders.

"They are in my prayers every day, Mary, but I worry, too." The bishop tried his best to console his niece, but his words didn't help.

Mary looked at her husband and her voice quavered. "Just thinking about them, on that small boat, somewhere in the middle of the Atlantic." She cradled the baby closer and kissed the top of his head. "What if there is a storm, Uncle? Or what if there is *no wind*? How long will it take to get across to New York? Will they have enough food? When will they be safe?" She had so many questions and no one had answers.

They all knew the family was in the belly of the *Cushlamachree*—somewhere on the stormy Atlantic Ocean, fighting the waves and hoping for a favorable wind. Laurence explained to them about the time difference between Ireland and America. Since it was morning in Galway, it would still be some hour during the night for the family.

Mary changed the subject away from her family's situation and blurted out that she and Dan were moving to Dan's parents' home in Galway. She told the bishop what Dan's work situation would be. The bishop already knew all of this from James Duval's letter, but he did not let on to the young couple that he knew Dan and his father would be working together for at least a few years.

"Well, that's wonderful news, my dear," the bishop said to his niece. "Not all of the Bodkins have left Galway! Have they now, Mary? *Crom a Boo!* Mary, *Crom a Boo!* The family continues! You will love living near the Claddagh, Mary. The Duvals' home is beautiful. Daniel, will you be selling your home in Castlegar?"

"I'll have to sell it, Excellency," Daniel explained. "I told my father I would be with him at work by next week. I've made arrangements with a friend who lives nearby in Tycooly. He'll try to sell it for me. Marty Costelloe is his name. I've known him for a while, and I am sure he will arrange a fair deal for me."

Bishop O'Donnell thought for a moment and then proposed what he had planned since the day he received James Duval's letter.

"Daniel, I might be able to help you out with this. Father McCann, you know him, I'm sure—the pastor at Saint Columba's.

He needs a new rectory. Your home is close enough to the church and would suit his needs well. If you are interested and he is agreeable, I am sure the diocese can work with you on the price and the other details."

"That would be a blessing, Excellency," Daniel said. "Thank you."

"I am scheduled to be in Castlegar at Saint Columba's on Maundy Thursday, to celebrate Mass with Father McCann and for the Washing of the Feet ceremony. Why don't you invite your parents to join us? Afterward, we can walk over to your house with Father McCann and maybe even close the arrangement. I'll have the diocese's vicar general, Monsignor Gurley, prepare a document, and we can just enter the number of pounds we agree on."

Dan was amazed at how quickly things happened when Bishop O'Donnell was involved.

19

MONTAUK LIGHTHOUSE

April 19, 1848

MONTAUK WAS THE EASTERN TIP OF LONG ISLAND. IT
was also the easternmost point in New York State. The Montauk
Lighthouse was authorized by George Washington and designed
to serve as a navigation aid for boats coming into New York Harbor. Since 1797, on a clear night, a lookout would see the signal of
the giant wicks from a distance of nearly five miles out at sea.

Late on the thirty-first night of the voyage, the *Cushlamachree*'s
mate on the watch called from his lookout basket, "Land ho! Captain, land ho!" The beacon from Montauk was visible to him off
the starboard bow. The sailor's call was loud and clear. It might
have been heard by the Masseys, in their cabin close to the lookout, but the mate intended to inform Captain Thomas and his
crew of the sighting—not the passengers. The Bodkins, and the
others in steerage, didn't hear the call. The usual rumble of the
hull cutting through the ocean, combined with mumbled conversations and snoring, kept any sounds from the upper deck from
being heard.

The captain's reaction to the call was minimal, as he'd expected
the sighting of the lighthouse during the night. "Hold the wheel

steady as she goes, mate," Thomas said to his first mate. The captain knew that with the favorable wind, abaft of the *Cushlamachree*'s beam, the southern shore of Long Island would be visible by dawn. The first mate kept the helm steady, and by daylight, the *Cushlamachree* had navigated many of the remaining one hundred and twenty-five miles of the thirty-three-hundred-mile voyage from Galway to New York.

Before dawn, on Wednesday, April 19, word of the "Land ho" call spread like a fire through steerage. The sleeping passengers awoke early, as the dull noise in steerage turned into excited chatter. The passengers wanted to be allowed on deck. They all wanted to see. Over the past couple of days, significant rumors had circulated that they were getting close to land. For days, the passengers kept looking north and west, each hoping to be the first to see land. Hoping to be the one to yell, "Land ho!"

For safety and security reasons, the captain had been strict with his allowance of deck time for the steerage passengers, but, because they could see land, Captain Thomas became generous and allowed everyone on deck. The *Cushlamachree* had been at sea for a month, and the captain knew how difficult it was for the passengers belowdecks. He understood their misery. He planned to allow them to stay on deck for the rest of the trip. They could go up and down the ladder as they wished, to prepare meals, maybe to sleep in the bunks, and to use the toilet bucket.

Of the one hundred and twenty-five steerage passengers who left Galway on March 19, a total of fourteen had died and been committed to the sea. Another nine were too ill or too weak to come up on deck, and they stayed in their bunks. Several others remained below to care for the sick.

For the first time, all of the Bodkin family would be on deck together as they had no possessions left worth stealing. Biddy did not sprint as she had in Galway. There was no pushing or jostling and no way to get up. A big crowd at the bottom of the ladder was waiting—everyone moved slower than they had on the day of departure. Mam and Da were weak from the voyage; they had each lost a significant amount of weight and needed help getting to the bottom of the ladder, through the crowd, and more help getting up. But they made it.

Once on deck the Bodkins moved toward the railings on the starboard side of the ship and looked north at Long Island. At dawn, it was chilly in the stiff breeze, but what Dominic saw was beautiful.

Land!

It was the first land they had seen since the western tip of Ireland. To Dominic, it looked like a massive stretch—miles and miles of long and wide, very white, sandy beaches with no landmarks, no houses, no man-made walls, and no sign of life. None of the beaches the Bodkins had seen around Galway looked anything like this beach. Only Da had seen beaches with sand as white as this before. Da had worked as a child in a townland called Ballyconneely in Connemara. Beautiful beaches existed along the coast of Connemara, but none were as long, or as wide, or as white, as the beaches he saw now. Dominic realized there was no wondering why it was called "Long" Island. Uncle Laurence's geography lessons had prepared him well.

The land and the beach became clearer to the passengers as they sailed closer. The *Cushlamachree* continued her westerly course—only a couple of miles offshore—as she sailed at full speed with a steady and favorable wind still blowing. Along the railing, the family stood arm-in-arm. Mam and Da were in the middle of their children. Patt and Nora were next to each other at one end of the line, eager to be Patt O'Donnell and Nora Jones once again.

Patt was looking everywhere in the crowd for Maria. He found her. She was with the Masseys, and though they caught

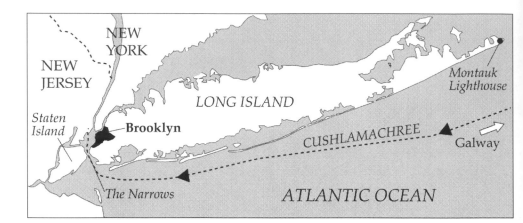

each other's gaze, she had to watch the children as Steven and Precious enjoyed the sight of Long Island. Maria and Patt waved to each other. *Maybe?* Patt thought. *Maybe? She touched her fingers to her lips. Maybe she blew me a kiss?* He would find Maria on the dock in New York.

The family spent the day topside, only going below to take care of necessities. Many passengers were back and forth to steerage all day, and that left enough room on the deck so those remaining topside could find a bulkhead to sit against while enjoying their first views of America. By mid-morning, the passengers saw signs of life. At first, it was smoke, then chimneys with smoke, then the houses with the chimneys came into view. Soon fishing boats bobbed on the sea between the *Cushlamachree* and the shore. A significant cheer arose among the passengers when two fishermen waved to the Irish immigrants crammed against the railings. *Maybe those men are Irish immigrants too?* wondered Dominic.

Boats the size of the *Cushlamachree* and larger, loaded with cargo on the return trip to Europe, passed them heading east. The passengers and crews waved to each other across the distance.

Other than long stretches of beach along the coast, all Dominic could see was flat and barren land. However, as they sailed west, more houses began to become visible—attached houses, reminding him of some of the homes in Galway. More and more houses. By late in the afternoon, there was still beach along the coast, but the buildings behind the beaches went on as far as Dominic could see. Most of the buildings seemed to be three and four stories.

"This must be Brooklyn, Da," Dominic said to his father, who was now standing next to him. "It is a much larger city than I had expected, Dominic," his father answered as he looked at the skyline in amazement. "Brooklyn is indeed a much larger city than Galway."

It was the beginning of spring, and beautiful trees were in bloom everywhere. Crab apple and pear trees with white blossoms. Cherry and maple trees with reddish flowers and large green-leafed trees—*Ailanthus altissima*, the tree of heaven. A tree the children knew grew in to Brooklyn, thanks to Uncle Laurence's botany lessons.

Hopefully, the passengers would see New York City tomorrow. Manhattan Island it was called. It would be bigger still.

Captain Thomas had shortened the *Cushlamachree*'s sails, and the boat was moving slowly.

"New Jersey is off the port," Captain Thomas told the passengers. "Staten Island is straight ahead."

Crewmen climbed into the rigging to lower the *Cushlamachree*'s sails, and the boat came to rest. The crew dropped the anchor in the Narrows as the sun was beginning to set off the port side. Several ships queued ahead of them. Word spread that they would have to wait for the inspectors from the customs department to get the ship's manifest from the captain and to assess the passengers' financial ability, as well as other information about their destinations, sponsors, and housing. The passengers all needed the name and address of a sponsor, and they needed some money to prove they wouldn't be a burden on the Americans. A destitute Irish immigrant would go back to Ireland.

A Health Department inspector would also board the *Cushlamachree* and review the health of the passengers. No one could come into America if they had typhus or cholera—or any other infectious disease—and an insane person couldn't get in. The sick passengers would be taken straight to a hospital, where they would await their almost certain death. The inspectors would decide who could enter the country.

The boats ahead of the *Cushlamachree* seemed to be waiting for the inspectors. There were several smaller boats that Dominic thought might be the harbormaster, the health inspector, or the customs agents. He wasn't sure what they were, but the smaller boats didn't have sails or men rowing with oars. Each boat had a long, large-diameter pipe protruding from its deck with smoke puffing from it. "Martin," Dominic reminded his brother, "Uncle Laurence told us about this type of boat. It's a harbor boat, and it has an engine that is powered by the steam created by heated water. The excess steam is coming out of that stack." The boys watched in amazement as the small boats glided effortlessly through the Narrows as they went back and forth between the boats ahead of them in the queue.

Martin and Dominic watched the harbor boats for a while and helped their parents back to the bunks. Dominic was worried about his parents. They did not show obvious signs of disease being present, but they did appear weak. Mam and Da would need support to get through the health inspection.

The shadows of early evening stretched against the Brooklyn buildings, and the gas lamplights turned on. Eventually, as night fell, everyone made their way back down the ladder to sleep in a filthy bunk for another night.

HOLY THURSDAY

FOR THE FIRST TIME SINCE THE *CUSHLAMACHREE* LEFT Galway, the night passed quietly in steerage. The ship was at anchor. The sound of the constant straining of the hull cutting through the ocean was gone. The excitement of Wednesday—seeing land for the first time, seeing Brooklyn and Staten Island, waving to the fishermen off Long Island—may have exhausted the passengers. The sheer volume of fresh air and sunshine they experienced by spending the entire day on deck were all good variables assisting a good night's sleep.

Dominic and Cate were the first two of the family on deck in the morning. The sun was rising through the fog off the starboard side of the *Cushlamachree,* and the Narrows' swells were reasonably calm. Nothing had changed from the situation at nightfall, other than three new ships were now anchored in the queue behind the *Cushlamachree,* and a fourth, still under sail, could be seen arriving from the east. The rest of the family, slowly but surely, came on deck and took positions along the bulkhead.

They waited.

Rumors spread that the customs inspector was coming today. The Bodkins had thirty-seven pounds left in Cate's bank and no worries there. They had a sponsor, and they had a place to live. Other families, however, were trying to get some money in their pockets—at least temporarily—and individuals had to get stories straight about who was meeting them at the dock and where they would be living.

Patt found Maria, and she explained she would have no problem passing the customs questions because she would be Mr. Massey's employee until after they disembarked in New York. How she was getting to Port Jervis, however, was still an unanswered question.

All morning the passengers watched the ships ahead of them, and they focused on a harbor boat which had one crewman and one man in uniform. Everyone on deck assumed it was the customs inspector. After noon, the skiff pulled alongside the *Cushlamachree,* and one of the crew threw a line to the man in uniform. The skiff tied off, a rope ladder was draped over the side, and the man in uniform climbed aboard. Across the crown of his blue cap was emblazoned in gold script:

UNITED STATES DEPARTMENT OF CUSTOMS

Captain Thomas greeted him personally, and the two men disappeared into the captain's quarters.

Most of the passengers were on deck, hushed with fear, for what seemed an interminable length of time. After half an hour, the inspector came out of the office holding the ship's manifest, which listed the passengers' names, ages, and other information. The inspector had a very solemn expression on his face. He was all business as he walked around the deck, asking passengers questions, checking off each name as he did so with the captain following alongside. He only talked to the adults, assuming the children would have the same answers as their parents. He did not speak to all of the adults—he was selective, it seemed, in the interest of his time. He quietly asked Captain Thomas, "Where is the Bodkin family?"

The family was against the bulkhead. The Bodkins were the largest family group on the ship, so Captain Thomas knew who they were. He brought the inspector over toward them. The captain pointed to the family and said, "Here they are. These are the Bodkins, Mr. Neylon. They are the ones you want."

Singled out, the Bodkins were petrified. No other passengers had been sought out by name as they had been. They had only seen the captain a few times on deck and had never spoken to him other than to say good morning. Now Captain Thomas seemed eager to garner favor with the inspector by identifying the family.

What had they done wrong?

Were they in trouble for something?

The inspector walked directly to Mam and Da, and his face broke into a broad and welcoming smile. "My name is Paul Neylon, and I am a friend of Father Bernard Fitzpatrick, from Saint Patrick's Church. He asked me to find you and welcome you to America." The family was stunned—with an immense sense of relief.

After Mam and Da had greeted Mr. Neylon, Dominic introduced himself and the rest of the family. Neylon explained that he would personally let Father Fitzpatrick know the *Cushlamachree*'s schedule. The customs man told the family that the health inspector would not get to the ship until Saturday and to expect Father Fitzpatrick to be waiting for them on the wharf on Sunday. The inspector wished the family well and indicated that he hoped to see them in church regularly at Saint Patrick's.

As he was leaving, the inspector said, "Dominic, may I speak with you a moment?" Dominic and the inspector walked across the deck and back over to the rope ladder so Neylon could exit the ship.

"Dominic, your parents are the oldest passengers on the ship, and they do not look well. Be sure you have them on deck when the health inspector arrives on Saturday. Find them a good place to sit and make sure they don't have to walk while the inspector is near them. Be sure they only answer the questions he asks. If he asks how they feel, be sure they tell him they are tired from the trip and need a few good meals. I will talk to the health inspector myself before he gets to the *Cushlamachree,* and your parents should have nothing to fear." Dominic thanked the inspector for his help. Neylon said, "Don't worry, young man. Father Fitzpatrick has a lot of friends."

Captain Thomas met the inspector at the ladder. They had a few private words, and Neylon left the boat. Later in the afternoon, one of the crewmen came over to the family and said Captain Thomas wanted to see Mam and Da in his cabin.

What now! Dominic thought.

Cate and Dominic helped their parents to the captain's quarters. The captain sat them in chairs at his dining table and closed the door. He produced two bowls of hearty soup and placed them in front of Mam and Da. He said to them, "Mr. Neylon asked me to help you. Today is Thursday. Come back here again, quietly, at this hour on Friday and again on Saturday. We have to do our best to give you some nourishment before the health inspector arrives."

Dominic, Cate, Mam, and Da thanked Captain Thomas—and the Lord—for his gifts on Holy Thursday.

As evening fell, the last family to come belowdecks brought a bucket of seawater to steerage and placed it in front of the bunk where Mam and Da were sitting.

For the first time on the voyage, the Massey family and Maria came down the ladder to be with steerage passengers. If the stench of the bunks or the sick and dying passengers impacted the Masseys, it didn't show. Dressed in their finest, but by now well-worn, clothes, they walked straight to Mam and Da.

Most of the passengers were Catholic and knew they should attend Mass on Holy Thursday evening—the Mass of the Lord's Supper. But there was no priest on the *Cushlamachree*. Surprisingly, Stephen Massey took it upon himself to lead an impromptu ceremony.

He read from his copy of the New Testament, "'A new commandment I give unto you,' the Lord said to his Apostles, as he washed their feet at the Last Supper on the night before he was crucified, 'that you love one another, as I have loved you.'" He knelt next to the bucket of water in front of Mam while Precious knelt in front of Da. "John and Eleanor, you are the oldest among us," Steven explained, "and you represent our community's strength in the search for freedom and opportunity."

Reverently, the Masseys washed the Bodkins' feet as the other steerage passengers bowed their heads in silent devotion.

21

GIFTS

DOMINIC WAS NOT YET FOURTEEN YEARS OLD, BUT already he had learned a lot about the sciences, mathematics, and language. He had also learned a lot about life. One of the essential things he had learned was to appreciate the value of a gift. Especially the gifts he received from his parents.

Mam and Da had given him the gift of life. The most valuable gift of all.

The hardships of life in Ireland in the middle of the nineteenth century made some Irishmen question the value of life, but not Dominic. His present conditions were not ideal, but he saw his future as being full of opportunity. Opportunities to grow, to advance, to improve. The chance to help others achieve their potential.

Dominic also appreciated that his parents had given up their lives in Ireland to improve their children's chances to succeed in life. Mam and Da could easily have decided to stay in Briarhill, live miserably, and die an early death caused by starvation or typhus, or dysentery. They could have taken the easy way out and left the children to be young orphans with no hope for the future, to be raised by older siblings, or maybe by an aunt or a distant cousin. They did not take the easy way, however, and were in the process of surrendering their lives for their children. Dominic understood the decision his parents made, and what they were doing now, and he appreciated their gift.

The education Dominic received from Uncle Laurence was another gift he treasured. His education was comprehensive, including history, geography, and astronomy. One history lesson was, by far, more interesting to Dominic than all of the others.

It was in the seventeenth century that many British citizens left Great Britain for the "colonies." They sailed across the Atlantic because of overpopulation, poverty, and the religious persecution commoners were experiencing in England and Scotland. In one form or another, they began a new homeland. The early colonists either lived with the American Indians or fought with them. The colonists started a new economy and enjoyed religious freedom, while still living under the control of the British monarch. The bravery and persistence of the colonists, combined with the bounty they produced from the land they farmed on the eastern coast of America, led to a level of economic success the British wanted to control—and tax.

Eventually, the American colonists recognized that the long arm of the oppressive British monarchy—the same monarchy their forefathers had escaped when they left England—had followed them to America. And so, the first shots of the Americans' Revolutionary War were fired.

The Americans, under the guidance of some strong leaders and generals, formed an army to fight the British. The American leaders declared independence from the British Empire and became the United States of America, on July 4, 1776. The first battle after that declaration of freedom was fought on August 27 and became known as the Battle of Brooklyn. The American revolutionaries, led by General George Washington, lost the first battle with the British, but the Americans did not give up. Washington's ragtag army fought again and again—up and down the Atlantic coast—all across the thirteen colonies.

Finally, in October 1781, the war ended when the colonial army won the Battle of Yorktown in Virginia. Two years later, the Americans were formally granted their independence when representatives of King George III signed the Treaty of Paris. In 1789, a new form of federal government was established, and General Washington was elected as the first president of the United States of America.

George Washington was one of Dominic's heroes.

So was the man who taught him about Washington, the Battle of Brooklyn, and the American Revolution—his uncle Laurence.

Dominic wanted to be as strong a person and a leader as his heroes.

Dominic watched the gaslights come on in Brooklyn for the second time. He thought about the eerie similarities between the oppression, the poverty, and the religious persecution the Irish were experiencing today in their homeland and what George Washington's Americans fought to escape seventy-five years earlier.

Across the Narrows, in his office in the rectory of Saint Patrick's Church, Father Fitzpatrick was busy about the affairs of his church during the holiest week in the Catholic Church's liturgical year.

Father Fitzpatrick's parish was growing, week after week. In addition to people moving to Brooklyn from Manhattan Island, many Irish immigrants, like the Bodkins, were getting off the boat and coming directly to Brooklyn every day. His new church was almost full for daily Mass. It was frequently full on Sundays.

The connections his parishioners had to the new immigrants—a sibling, a cousin, an aunt, or an uncle from Ireland—required the church to have a system. Someone from the parish had to be at the bottom of the gangway at the pier in Lower Manhattan to greet the arriving family members and lead them to their new home in Brooklyn.

Father Fitzpatrick planned to be there personally to meet Bishop O'Donnell's family.

On the afternoon of Holy Thursday, April 20, 1848, Customs Inspector Paul Neylon came to the rectory office, as he usually did at the end of his long workday. He found Father Fitzpatrick in his office and knocked gently on the door. "Excuse me, Father."

The priest looked up. "Paulie! Hello, Paulie. Come in, come in, sit down, please sit down."

"Thank you, Father. I wanted to let you know, Father, the *Cushlamachree* dropped anchor behind three ships from Liverpool in the Narrows last night." Neylon was a man of few words. "I met with its captain today, and I had him introduce me to the family."

They made it! Fitzpatrick thought. He confirmed with Neylon that every family member was aboard—everyone O'Donnell had told him to expect.

Neylon went on, "The medical inspector is a little behind schedule, and nine ships are at anchor ahead of the *Cushlamachree*, so he will not get to do their inspection until Saturday, and the ship should dock with Sunday afternoon's slack tide. Here is the list of the other three ships from Liverpool, Father. Some of our friends in the parish are waiting for two of these boats to arrive. We'll have to let them know that Sunday is the day."

Neylon was an Irishman from Corofin, County Clare, in western Ireland. He had immigrated to Brooklyn about twenty years earlier, joined the United States Navy, married a German girl, and worked at the Brooklyn Navy Yard. Now he wore the uniform of an inspector for the United States Customs Department. Every day he met the Irish Famine Ships after they dropped anchor in the Narrows.

"How did the family look?" Father Fitzpatrick asked.

"All of the children looked thin, as expected, but otherwise healthy, Father. The parents did not seem to weather the trip as well." Paul stayed ahead of Father Fitzpatrick's thoughts. "I will talk to the medical inspector to make sure he understands your special interest in the Bodkins."

"Thank you, Paulie." The priest smiled at his friend. "Holy Thursday Mass is at six o'clock this evening. Will I see you and Shirley there?"

Saint Patrick's Church was on the corner of Kent and Willoughby Avenues. Neylon would walk home to his house a few blocks away on Myrtle Avenue, and then he and his wife, Shirley, would walk back to the church for the Mass and the Washing of the Feet ceremony.

"See you tonight, Father. The Bodkins looked like nice people. I'm glad they made it across."

On the walk home, Paul thought about how to pose his question to Shirley.

Thirty-three hundred miles east of Brooklyn, Saint Columba's Church in Castlegar was full for Holy Thursday's evening service. Every resident of Castlegar and Briarhill was present. About sixty filled the church. Father McCann and Bishop O'Donnell were finished washing the feet of Saint Columba's most destitute parishioners. Everyone in the congregation was paying attention to the service but was also praying for the Bodkins. They had no way to know the *Cushlamachree* was at anchor outside New York Harbor and all the Bodkins were alive and safe.

The Duvals were in the front pew of the church, James and Ailis included. The senior Duvals were in Castlegar to help Mary and Dan with the final preparations for the move to the Duvals' Galway home. Seated toward the middle of the congregation were Jamie and Carmel Flynn, with their friend Mickey Bellew. At the end of the service, the bishop made a few comments about missing the large Bodkin family from the congregation and led a prayer to Saint Christopher for their safety.

After Mass, the four Duvals, Bishop O'Donnell, and Father McCann walked over to Mary and Dan's house and agreed upon its purchase by the Diocese of Galway to be the new rectory for Saint Columba's Church.

GOOD FRIDAY

THE GOOD FRIDAY SERVICE AT SAINT PATRICK'S Church in Brooklyn was the same lengthy, somber, muted service that was experienced by Catholics all over the world. Nearly everywhere throughout Christendom, the Good Friday service lasted three hours and included a substantial amount of kneeling and chanting, integrated with periods of silent prayer. Its conclusion—at three in the afternoon—was designed to commemorate the hour of Christ's death on the cross.

Father B.J. Fitzpatrick led his parishioners through the three-hour service. On the most solemn day of the liturgical year, many businesses were closed and children did not attend school, so the pews were full. Parishioners lined the walls along the side aisles and stood on both sides of the center aisle. The reading of the Passion, the Veneration of the Cross, various litanies, and the homily dominated the service.

B.J. had spent hours working on this year's sermon. The knowledge that he had people he considered to be family and friends still enduring the harsh voyage from Ireland, yet only a few miles from Saint Patrick's altar, weighed heavily on his preparations. The fact that he did not have anywhere near enough room in his tiny rectory for nine long-term visitors had not left his thoughts for many weeks. This week, however, his problem became the subject of significant prayer. He needed help, and he spent all of Holy Week praying for it.

The pulpit in Saint Patrick's Church provided the church's pastor a suitable place to proclaim the word of God in the reading of the gospel each day at Mass. The impressive structure also gave a pastor a significant position of authority as he stood before a church full of his parishioners each Sunday when he described to them the fires of hell associated with the evils of sin and the joy associated with tithing. Today, as he climbed the four marble steps into the rounded, canopied, mahogany pulpit to address his congregation, he prayed for guidance. He spoke to his parishioners for about thirty minutes. Except for the occasional baby making the noises babies make, the church was silent and his congregation attentive.

Paul and Shirley Neylon were seated in the fourth row of the church, on what Catholics call the "gospel side." Paul sat by the aisle. Saint Patrick's Church was a predominantly Irish parish, but there were also many Italian and German immigrant parishioners. The Italians and the Germans had been in the neighborhoods of Brooklyn Heights and Fort Greene longer than most of the Irish, who now dominated the nearby Vinegar Hill and Clinton Hill neighborhoods. Sitting next to Shirley Neylon was Giuseppe Visconti and his young son, Joey. Two rows behind the Neylons sat a young family of Germans, Eugene and Liesl Etzkorn.

No other parishioners were waiting for passengers on the *Cushlamachree*, but Susan Caulfield, Kathleen McSherry, and Luke Smith sat anxiously in the pews as they prayed for Irish sisters and brothers who had arrived in the Narrows on the ships that sailed from Liverpool. Their siblings were from Waterford, Kildare, and Milltown Pass.

All of Father Fitzpatrick's parishioners knew each other, and his sermon had to address their concerns. He talked about having faith and hope on this Good Friday, and he spoke about charity. He stressed the faith his parishioners needed related to believing that, on Easter Sunday, Christ would rise from the dead. He compared their faith to the hope Christ's disciples must have had more than eighteen hundred years earlier. "Charity," Father Fitzpatrick said from the pulpit, "is what this parish of immigrants is about. Christ gave his life to save each of ours. We all came from nothing. We had nothing in Ireland, or Germany, or Italy, but now we have something here in Brooklyn. At least we have hope. Some of us have more, and some of us have less, but every one of us has something to share. Those who follow us to these shores will need our help as individuals and as a parish. We must make their lives livable."

Shirley leaned toward Paul and whispered, "Let's find Father after church and tell him we'll do it."

The solemn service ended as scheduled, at three o'clock, and everyone processed down the central aisle and out the front door.

Good Friday was a day of fasting in the Catholic Church, and therefore there was no reception with cookies and liquid refreshments after the service. So, Paul and Shirley caught up with Father Fitzpatrick on the path to the rectory. Shirley told him what was on their minds.

Out on the *Cushlamachree*, it was a warm, sunny day, and it was unlike any Good Friday the Bodkins had ever experienced before. The temperature was as warm on this April 21 as it would be on the warmest day of the summer in Galway. The colors of the buds on the trees were visible from the deck. Some were pink, some were yellow, some were white, but all reflected the new life that occurred in nature every year.

Word spread throughout the ship that Stephen Massey would lead a Good Friday service, and a crowd of passengers gathered on the forecastle. About eighty of the passengers and crew participated. The textile merchant from New York began by leading several hymns, with which everyone was familiar. He did scripture readings from the New Testament and led the assembled passengers around the deck, replicating the Stations of the Cross by stopping fourteen times, to lead them in prayer. The passengers all knelt and said the rosary to conclude the service at around three in the afternoon. Dominic was impressed by Mr. Massey's leadership of the service, and he was amazed by the camaraderie that existed among the passengers after their long voyage. All of the initial uncertainty Maria Teresa Jones had expressed about Massey had long ago disappeared. He seemed to be a gentleman and a scholar.

After the Good Friday service, Dominic and Cate quietly brought Mam and Da to Captain Thomas' quarters, where he again had hearty bowls of soup to share with them. The captain showed the same friendship and cooperative spirit to the Bodkins that Dominic had just seen among the passengers at the conclusion of the Good Friday service. They devoured the soup, but Dominic was anxious about his parents' upcoming health inspection.

As evening fell, Dominic thought, *Two more nights and our new lives will begin.*

JUST A SMILE

January 23, 1902
Saint James Cathedral, Brooklyn

8:30 AM: *People I knew from years ago, neighbors, relatives, and others I didn't know at all kept coming through the cathedral's big doors. I wondered if there would be enough seats in the pews.*

I saw a lady talking to Cate. She was an old friend—probably about seventy years old now—standing arm-in-arm with her daughter and son-in-law. More than a decade had passed since the last time I'd seen the woman. She came over to me, we hugged, and she kissed me on the cheek. She still had a beautiful smile.

"I'm so sorry, Martin."

Once again, I found meself entertaining a memory I shouldn't have been having at me brother's funeral ...

It was Good Friday and I remembered I couldn't sleep that night. From the monotonous sounds of quiet slumber surrounding me, I judged I might be the only one in steerage who was awake.

Over the weeks me mind had grown to be at ease with the dangers and insecurity of the temporary living conditions provided on the Cushlamachree. But that was all due to change tomorrow—or the next day—and whatever we would find in Brooklyn wouldn't be temporary. It would last forever. The reality of that permanence generated a level of anxiety in every one of us. Me personal fears had kept me from sleeping since the day we dropped anchor in the Narrows, and I needed some fresh air and solitude to commit myself to me unknown future. But Patt was on one side of me snoring and Lawrence on the other. Me little brother seemed to have developed extremely sharp elbows and kept moving closer to me. I had to climb over me cousin to get out of the bunk, and I did it successfully without waking him. I made the way to the top of the ladder and opened the hatch. The chilly night air was invigorating—but I wasn't alone.

Maria had wrapped herself in a blanket and was sitting on top of the boat lines coiled up on the forecastle. She was older than me—but only a few years—and of course I had noticed she was pretty, but tonight, with her tousled red hair mostly stuffed into her white linen nightcap, I imagined her differently.

"Hello," I whispered, even though there was no one else on deck. "You couldn't sleep either?"

She smiled when she saw me, pulled the blanket tighter around her shoulders, and tucked it up around her chin. "No, I couldn't." Her eyes told me to sit next to her and I did.

"I'm frightened, Martin. So much is going to change—so fast." Maria looked toward the gaslights twinkling on the Brooklyn shoreline, and I knew what she meant.

"I agree. Every one of us will begin a new life in a day or two, and we all have doubts and fears."

She tucked the blanket under her knees and gazed across the Narrows. "You shouldn't be afraid, Martin." I didn't remember if she took my hand or if I reached out for hers, but there we were, sitting and *talking about our futures. "You have your family. They're all strong. You know where you're going and have someone to meet you. You will be together. When we walk down the gangway in New York, you will go to Brooklyn, and I'll head for Port Jervis and probably never see anyone on this boat again."*

"Do you have to go to Port Jervis?" I asked.

"I do." She fiddled with the blanket. "Before my mother died, I promised her I would come to America and live with my cousin Denise."

"What about Patt?" I asked, with a level of caution that surprised me.

"Patt's sweet, Martin. But ... he's not for me. Perhaps I'll find someone in Port Jervis. Perhaps never."

"Maybe," I thought quickly, "you could just visit your cousin and then come back to New York. If you kept working for Mistress Massey, we could all see each other once in a while."

"It's too late to change my plans now. I overheard the Masseys discussing that they will offer my position to Cate. They've liked her since the day we all met on the quay. Mistress said Cate was good with the children."

Mesmerized, I watched as Maria brushed at a tear that ran down her cheek.

"I'm probably upset about nothing, but I made a promise to my mother and I have a plan. A person can't just change everything on a whim." She tucked a long red curl back under her nightcap. "That's not the way I do things."

Maria turned toward me. "Thank you for listening." She looked straight into my eyes and smiled. "I'm happy I got to know you, Martin."

She kissed my cheek ...

24

HOLY SATURDAY

THE DAY BEFORE EASTER WAS AGAIN AN UNUSUALLY
warm day by New York standards. The temperature rose to above
eighty degrees Fahrenheit by two o'clock in the afternoon, and
the sky was clear. The sun was intense, and the fair-skinned passengers from Galway could feel its rays burning their skin. It was
too hot in steerage, and everyone who was able climbed the ladder and found a little bit of shade on deck. Naturally, the shadiest
places on deck kept changing based on the angle of the sun. Since
Wednesday, when the *Cushlamachree* anchored in the Narrows, the
harbor master's crew had pulled a skiff alongside several times
and dropped off fresh water for the passengers and crew. The
water was a godsend. Dominic did his best to keep his parents
hydrated and sitting in whatever shade was available.

The passengers saw what they assumed was the medical
inspector's skiff tied alongside a vessel fifty yards ahead of the
Cushlamachree in the queue of ships waiting to enter the harbor.
Dominic anticipated the inspector's arrival later in the afternoon.

For the third day, at around three o'clock in the afternoon,
Cate and Dominic helped their parents to the captain's quarters,

and he again shared his soup with them. Captain John Thomas had evolved, over the past two days, into an angel of mercy for Mam and Da. The soup gave the parents more energy for a few hours, but then they resumed the extreme lethargy they had experienced for the last two weeks.

The health inspector arrived on board, and Dominic's parents were among the first to be examined. The man from the New York State Department of Health, Dr. R.A. "Red" Mahoney, was originally from County Cork but had arrived in America nearly thirty years ago. He was sixty-five years of age and was a tall and trim man. He walked with a slight limp. The doctor was a man of tremendous patience, with an excellent medical background. He lived with his wife and family in Brooklyn, and, like the Neylons, the Mahoneys were also parishioners of Saint Patrick's Church. He placed a lot of trust in a man's word.

He said, "Mr. and Mrs. Bodkin, you look well today after your long voyage. Welcome to New York! I am pleased you will be staying with Father Fitzpatrick. He will look after you and help you with any medical needs you might have. I am happy to pronounce you medically fit to enter America, and I wish you the best of luck with your health and your new lives in America. I hope to see you many times again at Sunday Mass." Dominic wondered if someday he could be the caring, perceptive person Dr. Red Mahoney was. *Maybe,* Dominic thought, *I might become a doctor someday.*

Dominic grasped Dr. Mahoney's hand and thanked him for his favorable opinion. He thought about the long reach of Uncle Laurence. The bishop had reached out to his friend from the seminary at Maynooth, Father Fitzpatrick, and his sphere eventually influenced two men Bishop O'Donnell did not even know, first Paul Neylon and now Red Mahoney. Once again, the Bodkins were the beneficiary of Uncle Laurence's assistance.

Later in the afternoon, it was still warm on the *Cushlamachree's* deck. Luckily for the passengers, as the sun began to set, the evening temperature came down, and the passengers were able to move back belowdecks for the last night of the voyage. The murmur of anticipation in steerage continued well past midnight. Almost no passenger was able to sleep. As Dominic tried to sleep, he thought about the *Cushlamachree* moving into the harbor. The passengers would disembark tomorrow and begin the rest of their lives. Some of them would stay in New York City. The hawkers on the wharf would lure them with the offer of inexpensive housing in one of the worst slums in the world, the hellhole known as the Five Points. The Bodkins, and many others, would cross the East River and take up residence in Brooklyn. Dominic imagined Brooklyn and what plans Father Fitzpatrick had for the family. The Masseys would leave the wharf at the seaport, on the lower east side of Manhattan, and return to their Gramercy Park home, which was less than five miles north. Stephen and Precious would have to find a nanny to replace Maria Teresa. Maria would find her way to Port Jervis and try to locate her relatives from County Longford. Patrick O'Donnell and Nora Jones talked, quietly on this last night, about their new family, the Bodkins, and also about what they might find in Harrison, New York.

As he searched for sleep on his last night in steerage, Dominic thought, *Brooklyn, New York, and Briarhill, Ireland, are different worlds. I hope I'm ready.*

Captain Thomas and his first mate watched the gaslights twinkle in the Brooklyn streets. The water was calm on the Narrows, and tomorrow would be a slow but stressful day as the two men would guide the *Cushlamachree* into her berth.

Back at his home on Lafayette Avenue, Red Mahoney knelt by his bed and said his evening prayers. He knew the rules—and he had bent them—but he prayed he had made the correct decision about John and Eleanor Bodkin.

Eventually, sleep came for most.

25

FATHER BERNARD
JOSEPH FITZPATRICK

April 23, 1848

"MÁIRE!" B.J. FITZPATRICK CALLED FROM THE FRONT
door of the rectory to his housekeeper, who was in the kitchen,
already busy preparing Easter dinner.

"MAH-ree!" he called louder. "MAH-ree! *Tá mé fágáil don bhád
farantóireachta,* Máire!" I'm leaving for the ferry, Máire! he called
to her. The seventy-one-year-old priest was a little exasperated as
he rushed around the rectory after saying Easter Mass before a
full church at Saint Patrick's.

Máire came rushing from the kitchen, wiping wet hands on
her apron. *"An t-Athair* Fitzpatrick, do you think you should bring
your overcoat? If the Bodkins are late to arrive, you will get cold
when the sun begins to set."

She reached for his black coat, which was hanging on its
usual hook by the front door. The days had been warmer than
usual during every day of Holy Week, but the nights were still
seasonally chilly.

"I will be fine, Máire. Paulie Neylon has assured me the *Cush-lamachree* will dock right on time."

"*Go han-mhaith, Athair.*" Very well, Father.

Máire knew she couldn't win this argument. The man hated to wear a coat. She mumbled, "Stubborn man," shook her head, and hung his overcoat back on its hook.

She gave him a satchel with an apple, some cheese, and bread—his favorite lunch. Such a little bit wouldn't ruin his Easter dinner.

Thank you, Máire.

"*Bí cúramach os a chionn, Athair.*" Please be careful over there, Father.

Máire had not been back to Manhattan since the day five years ago when she arrived in America, but she knew firsthand the dangers faced by the arriving Irish. On the day she arrived, Father Bernard Joseph Fitzpatrick was on the wharf, meeting newly arriving parishioners. Almost as soon as twenty-year-old Máire stepped alone onto the dock at South and John Streets in Lower Manhattan, she was accosted by two Sicilian men. They intended to feature the beautiful young Irish woman as a new attraction in their brothel on Mulberry Street. After a physical scuffle with the two thugs, Fitzpatrick rescued Máire and brought her back to the safety of his rectory.

Máire, who was from Mulranny in County Mayo, could not speak English when she arrived in New York, and Father Fitzpatrick had helped her to learn the language during the years she had been his housekeeper. However, when he was agitated about something, they frequently slipped back into Irish.

"*Beidh mé ar ais ag an am dinnéar, Máire. Geallaim.*" He promised Máire he'd be back by dinnertime and rushed out the door.

The short ferry ride to Lower Manhattan gave Fitzpatrick time to think back on his childhood and his lifetime of knowing Laurence O'Donnell. When B.J. was a teenager, his mother was a nervous little woman who was overwhelmed by having to raise a small boy who had a penchant for finding himself in trouble. She called him "Bernie." Her only other child was a daughter who was the perfect child for whom every mother prays.

The Fitzpatrick family lived on the Wellington Quay in the Temple Bar section of Dublin. The second-floor rooms in which they lived were one street away from the Ha'penny Bridge, on the south bank of the River Liffey. Temple Bar was the seediest, most crime-ridden section of Dublin, and it was notorious for offering many ways in which a young boy could get into trouble, if he was so inclined. Prostitutes, pickpockets, and petty thieves ruled Temple Bar—night and day. As a teenage boy, B.J. knew them all.

After one of B.J.'s more severe transgressions, his mother decided that he was too much for her to handle. Bernie was going to represent the family in the priesthood. Young B.J. understood more clearly what his mother meant when she said, "Bernie, get the hell out of the house!"

A few days later, nineteen-year-old Bernie found himself knocking on the door of the Catholic seminary in Maynooth, County Kildare. A tall, young priest, Father Jack Tracey, answered the door. The bespectacled Tracey stood six feet nine inches tall and appeared five inches taller with the black, three-peaked biretta that Catholic priests wear on their heads. Father Tracey was the tallest man B.J. had ever seen.

B.J. looked up at Tracey. "Good day, Father. My name is Bernard Joseph Fitzpatrick, and my mother has evicted me from her house. Will you help me to be a better person? Will you teach me to be a priest?"

Tracey shook his head in dismay, as he met yet another young man who was evidence of the negatively trending Irish Catholic priesthood.

"Can you read, Fitzpatrick?" Tracey asked his young visitor.

B.J. nodded.

"Can you write your letters and your numbers?"

"Yes. I can, Father."

"English and Irish?"

"Yes, Father, both." B.J. had passed the entrance examination.

Fitzpatrick was the second seminarian admitted that day. The first "knock, knock, knock" of the big iron clapper that morning had brought the face of a man named Laurence O'Donnell. O'Donnell had surprised Tracey in that he seemed to be well-educated and a gentleman.

Tracey told Fitzpatrick to follow him, and together they walked down a street and around the corner to McHugh Hall, where the novice seminarians lived. Tracey led Fitzpatrick up a flight of rickety stairs to a room that had the number 210 painted on the door. The tall priest did not knock. He opened the door and walked in. Sitting on one of the two beds in the room was O'Donnell, a tall, good-looking young man who was a few years older than Fitzpatrick. Father Tracey introduced the two novitiates and left them alone.

The two young men endured a few awkward moments of silence, then began to explore why they were each at the seminary.

"Do you really want to be a priest?"

"Which bed do you want?"

Then the family questions. "Brothers?" "Sisters?" "Where do you live?" "What about schooling?"

"Are you hungry?"

B.J. said he was always hungry.

O'Donnell explained he had recently completed his studies at Saint Patrick's College, on the other side of Maynooth, so he knew his way around the small town. "I know a pub, McCabe's Pub. It's only a ten-minute walk."

He was right. As Fitzpatrick would learn, Laurence O'Donnell was usually right.

Ten minutes later, they were sitting at McCabe's Pub with the foam of two pints rising in front of them. They ordered some food, and they continued the individual background checks they had begun back at McHugh Hall.

O'Donnell told Fitzpatrick all about Oughterard, Galway City, and the outlying areas of County Galway.

Fitzpatrick told Laurence about Dublin, accentuating its seedier side. "In fact," B.J. admitted, "this is my first time outside of Dublin."

The two new friends shared a meal of potatoes and ale. The boxty loaf was straight out of the oven. Four pints later, Laurence O'Donnell and B.J. Fitzpatrick found themselves stumbling out of McCabe's Pub and heading back in the direction of the seminary. August 26, 1800, was their first day as novices at the Maynooth Seminary, and neither man considered spending the first night getting drunk at a pub to bode well for future "men of the cloth." Morning Mass with the seminary's rector and the other novitiates was in four hours. It would be a stressful morning for the new roommates.

Nearly half a century later—Easter morning, April 23, 1848— Father Fitzpatrick's ferry approached Fulton Ferry's dock in New York City. He found himself smiling at the memories of Laurence and their years together in Maynooth. He almost laughed out loud when he thought, Bishop *Laurence O'Donnell!* Pastor *Bernard Joseph Fitzpatrick!*

From his seat on the ferry, he could tell the *Cushlamachree* had not yet arrived at her dock. The tide was still coming in, and he judged it would be several hours before the Bodkin family walked down the gangway. The Easter dinner of turkey and ham Máire was preparing at the rectory would be ready about the time he arrived with his new family.

Father Fitzpatrick's ferry docked in Lower Manhattan, just below the pier at South and John Streets. The seaport's docks were busy with several ships—some unloading passengers from Europe but most loading cargo destined for ports all over the world. The docks were full of families meeting passengers and hucksters trying to gain some sort of advantage over the starving, exhausted, and unsuspecting arriving passengers. Street vendors were selling food to passengers who had not eaten real food for more than a month. Landlords were aggressively trying to rent their hovels for inflated prices.

B.J. was able to quickly identify the pickpockets and prostitutes working the dock this Easter morning. One character reminded him of Séamus Garfull, the sneakiest pickpocket in all of Temple Bar, and another looked like a redheaded whore he knew in Dublin named Nessa. Everyone called her Nasty Nessa because of her reputation for spreading diseases to her clients. Many years ago, in the shadows under Ha'penny Bridge, B.J. once heard someone say a man took his own life because a disease she gave him affected his brain. The political operatives from the Tammany Society were also on the dock. They were right next to the slumlords, pickpockets, and prostitutes—working to gain favor with the voting-age Irish men arriving in New York. Over on South Street, B.J. saw the man everyone in New York knew as an aggressive, up-and-coming political operative named "Boss" Tweed, holding court with a couple of his policemen cronies. It may have been Easter Sunday, but on these docks, it looked like any other working day.

Fitzpatrick walked north a few hundred yards to Fulton Street and admired the area known as Schermerhorn Row with its Federal-style warehouses. He passed his favorite seaport eating house, Sweets Restaurant. The eatery was built on two floors and had two addresses: downstairs was 2 Fulton Street, upstairs was 4 Fulton Street. B.J. loved Sweets' oysters and clams—but also the whiskeys lined up behind the mirrored bar.

Father Fitzpatrick stayed in the seaport area. He knew not to venture toward the midsection of Lower Manhattan. A few blocks north, and away from the East River, was the notorious Five Points, where four streets—Anthony, Cross, Orange, and Little Water—converged at the same corner. One block away was Mott Street, densely populated with Chinese immigrants, crowded tenements, and women—both young and old—from many countries, selling themselves in brothels.

Nothing good ever happened in the Points, and although he assumed he would be safe anywhere while wearing his black cassock and biretta, the priest knew it would be better for him to stay near the docks.

Fitzpatrick was getting chilly, and a seat on a bench in the sun looked appealing to him. *I should have worn my overcoat*, he thought, as he ate the apple, cheese, and some of the bread Máire had packed. He read his daily prayers and waited for the Bodkins.

26

AMERICA!

April 23, 1848

SUNDAY MORNING, APRIL 23, 1848, DID NOT SEEM LIKE Easter Sunday to anyone on board the *Cushlamachree*. At around ten o'clock in the morning, it took the efforts of every crewman to raise the anchor. The ship began to move through the Narrows. Around eleven o'clock, the crew trimmed half of the ship's sails, and the *Cushlamachree* eased forward into the last part of the voyage. Almost all of the passengers were on deck in the beautiful sunshine. They had all of their belongings and hoped never to see steerage again. Dominic found a place near the first mate, so he could observe the process of navigating the ship along the narrow shipping lane between Brooklyn and Staten Island. The water in the Narrows was deep enough for the oceangoing vessel, but the current was swift. The Narrows flowed into Upper New York Bay between New York and New Jersey, where the *Cushlamachree* quickly approached another small island known as Governors Island. The captain navigated the waters on the eastern side of Governors Island—the very narrow Buttermilk Channel. The Vinegar Hill section of Brooklyn was close enough off the starboard that the passengers called "Happy Easter!" and waved hello to a group of people strolling on the shore. The *Cushlamachree* continued to sail across the southern tip of Manhattan against the problematic currents of the East River.

"Would you look at this, Cate! Nellie! Can you see it?" Biddy called to her sisters.

"Look at them, Nell!" Nora said as she lifted her little cousin so she could take in the sights of New York Harbor.

Ahead of them, on both the Manhattan and Brooklyn banks of the East River, were the masts of forty to fifty of the largest sailing ships they had ever seen. The ships were all moored into piers, bow to stern. The masts of the majestic ships—seemingly motionless in their berths—were positioned in rows like pine trees in a dead forest, connected by spiders' webs of riggings and furled sails. In the middle of the river were a dozen more vessels moving in both directions, some under sail, some steam-powered. Those ships arriving in New York were sailing up the East River to a berth, and those headed downriver were going out to sea—to Europe, to Africa, or south to ports on continents unknown.

Nellie was frightened by all of the ships' activity and looked around for Sadhbh. She found her friend, still beautiful in her white and gold silk gown, hovering by Captain Thomas and Dominic on the bridge. Nellie was happy to see Sadhbh guiding Captain Thomas, and the little girl waved to her friend to thank her for keeping them all safe. Dominic saw his sister's wave, and he called, "Hello, Nellie," as he waved back.

Dominic was amazed at how Captain Thomas maneuvered his ship. The treacherous entry into a pier on the East River was more achievable with the favorable currents of a slack tide. The slack tide would last for an hour and a half to two hours after either a high or low tide. This afternoon a high tide would be reached at around two o'clock in the afternoon, and the captain's goal was to dock the ship at the South Street pier after two o'clock but before three. The *Cushlamachree* kept advancing slowly with only a slight breeze. The conditions were perfect.

Dominic's heart beat faster than usual with excitement. New York City was massive. Was he ready for this?

The passengers lined both the port and starboard rails. Those on the port railing looked at Manhattan, and those on the starboard continued to marvel at Brooklyn. The passengers on the port side could see the pier where they would dock. Excited voices drew the passengers from the starboard side over to them, and now everyone was looking at the pier.

Dominic could hear the tension in the exchange between Captain Thomas and his first mate. Thomas gave sharp, crisp commands about the sails and the rudder. After the thirty-three-hundred-mile voyage from Galway, the last two hundred yards would be crucial. The captain allowed the ship to sail, ever so slowly, just past the pier and ordered the large sail dropped. The rudder was pulled hard to starboard, and the two small sails swung to catch the breeze, which was again a little abaft the beam. Only a minute later, Thomas ordered the small sails dropped. The *Cushlamachree* turned to the port, and—with enough forward drift—slid gently toward its berth.

At the ship's bow, the crew had positioned themselves at both the port and starboard sides of the *Cushlamachree*—a length of the boat's lines in their hands. As the ship edged into its slip, the dockhands prepared to throw dock lines to the crewmen on board. Dominic saw that on the first mate's shout, lines were thrown in both directions, caught and tied to large iron cleats located on the pier and the ship's deck. The position of the lines created the effect of a spring, and the *Cushlamachree* came to a halt.

A roar went up from the passengers—"Hip, hip, hooray!"— for the crew.

The crowd of people awaiting the arrival of the *Cushlamachree* was much larger than the one at the departure from Galway. People on the pier were waving to relatives and friends on board. Cheers of "Hooray! Hooray! Hooray!" and "America! America! America!" were heard everywhere.

Dominic noticed a contrast. The people onboard wore filthy rags that were tattered and torn by the end of the voyage, while the people onshore wore fancy clothes of multiple colors and plaids. The men ashore had large floppy hats and neckties, and many were wearing colorful suspenders, and the women wore colorful dresses with big hoops in their skirts. Some had parasols.

Many passengers shared prayers, tears, and hugs of farewell. Dominic joined his parents, his siblings, and Patt and Nora. They all hugged and smiled—and cried. Patt found Maria Teresa, and they hugged. It was the first time they had ever touched each other.

The Bodkins all looked at the crowd, and they tried to find Father Fitzpatrick. Mam and Da knew him, but the children were too young to have any memory of the priest. Patt O'Donnell and Nora Jones had no recollection of the man who was the other priest with Uncle Laurence at An Spideál fourteen years ago.

The dreadful voyage was over, and the Bodkins were all alive. The crew fastened the gangway, and the passengers pressed to get off the *Cushlamachree*. Biddy and Dominic remembered their race across the ship's deck on the first day. No one raced today. It would take some time, but they would all get off. Two by two, the passengers came down the gangway, amazed at what they saw, looking toward the pier as they walked, some looking for a brother or a sister—someone they knew. Some looked for a friend from Sligo, or Connemara. Still, most of those disembarking the *Cushlamachree* were looking for someone from County Galway. The passengers who were sure no one was meeting them looked ahead with fear. But they all had hope, clutching each other's arms for stability and strength as they walked.

The Bodkins waited their turn at the top of the gangway. Dominic took Mam by the arm, and they led the family down. Da and Cate were right behind them. The others paired together and followed. At the bottom of the gangway, Dominic stopped and moved back a step to allow Da to move up and be next to Mam. Together Mam and Da took the first Bodkin steps onto American soil. Dominic and Cate came next, then Biddy with Nellie … then Martin with Lawrence and John. Patt and Nora walked down the gangway last. Ten yards onto American soil, they all stopped, huddled together in celebration, and clung to each other.

Da's head turned when he heard a man's voice say, "Hello, John Stanley." He reached his arms out to embrace the man standing in front of them, "Hello, B.J. We meet again."

27

CHAOS ON THE PIER

TO THE IRISH, IT WAS A "QUAY," BUT IN BROOKLYN everyone knew it as a pier. The wharf at South Street in Lower Manhattan was about two hundred feet across and fifty feet deep. The surviving one hundred and sixteen passengers, plus the crew of ten, joined the welcoming crowd of another hundred on the pier. Some in the waiting crowd had vegetable carts. Some were roasting chickens, ribs of beef, onions, even potatoes. They cooked over red-hot, smoky fires. The smell of the sizzling beef and chicken fat was so enticing to the hungry passengers and crew that many were spending their remaining money to get some food into their empty bellies. Street hawkers approached the passengers with offers of lodging, work, transportation, and ale. The hustlers sometimes even said to the male passengers that female companionship was available.

Four street musicians were playing for coins in the middle of the crowd. The musicians produced ballads and love songs in the passengers' native Irish language. The troupe had just a fiddle, a flute, and a bodhran, which blended magically with the sweet but strong voice of a beautiful young woman. She had black hair and brilliant blue eyes, eager to steal a man's imagination. Her songs filled the new immigrants with the hope that much of what they loved about Ireland would be found on the streets and in the neighborhoods of New York.

Newly reunited families were hugging, kissing babies, back-slapping, smiling, and weeping with joy. The passengers were juggling greetings and farewells, pursuing endless solicitors, and buying food. Several passengers were having trouble getting used to standing on firm land for the first time in thirty-six days, and their equilibrium was disturbed enough to merit medical attention, but the only assistance available was water and a seat on the pier. Mam had to sit down, and Dominic waved his hand like a fan to cool her face. He made sure she had water to drink. Da was exhausted from the trip, but he was energized by being reunited with the familiar face from County Galway.

"John, I don't think we have seen each other since Laurence's fiftieth birthday celebration." B.J. Fitzpatrick stood with his arm around Da's shoulder. "I believe you are right, B.J.," Mam said. "Years ago, at Saint Columba's."

B.J., Da, and Mam did not know each other well and had only been together on a couple of occasions—at events with Bishop O'Donnell—but today they were like long-lost siblings.

Cate stepped forward and embraced the priest. Fitzpatrick marveled at what a beautiful young woman she had become. "You were just a baby, Cate." For the first time, he met Dominic, Biddy, Martin, Lawrence, John, and little Nellie.

Patt smiled and extended his hand to the priest. "Father Fitzpatrick, I'm Patt O'Donnell, and this is my sister, Nora. Nora Jones."

"Ahh, Patrick! Nora! You were both only three when Laurence and I brought you to your parents at An Spideál. What a week it was for everyone! And here you are with me in America. Look at how much of a great change the years have made in you!

Catherine and Peadar must have done a wonderful job of raising you both." B.J. had tears in his eyes.

"Your uncle Eamon should be here shortly. I sent a message to him on Holy Thursday that you would arrive today, and I am sure he will be here."

Fitzpatrick saw his parishioner Luke Smith standing with several passengers who had arrived on a ship from Liverpool. Luke introduced Father Fitzpatrick to the new members of his congregation. They were Smiths, Caulfields, and McSherrys. Luke would help all of the new arrivals reunite with their families in Vinegar Hill, and Father Fitzpatrick invited them all to the rectory for Easter dinner.

The Massey family and Maria came to join the Bodkins, and Dominic introduced them to Father Fitzpatrick. The Masseys were still the best dressed of all of the passengers, but Mr. Massey's cravat was gone, he had not shaved for several days, and his suit looked well-worn. The coiffure Mistress Precious had when she boarded in Galway was gone, and her hair hung in dirty and greasy ringlets around her shoulders, like all of the other female passengers'. Her dress was wrinkled and stained, but she still carried her parasol. Maria had done well with the Massey children—they looked as neat and clean as they had the day the *Cushlamachree* departed from Galway. Mr. Massey had already procured the services of a porter to maneuver the family's trunks off the *Cushlamachree*, to wait for the Masseys' carriage. Stephen brought relief to everyone when he announced that Maria would travel to Gramercy Park with his family, and, in a day or two, his coachman would drive her to Port Jervis.

A large coach, pulled by four Morgan horses, arrived in a rush at the top of the wharf and stopped on South Street. An older man climbed out and looked around the crowd, trying to locate someone.

A wealthy man, Dominic thought when he saw the fancy coach and the man dressed in a grey suit and matching silk top hat. He had a cane like the one Mr. Massey carried. Father Fitzpatrick saw the man and his coach, and the priest waved toward him and called out, "Mr. Hickey? Eamon? Eamon Hickey?" The man heard Fitzpatrick's call and waved back as he came over to the large group of passengers gathered around the priest.

"Father Fitzpatrick?"

The two men shook hands, and B.J. turned to introduce the others, but Patt had already extended his hand.

"Uncle Eamon, *dia dhuit*, Uncle Eamon, hello. I am Patrick, and this is Nora."

"Patrick! Nora!" Hickey exclaimed. "I never thought this day would come when I finally saw you again. You were such small children when I left An Spideál."

"Our parents send their love and greetings, Uncle."

"Aunt Gabriela is not with you, Uncle?" Nora asked.

"It is a long carriage ride to and from Harrison, Nora. Thirty miles each way. She is at home anxiously awaiting our return."

The Masseys' polished black carriage arrived, and suddenly it was time to say goodbye to the Masseys, Maria, Patt, Nora, and Eamon Hickey.

Father Fitzpatrick did not know what to think. Would he only know Patt and Nora for these few moments on the pier? He had looked forward to meeting the children for years.

Again, as it had been on the quay in Galway, there were hugs of farewell and promises to visit. However, the likelihood of visits between the Bodkins, Patt, Nora, and Maria seemed much higher than the likelihood of receiving a visit from Mary and Dan Duval from Galway.

The porter loaded the trunks on the Masseys' carriage, and Maria supervised the children, getting them into their seats.

She was still clutching her only bag, as she had on the quay in Galway—with the strap over her shoulder.

When Mr. Massey got to Cate, he had a serious look on his face. "I know you have just arrived, Cate, and you plan to live in Brooklyn with your family. But America is the land of opportunity, Cate, and Precious and I want to offer you your first opportunity. Please come to Gramercy Park to live with our family and help us raise our children. I work all day and many evenings. Precious has many social responsibilities. We do need constant assistance with the children," he explained. "You'll have your own bedroom, a sitting room, and your own bath. You will join the children for meals prepared by our housekeeper, and we will also pay you a stipend." Massey's salesmanship was evident as he continued his offer. "One day a week will be your day off, and if you want, my coachman will bring you to the ferry in Brooklyn and return for you at the end of the day. It only takes two hours to get from our house in Gramercy Park to Brooklyn, so you could visit your family each week if you wanted."

Cate was overwhelmed. "One hour in America, and I already have a job!

"Mam and Da," she said. "Should I do it? I want to do it. May I accept Mr. Massey's offer?" Of course, Mam and Da agreed.

Opportunity! Dominic thought. *The land of opportunity!*

Arrangements were made for the Masseys' coachman to meet Cate at the ferry pier in New York in five days.

Eamon Hickey's driver retrieved Patt and Nora's bags, and the large coach left for Harrison with the Bodkins' cousins waving goodbye.

The suddenness of all of these changes stunned everyone.

The United States Department of Customs employees were not working on Easter Sunday, and Paul Neylon had volunteered himself—and the government's skiff—to ferry the Bodkins from New York to Brooklyn. With his boat, he could bring them into the Navy Yard, leaving a short walk to the rectory.

Neylon arrived on the pier and docked between the *Cushlamachree* and the Fulton Ferry, as the Masseys' carriage was pulling away.

With only their small bags to carry, it was only a few yards to Neylon's skiff. Everyone helped Mam and Da onto the small boat.

"I am tired of boats, John," Mam moaned to her husband as her children secured her on the middle seat of the boat's uncomfortable bench, "and I never want to be on another as long as I live."

The trip to Brooklyn lasted less than half an hour, and the Bodkins headed to the rectory with Father Fitzpatrick narrating the sights in their new neighborhood. The spring buds and flowers were on the trees as they walked along Clinton Avenue to Myrtle. The walk to the rectory became difficult for Mam and Da, but they couldn't stop now.

Da was proud of his family. Against the odds, they had all made it alive from Briarhill to Brooklyn.

28

WELCOME TO BROOKLYN

THE CLOTH SIGN HANGING OVER THE RECTORY DOOR flapped in the gentle breeze as the Bodkins approached the entrance. The white banner with green letters welcomed today's arrivals in their native Irish:

FÁILTE GO BROOKLYN

New York did feel like Ireland to Dominic. Beginning with the fishermen he saw off the coast of Long Island, almost everyone they saw looked like an Irishman. Boys and men with red hair and freckles. Girls and women with black hair and blue eyes. The Irish were everywhere—though there were Chinese and African laborers on the pier, an unusual sight for a boy from Briarhill.

"*Máire!*" Father Fitzpatrick called from the front door.

"MAH-ree!" he called louder.

"*MAH-ree! Tá muid sa bhaile, MAH-ree!*" *Máire!* We're home, Máire!

Máire rushed from the kitchen to greet the family with a welcoming committee. Following Máire were Red Mahoney and Customs Inspector Paul Neylon. Shirley Neylon came out of the

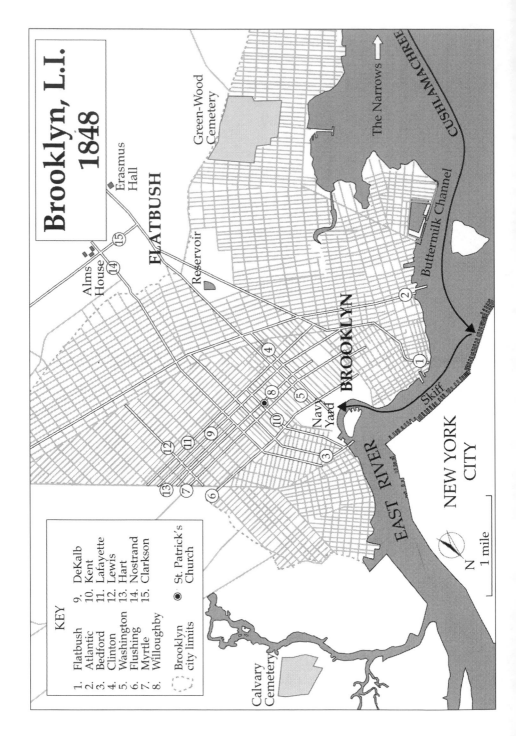

Brooklyn, L.I.
1848

KEY

1. Flatbush
2. Atlantic
3. Bedford
4. Clinton
5. Washington
6. Flushing
7. Myrtle
8. Willoughby
9. DeKalb
10. Kent
11. Lafayette
12. Lewis
13. Hart
14. Nostrand
15. Clarkson

St. Patrick's Church

Brooklyn city limits

FLATBUSH

Erasmus Hall

Green-Wood Cemetery

Alms House

Reservoir

BROOKLYN

Navy Yard

The Narrows

CUSHLAMACHREE

Buttermilk Channel

Skiff

EAST RIVER

NEW YORK CITY

Calvary Cemetery

N

1 mile

kitchen, where she had been helping Máire and some other parish women prepare Easter dinner.

Everyone introduced themselves, and Saint Patrick's parishioners made the Bodkins feel at home.

"Were you warm enough, Athair?" Máire asked in English, as Father handed her his biretta to place on its stand. *Hmmmm*, he thought. "I was fine, Máire, but next time I'll follow your advice." Máire smiled … she knew he never would.

Dominic peeked into the kitchen and saw a short, thin woman with white hair stirring gravy for the turkey while at the same time preparing another dish with small onions in a creamy white sauce. Dominic introduced himself. She said her name was Dorothea, and she welcomed him to the parish. A woman of few words, she went back to stirring the gravy.

The crowd in the rectory grew significantly larger with the entrance of Luke Smith and his contingent of new arrivals from the Liverpool ships.

Dr. Mahoney had met all fourteen of the newly arrived Irish men, women, boys, and girls while they were still passengers on their ships in the Narrows. He spent time speaking with each of them.

In 1818 Mahoney came to New York in the steerage of a packet ship. After Red arrived, he worked odd jobs in Brooklyn for several years. He painted houses and worked as a plumber. Before his medical education began, Mahoney worked as an apprentice in the practice of another Irish immigrant doctor. Red saved enough money to enter medical school and became a student at the College of Physicians and Surgeons of the City of New York, studying under the faculty of Columbia College. After the completion of his education, Red opened his general medical practice and worked to serve the growing population of Brooklyn.

Red was well beyond retirement age when he closed his practice and joined the New York State Health Department. He had seen it all in his three years of performing medical inspections on immigration ships. His job as a health inspector was to identify those immigrants who were either a financial risk to New York State because of their health or those who were a medical danger to other residents of New York. If he identified passengers with either type of risk, his responsibility was to restrict their entry into New York by sending them to the hospital to allow them to recover. They never did.

Typhus was the most common disease on the Irish Coffin Ships. Caused by a bite from an infectious agent, like a rat or lice, it could not spread from person to person. On the *Cushlamachree* Mahoney had talked to Mam and Da for only a few minutes, but he saw they both had the beginnings of a rash on their upper chest and throat area. They both had typhus.

He knew Father Fitzpatrick would provide anything Mam and Da needed, both financially and medically. Mahoney did not follow the state's rules as he should have applied them to the two senior Bodkins, but Father Fitzpatrick's word allowed him to look the other way.

After everyone had been in the rectory for half an hour, Máire told Father Fitzpatrick that dinner was ready, and he led the assembled families in grace.

> *Bless us, O Lord, and these your gifts*
> Beannaigh sinn, a Thiarna, agus na bronntanais seo uait
> *which we are about to receive from your bounty,*
> a bhfuilimid le glacedh ó do rath,
> *through Christ our Lord. Amen.*
> trí Chríost ár dTiarna. Âméin.

Then Fitzpatrick led the way through the supper line.

Dominic, who was near the end of the line, filled his plate and found an empty seat in the drawing room next to Dr. Mahoney, who was deep in conversation with Father Fitzpatrick.

Mahoney and Fitzpatrick cut the conversation short when Dominic sat down.

The two men and Dominic sat in silence for a few minutes while they enjoyed their dinners.

"Real food!" Dominic said as he began to devour his meal. "Dr. Mahoney, how old do you have to be to become a doctor? I'll be fourteen in three weeks." Mahoney explained the process of becoming a doctor and that in New York, the minimum age for licensure was twenty-one.

Meanwhile, Father Fitzpatrick went back to the dinner table and filled another plate with turkey and gravy. On his way back, he asked Cate and Biddy to come and sit with him.

"This is all delicious, Father. I hope when I get to the Masseys' home next week, I discover that mistress's cook is half as wonderful as Máire," Cate said. They all sat together, and Red Mahoney took over the conversation.

As a doctor, he knew how to deliver bad news to families in a factual yet compassionate manner. He explained the rash that was evident on their parents. He gave his diagnosis as typhus, most likely caused by lice in steerage.

"As long as the rest of you do not present a rash, fever, headache, or chills, you are safe and you cannot contract typhus by contact with your parents," he said.

"What will happen next?" Dominic asked.

"The symptoms will escalate fairly quickly, Dominic. Your parents will develop high fevers, muscle pain, and severe headaches. Your parents' mental condition will devolve into confusion, and they will appear to be in a stupor—out of touch with reality. Eventually, they will not know where they are or who you are."

Mahoney told the three oldest Bodkin siblings that the potential for recovery was slim. He assured them he would do everything possible to keep their parents comfortable but had to tell them, "Most likely, they will both die within weeks."

Father Fitzpatrick took over from Mahoney to console Dominic, Biddy, and Cate. He talked to the siblings about strength, healing, and celebrating life—all of the things a priest says when he is consoling a family.

Mam and Da's health situation made the priest's explanation of the Bodkins' housing arrangements a little easier for the family to accept. Father Fitzpatrick went on to tell the three oldest Bodkin siblings that the Neylons had offered to take John, Nellie, Lawrence, Martin, and Biddy to their home and care for them. In Mam's absence, Biddy and Shirley would function as the young children's mother.

"Cate is leaving for the Massey house in Gramercy Park in less than a week, and Dominic, you will stay here in the rectory to care for your parents, with Dr. Mahoney's guidance, of course, until the end."

Dominic's head was spinning with today's events.

They had docked in New York after a thirty-eight-day trip from the cottage in Briarhill. The family stepped onto the pier in Lower Manhattan only six hours ago.

Patt and Nora had left for Harrison.

Cate had taken a job in New York.

Mam and Da were dying, and Father Fitzpatrick was dividing the family, with most of the children living at the Neylons' home several blocks away.

Across the room, the Neylons were getting to know the four younger Bodkin children. They were all smiling and happy.

Dominic hoped he was ready for the next chapter of his life.

29

MAY THE ROAD RISE
UP TO MEET YOU

January 23, 1902
Saint James Cathedral, Brooklyn

8:37 AM: *Catholic funerals were remarkably similar events. They didn't change much over the years. Only me relationship with the deceased distinguished the inevitable occasions—a friend or business associate, a distant relative, a brother, a sister ... or a parent. Today, January 23, 1902, stood out because there was a larger crowd than usual, and a lot of dignitaries. Me brother knew everybody in fookin' Brooklyn.*

In contrast, I remembered the morning of July 11, 1848, as though it were yesterday. The day before that, however, was a surprising blur, entwined in the cobwebs, which seemed to have invaded me brain several years ago. Da died the day before—so I should have remembered it clearly, but I didn't. I only remembered his funeral ...

* * *

Spring had become summer, and today would be New York's warmest day. The heat and humidity in Brooklyn had been unbearable for nearly a week, and the rain overnight brought no relief.

It was still early in the day and sweat was already dripping down 'tween the cheeks of me backside. Father Fitzpatrick looked very uncomfortable in his priestly garb. The morning sun caused beads of sweat on his forehead as he stood in the cemetery behind Saint Patrick's Church.

Da's casket, a simple pine box, was suspended atop three wooden boards over a freshly dug pit. The loose, slightly raised dirt of me mam's final resting place was only a few feet away from Da's. Some single flowers lay on her grave. Many had wilted since the last day someone stopped to say a prayer.

It was the fever that got 'em, as Mam knew it would be.

We were standing along the length of Da's casket. Biddy was arm-in-arm with Lawrence, and Dominic stood with his arm across John's back, his hand clutching John's shoulder. Cate was holding Nellie's hand. Poor little Nellie was weeping and trembling.

Father Fitzpatrick touched his right hand to his forehead and began the burial service.

"In nomine Patris, et Filii, et Spiritus Sancti. Amen."

I made the sign of the cross and repeated, "Amen." The priest was on the other side of the casket. He dipped his brush into the holy water bucket and walked the length of the wooden box, sprinkling the sacred water from one end to the other. He looked solemnly at us, and then at the Neylons, Red Mahoney, and Máire—the only mourners who walked from the funeral Mass to the little cemetery behind the church. We had just met these people, and now, suddenly, they were our family. We were orphans.

"Let us begin with an Our Father in our native Irish tongue," Fitzpatrick continued.

**Ár aAthair atàar neamh,
go naofar d'ainm;**

go data do ríocht;
go ndéantar do thoil ar an talamh
mar a dhéantar ar neamh.

Tabhair dúinn inniu ár n-arán leathúil
maith dúinn ár bhfiacha
mar a mhaithimidne dár bhféichiúna féin;
agus ná lig sinn i geathú,
ach scor sinn ó ilc.
Âméin.

He recited other prayers—some in English, some in Latin—and everyone responded, "Amen."

Me own mind did not focus on Father's burial; maybe his death was too much to deal with. The thoughts were about me mother. I could remember her saying, "Martin," talking to me, but the sound of her voice was gone. Her funeral was a month before. She had lived in America for forty-five days.

Earlier that morning, I was stunned to overhear Father Fitzpatrick say to Dr. Mahoney, "The bishop may well ask me to send them back to Galway. It will be weeks before I receive an answer to my letter."

When Dominic heard what Father Fitzpatrick said, he declared he was not going back to Ireland, and Cate already had a good job working for the Masseys. I had to tell Father Fitzpatrick that we were all staying— together.

Da and Mam had given their lives so we could live in America. Uncle Laurence would not make us return to Galway. Would he?

"Eternal rest grant unto him, O Lord.
And let perpetual light shine upon him.
Amen."

Fear overtook me. Can we fend for ourselves in Brooklyn? How can the seven of us stay together? Why has God done this to us? We will survive!

Me parents had planted a seed in Brooklyn. A seed from which a large tree could grow. They were now buried next to each other in a cemetery behind our church. A church in which they had never even attended Mass. Why did God do this to them?

"In nomine Patris, et Filii, et Spiritus Sancti. Amen."

A flower fell from me hand, onto Da's casket.

Until we meet again, dear Da, may God hold you in the palm of His hand ...

30

GRAMERCY PARK

BEING WITH HER FAMILY AT THE RECTORY FOR JUST one night after Da's funeral was as good for Cate as it was for her siblings. But now she had to return to work.

Cate was relieved to see Precious Massey standing next to the carriage at the Manhattan dock of the Fulton Ferry. They were not just employer and employee anymore. Cate and Precious had become friends. They embraced, and they clung to each other and sobbed before heading back uptown to the Gramercy Park mansion. Although Cate was numb with grief, talking about the details of Da's wake, the funeral Mass, and the burial made her feel better. She shared every minute of the last two days with Precious, who was as interested, attentive, and compassionate as she had been after Mam's death. She asked about the ceremonies and inquired how everyone was handling the loss of their second parent.

"The Neylons were with the children every moment," Cate said, "and Dr. Mahoney was at all three functions, helping to console the family. Only a few other people from the parish attended the funeral Mass, and the big church seemed quite empty. It was too bad Da and Mam had not met any of their Saint Patrick's neighbors. Father Fitzpatrick's parishioners seemed like nice people," Cate mumbled as the carriage clattered along the cobblestone road. "The wake was at the rectory, where Máire and the older woman, Dorothea, provided meals, pies, and sweets for everyone.

"Dominic seems to have become quite a young man. He relates well to all the adults, and the younger children look to him for advice and direction. He has a difficult road ahead of himself, and he will need help to deal with everything. Mrs. Neylon is tremendous with the children, but Dominic and I are aware they can't live at the Neylons' home forever."

"Have you any word yet from Bishop O'Donnell?" Precious asked about the man she had never met but about whom she had heard so much over the past four months.

"Not yet," Cate answered. "Father Fitzpatrick wrote to him when Mam passed, but it was only a month ago, and he has not heard back. He wrote again three days ago when Da died, but it could be two or three months before Father receives a response." The Catholic communication network was efficient—on horseback—but it took time for a letter to make its way across the Atlantic, and the wait for a response could seem like an eternity, especially when it pertained to death. Fitzpatrick had informed Laurence in the first letter that Da's health was failing rapidly, so he would not be surprised when he received the second letter.

It was late afternoon as the Masseys' carriage driver made his last turn around the square in the middle of Gramercy Park and delivered Cate and Precious to the front steps of the three-story house. Cate concluded the narrative of her father's funeral with Precious as they stood on the sidewalk in front of the house.

"I told Dominic that I would come to Brooklyn as often as possible to help him with our brothers and sisters. Biddy is a big help, but they will need more. I will have to make the trip each week, mistress. I hope, under the circumstances, you would allow me to be away from the children for two days some weeks, rather than just one. Certainly, I would not expect the stipend for the extra day off." Precious told Cate she would discuss the matter with Mr. Massey that evening.

Mistress Massey walked up the stone steps to the wrought-iron-framed portico, which protected the leaded glass, framing the front door.

Cate went through the iron gate on the sidewalk and down the steps that led to the basement door from which the Masseys' servants entered their small living quarters. She changed immediately into the grey dress, white apron, and little hat she wore all day, every day, while she was taking care of the Massey children.

Before she could gather the strength to go upstairs to collect the children, she sat on the edge of her bed to pray for her parents, for her brothers and sisters, and herself.

Her parents' deaths were something from which she would never recover. They were gone—may God bless their souls, she prayed. Dominic, Biddy, and the other children would never recover from the loss either. But everyone else, it seemed to Cate, had forgotten her parents already. The day after Da's funeral, all of the men in the parish were back at their jobs, and women did their housekeeping. Children sat at desks in school. Father Fitzpatrick said the seven o'clock morning Mass and then listened to the sins of his congregation. Dr. Mahoney did more physical examinations on newly arrived packet ships. Paul Neylon checked names off a ship's manifest. In the afternoon, Neylon reported to Father Fitzpatrick on the arrival of another new parishioner. Mistress Massey played backgammon with her friends in the afternoon and had another social engagement for dinner. The Masseys' carriage driver groomed the horse and went to his apartment above the stables.

Cate, Dominic, Biddy, Martin, Lawrence, Nellie, and John would all cry more today and again tomorrow. So much of their world had come to an end—and what was left was filled with uncertainty. Poor Mary probably did not even know yet that Mam had passed away. She couldn't know her father was also gone. She would weep when the news arrived in Galway City.

Cate rose from her bed and made her way up the narrow back staircase to the kitchen, where she collected the children from the cook, who had filled in as nanny over the last few days. Supper for the children was almost ready, and Cate stood in the dining room for a moment—stunned. As much as she didn't want to accept reality, she was back at work the day after she buried her father.

Life had moved on. She and Dominic would wait for Uncle Laurence's letter to make any decisions, but it would be months before the siblings would get any guidance. In the meantime, Cate would keep working. Before she left Brooklyn, Dominic told her he would talk with Father Fitzpatrick regarding the children's schooling, and he would find a part-time job for himself.

GALWAY

July 1848

ON STRETCHES OF THE TRIP FROM ATHLONE, THE messenger was able to keep his mount at a gallop. The roads were clear of travelers on the overnight ride; he and his mare were able to see the path under the light from a full moon. But now, entering the heart of Galway City, the horseman had to walk—keeping a tight rein on his horse. He had learned the mare would easily get spooked by the peasants' fires along William Street. In the pre-dawn light, peasants stoked their fires with scraps of wood or chunks of peat from a charitable shopkeeper. The man and his horse turned off William and heard a cock crow as they passed Lynch's Castle, announcing the beginning of another summer day. The end of his route—the Catholic bishop's rectory—was only another hundred yards down Lower Abbeygate. Bishop O'Donnell's housekeeper would be in her dimly lit kitchen, preparing breakfast and expecting the mail delivery from Dublin.

After his breakfast, the bishop sat at his desk and opened the packet of mail, which included a letter from B.J. Fitzpatrick. The letter had been mailed from Brooklyn five weeks earlier.

Saint Patrick's Church
Brooklyn, New York, USA
7 June 1848

Dear Laurence,
I am beside myself with grief to tell you that your sister, Eleanor, passed to her heavenly reward this morning. Her loving family surrounded her, and she showed the strength of her spirit until the last moments.

The children are beside themselves. They knew the end was near, so they expected the loss of their mother.

They also all know, and I believe they understand, as much as they are able (considering the difference in their ages), that their father is quickly going down the same path to heaven as their mother just traveled.

Young Dominic's strength and maturity will help the children through the loss of their mother and the impending tragedy of the death of both parents.

It is difficult for Cate, living and working in New York City, with the family she met on the crossing, but she has been able to travel between New York and Brooklyn regularly and was with her mother at the end.

All of the children are emotional about Mary's absence.

Dominic and Cate have been clear with me to beseech you to tell Mary about her mother's death and the truth of the situation related to her father's declining health.

My dear Laurence, I fear that within weeks the children will be orphans, and I request your guidance as to their future.

My parishioners will help me to care for them, but without
parents, I fear for their ability to survive to adulthood and become
contributing members of our society.

Please write to me with your considerations for the future as
soon as possible.

My prayers are for Eleanor and John. May the Lord welcome them.

As Always,
I am Your Brother in Christ.
B.J.

It took the bishop until after noon to get a message to Mary. She was in the rectory within the following hour. Whenever Mary talked to Uncle Laurence, it seemed as though the world changed. Most of the time, the changes her uncle orchestrated meant good things were happening for Mary, but July 12, 1848, would be different.

They sat next to each other on the couch in his study, and, not knowing any way to soften the news he was to deliver, the bishop went straight to the point.

"My dear Mary, your mother has passed away. Your siblings and your da were all with her at the end. She took her last breath in Father Fitzpatrick's rectory, and no doubt, it was typhus." The sudden reality of a mother's death would always be a shock to her child and Mary sat in stunned silence, then wept as her uncle continued with Da's near-death situation.

"Oh, Uncle Laurence," Mary asked. "What must I do? I should be with my sisters and brothers. I have to help them. But Dan is just taking over his father's business, and, Uncle, I have told no one—except my husband and his parents—but I am with child again, and I fear for my unborn's life to make such a trip. My family needs me, Uncle. I must go."

The bishop could see the distress his niece was enduring and held her hand as he tried to decide the best action. "When should your child be born, my dear?" Laurence asked, but before Mary could answer, she heard a light knock on the study's door, and it opened quietly.

Monsignor Terence Gurley stuck his head around the door without entering the room. Gurley was several years younger than the bishop, but he had been the vicar general of the Diocese of Galway since the formation of the diocese, in 1831. He knew more about the diocese—its politics, finances, operations, as well as its darkest secrets—than Bishop O'Donnell, who had only been the bishop of the diocese for four years.

"Excuse me, Mistress Mary," Gurley apologized. "Pardon my interruption, Excellency, but we have a meeting with the barristers, Cassidy and Cogan, within the hour to discuss the matter concerning the newspaper publisher. Would you like me to go alone?"

"That's a good idea, Terence. Perhaps I'll meet you later. Please give my apologies to Padraig and Thimity and let them know I'll join you as soon as possible." Gurley nodded and quietly closed the door.

"I'm sorry, Mary. I was asking, when do you expect your new little one?"

"On New Year's night, when I set the extra place at the dinner table to honor Mam, I may well have her new grandchild in my arms," Mary said, making light of the Irish tradition of honoring the dead at New Year's. "Mary"—the bishop became somber again—"bear in mind that you may well be setting two empty places for this New Year's dinner."

Laurence recognized a look of resignation in Mary's eyes and said, "Go home, my dear, and break the sad news to Daniel and his parents.

"Meanwhile, I have an idea or two I have to discuss with Monsignor Gurley. Let's meet here again tomorrow at this time."

She left the rectory and walked along Middle Street, making her way across town to the rickety old Claddagh Bridge over toward the other side of the Corrib. She headed for the Duvals' home with her sad news.

The bishop walked in the opposite direction, toward the end of Abbeygate, onto Saint Augustine Street. He hurried in the direction of the Hall of the Red Earl, and the meeting with Gurley at the barristers' offices on Courthouse Lane. He had much more on his mind than the matter with the newspaper publisher.

After speaking for two hours with the solicitors, the monsignor and the bishop stopped at the King's Head on High Street for some black bread and a pint.

"Terence, my meeting with Mary earlier was to tell her of the death of her mother in America. Her mother was, of course, my younger sister, Eleanor. The same fate is expected for Mary's father any day now. My nieces and nephews will be orphans soon—only months after arriving in New York. For the moment, they are in the caring hands of our old friend Bernard Fitzpatrick and his parishioners, but I have to see the situation personally. I have to know there is a plan for their survival.

"I want you to take over the affairs of the diocese for me, Terence. I will make every effort to ensure I return as quickly as possible, but the trip back and forth across the Atlantic will take at least three months."

Gurley ordered two more pints.

"Excellency, I would be honored. Now is a quiet season in the church calendar, and it will be several weeks before anyone notices you are gone."

At the same time, on the other side of the River Corrib, Mary had finished telling Dan and his parents the sad news.

"Daniel, I need to be with them," Mary said to her husband as they sat around the dinner table with his parents, "but I fear for our unborn child." They all agreed that a trip at this time would be too dangerous for both Mary and the unborn child.

After dinner, Dan and his father were alone, and James said, "Daniel, things rarely work out exactly as planned. I can delay my exit from the company for a few months, or I can make other arrangements. You need to travel to America with your wife and children. Have no concern about the cost associated with the voyage. When your new baby is strong enough, Mother and I will pay the fares for comfortable passage for you and your family."

32

TIGH Ó MORÁIN

August 26, 1848

AS THE PASTOR OF SAINT COLUMBA'S CHURCH, FATHER
Kevin McCann inherited his horse from the church's previous
pastor, Father Andrew Martyn, who had been gifted the Irish cob
by Laurence O'Donnell.

O'Donnell named the cob Georgie—an unusual name for a
horse—and a not-so-subtle insult to the obese English monarch
at the time, King George IV. The short, sturdy, black and white
Georgie had been a farm horse for the first several years of his
life, pulling a turning plow for a farmer's potato patch in Two
Mile Ditch. O'Donnell bought him from the farmer for transportation around the townlands comprising his parish. Before Saint
Columba's, O'Donnell traveled *to* his parishioners; he would say
Masses at their homes and baptize babies or perform marriages
in a local barn in Castlegar. He held funeral services at the home
of the deceased, and then the mourners would walk to the cemetery for the burial.

Georgie moved slowly, but securely, as he carried Father Kevin along cart tracks that had been cut by farmers' two-wheeled wagons over decades, along the road from the rectory in Castlegar to Briarhill.

It was August 26, 1848, and John and Eleanor Bodkin's friends and family were gathering at the couple's favorite pub, the Tigh Ó Moráin. Ó Moráin's was nothing more than a one-room cottage with a bar, a couple of stools along one wall, and four tables with chairs.

Father Kevin was to lead the group in a final prayer for their deceased friends. Kevin was purposely a little late for the gathering—so as not to be the first mourner—but as he bowed his neck to enter the pub's low door, he presumed he might well have been the last to arrive.

"Father Kevin! Glad you arrived safely," a five-months-pregnant Mary Duval greeted her pastor at the door. "Thank you so much for coming, Father. Come in, come in. Let me make sure you know everyone."

Jamie and Carmel Flynn and Mickey Bellew stood and embraced their pastor. Mary took Father Kevin around the room and introduced him to everyone else. Michael Diskin had a cup of Ó Moráin's famous *poitín* in his hand for the priest.

"Father Kevin, this is Michael Diskin. He was a friend of my da's," Mary said.

"*Dia dhuit*, Father!" Diskin welcomed Father McCann. "I worked with John on the 'Walls,' and I came here to Ó Moráin's sometimes with John and Eleanor. Their daughter Cate and I were godparents for the youngest son at your church, but that was years before you were there. I loved John as a brother. We will all miss them both."

"Cormac," Mary said, turning to Cormac O'Donnell, "come and meet Father Kevin McCann. He is the pastor at Saint

Columba. Cormac is Bishop O'Donnell's cousin, Father—and this is his wife, Ciara."

"*Dia dhuit*, Cormac, Ciara," the pastor said to the couple. "I'm very sorry for your loss. John and Eleanor were wonderful people, and Eleanor was a saint, too. Raising eight children in these times! And all as smart, and as nice, as Mary here."

Mary smiled at the compliment as she led the priest around the small room to introduce Patt and Bernard Flatley, and another cousin, Robert O'Donnell.

"Finally, Father, this is my godmother, Mary Kirwan, and her husband, Peter."

Mary Kirwan said, "*Dia dhuit*, Pastor. We have been to your church. As Mary said, I am her godmother, and my Peter was the sponsor for her brother, young Martin." Peter Kirwan gave Kevin another drop of *poitín* as the priest said, "It's good to see 'the Fourteen Tribes of Galway' are represented by the Kirwans here tonight."

Then the child in Mary's belly asked her to sit for a while.

Everyone sipped a drink and listened as Jamie and Carmel told exaggerated stories about John and Eleanor from the time when the couple first met at the Forge in Moycullen. Jamie's rendition of the nights in Moycullen blamed Da for keeping them out so late each night.

Mary's family told stories of Mam growing up on the farm in rural Oldchapel—raising sheep and pigs and working hard on the farm. The O'Donnell children had fun playing on the shores of Lough Corrib.

"What will your brothers and sisters do, Mary?" Jamie asked. "Who do they live with in Brooklyn? Will they return home?" Dan answered part of the question, telling everyone about Father Fitzpatrick and the Neylons, and Cate living in New York City.

Mary followed with, "We will all go to New York after my baby is born and is strong enough to make the voyage. It may be a year from now before we leave, but Uncle Laurence is planning to travel with us. Our plans are uncertain, and we may well be leaving Ireland for good. We may be moving to America."

"My God, child! Will no Bodkin blood be left in Galway?" Flynn pleaded with Mary. All of the others in the room murmured disapproval of Mary's plan. "We have no choice," she countered. "Mam and Da's wish was for the children to have the freedom and opportunities America offers. We cannot deny their wish."

Father Kevin shifted the conversation by speaking a few words about life and death—heaven and earth. He prayed a few Aves for John and Eleanor and asked Flynn, who had the singing voice of a tenor, to lead a few traditional Irish tunes, appropriate at a wake for the deceased. Then a few moments of silence.

Michael Diskin walked to the bar for another pint. Slowly, most followed his lead, and the conversations resumed. The warm sound of Irish laughter and storytelling reentered the room.

Dan and Mary were the first to leave, having a long ride home. Father Kevin was next. He climbed on Georgie. "Home, boy. Home, Georgie." He held on, comforted that Georgie knew his way back to the rectory.

Finally, Jamie closed the door of Tigh Ó Moráin's behind him and locked the latch. Da would not have been surprised by Jamie's being the last to leave. As the Flynns walked home, Jamie thought he could feel the warmth of his friend's smile.

BROOKLYN

August 1848

DURING THE HOTTEST AND MOST HUMID SUMMER
Dominic and his family had ever experienced, everything growing in Brooklyn was green. Workers performing hard labor
perspired; boys played games in the streets without shirts; mothers sat in the shade, waving fans near their faces; businessmen
walking to and from offices took off their jackets.

"Dominic," Father Fitzpatrick said one evening in late summer, "a friend of Saint Patrick's Parish, who is a personal friend
of mine from my seminary days—E.A. Murtha is his name—is
the headmaster at Erasmus Hall Academy in Flatbush. For several years, Headmaster Murtha has been encouraging me to send
him good students. So far, I have not had a student I thought
would benefit from such a fine education, but at last, I believe
you would do well at Erasmus Hall. You seem to be advanced
academically, and Bishop O'Donnell tells me you were his prized
student and have tremendous potential. I recommend we go to
Flatbush tomorrow, so Headmaster Murtha can meet you and
administer the entrance examination."

Dominic was excited. *Finally! A school!* he thought.

"Thank you, Father, but what about my brothers and sisters? Will they also be going to school?"

The priest measured his answer. "Dominic, I believe the results of your entrance examination will qualify you for admission to the academy's secondary school program. Your younger brothers and sisters, however, will have to spend time at the elementary levels to begin their schooling. Appropriate schools for them are available right here in the parish. Biddy—even though she is older—is not as academically advanced as you, and the public secondary school system will suit her best.

"Matriculating at Erasmus Hall Academy will require a commitment on your part, Dominic," Fitzpatrick continued. "In addition to the rigorous academic program, you will walk nearly an hour from the rectory to Flatbush every day for your classes."

Dominic was so excited he had trouble sleeping that night. After only four months in America, Father Fitzpatrick was talking to him about going to secondary school.

As promised, after morning Mass, Dominic and Father Fitzpatrick hitched Capuchin to the carriage, and they left for the trip to Flatbush. Capuchin, a chocolate-colored mare, lost no time trotting along Washington Street, past a large undeveloped park-like area with a lake. "Washington's army fought several battles on this site during the Revolution," Fitzpatrick instructed. Dominic smiled and listened intently to the priest's history lesson, but even though he had never seen this part of Brooklyn, he already knew all about Washington's Battle of Brooklyn.

In almost no time, they were in Flatbush. "Flatbush is a separate community from Brooklyn," the priest explained. "Its residents tend to be more affluent than my parishioners, and also, they seem to have been in America longer than most of us. Flatbush is a safe community and an excellent location for the academy." The houses were farther apart from each other than they were in Brooklyn, and Dominic noticed that they were neat and well maintained.

Quickly, they were surrounded by mature oak trees and red brick pathways connecting three small buildings and a sign that read:

ERASMUS HALL ACADEMY
THE HALL

EUGENE ANDREW MURTHA
HEADMASTER

The carriage came to a halt, and a smiling, dark-haired man bounded out the door of one of the buildings to greet them.

"Hello, B.J.!"

"*Dia dhuit,* Eugene! *Bhí sé ró-fhada, mo chara!* It has been too long, my friend."

The two men shook hands and grasped each other around the shoulders. Father Fitzpatrick repeated, "Entirely too long, my friend! This is the young man I told you about, Gene.

"Dominic, this is my old friend Headmaster Eugene Murtha. Gene, this is Bishop Laurence O'Donnell's nephew Dominic George Bodkin." Dominic and Headmaster Murtha shook hands.

"I understand you have recently lost your parents, son. I'm very sorry. Where did you live in Ireland, Dominic?"

"Thank you, Master Murtha, I miss them terribly. We lived in Briarhill. Our family home was a small cottage—a few miles outside of Galway, sir. My father's family was from Galway, and my mother grew up in Oughterard with Bishop O'Donnell. It was actually outside of Oughterard, sir, in Oldchapel. Is your family from County Galway, sir?"

"No, Dominic, we were from County Dublin—a small town called Lucan. It is not too far west of Dublin. Father Fitzpatrick and I met in Maynooth when he was in the seminary. Come inside, and we can talk more in my office."

Father Fitzpatrick needed to tend to Capuchin and the carriage. He said that he would find them later.

Headmaster Murtha and Dominic walked together into the largest of the Erasmus Hall buildings and down a long hall to the headmaster's office. Murtha sat behind his desk, and Dominic took a seat in a chair facing him.

"How was your trip across, son?" the headmaster asked.

Dominic told him about the experience of leaving Galway and about leaving Mary and Dan. He related stories about life aboard the *Cushlamachree* and told accounts of Captain Thomas and the navigation he learned from the captain. He told the headmaster about the Masseys, Nora and Patt, his brothers and sisters, and his parents.

Headmaster Murtha started a conversation about the history of Ireland, and Dominic told him of the Bodkins, being one of the Fourteen Tribes of Galway. They talked about the Great Famine. They spoke of New York Harbor, Brooklyn, and the American Revolution. Dominic understood the entrance examination had started when the conversation moved from the history of Ireland and the American Revolution to the use of the polar star in navigation across the ocean and the length of time it took to cross the Atlantic.

They talked more about science and mathematics. And then about emperors and wars, about the pyramids and the oceans. The headmaster asked about the bones in the body and about the stars and the planets.

Dominic had the strangest feeling Uncle Laurence was sitting next to him, guiding him through.

"Looking to the future, where would you like to be in five years, Dominic?" the headmaster asked.

At that moment, Father Fitzpatrick stuck his head in the office's door and asked, "May I come in, gentlemen?"

The examination ended.

They left the headmaster's office, and Murtha gave his two visitors a tour of the buildings and classrooms that were dusty and empty on an August afternoon. They made their way back to Capuchin and the carriage. Headmaster Murtha ended the appointment by inviting Dominic to join the Hall's first-year program in the secondary school.

"Classes commence in two weeks, Dominic. Will you join us?"

"Thank you, Master Murtha! I will be here." Dominic beamed.

The two men and Dominic shook hands, and Father Fitzpatrick climbed back into the carriage—but Dominic hesitated.

"I'd better walk, Father. I need to know how long it will take on the first day of school."

They left Erasmus Hall at the same time. It took Dominic less than three-quarters of an hour to get back to the rectory. It was a three-mile walk.

He was ready.

THE HALL

FATHER FITZPATRICK'S YOUNG IRISH HOUSEKEEPER was always in the kitchen well before dawn to prepare the priest's breakfast. Each morning Máire ironed his cassock. She laid out a starched Roman collar, clean underwear, and matching socks. On September 11, 1848, after she ushered the priest out the rectory door for morning Mass, she began a new routine.

Over the few months that Dominic had lived in the rectory, Máire had developed a fondness for him. For breakfast, on his first day of school, she prepared a steaming bowl of oatmeal and sprinkled a generous helping of brown sugar on top. Then she packed a satchel with some lunch—a wedge of cheese, a sweet roll she had baked yesterday, and an apple for his afternoon snack. *It's a long walk and a long day for a growing boy*, Máire thought as she added a handful of ginger cookies to the sack.

"Dominic!" she called from the bottom of the staircase to rouse the sleeping teenager. "DOM—!" Máire stopped in the middle of her word as a fully dressed Dominic rushed down the stairs.

"Good morning, Máire. The oatmeal smells grand!"

"Take your time eating, Dominic." She placed his satchel by the front door so he wouldn't forget it. "It looks like it might rain this morning. Do you want to wear Father's overcoat?"

Fourteen-year-old Dominic did not like the idea of wearing the old priest's overcoat on his first day of school, and, in between mouthfuls of oatmeal, he mumbled, "Thanks, Máire, I'll be all right."

"Be sure to wash your teeth before you leave." Dominic raced up the stairs to the bathroom and bounded back down less than a minute later. At the front door, Máire handed Dominic two silver dollars and smiled. "Father Fitzpatrick left this for you to buy your textbooks."

Unexpectedly—to both of them—she gave him a big hug. "Good luck today, Dominic, I'm proud of you." She kissed him on his forehead. "Be careful on your trip."

He bolted down the front steps and took off along the street—he found he was almost running. Less than five minutes later it started to rain. He darted between the storefronts that lined Washington Street and had to race at full speed on a muddy part of Flatbush Avenue that bordered the park. By the time he arrived at the gates of Erasmus Hall—out of breath, soaking wet, and very early—he thought his first day of high school was off to an inauspicious beginning.

Inside the front door of the Hall's main building, Headmaster Murtha was sitting on a chair to greet the students as they arrived. The headmaster would sit and wait every morning to monitor the gentlemanly appearance of his students as well as their timely arrival. But today, the headmaster had a sheet of paper for every student, containing a list of books needed for each class. This morning, he also had a couple of towels for his soaking wet students. "Welcome, Dominic!" the headmaster greeted his new pupil. "Here's the list of your required texts.

The master of each class will have a supply of books—enough for every student to buy one."

Dominic worried the two dollars Máire gave him wouldn't be enough. He looked at his list as he walked down the corridor.

First Form Latin
Basic Mathematics
English Literature
Introductory Biology
Music Appreciation
Gentlemanly Behavior
World History
English Composition

Was he as surprised as he was nervous—or was he just anxious to begin?

Through the fall, a snowy winter, and into the spring, Dominic was pleased with how his first year at the Hall evolved. He had new friends and was performing well in school. The only class in which he had to work hard was English Composition.

His English Composition master was a young man named Emmett Callow. He was a strict teacher but an excellent instructor who demanded students write passages in a journal every day. He taught them about writing prose, how to compose reports on books they read in literature class, and, in the last week of the spring semester, Callow taught his class the mechanics of writing a letter.

The final homework assignment of the year was to write a "thank you" letter to someone you knew. Dominic was excited about writing a letter—he would get to mail it to Ireland—and he might get a response!

April 23, 1849
Bishop Laurence O'Donnell
Bishop of Galway
Chancery Office on Abbeygate
Galway City, Ireland

My Dear Uncle Laurence,
I pray my letter finds you in good health and that the fears of disease and starvation have diminished among those remaining in Ireland.

In the names of my brothers and sisters, I will tell you that we miss our loving parents terribly. However, with your assistance from Galway, the supervision of Father Fitzpatrick, and his parishioners (Mr. and Mrs. Neylon, in the particular), we find ourselves well cared for.

As I think you already know, I am a first-year student at Erasmus Hall Academy in the Flatbush neighborhood of Brooklyn— those familiar with the school call it "the Hall"—and my first year is quickly coming to a close.

I am taking the opportunity, provided by a rainy Sunday afternoon, to write you a sincere thank-you for all the preparation in my studies which you gave me before the family left Briarhill.

My courses are excellent, and the masters are demanding men. Still, the knowledge you imparted to me in Latin, biology, history, reading, writing, and arithmetic have prepared me well for the challenges of my first year of school. Most of the fellows in my class did not know the first word of Latin and forced the master to crack them with his stick when they did not learn quickly enough. Please do not get the impression my first year at the Hall has been a waste of my time. I now have a greater appreciation

*of music and song, and I have learned a great deal as to how a
gentleman behaves.*

*I have also made good friends among the fellows here. Most of
my classmates live in Flatbush, and boys named Jimmie and Jackie
are my best fellows. They try to call me "Dommie," but I tell them
my name is Dominic.*

*Thank you, dear Uncle, for everything you have done to
prepare me for my education, and all you do to this day for my
brothers and sisters. We all miss you and pray that you will come to
visit us in America soon. Please send me a letter of reply to tell how
you are faring and about life in Galway in general, and please say
a hello to my sister Mary.*

*Your Loving Nephew,
Dominic George Bodkin*

*P.S. The Hall's Headmaster Murtha (a friend of Father Fitzpat-
rick's from old Ireland and maybe you knew him from years ago
also) said it was a proper gentleman's good behavior for me to tell
you that I am first in my class at the Hall!*

After months and months had become four full years of walking
from his home to Erasmus Hall, Dominic knew everything that
was along Flatbush Avenue. He knew what he would see with
every step. His trip each morning was at precisely the same time.
The afternoon's walk home might vary a little, but in the morning,
his routine was the same.

He knew who he would see on every corner and at every turn
on Flatbush. At first, he didn't know their names, but over time,
he took a minute to stop and introduce himself to one passerby

and then to another, and now he knew almost everyone who was walking—on the same schedule he was.

"Hello, Dominic!"

"Hello, Mr. Griffin!"

"Good morning, Bodkin!"

"Looks like rain today, Mrs. Oliver!"

On every corner, at every turn, there was a different greeting to—or from.

With so much new home construction going on in Brooklyn, many of the people he got to know were construction workers. They were laborers, plumbers, stonemasons, and painters. He got to know them all and noticed the start of every new brownstone. He watched the progress, from digging the dirt for the foundation to putting up the walls for the ground floor and the first floor, the second and the third. As a game to entertain his mind on each day's commute, Dominic guessed how much the workers would complete the next day and by the end of the week.

One day he noticed that since he had walked by the day before, there was a new sign on the corner of Flatbush and Winthrop:

FLATBUSH ALMSHOUSE

At the bottom of the sign was an arrow which directed the traveler to turn left, to the east. Dominic knew what an almshouse was, but he did not know one was so close to where he walked each day. He thought back to his mam, explaining how his father worked on the Famine Walls so that the family didn't wind up in Galway's workhouse. He remembered his mam's warning, "At the gate to the workhouse, the keeper would yell, 'Adults this way, children that way.' Families would be separated forever."

In the days after their parents died, the Bodkin children realized they were now a family of orphans. "Will we be sent to a workhouse in Brooklyn?" Dominic remembered asking Biddy one day.

At the end of each school day, Dominic cleaned the slate boards and emptied the classroom wastebaskets to help pay his tuition. Frequently, he had the opportunity to talk with the headmaster while he cleaned. "That is correct, Dominic, the Flatbush Almshouse is very close to us," Headmaster Murtha answered Dominic's question later that afternoon.

"Orphans, too, Dominic? Yes. Many orphans. In total, the almshouse has more than a thousand inmates. The mentally ill, orphans, deaf, dumb, and blind. Those suffering from drunkenness, too. You know, we Irish have a lot of drunks. It is a terrible situation, Dominic. The city is in charge of running the almshouse, but they can't find enough employees to care for all the inmates. Some inmates have to work on the farm that is part of the almshouse, some citizens volunteer to help, but there are never enough."

The last chalkboard was clean, and Dominic collected his homework assignments and got ready for his walk home.

"On a different topic, Dominic, Mrs. Murtha has asked me to invite you to supper one afternoon before graduation. She wants to be sure we have a plan in place to stay in contact with you and to help with your further education after you graduate from Erasmus Hall."

On his way home that afternoon, Dominic made a right turn off Flatbush and walked along Clarkson to Nostrand Avenue. He was in an area of Flatbush he had never walked before.

In front of him were five huge red brick buildings which opened onto a large stone courtyard. A sign announced to Dominic that he stood at the entrance to the Flatbush Almshouse.

He walked alone through the square and, though he saw no people, he could hear the inmates inside. Sometimes he heard old people, moaning and screaming. Sometimes it was children, yelling. Then, an infant, crying.

As Dominic stood in the square listening to the noises, a large, enclosed, horse-drawn Police Department wagon clattered across the square before coming to a stop. Police Department wagons, known as "paddy wagons," were used for more than transporting common criminals to jail. A family—he presumed—consisting of a mother, a father, their three boys, and a daughter, were ushered out the rear of the paddy wagon, and up the steps of a building marked: ADMINISTRATION BUILDING. They walked by a handwritten poster that proclaimed. "HELP WANTED," and into the building, as the big iron doors slammed shut behind them with an ominous boom that reverberated throughout the quadrangle.

Something about the scene of an impoverished family being interred in an almshouse, while they walked past a Help Wanted sign, struck Dominic as oxymoronic. Why didn't they hire the father so he could feed his family?

The empty paddy wagon pulled away and clattered back across the square and out onto Clarkson.

Dominic stood by himself on the square for a few minutes longer and then resumed his walk home.

On the first Saturday morning in June of 1852, only weeks before his graduation from the Hall, Dominic walked his usual route from Saint Patrick's along Washington Street to Flatbush Avenue. He walked along Flatbush at the same hour as he did on school days, but today was Saturday, and the streets were quiet. He saw none of the faces that had become so familiar to him.

At Clarkson, he followed the directional arrow to the left and walked to the Flatbush Almshouse. He crossed the square to the administration building, climbed the steps, and passed the Help Wanted poster that was still there. Dominic looked closely at the sign. He saw no small print.

It did not say: "NO IRISH NEED APPLY."

An hour later, Dominic walked out of the Administration Building with an agreement to be at the Laundry Building at seven o'clock in the morning on the Monday after graduation. Dominic was proud of himself. He had a job in the Linen Room. If he proved he could perform linen folding, he would be promoted to housekeeping and cleaning, and then maybe to the farm. Eventually, he hoped to work in inmate care.

He was excited and almost running on his way home along Flatbush Avenue. He couldn't wait to tell his brothers and sisters—and Father Fitzpatrick.

Dominic had a job. Da would have been so proud.

DINNER AT THE HEADMASTER'S

June 1852

"I'M HOME, ELLEN!" GENE MURTHA CALLED TO HIS wife from the front door of their house, located in a far corner of Erasmus Hall's campus.

"Ellen, I'm home," he repeated.

She greeted him in the hallway, and as he hung his suit coat on a hook, he said, "Before I forget, I talked to Dominic about supper, and he is coming next Tuesday. He was appreciative of the invitation and is looking forward to it." Having been married to the headmaster of Erasmus Hall Academy for more than twenty years, Ellen Murtha knew how to prepare a hearty meal for a teenager. She already knew what she would serve.

"I'm glad he is coming, Gene. You've never had a nicer boy at the Hall."

"Or a smarter one!"

"By the way, I had a visitor today," the headmaster said. "John Taylor. He is one of the Hall's trustees. I'm sure you know him."

"I do, Gene. Quite a philanthropist also, as I remember."

"That's correct, dear; he's the one. Taylor, and several of his associates, have opened what will be a 'nearly free' library over on Atlantic Avenue at Clinton. He said it would cost less than a dollar a year. The 'Brooklyn Athenaeum and Reading Room,' he calls it. And listen to this, Ellen! He asked me to be on the board of trustees! Me! I can't believe it. He asked me, just the headmaster of a little old school, to be a trustee.

"We, the board that is, will get to decide what books we will have in the Reading Room. We will have a budget to use for new books each month—both textbooks and novels. Probably some poetry, too. I'll be on the Acquisitions Committee, also the Membership Committee. The board will be an opportunity for me—for us.

"I will be able to promote the Hall to the other trustees with whom I will serve. There are several I don't know. The most prominent is Mr. Peter Wyckoff. He's a banker. They say he is the brains, or at least the money, behind the General Hospital of Brooklyn. The Catholic Church is involved, too, of course. I hear the archdiocese in New York City is going to create a separate diocese in Brooklyn. Well, I guess that means the Pope is going to create a new diocese. They are bringing Monsignor Loughlin over from the cathedral in New York to be the new bishop. The Pope approved it last week. Bishop Loughlin is not going to be on the board of the Athenaeum himself; he'll be too busy. He's appointing one of his young priests, a Father McGoldrick. He's young, but Mr. Taylor indicated he is a real 'up-and-comer.'

"There's a doctor on the board, too. I don't know him. He's a physician named Red Mahoney. Retired, I think. Unfortunately, there's no compensation. But I received ten memberships I can give to the boys. They'll love it."

"That's wonderful news, Gene, congratulations! It sounds as though it is both an honor for you, as well as an opportunity! You deserve it." Ellen hugged her husband.

"Would you be allowed to give one of the memberships to a graduate?"

"I don't see why not, Ellen."

⟨⟨⟨⟩⟩⟩ ⟨⟨⟨⟩⟩⟩ ⟨⟨⟨⟩⟩⟩

Ellen Murtha loved to cook. For Christmas, Gene gave her one of the new wood-fired cookstoves all of the finer families had. With her new stove, Ellen could roast meats, boil potatoes, keep vegetables warm, and bake—all at the same time. The Murthas were not wealthy, but they were not poor either. Headmaster Murtha's compensation was not substantial, but it was generous in that it included a house on the Hall's campus for his family to live in. It was Ellen's responsibility to maintain the house, and since she spent much of her time in the kitchen, she had the best culinary equipment Gene could find.

⟨⟨⟨⟩⟩⟩ ⟨⟨⟨⟩⟩⟩ ⟨⟨⟨⟩⟩⟩

On the following Tuesday afternoon, the roast of beef had been twirling on the spit-jack for several hours. Scalloped potatoes had replaced an apple pie in the baking compartment, and Ellen saw that the tops of the potatoes were browning nicely. Spinach was ready on the warming griddle, and the aroma of the cooling apple pie competed for her attention with the garlic-seasoned roast of beef.

Dominic and the headmaster walked across the Hall's campus together and arrived at the Murthas' home by the time Ellen had completed all of her preparations.

"Dinner is ready, Gene. Hello, Dominic, how are you today? I'm so glad you could come. Your place is over there." Ellen motioned to one of the three chairs set at the table.

"Hello, Mrs. Murtha. It's nice to see you again. Thank you for inviting me. Everything smells grand."

The headmaster sliced the beef, Dominic passed the potatoes and the spinach, and Ellen poured them each a glass of apple cider.

"This is delicious, Mrs. Murtha," Dominic said after his first forkful of beef.

The silence around the table confirmed Dominic's praises.

"Wonderful, Ellen." The headmaster winked at his wife.

As Mrs. Murtha cleared the dinner dishes and set out new plates for the apple pie, Dominic told the headmaster and his wife about his trips to the Flatbush Almshouse and about his new job.

"That is great for you, Dominic. I am sure you will do a good job and advance quickly," Ellen said by way of congratulations.

The headmaster beamed. "Wonderful, Dominic. This will be a good start for you. A great experience for the future!

"Speaking of graduation, I've learned during the last week that Brooklyn has a new library—a reading room—and the library is looking for members. It is over near where you live; it's called the Brooklyn Athenaeum and Reading Room. A library would be a good place for you to further your education. Maybe even to prepare you to apply to a university."

"I like the idea of going to a university, Headmaster Murtha, and I am pretty sure I know where the new library is, but I will be giving most of the money I save from the almshouse to support my family. I could never afford a membership to the Athenaeum."

Ellen finished serving big pieces of apple pie to everyone, and she rejoined the two men at the table.

"Some coffee, Dominic?" she asked as she poured her husband a cup from her new hourglass-shaped coffee brewer.

"No, thank you, Mrs. Murtha, but may I have another glass of cider, please?"

Ellen poured the young man another glass.

"Well, Dominic, Mrs. Murtha and I would like to give you a membership to the Reading Room as a graduation present." The headmaster slid an envelope containing the membership card across the table to his prized student.

Dominic was stunned. He never thought he would receive a gift—just for graduating from Erasmus Hall. He was thrilled, and he thanked the Murthas profusely.

"Dominic, I have a question for you. A question I asked you several years ago." The headmaster said as he dropped a lump of sugar into his coffee cup, "The day Father Fitzpatrick first brought you to the Hall, you didn't have an opportunity to answer the question the first time I asked. 'Where would you like to be in five years?'"

CASHMERE, STRAWBERRIES, AND CREAM

AFTER THE WEEKS OF DREARY DAYS AND SLEEPLESS nights on the *Cushlamachree*, late afternoon of Easter Sunday, April 23, 1848, held excitement and changes beyond Nora's wildest imagination.

"*Ciao! Signorina!*" Eamon Hickey's young, neatly mustachioed coachman tipped his cap to greet Nora, and offered his hand to assist the green-eyed Irish girl into her uncle's carriage. "Hallo, Miss Hanora Joneza! You like America? No?" He smiled, as he leaned close to grasp her elbow. "And my very buono Heeaster to you, Miss Hanora." She was weak from the voyage and thankful for his help on the carriage's steep steps.

The young man's voice was deep and loud. But his accent, and his words, were foreign to Nora. *Did he say happy Easter? Is this how American boys talk?* She took a chance. "Happy Easter to you also, good sir." She didn't return his smile, mortified at her wretched appearance after the long crossing. Strands of greasy auburn hair stuck to the sunken cheeks which now blemished her pretty face. There had been no bath day last night, while the *Cushlamachree* sat at anchor in the Narrows. It had been more than a week since a bucket of salt water had flushed the filth from her body. She knew she smelled worse than the tail end of her uncle's horse.

"Let's get going, Sylvio," Eamon barked impatiently at his coachman.

Sylvio flicked the lead mare with his leather whip, and the four horses lurched forward—up South Street past the Masseys' coach.

Nora watched as Patt craned his neck to look through the carriage's rear window, trying to get one more glimpse of Maria. He fantasized about her, and they made eye contact for a final time, but she had devastated him. Maria told him on the wharf that he was a sweet boy—good looking, funny, and it was nice knowing him—but she didn't have feelings for him. Nora saw her brother's sadness and squeezed his hand. *He'll get over her,* she thought as she waved goodbye.

In the blink of an eye, the journey from Moycullen to America was over. The *Cushlamachree*, the Masseys, and the Bodkins were all gone.

Sylvio made a fast trip of the distance between the *Cushlamachree*'s dock at New York City's South Street wharf and the sleepy community of Harrison. The sights and sounds of the big city astounded Patt and Nora on that Easter afternoon, but quickly Uncle Eamon's coach was off the city streets and roaring along country roads. The scenery changed from the office buildings in Lower Manhattan to park-like settings, then farmland, and finally rolling hills rimmed by babbling brooks twisting through the wooded properties of large homes and estates in Westchester County.

Patt and Nora's introduction to Eamon Hickey was eye-opening for the seventeen-year-old Irish immigrants. The elderly Eamon strained to make his voice heard over the noise of the coach's wheels as they clattered along Boston Post Road. "You can take the Post Road from New York all the way to Boston," he told his nephew. "I first moved here in 1837—when I came to Harrison to work in the china factory." The horses slowed to a trot as the Post Road wound along a narrow, winding stretch. "We are almost home, Nora. Harrison is not too much farther, now," he said to his young, wide-eyed niece.

"Patt." Nora nudged her brother with some new energy, as she nodded her head toward a large home. "In Ireland, we would call these homes castles."

"After about five years of working hard at the factory," Eamon continued, "I was moving up the company's ranks, and I became the owner's second-in-command. He liked the fact that I didn't let the Italians come to work drunk and lazy. 'A day's pay for a day's work,' I told them. 'Sleep at home if you want to sleep.' Eventually, the old man who owned the factory died—and now it is all mine. Ha! Ha!" Eamon roared with laughter. "Now, I'm the old man who owns the china factory!"

Sylvio brought the horses to a walk as he guided the coach into an entrance between two stone pillars. The carriageway continued for about a quarter of a mile, and finally, Patt and Nora saw Uncle Eamon's house.

"Surely, this would be a castle in Ireland," Nora said with a smile.

In the spring of 1858—after ten years in Harrison—Nora knew that taking a stroll around the grounds on April mornings was invigorating. She finished her breakfast of strawberries and whipped cream, wrapped a cashmere sweater around her shoulders, and left the house through the French doors in the dining room.

"Isn't it a beautiful morning, Anthony?" Nora said to her groundsman, who was busy planting a row of herbs in the kitchen garden.

"Good morning, mistress. It certainly is. These plants are the oregano you asked for at the end of last season, ma'am. Some basil will go in right behind the oregano."

"It looks grand, Anthony. Thank you."

Nora walked along the brick pathway separating the kitchen garden from the formal garden. She noticed that the hedges and trellises required some attention from Anthony after a harsh winter, but she saw that the stems of the rose bushes were green. *A good sign,* she thought. *It is definitely spring.*

The path continued toward a creek that formed the eastern boundary of the estate. The yellow and white daffodils along the bank of the stream were in full bloom, as were the purple flowers of the crepe myrtle bordering the brick path. Nora picked a few daffodils to place on the windowsill in the kitchen of her Westchester mansion.

The ten years that had passed since she and Patt left Galway Bay on the *Cushlamachree* had been filled with changes—often, the changes were life-altering. As she meandered back through the garden, Nora reflected on her first decade in America and an invitation to a reunion party she had just received from Cate Bodkin. She wondered what it would be like to see the Bodkin family after all these years.

Nora remembered writing her first letter to Cate at Gramercy Park. It was three months after they all arrived on the *Cushlamachree*, and Nora had a lot of news for the Bodkin cousins.

July 4th, 1848
9 O'Clock PM
Harrison, New York

Miss Catherine Bodkin
In the care of Mr. and Mistress Steven Massey
Gramercy Park, New York City

Dearest Cate,
I apologize for not writing sooner. So much has transpired since
Patt and I left everyone on the quays in New York.
If you will remember, my uncle Eamon came with his coachman
to retrieve us to Harrison. We were surprised when he met us on
the quay without our aunt Gabriela. When we arrived at Uncle's
beautiful home in Harrison, we learned the true reason for our
aunt's absence. She was indeed quite sickly, and Eamon feared she
could not make the trip. As it turned out, he was correct. Aunt
Gabriela passed away within a short few days of our arrival at
Uncle's home.

His home is beautiful, by the way. It reminds me of an Irish
castle. Patt and I are just now learning the location of all the
rooms and our way around the grounds.

We buried Aunt Gabriela in a cemetery which abuts Uncle's
acreage, just on the other side of the pond. It is a lovely spot and
reminds me of the hills around certain parts of Lough Corrib, at
our home.

I must prepare you—my news only gets worse. Two days ago,
Patt and I received a letter from our mother to tell us our beloved
father, Peadar, died less than a fortnight after we sailed from Gal-
way Bay. This news is all terribly saddening, and we have fears for
our mother living alone in Moycullen. As you will remember, she is
not young herself.

Uncle Laurence came to be with our mother in Moycullen. He performed Father's funeral at the church, and also the prayers at his grave. He stayed with Mother for a few days but then returned to Galway to attend to his duties at the diocese.

I hope your news of New York City and Brooklyn is better than ours. Harrison is today celebrating a holiday—Independence Day, everyone calls it. Rifle shots and explosions of celebration have been heard all day and have continued into the evening.

Please express our love to your mam and da, and all of the boys and girls. Give little Nellie a special hug from me!

Fondly,
Nora

Cate received Nora's letter a week after it was sent from Harrison—two days after the Bodkins buried Da. Again, Cate cried for her da and her mam as she responded to her cousin's bad news with bad news of her own.

For several years the two women exchanged letters, and as each posted a message to her friend, she looked forward to receiving a response, but it seemed neither ever replied with good news.

In 1852, Cate wrote a letter to Nora to tell her the oldest Bodkin sister, Mary, and her sons, Lucas and Danny, had arrived in Brooklyn, and that Mary's husband, Daniel, had tragically died on the ship while crossing the Atlantic. The entire Bodkin family was living in Mary's new house on Bedford Avenue.

Later that same year, Nora sent a message to tell Cate her mother died in Moycullen. She said Uncle Laurence again performed the funeral and the burial.

Three years later, Nora and Patt—although twenty-four-year-old adults—became orphans, for what they counted as the third time in their lives. Nora wrote to Cate that her uncle Eamon died. She didn't know what was going to become of herself and her brother.

Still later that year, Nora received a letter from Monsignor Terence Gurley, vicar general of the Diocese of Galway.

Nora read his letter with great sorrow.

DIOCESE OF GALWAY, ABBEYGATE
GALWAY CITY, IRELAND
25 June 1855

Dear Nora,
It is with great sorrow that I inform you of the death of your
uncle Laurence.

The second bishop of Galway, Laurence O'Donnell, died
from the fever on 23 June 1855. We buried the bishop behind the
Dominican priory on the Claddagh. The priory was his favorite
place on earth.

Your uncle worked tirelessly to help the victims of the Great
Famine, and I will remember forever his efforts and kindness on
their behalf.

Nora, please know that as his niece, and one of his few living
relatives, you had a special place in his heart.

Either Thimity Cogan from our solicitor's office or I will be in
touch with you again in the very near future.

For the Love of Christ,

Terence Gurley †
Vicar General, Diocese of Galway

In Brooklyn, all of the Bodkin siblings received the same letter from Vicar General Gurley.

Nora wrote to Cate to inform her of the sad news of Uncle Laurence's passing, and Cate wrote to Nora to tell her the same. The letters crossed in the mail between Brooklyn and Harrison.

Nora's letter to Cate also contained some good news for once.

July 29th, 1855
10 O'Clock AM
Harrison, New York

Miss Catherine Bodkin
In care of Mary Duval
2308 Bedford Avenue, Brooklyn, New York

Dearest Cate,
Patt and I send our best wishes.

I assume you and your brothers and sisters have received a letter from the vicar general in Galway informing us all of our uncle Laurence's death.

It is so sad.

His passing seems to be the end of our final link to our beloved Ireland.

In the way of good news, Patt and I were surprised by some last week when we received a visit from Uncle Eamon's attorney. He is a man from Rye, New York—the small town which is next to Harrison. He seems to be a knowledgeable fellow.

As it turns out, Uncle Eamon's last known will identifies Patt and me as Eamon's only living relatives!

In his will, Uncle made some gifts to the church and a couple of local charities. But he bequeathed the china factory, his home— including the acreage—and his financial accounts to Patt and me.

Patt is in the process of learning the operations of the china factory. He is getting to know the employees, writing to the customers, and meeting our suppliers. I fear my poor brother may be working himself to death.

In the meantime, I am involved with the staff here at home to make sure everything continues to be at the level of perfection which Uncle Eamon demanded, and to which I have become accustomed in the short number of years I have lived here.

We must make arrangements to visit you in Brooklyn. I have heard of families who have summer homes in Brooklyn, and Patt and I would like to explore such possibilities.

I hope to see you soon. Please extend our greetings to your brothers and sisters.

Fondly,
Nora

Weeks after learning of Uncle Laurence's death, Nora opened the promised correspondence from Thimity Cogan. The same letter was received by all of the cousins.

Cassidy & Cogan
Solicitors
No. 69 & 70 Courthouse Lane
Galway City

Padraig W. Cassidy
Thimity C. Cogan
2 August 1855

To the Beneficiaries of the Estate of
Laurence O'Donnell, Bishop of Galway

Gentlemen and Ladies,

Yesterday, interested parties to the last will and testament of our late bishop, Laurence O'Donnell, gathered at our Courthouse Lane offices in Galway City.

Those gathered included the man we anticipate will be appointed by the Holy See as the next bishop of Galway, Monsignor John McEvilly. Also present was the vicar general of the diocese, Terence Gurley, and the late Bishop O'Donnell's housekeeper, Mrs. Kitty Carr, who was accompanied by her son, Father Thomas Carr, presently serving at Saint Patrick's College in Maynooth.

The reading of the deceased's last will and testament revealed the following beneficiaries of his estate. (I have not included all of Bishop O'Donnell's specific bequests, or the percentages of residual gifts, as some of the information still requires calculation and estimation.)

> *The Diocese of Galway, Galway, Ireland*
> *Saint Columba's Church, Castlegar, Ireland*
> *Father Kevin McCann, Castlegar, Ireland*
> *Saint Nicholas West Church, Claddagh, Galway, Ireland*
> *Dominican Priory, Claddagh, Galway, Ireland*
> *Dominican Cemetery, Claddagh, Galway, Ireland*
> *Monsignor Terence Gurley, Galway, Ireland*
> *Catherine (Kitty) Carr, Galway, Ireland*
> *Mary Duval, Brooklyn, New York*
> *Danny Duval, Brooklyn, New York*
> *Lucas Duval, Brooklyn, New York*
> *Catherine (Cate) Bodkin, Brooklyn, New York*
> *Adelia (Biddy) Bodkin, Brooklyn, New York*
> *Dominic George Bodkin, Brooklyn, New York*
> *Martin Robert Bodkin, Brooklyn, New York*

Lawrence Bodkin, Brooklyn, New York
John Stanley Bodkin, Junior, Brooklyn, New York
Nellie Bodkin, Brooklyn, New York
Patrick O'Donnell, Harrison, New York
Nora Jones, Harrison, New York

As you may well know, Bishop O'Donnell was a wise man, and to say the least, shrewd with his financial dealings.

A partial list of his assets is as follows:

Various financial accounts at the Bank of Ireland
Several bags of coins
2 silver chalices
1 Irish cob
1 riding carriage
Galway hooker on Galway Bay
Curraghs on Lough Corrib, near Oughterard
Several parcels of County Galway real estate:
    Cottage and acreage in Briarhill
    Cottage and acreage in Oughterard
    Cottage in Moycullen
    Cottage in An Spideál
    Residence in Galway City
    Commercial rooming house in Eyre Square, Galway City
One parcel of County Kildare real estate:
    Cottage and acreage in Maynooth

I am confident my investigation will discover additional assets. The process of administering Bishop O'Donnell's estate is complicated, and it will take some time. Please advise me as to your wish for the disposition of the assets listed above. Some of you are familiar with individual parcels of the real estate and may wish to *claim possession of those properties. The alternative, of course, is the assets be sold, liquidated to cash, and the balances distributed following the percentages delineated in the deceased's last will and testament. For your information, the bishop made specific bequests of the two chalices (the diocese), the Irish cob (Father McCann), the rooming house (Kitty Carr), and the hooker (Monsignor Gurley). I hope to have all matters concluded within three months.*

Yours truly,
Thimity C. Cogan, Solicitor

It took longer than Cogan had suggested, but he liquidated all of Uncle Laurence's property within a year and issued checks drawn on the Bank of Ireland to his beneficiaries.

THE BOYS' CLUB

January 23, 1902
Saint James Cathedral, Brooklyn

8:43 AM: *The icy January wind whistled through the vestibule each time someone opened one of the cathedral's big doors, and me fookin' feet were starting to feel cold. But it was almost time to begin. The clergy was arriving, and the pallbearers lined either side of Dominic's casket. They were me sons and nephews—mostly sons—and they reminded me of meself when I was younger. Me and me brothers had some good times back in our younger days ...*

***

Back in January of 1858, Dominic was twenty-three—a year older than me—Lawrence was twenty, and the Angel eighteen. We thought we were men. Each of us had suitable, steady employment in Brooklyn, and with our combined incomes, we could afford to rent a flat of our own, and we wanted a place to live without our sisters. So, we moved out of Mary's house. Only a few doors away, mind you—still on Bedford Avenue—but we were away from the girls. We knew our neighbors called our new home "the Boys' Club." It was a little disconcerting, but they were probably right.

One Friday morning, a few months into our Boys' Club experience, the others were already up by the time I got out of bed and made me way into the kitchen. The Angel and Lawrence were rushing through breakfast before they had to leave for work.

The temptation to torment Lawrence had never left me, and without saying a word, I smacked him on the back of his head on me way past the eating table.

"Eejit! Lawrence growled back at me. In retaliation, he swatted at me hand, but as usual, he missed.

"Eejit? Eejit?" I reached for Lawrence and encircled his head with me left arm. With his head held securely in the crook of the elbow, I dug the knuckles on me right hand back and forth across the top of his scalp. "Damn it, Martin! That hurts," Lawrence complained. "Stop! Please stop!" he whined. I twisted the knuckles even harder for a few more seconds and let me brother out of the headlock. I smacked him in the back of the head again and questioned whether he would ever toughen up.

"Eejit?" I asked incredulously. "You're the eejit, you arsehole. Not me." Admittedly, the truth escaped me sometimes when I was young.

As usual, the Angel watched us and chuckled with amusement. He was always glad I picked on Lawrence and not him. The little Angel among us was now a man—almost as big as me and still growing, already tough and confident enough to seek a path of his own. He had completed his schooling and worked as a plumber at Drennan's Brownstones—a construction company that was building new row houses on nearly every street in Brooklyn.

Lawrence also worked for Drennan's as a stair builder. Their employer, Patrick Drennan, had so many brownstones under construction at the same time that even when Lawrence and John were not working on the same house, they were almost assuredly working on the same street. They always walked to and from work together, starting at seven thirty in the morning and ending at four. Plumbers and stair *builders were in demand, and they could work every day if they wanted. They usually worked six days.*

Everyone who knew the four of us said I was the one who should be a construction worker, but I put on a tie each morning—Monday through Saturday—and went to me job as a clerk at an ironmonger's shop a few streets from home. The retail ironmongery business was booming. We sold tools and construction supplies to contractors—like Drennan's—and equipment and hardware items to the homeowners who bought the houses Drennan's built. Work didn't start until eight in the morning, so I had a little more time for breakfast.

"Hurry with your breakfast, John!" Lawrence said to the Angel. He was still massaging his sore scalp. "It's after seven already. We're going to be fecking late."

Arrogantly ignoring me younger brother's discomfort, I cracked four eggs into a small bowl and began to scramble them. Mary had asked me to remind everyone to come to her house for dinner tonight. She wanted me to tell everyone not to be late because Patt and Nora were coming, too. John stopped next to me at the stove, and I relayed Mary's message.

"Hurry up, John," Lawrence prodded the Angel.

I dumped the eggs into a frying pan sizzling with butter.

The Angel stacked his empty breakfast dish in the kitchen basin with the others and hustled toward the door ahead of Lawrence. "We're going to be late!" Lawrence said again, smacking the Angel in the back of his head as he rushed out the door after him.

"Dominic is already at work," Lawrence yelled back to me on his way down the steps, "but we'll see him later today. He's painting a house on the same street where we are working this week. Don't worry. I'll remind him about tonight."

"I can't wait to see Nora and Patt. We have so much to talk about," the Angel called to me as he and Lawrence reached the sidewalk and headed down Bedford ...

38

REUNITED

April 1858

AT MARY'S HOUSE ON BEDFORD AVENUE, SHE AND
Cate were awake early, preparing for the tenth crossing anniversary and reunion party with Patt and Nora. Mary was on her
knees, scrubbing the downstairs floors, and Cate was dusting
the bedrooms on the second floor. They wound up sitting on the
staircase together while they took a break from their chores.

"It is certainly easier to clean the house without the boys being
here," Mary quipped to Cate.

"They made a mess everywhere," Cate answered.

"I wonder what Patt and Nora will be like," Cate mused. "From
what she says in her letters, they seem to have been fortunate in
the way their lives have turned out."

After the liquidation of Uncle Laurence's estate, the checks
they all received from Solicitor Cogan—nearly two years ago—
had been a godsend for the Bodkins. Not that they needed
the money to pay immediate bills, or went out and purchased
things they didn't need, but the money gave the family a sense
of security about the future they had never experienced before.

Remembering lessons learned as children in Briarhill, the Bodkin siblings were, for the most part, a thrifty group of young men and women. Most, but not all of them, saved the inheritance from Uncle Laurence.

Dominic, Lawrence, and Martin walked the few blocks to the Emigrant Savings Bank together, and the clerk behind the teller's cage, a young man named Liam Finneran, helped them deposit the checks from the Bank of Ireland into their already existing savings accounts.

Dominic was saving for medical school.

Martin had an eye for a particular lady who had just moved to Brooklyn from New Jersey, and he was saving for the day when he would be a family man.

Lawrence always saved all of his money. After paying his rent, he rarely spent a dime of his own money.

John, unlike his brothers, spent most of his money and saved a little. He had a jar in his bedroom with his small savings.

Mary and Biddy put all of theirs in an account at the Emigrant. They called it the "rainy day fund."

No one was quite sure what Nellie did with her money—but if she spent it on something, she had nothing to show for it.

As Cate finished dusting the last bedroom, she decided to spend some of her savings on a pretty hair pin for tonight's party. *I'll bet Nora has a beautiful dress to wear tonight!* she thought.

On Friday night, the four Bodkin men cleaned up after their day at work and, as instructed, they arrived at Mary's right on time.

A coachman stopped a shiny, black carriage at the front of the house and from it emerged Patt O'Donnell and Nora Jones. Cate opened the front door to greet the cousins.

Nora was wearing a beautiful silk dress with a big skirt and a colorful bonnet. Her hair was perfectly coiffed. Patrick had a short-trimmed beard and wore a dark suit, like the ones James Duval wore around Galway, Mary remembered.

Patt bounded to the top of the steps and gave Cate a big hug. Nora was right behind her brother, slowed somewhat by the crinolines under her skirt, but just as excited to be seeing her cousins again.

"Nellie, you've grown so much!" Nora said as she embraced her youngest cousin.

Hugs, handshakes, kisses, and backslaps went around the parlor as the cousins were reunited. Dominic introduced Patt and Nora to Mary's sons for the first time, and the cousins from Harrison expressed belated sympathy to Mary for the loss of her husband.

"I love your house, Mary, and Bedford Avenue seems to be a nice street. Do you like your neighbors?" Nora asked as Mary gave her a tour of her home.

"Thank you, Nora. We love it. Brooklyn is certainly a city, and it has changed over the years, but our neighbors are friendly people—mostly Irish. My sons have many friends, and they are always outside playing together. We have plenty of room now that our brothers have moved to their own place. The third floor has two spare bedrooms and a bath. I hope you and Patt don't mind sharing a bathroom for the night?"

"Patt and I can share a bathroom for a single night, Mary. We'll be fine. Your home is so big! It must be expensive to maintain."

"My late husband's parents have been generous. Danny and Lucas are their only grandchildren, and the Duvals help us a lot.

"Let's get back to the others, Nora," Mary said, leading Nora back down the stairs. "Harrison is country living. Isn't it?"

⟨⟨⟨⟩⟩⟩ ⟨⟨⟨⟩⟩⟩ ⟨⟨⟨⟩⟩⟩

Patt, Dominic, and John were in the parlor, catching up on the last ten years and each other's plans.

"Medical school! My God, Dominic, that's exciting! When can you apply?" Patt was not surprised by Dominic's dream.

"It will still be a few years, Patt. I graduated from secondary school back in '52, but I've not been able to afford any university. The route I'll have to follow to medical school might be an apprenticeship."

"Do you have one established, Dominic?"

"I'm getting close. Our old friend Dr. Red Mahoney has been introducing me to other doctors, and hopefully, someone will work out. In the meantime, I spend many hours at the Athenaeum Reading Room. I'm learning as much as I can and saving every cent from my work. The tuition at the University of the City of New York can be as much as three thousand dollars.

"I hear you are operating a china factory in Harrison, Patt. How is that working out for you?"

"I've got a lot to learn, Dominic, but it's going to be good. I'm sure you know Uncle Eamon's story. It's been hard work for me since he died, but I'm getting used to it.

"What about you, Angel? You are working as a plumber?"

"I am, Patt, and it's all right for now. I work every day with Lawrence, and we see Dominic on the job pretty regularly. I'm not sure I want to spend the rest of my life being a plumber, though. I'm looking for another way I can fulfill my dreams. I need something more creative. But I don't know what it is yet."

In the kitchen, Nora was helping Cate and Biddy, as they prepared some meats and cheeses to serve the others. Their conversation was a continuation of the many hours they spent talking about boys on the *Cushlamachree*, except now it was about *men*.

"You must have more men worth courting in Brooklyn than I have in Harrison, girls. Don't you have anyone you could go after? No one that you are interested in?" Nora quizzed her cousins.

"Brooklyn has plenty of men, Nora, but neither of us is ready for that. Someday though! What about you?" Biddy asked. Biddy talked to more men than Cate did, so she was comfortable responding to Nora.

"I'm too busy with the house now to worry about men, Biddy. But soon, I hope! It may be difficult in Harrison, though. Patt and I don't have close neighbors, and it will be difficult to meet someone.

"How is Nellie?" Nora asked her cousins. "I haven't seen her since we arrived."

"Nellie is very quiet, Nora. I won't be surprised if she has already retired for the night," Cate said with a serious note to her voice.

As the evening moved along, everyone laughed and joked. The cousins all reminisced about Mam and Da and the voyage. The boys teased Biddy and Nora about Damen Goldyn, and how much of them Biddy's *búachaill* may or may not have seen.

NELLIE

NELLIE REMEMBERED MOST OF THE THINGS THAT
happened in her life when she was a six-year-old in Briarhill, but
she did not have a clear recollection of too many things that happened when she was five, and even less of what happened when
she was only four.

She remembered nothing of her life before she was four. As
the baby of a family—almost by definition—your siblings were
all bigger than you were, and, of course, smarter than you were.
Those were her first memories. She was living in a world of giants.
She was living in a world where everyone was smart, and she was
not. Everyone thought she was needy, and someone was always
taking care of her, never allowing her independence.

She was six when she first met Sadhbh.

Nellie had ventured over the meadow, behind the cottage in
Briarhill, toward a stream to pick some daffodils. At first, Nellie
thought she was asleep and dreaming. A good dream about a
beautiful girl who was about eighteen years old, with long, curly
blond hair. Sadhbh was a statuesque girl, wearing a flowing,
diaphanous gown made of gold and white silk. The girl floated;
she hovered next to Nellie.

Nellie couldn't remember whether she had given Sadhbh her name or if Sadhbh had told her what her name was. Sadhbh meant "sweetness and goodness" to Nellie.

Sadhbh smiled at Nellie and said, *"Dia dhuit, mo stór."* Hello, my treasure. The two became friends. They played together, and Nellie learned about life from Sadhbh.

From the beginning, Nellie's relationship with Sadhbh reinforced in Nellie that her obligation in life was to care for others. But to do that, Nellie had to care for herself. Sadhbh knew this was a difficult concept for a little girl, but she told Nellie she would always be with her, to help along the way.

"Never give up, my sweet Nellie." The beautiful fairy said to Nellie, "Never give up, *mo stór.*"

In the meadow—on that first day—Nellie realized her visit with Sadhbh was not a dream when she heard her mam's voice calling her to come back to the cottage for supper.

Today, eleven years into their friendship, things hadn't changed too much, except that they were about the same age now. Sadhbh seemed to like Brooklyn, but Nellie saw that her friend longed for the peaceful meadows and fields in Briarhill and the flowers along the banks of the stream near their cottage.

By virtue of the order of birth—with four boys in between— Nellie's sisters were so much older. They were more like mother figures to her than sisters. Mary was a married woman when Nellie was six, and she had a baby of her own by Nellie's seventh birthday. In Nellie's earliest memories, Biddy and Cate were teenagers. To Nellie, they were teenagers who behaved more like adults. They acted like the mature Mary or even Mam herself.

Da seemed like a nice man. Of course, she knew he was a nice man, and he loved her, but she hardly knew him. When she was a child, Da worked all day, and as his eighth child, when he came home from work, Nellie was Mam's responsibility.

Nellie had beautiful memories of her mam during those years in Briarhill—and her few days in Brooklyn. She remembered sleeping next to Mam in Briarhill. Riding in the cart huddled against the cold on their way to Galway, and lying all day and night, being protected by Mam in the smelly, disgusting steerage bunk on the *Cushlamachree*.

She could recall her brothers, who ran and played games in the fields around the cottage in Briarhill. She also remembered getting her brothers' hand-me-down clothes and an uncle, a priest, who came to Briarhill and told stories—stories which she never understood.

⬦⬦⬦ ⬦⬦⬦ ⬦⬦⬦

Nellie was in her bed. The ten-year reunion party was still going on downstairs, and it had been more fun to talk to Nora and Patt again than Nellie had anticipated—especially Nora.

Nellie remembered their conversations from long ago. Nora told her things about her father and sailing away from Inis Mór on the curragh. About her mother's dying.

Nora was seventeen at the time of the crossing. Nellie was seventeen now, and Nora had made that connection tonight, mentioning the coincidence to Nellie.

As she sat on the bed in her room, Nellie knew she shouldn't have stolen away from the party just to be alone, but she had. It was what she always did. Usually, no one talked to her, and what they talked about among themselves wasn't particularly interesting to Nellie.

When Nellie tried to start a conversation, her sisters and brothers would just look at her and seldom did anyone respond. As a result of being ignored for years, Nellie had the habit of not trying to talk with anyone. Usually, she could wander off with Sadhbh and be sure no one missed her. She had places where she and Sadhbh could hide for days at a time, and no one seemed to notice she was gone. Nellie assumed they didn't care.

Tonight, though, Nellie thought she'd made a mistake. She should have stayed downstairs and talked with Nora. She wanted to talk more to Nora, and Sadhbh agreed.

"Maybe it's not too late," Sadhbh whispered to Nellie as she heard the Bodkin brothers saying goodbye.

The reunion party was ending.

From her second-floor bedroom, Nellie could hear her family preparing to go to bed. Doors closed. Kerosene lamps extinguished. Her sisters' footsteps in the hallway. Patt and Nora's footsteps, creaking the stairs as they headed to the third floor. Windows adjusted. More doors were closing.

Silence.

Nellie knew which bedroom Nora was in upstairs, and she wanted to talk to her again tonight. She knew her sisters would fall asleep quickly—especially since Martin brought a jug of *poitín* to the party.

If she waited until they were asleep, they would not hear creaking on the stairs as she went up. She was sure they wouldn't hear Sadhbh. Their hiding place was upstairs, and together with Sadhbh, she had crept to her spot many nights without being detected.

"Let's go," Sadhbh said confidently.

It was dark as Nellie and Sadhbh made their way to the third floor. They knew to stay on the right edge of each step to reduce the creaking. It worked again.

Two quiet knocks on Nora's bedroom door.

Knock. Knock.

"She's awake," Sadhbh said.

"Nora? Are you still awake?" Nellie whispered.

Nora rolled over in her bed to see who was at the door.

"Nellie?"

"Shh!" Sadhbh followed Nellie into the room, and Nellie closed the door behind them. "Can we talk, Nora?"

Nellie came over to Nora's bed, and Nora smiled. "Certainly, Nellie. Sit with me."

"I'm sorry I snuck away earlier. I tend to do that. I wanted to talk to you more, but I was afraid, with my sisters there."

Nora shared a blanket, which she put around Nellie's shoulders. Sadhbh never needed a blanket over her gold and white silk gown.

The cousins talked until morning, and by dawn, Nora had a good understanding of the loneliness Nellie continued to feel, even ten years after her mother's death.

⬥⬥⬥ ⬥⬥⬥ ⬥⬥⬥

The rising sun was filtering through the third-floor window, and people were stirring throughout the house, so Nellie, and a smiling Sadhbh, quietly went back to her bedroom while Nora prepared to leave for home.

Patt and Nora's carriage returned for them, and it was time to bid the cousins from Harrison goodbye. Nora looked weary.

"Are you all right, Nora? Wasn't your bed comfortable? You look like you've been up all night!" Cate said to her cousin.

"I was. I was talking to Nellie, Cate. She wants to go back to Ireland—back to County Galway. She's sure of it, Mary. She has saved all of her money from Uncle Laurence, and she said she wants to go home, to try to live on her own.

"She has enough money to go there, and to get back here if it doesn't work out. She suggested that maybe she could stay with your in-laws. Maybe the Duvals might need someone who would be a help to them."

"Oh my God!" Cate said. "What have we done?"

"But we will miss Nellie, Nora. We will miss her," Biddy expressed, not just to Nora but to her sisters as well.

"It's a little late to be worried about that, Sisters," Mary said. "I'll write to the Duvals and Cate, you write to Monsignor Gurley. Maybe he will have an idea about employment at the diocese."

Patt and the coachman had the carriage packed.

"Let me know what you learn from your letters to Galway. I'll help any way I can." Nora got in the carriage.

The sisters waved goodbye as the carriage pulled down Bedford Avenue, and they walked back in the house to figure out what to say to Nellie, their baby sister.

MARIA TERESA

1861

MARIA TERESA'S FATHER PASSED AWAY WHEN SHE WAS twelve, and her mother, Teresa Reel Jones, raised her only child.

It was just the two of them—mother and daughter—best friends. Her mother taught Maria how to read and how to write in English. She taught Maria to love life and never give up.

Under her mother's loving tutelage, Maria faithfully worked on her "sampler," a sheet of fabric with several different colored thread stitches. Maria's stitches were in the form of letters, numbers, and symbols. She made a few stitches every day and used a different color for every new letter or number.

A B C D E F G H I J K L M N O
P Q R S T U V W X Y Z

and

1 2 3 4 5 6 7 8 9 10

and

a b c d e f g h i j k l m n o
p q r s t u v w x y z

It was precise and time-consuming work. Maria's stitches were perfect, and she knew all of her letters and numbers. The symbols she stitched were artistic. Each had a meaning related to her life as a child in Edgeworthstown, County Longford.

Young Maria's stitches improved with each letter and each number. Her mother said the stitches in her signature line were perfect:

MARIA TERESA JONES × × HER SAMPLER
WROUGHT IN THE YEAR 1842 ×× AGED 10

When Maria was almost sixteen, her mother caught the fever and died on Christmas Day in 1847. Young Maria Teresa was alone. Her mother told her before she died that she had saved a little money, and Maria knew on that Christmas morning she was going to America. She had to leave.

After her mother's death, with the help of her few remaining relatives, she completed all the arrangements necessary for her to leave Edgeworthstown.

Three months after her mother's death, Maria left the dock in Galway—with the Masseys, the Bodkins, and the other hearty souls on the *Cushlamachree*. She had one small bag. It contained a change of clothing and her only other possession—her sampler. The sampler was Maria's only link to her mother, and it was going to America with her. If she was someday blessed to have a daughter, Maria would use her sampler to teach her little girl to read and write.

Ten years after the *Cushlamachree* docked at the pier in Lower Manhattan, her life had evolved the way she had hoped it would.

Maria liked Port Jervis when she first arrived. She lived with her cousin Denise and her husband, Jack O'Leary, who had arrived in New York two years earlier, in 1846. The young couple had two children, and Maria enjoyed helping her cousin care for them. She became acquainted with a few people in Port Jervis, in addition to her family, but not many. The homes in Port Jervis spread out over the countryside, and as it was in Edgeworths-town, there was a significant distance between homes. Families could not walk down the street to shop. They had to ride to town in a carriage.

She found Port Jervis calm and quiet. It was too calm and too quiet, and after traveling back to New York City once with her cousin's family, she thought city living might be more to her liking. Maria wanted to have neighbors who lived close. She wanted to be with people who greeted each other on the sidewalks while walking with their children and shopping in stores on the street corners.

By February of 1855, she had made an arrangement to live with other relatives in New York City and to look for work as a factory girl, and maybe she would be able to find the Bodkins from the *Cushlamachree*. Perhaps she could locate the Masseys and go back to work for them. The Massey children were seven years older now. Maria loved children and wanted her own someday but wondered if the two teenage Massey children were more than she could handle.

Then she received a letter. She thought the message was sweet—very sweet.

Miss Maria Jones
Port Jervis
February 26, 1855

My Dear Miss Jones

I hope you will forgive me when you read this note for the free-
dom I use when addressing you in the unguarded manner. I would
feel happy in being acquainted with you before this time, but the
disagreeable weather we had this time back and other affairs have
prevented me from going to Denise's to see you.

I have heard today that you are going to New York in a few
days. Now if you are not in too great a hurry to go there, I would
like to see you before you would go. There is nothing that would
give me more pleasure than to think we would be good friends
before you go. If you think proper of what I propose, let me know
when and where shall I have the pleasure of seeing you. I hope you
will excuse this hurried note and I being unacquainted with writing
love letters if this is not done in the best stile.

I Remain Yours Truly,
Patrick Drennan

In the past months, Maria had seen Patrick Drennan in Port
Jervis several times while she was shopping with Denise and
her children. They had never met. They had never spoken. But
they had made eye contact a couple of times, and she thought
he smiled at her once. Patrick looked several years older, but she
thought he was good-looking, and the quality of his horse and
carriage let on that he was a successful man.

She decided to delay her plans to move to New York for a few
days and asked Denise's husband to deliver a note of response to
Patrick Drennan—she wanted to meet him.

Patrick and Maria were married a week later on March 16, 1855.
They lived in Port Jervis in a house Patrick built. His business
was home building and his craft widely regarded. Their daughter,
Mary, was born before the couple's first wedding anniversary.

Patrick's business continued to grow, and his reputation led to requests for him to build homes in Brooklyn and New York City. The flood of European immigrants to New York had created a housing shortage in Brooklyn. Patrick and Maria saw the potential of moving the family to the fastest-growing city in America.

Maria was pregnant with the couple's second child when the family moved to Brooklyn in the fall of 1856. After being in business for two years in Brooklyn, Patrick's company, Drennan's Brownstones, was building new homes on almost every city block from Clinton Hill out to Bushwick. The years flew by for Maria and Patrick. In the fall of 1861, they lived on the corner of Lewis and Jefferson Avenues. It was a new and growing neighborhood in Brooklyn, and Patrick assured her their new community would be large very soon.

The families along Lewis and Jefferson had the same names and were the same neighbors that people everywhere in Brooklyn had. There were Italians, Germans, Jews, English, and of course, the Irish. The Carmines, the Greens, the Newmans, the Phelpses, the Ripleys, the Hennens. Maria knew everyone on Lewis Avenue. The children loved the neighborhood. It was almost exactly what Maria was hoping for when she heard the men groaning "HEAVE … HEAVE … HEAVE" as the *Cushlamachree* moved away from the quay in Galway thirteen years before.

Late one October afternoon, Maria was shopping at Miklas' Butcher Shoppe on Lafayette Avenue, and she decided to take a walk on the way home. She liked walking in this area with the children. They walked along Lewis, across Lafayette, DeKalb, and Hart. Today she made it to Willoughby. The leaves on the trees had reached the peak of their change from summer's green to autumn's shades of reds and oranges and gold. Brooklyn was beautiful. The air was crisp and refreshing. The sun was getting lower in the sky, and the gaslights on the streets would be on before dinner. Smoke from Brooklyn's coal-fired furnaces came from many of her neighbors' houses. It would be the first cold night of the fall, but Maria knew she had plenty of blankets for the children. They would all be warm in bed tonight.

290 CLINTON AVENUE

December 20, 1894

IT WAS FIVE DAYS BEFORE CHRISTMAS 1894 AS THE SS
Gallia pulled closer to New York Harbor. In the warmth of the ship's
elegant dining room, Dominic stood at the windows and performed as a tour guide for most of the other first-class passengers.

"Brooklyn is on the right. New Jersey is over on the left," he said.

"There!" He pointed. "Ahead on the left—it's hard to tell it's
an island from the view we have, but that is Staten Island. The
entrance to the harbor is called the Narrows because of its narrow
strip of navigable water for the larger ships entering the harbor."
Dominic commanded the attention of the crowd at the windows.
"It is said, the Narrows was where Giovanni da Verrazzano
anchored when he first arrived in New York in 1524."

Almost in unison, everyone shifted their gaze from the starboard side of the *Gallia* to the bow. Lady Liberty—the Statue of
Liberty—was in front of them.

Further ahead, spanning the East River between Manhattan
Island and Brooklyn, was a bridge. "Dominic, would you look at
that!" Father McCann said with amazement as he pointed toward

the structure. "Isn't it grand, Dominic? The deck looks like it's suspended by hundreds, maybe thousands, of cables, strung like a harp."

"Father Kevin," Dominic said to the priest, "it's called the New York and Brooklyn Bridge, and it is hanging between those two magnificent stone towers embedded in the river. The bridge opened a few years ago, and many Brooklynites walk across it every day to get to jobs in Manhattan. Without those cables, Father, Brooklyn would not be growing as it is. My coachman is going to meet us at the pier, and you and I will ride across the bridge this afternoon on the final leg of our trip home."

As Captain Boehmcke approached the Mallory Shipping Line's Pier 16, the *Gallia* was barely moving. On the dock was a warehouse with a sign that read: "FULTON FISH MARKET," and Father Kevin saw as many as twenty fishmongers pushing wheelbarrows, loaded with fish and ice, toward several horse-drawn wagons parked in a line along South Street. He was amazed to see another ship loaded with bananas that had docked at an adjacent pier with signage indicating: "CUBA and MEXICO."

Two harbor pilot boats guided the *Gallia*'s bow into its berth. The ship came to a halt, and the crew tied the ship's lines to the large cleats on the pier. The passengers would all wait for a barge that would take the new steerage arrivals to Ellis Island, where they would endure the immigration process and a physical examination by medical personnel.

Dominic and Father Kevin McCann would not transfer to the barge since first-cabin passengers and American citizens had their physical examinations and customs inspections performed aboard ship. For the first-cabin passengers who were just visiting America—rather than immigrating—processing would be easier, no long wait in the lines at the newly opened Ellis Island Immigration Center.

Dominic sought out Captain Boehmcke on the bridge. The two shook hands and grasped each other by the shoulders, as men often do. "Safe travels, my friend," Dominic said.

In a few hours, Dominic and Father Kevin would be in Brooklyn.

Across the river at 290 Clinton Avenue, Lawrence's wife, Maggie, and Annie Corliss, her housemaid, were putting the finishing touches on the Christmas decorations around the front door.

"Mr. Alpers!" Maggie called from the front hall to Dominic's longtime personal coachman, who was having some lunch in the kitchen. "Will you help Annie and me put the garland on the top of the door? After that, don't you think it will be time to leave for Manhattan to pick up Dr. Bodkin?"

"You're right, Mrs. Bodkin. Let me help you, and then I better be on my way."

Alpers moved the ladder, climbed near the top of the front door, and after about three attempts, positioned the garland of pine needles to Maggie's liking.

"I'll be back with Dr. Bodkin and Father McCann in a few hours."

I'm a little early, Alpers thought. *If there is not too much traffic on the bridge, I might be able to have a minute or two for a bit of a taste at the bar.*

Alpers bounded down the front steps and drove his carriage to DeKalb and onto Flatbush Avenue. He headed toward the Brooklyn-side entrance to the New York and Brooklyn Bridge.

Before they could disembark the *Gallia*, both Dominic and Father McCann had to receive physical examinations. The crossing had been easy for the priest, who was in good health. He was a moderate drinker and still in his seventies. He anticipated the physical examination would be cursory. However, Father McCann's physical was not what he expected at all. It was only a wink and a nod.

He stood in his cabin and waited with Dominic for the health inspector to arrive.

One knock on the door and it opened.

"Hello, Body, old boy! I didn't expect to find you in here," Aaron Y. Hanson, M.D., said with surprise. He had always called Dominic by his medical school nickname, "Body."

"Well, hello, Aaron," Dominic replied.

The two doctors shook hands, and Dominic introduced the priest to his old classmate.

"We graduated from the Medical Department together back in '66, Father Kevin," Dominic said.

"Those were the days, eh ...," Hanson said with a smile.

"You were a good student, Body, old boy. What was it then ... first in our class, eh? That was it, Father," Dr. Hanson paid tribute to his classmate. "Body was first in our graduating class! How was your crossing? You look well, eh."

"It was a fine voyage, Aaron. My old friend Bruce Boehmcke was the captain, and the sailing was smooth. The cabin accommodations and the meal service were both excellent. My friend Father McCann here is from Ireland. He is on his first visit to America and will be staying with me for a few months while he gets to see the sights."

"Well, perfect for you, Father McCann. Welcome to America. I hope you have good weather for your visit. The New York City winters can be nasty, eh, Body, old boy! Gentlemen, I'll have to carry on, now, eh. There are several passengers I have yet to review, and I'm afraid they will not all be as healthy as the two of you. I told the wife I'd be home for a proper supper," the doctor said. "Ever get married, old boy, eh?"

"Too busy for women and any of that, Aaron. Delivering their babies takes too much time."

"It's a little late for that anyway, Body. Time to retire, eh. That's what I'm thinking. How about you, old boy?"

"Not yet, Aaron. But my nephew Marty just began his practice. He's been taking care of my patients while I've been traveling, and his brother George is in the medical department up at Columbia right now. They might be able to help me when it's time to hang up the old stethoscope."

"Sounds like a plan. See you around, Body. Have a merry Christmas. Nice meeting you, Father."

As Hanson moved on to the next cabin, Dominic and Kevin collected their suitcases and headed across the deck.

The wharf was as crowded with welcomers as it had been fifty years earlier when Dominic first came down the gangway of the *Cushlamachree*.

Standing on the pier, Father Kevin looked around in amazement at the New York City buildings that seemed to be reaching to the sky.

"So many fecking people, Dominic. Excuse my language." The priest blessed himself with the sign of the cross. "So many buildings."

Since he first arrived at Saint Columba's—more than a half-century ago—Kevin McCann had been the most devoted pastor his Castlegar parishioners could imagine. Every year he was required to go to Galway, for a day or two, on diocesan business. Once, about twenty years ago, he went to Dublin to attend the installation of a new bishop of the neighboring Diocese of

Dublin. Other than those trips, he had never been outside of Castlegar and the tiny, rural townlands that constituted his parish. Kevin's life was ministering to his parishioners. The sights he saw in New York City as he stepped onto the pier, and the emotions he felt at that moment, were nearly overwhelming.

"This is a different world, Dominic," he said as they walked along the pier. "It's bigger—and busier—than in my wildest fecking dreams." He blessed himself again.

"Here he is, Father! There's our carriage."

"Mr. Alpers!" Dominic waved and called ahead to his coachman. Alpers saw Dominic and called back, "Doctor! Hello, Doctor!"

"Mr. Alpers! Hello. This is great! Everyone is right on time. Father McCann, this is John Alpers. John, Father McCann was our pastor at Saint Columba's, back in Briarhill."

"Welcome to New York, Father. How was your voyage, Doctor?" Alpers asked as he picked up the suitcases.

"It was fine, Mr. Alpers. Fine. Good to be home, though," Dominic answered as the men climbed into the enclosed carriage. Alpers flicked the horse gently with his leather-handled whip, and they headed along South Street and back over the bridge into Brooklyn.

McCann held on to his seat as Alpers maneuvered the two-wheeled carriage through traffic on the brick and cobblestone streets. He saw there were sidewalks in front of businesses and homes. Grocers, haberdashers, cobblers, and butchers were on every corner. Men rushed along the sidewalks in business suits and overcoats. Women, wearing fancy hats and warm coats covering their colored dresses, looked in store windows, carrying packages from the shops where they had already made Christmas purchases.

Alpers pulled the carriage to a halt in front of 290 Clinton Avenue, and it was exactly what Dominic had described to Kevin. It was the most substantial home on the block—redbrick, with a porch wrapping all across the front and around one side. The house was three stories tall, with decorative cornices at the roofline. In front was a lovely yard, and Dominic said, "My lot has some grass and a small courtyard out back." The other homes on Clinton were all large Victorians, but not as significant as Dominic's.

McCann noticed the homes on Clinton were different from every house they had passed for blocks. The others were the brownstones, of which Dominic had told him so much. The large brownstones Kevin had seen typically connected to another on either side, and each had about a dozen steps from the sidewalk to the second floor, with wrought iron handrails and fencing. Dominic told him that the two steps on the side of the home went to the lower floor, where the maid or servants usually lived. Each house had the grandeur of a small castle.

Alpers brought in the suitcases, and Dominic and Kevin followed him up the steps to the front porch.

Maggie was in the parlor, admiring her Christmas decorations, when the carriage arrived home. She came out to greet the travelers and led them into the parlor. The fireplace had several logs blazing, helping to take December's late afternoon chill off the room.

Kevin took a seat and admired the decorations and furnishings. He noticed what struck him as peculiar, but beautiful, statues of a pair of small donkeys in the parlor. The two donkeys, already decorated for Christmas, wore tiny Santa Claus hats. Maggie saw Father Kevin admiring them and told him they were Dresden porcelain.

"Father, I am sorry Lawrence is not here to welcome you to our home. He is away, investigating some real estate. Beachfront property, out east on Great South Bay, I think. A place named for an Indian or something. Patchogue, was it? Maybe that's it. He took the train. Half those little towns have names of Indian tribes, or fish, or clams. Too confusing for me. I've never been there. The beach in New Jersey is my favorite. It's very civilized there. Anyway, Lawrence will not be home until tomorrow evening's meal. Let me show you around the house."

Kevin was exhausted from the trip, but the polite priest said, "Of course," and listened to Maggie as she described the beautiful woodwork and the hardwood floors, the glass and porcelain doorknobs, crown molding, high ceilings, big windows, several bedrooms, parlor, den, living room, dining room, kitchen, a dumbwaiter, multiple fireplaces. "We have a coal-fired boiler in the basement, and," Maggie concluded, "there's indoor plumbing, too."

They returned to the parlor, where Dominic was waiting.

"Could I offer you a glass of wine before dinner is ready?" Maggie asked Kevin, immediately winning the priest's friendship.

"I'd love that, Maggie, thank you."

Kevin sat in the parlor with Dominic and said, "This home is like a castle, Dominic. It's grand; you're rightfully proud of it."

Annie Corliss heard a knock at the door and went to answer it. She came back into the parlor and said, "Excuse me, Doctor, but Mr. John Caputo needs to speak with you." A moment later, Dominic came back to the parlor. "Mary sent him over from the office. Looks like twins," Dominic said. "Mary heard the *Gallia* had docked and assumed I was at home. I'm off to the hospital, Maggie. Sorry, I'll miss dinner, but the Caputo twins won't wait. I shouldn't be too late."

Dominic asked Annie to get his hat and coat. Mr. Alpers brought the doctor's carriage back around to the front of the house, and the two men quickly left on the short trip to the hospital.

Father Kevin was amazed. Less than an hour at home and Dominic was at work already. Maggie, on the other hand, was not surprised at all.

"This happens all the time, Father Kevin. It will be unusual for Dominic to be with us at dinnertime during your visit."

Annie came back into the parlor and announced she was ready to serve dinner. They walked down the hallway, and past what Maggie explained was Dominic's medical library. In the hall was a beautiful marble pedestal holding a bronze bust of a boy and a girl. Father Kevin knew from conversations with Dominic that, years ago, Maggie and Lawrence lost a child during childbirth, and Kevin wondered, *More than one?*

"Tonight's dinner," Annie announced proudly, "is a loin of lamb with rosemary and garlic, roasted red potatoes with parsley, string beans saved from the garden, and mint jelly, of course." The flickering light from two candles lit up the fine china, crystal stemware, and sterling silverware of the place settings, which seemed lost at the end of the long dining room table. Annie served the lamb on a china platter.

"The wine tonight is a fine French red wine, a Bordeaux, Father Kevin, a St. Julien 1893. It pairs beautifully with the lamb," Maggie proudly told the priest. Annie poured them each a glass, and they toasted to the end of the voyage on the *Gallia*. Kevin expressed his regret that Dominic and Lawrence were not with them for this excellent meal.

Maggie and Kevin ate dinner and got to know each other over the next couple of hours. The attractive woman, who was in her middle fifties, wore diamond earrings, two giant diamond rings, and a similarly large amethyst brooch. Kevin was impressed by Maggie's level of sophistication. He was curious about what appeared to be the substantial wealth accumulated by the wife of Lawrence Bodkin, in the mere four decades since Lawrence, a skinny—and not very healthy-looking—nine-year-old boy left Saint Columba's parish with his family. As Kevin remembered their departure, they had all of their possessions in two bags.

Kevin tried to find an answer.

"I am looking forward to meeting Lawrence tomorrow evening. He must be successful. When did you and Lawrence meet each other, Maggie?"

WORKING FOR THE BOSS

February 1862

IN FEBRUARY 1862, THIRTY-SEVEN-YEAR-OLD BRIAN Byrne's real job did not take up much of his day. He worked for the City of New York and was in charge of the city's growing park system. The city's parks, as well as the associated recreational venues, had been closed for the winter for three months. Every year from November 15 until March 17, Brian worked on the Saint Patrick's Day Parade in New York City. Everything he did—all day, every day—was aimed to ensure the success of the parade.

The Tammany Hall political machine paid Byrne's salary, and a man named William Tweed was his supervisor. Nobody called the supervisor William or Bill, and indeed not Billy. Like everyone else, Brian called him "Boss." Boss Tweed was aggressive, and he could be ruthless, but on March 17, Boss wanted a day of free fun, food, and drink for the Irish voters of New York City to remember when they went to the voting booth.

New Yorkers marched in the first Saint Patrick's Day Parade in 1762, and, as the chairman of the Ancient Order of Hibernians, Brian Byrne was now the director of the 100th-anniversary parade. The honor was a little overwhelming. The power was exhilarating. The risk of failing Boss Tweed was frightening.

The parade would start at the old cathedral in Lower Manhattan, on the corner of Mott and Prince Streets.

Byrne had checklists for the parade. He had revised, and revised, his lists over the past several years. He had sheets of paper filled with the names of marchers, politicians, and sponsors. There were bagpipers, bands, hospitals, fire houses, police precincts, and civic associations. Under the category of "Irish families," Brian had another list. The families were, for the most part, alphabetized—Ahern, Burgoyne, Clarke, Connolly, Dalton ... McKee, McNally ... O'Leary, Quinn. He tried to keep track of the numbers to help with his estimates of how many would be marching. So many men were in the South fighting the war he knew a huge turnout would be difficult to achieve.

Brian Byrne wanted the 1862 Saint Patrick's Day Parade to be the biggest and best. The challenges would be significant, however. The Civil War was raging, and the politics and social equilibrium of New York City were hopelessly divided. Half of New York praised Abraham Lincoln, and the other half ridiculed him. The rumors of the president's instituting a national draft, to fill the Union Army's ranks, had Irish families on edge. "Rich people could buy their way out of the draft," one rumor implied. The other story, that thousands would die in the war with the South, was already proving to be a fact.

The government was recruiting new immigrants into the Union Army right on the pier. The "recruits" were getting off Irish Coffin Ships, saying goodbye to their families, being outfitted as soldiers on the docks in Lower Manhattan, and immediately boarding army transport ships headed to ports and battlefields in the South. Many other New Yorkers were enlisting to support the Union cause. New York provided more soldiers for the Union than any other Northern state, and the Irish had earned the well-deserved reputation of being fierce fighters on the battlefield.

At the same time, many native New Yorkers, including some of Irish descent, despised the newly arriving Irish immigrants. Much of the natives' disdain for the new immigrants had roots in economics. The new Irish immigrants would work for little money, earning them comparisons to the runaway slaves living freely in New York.

The parade route passed through the Five Points on its way to city hall. Several rival gangs controlled the area. Half of the gangs had new Irish immigrant members. The other half had native-born American-Irish members. The native-born outfits called themselves "Nativists," and they hated the new Irish immigrants. The gangs included the Forty Thieves, the Plug Uglies, the Dead Rabbits, and the ruthless Bowery Boys—led by the notorious Bill "the Butcher" Poole.

Brian was concerned that the largest Nativist gang, the Butcher's Bowery Boys, would try to disrupt the parade. Brian knew their enemies—the Dead Rabbits, led by John Morrissey—would defend the marchers' right to parade for Saint Patrick. This fear of violence was one of the topics Brian would have to resolve with Boss Tweed.

Byrne needed marchers, and he required bands to play music for the marchers. He needed sponsors to provide drinks and food for everyone, and more sponsors to pay for the ferry trips from Brooklyn to Lower Manhattan and back again. This year the chairman of the Ancient Order of Hibernians was working hard to get people to march for Saint Patrick. He came to Brooklyn at least twice a week to recruit new Irish families and talked to families on the street corners, drank beer in the taverns, and went to the churches.

On Sunday, February 23, 1862, Brian went to Saint Patrick's Church in Brooklyn. After surprising himself by staying awake through the sermon, he walked over to the rectory and introduced himself to Father Bernard Fitzpatrick to share his concerns about the upcoming parade.

The two men shook hands, and the elderly Fitzpatrick showed Byrne to a sofa in his office. "Good luck to you with your parade, Mr. Byrne. It's not much of a year for festivities."

"I know, Father. The war and the unrest in the city are causing us problems this year. That's why I need new sponsors. My regular sponsors are putting a lot of money into the war effort and withholding their usual stipends from the Hibernians. I need more men marching, too, Father. Many of my regulars are off to fight in the war. You could help achieve my goal of having the largest Saint Paddy's parade ever if you will mention the parade at your Masses over the next few weeks. Your parish is a natural to support the parade—this being Saint Patrick's Church, and all."

Fitzpatrick didn't have to think for long.

"I will do that, young man. It makes sense. Let's see … there will be three Sundays before March 17. At the end of each Mass, during the parish announcements, I'll encourage marching in the parade—to honor our patron saint, I'll tell them. I'll march myself, and I'll see how many of my parishioners I can bring along for you. You have to understand, Mr. Byrne, that many of my parishioners are of very modest means," the pastor went on.

"The Hibernians will pay for the ferries, correct?

"And lunch and dinner will be provided, right?

"And all the beer they can drink?

"Will they be allowed to carry their Irish flags?

"Will Archbishop Hughes be there?

"How about Bishop Loughlin?"

Byrne wrote a few things on his notepad.

"You have a lot of questions, Father. Luckily, I can answer 'yes' to all of them." Byrne wrote down: "Loughlin."

"The archbishop marches every year, and I was with Bishop Loughlin last week when he committed to marching, right along with the archbishop. Thanks to our sponsors, and the Tammany Society, the ferries will run for free all day. We will have free food and drinks all day. You can promise your people all of that, Father. Not only may marchers carry flags of Ireland, but we will have small flags to give the children and a large banner to identify the marchers from Saint Patrick's Church. A green and white banner it will be, with green shamrocks—it will say: 'ERIN GO BRAGH!'"

Father Fitzpatrick knew some of his parishioners had attended the parade in past years. Still, he was excited about the prospect of his parish's being well represented and marching for the glory of Ireland and Saint Patrick himself.

"The Duvals and the Bodkins are one of our largest family groups, Mr. Byrne," Father Fitzpatrick went on to tell the chairman of the Ancient Order of the Hibernians. "I'll talk to them before this Sunday's Mass to make sure my announcement from the pulpit is well received. This is quite a family, and they have a lot of friends."

Byrne and Fitzpatrick concluded the meeting, with Byrne promising to stop at the rectory for a progress report each week.

Brian Byrne didn't like lying to a priest, and he had a lot of work to do to deliver on what he had promised.

He needed the Boss to get more sponsors for the ferry—the beer, the food.

The archbishop of New York and the new bishop in Brooklyn would march in the parade, but he still needed to invite them. *Maybe,* Byrne thought, *I should ask them to say Mass together at the cathedral at the start of the parade.*

B.J. Fitzpatrick sat in his office for a while after Byrne left, and he wondered about how he should approach his parishioners.

LÁ FHÉILE PÁDRAIG
FAOI SHONA!

March 17, 1862

EIGHTY-FOUR PARISHIONERS FROM SAINT PATRICK'S Parish accompanied Father Fitzpatrick to the cathedral in Lower Manhattan to join Archbishop Hughes and Bishop Loughlin, where they would celebrate a Mass to open the parade.

The Duval and Bodkin families all rode in Fulton Parade Ferry #6 as it left the Brooklyn side of the river, along with several others from the parish and communities farther east in Brooklyn. The Bodkin men rode in the stern of the ferry with Lawrence's wife, Maggie, and Martin's girlfriend, Pamela Densmer. They shared the pages of a single copy of the *Brooklyn Daily Eagle*.

Martin and Pamela had been courting for about a year, and they were making plans to be married.

"Martin, will we be as happy as Lawrence and Maggie seem to be?" Pamela asked Martin. They huddled together as the ferry cut through the small waves in the East River.

"Lawrence tells me they want to have a lot of children," Martin replied. "I'd like to have a big family too, Pamela. How many children might we have, my darling?"

Pamela had moved to Brooklyn from Hoboken, New Jersey, just before the young couple met at one of the dances sponsored by the Christian Mission. The young men and women from Saint Patrick's Parish often went to the Christian Mission dances because Father Fitzpatrick was a little old-fashioned when it came to relationships, and he thought physical contact between unmarried men and women was a sin.

Pam's family was from Naas in County Kildare, about twenty-five miles south and inland from Dublin. Her parents, Richard and Anna Densmer, had six children, of whom Pamela was the third oldest. Her father died in 1849, and the next year Anna braved the Atlantic with her six children and settled in Hoboken.

Martin and Pam had traded stories about their lives in Ireland. She had never been to Galway, or anywhere near Briarhill, and Martin had never been to Naas, or Dublin, or even to County Kildare. Martin gathered her family had substantially more financial resources than he and his siblings.

"I'd like to have a large family too, Martin," Pam answered. "As many children as we can manage." After a pause to collect her thoughts, she continued, "Martin, I've talked to Maggie, and she is concerned that she and Lawrence have been married for more than a year and have not conceived a child yet. I hope everything will work out for them. But Maggie is worried."

Lawrence's progress at the coal yard had seen him rise to a significant management position. He and Maggie were becoming comfortable financially, but they had no baby on the horizon.

Pam looked around the back of the ferry at the Bodkin men. They were a good family, and she was happy to be with Martin. John, the Angel, was a good young man, but at twenty-three, he was sowing some wild oats. He had a job that provided reasonable income and recently was talking about moving out of the brothers' house into an apartment with several of his friends. His friends included two women she and Maggie had agreed were not appropriate friends for John. Especially if he had any interest in being called "the Angel."

Pam studied Dominic. She wasn't sure about the oldest brother, who was different from the other boys. In the expanded Bodkin and Duval household, Dominic was certainly the male leader. He was not a father figure, but he was a leader. Dominic was a man who had a vision for himself. He had been a house painter for years, but he had a dream of becoming a doctor. Pam wished Dominic had a girlfriend, but she worried a little about Dominic's potential as a family man. He told her recently he had "no time for such activities." The influence of Father Fitzpatrick had a significant impact on Dominic's life. Dominic was a daily communicant at the earliest Mass, and he would never go to one of the dances at the Mission because Father Fitzpatrick did not approve of them. Right after the family arrived from Ireland, Dominic was disturbed by the number of men, and even some women, who drank alcohol to excess. These included many of Saint Patrick's parishioners and even, at times, Father Fitzpatrick himself. At an early age, Dominic decided that alcohol was the root of all evil and that the road to good health went along the path of total abstinence.

Pam hoped next year she and Martin could start their own family. A new family of Bodkins.

⸙ ⸙ ⸙

Mary Duval and her teenage sons sat among the other families with children, near the bow of Parade Ferry #6. She was seated next to a pretty, pregnant, red-haired woman who was about her age and who was busy with five small children of her own.

"My name is Mary Duval, and these two fine lads are my sons, Lucas and Danny. Lucas is fifteen and Danny fourteen," Mary introduced herself.

"Ah! Mary, I love your name! My oldest here is named Mary. She's seven. And this is Julia, six, and Teresa is three—Jeremiah is almost two. My infant here is Thomas," the red-haired woman said as she tried to keep Teresa from pulling Thomas' hat off. "My name is Maria. Maria Drennan." The harried woman tried to smile as she scooped Teresa into her arms. "I'm excited to make this trip into the city for the parade. I love the city! And I love any parade! My husband, Patrick, says that where we live, up at Lewis and Jefferson—they call it Bedford—will be as large as a city soon, but it still seems like country living to me."

"I've never been over in that direction," Mary replied. "We live on Bedford Avenue, but not near Lewis and Jefferson."

"Today is a great day for a parade!" Maria said as she continued to try to keep Teresa away from Thomas' hat. "With the 69th Irish Brigade leading the parade, I hope we will be safe today. I hear those Nativists can be nasty people. Why do they hate us so much?"

"Are you with our Saint Patrick's Parish group?" Mary asked, avoiding her new friend's question.

"No," Maria answered. "We belong to a small mission parish, Mary Queen of the Isles. They say we'll get a real church soon. Patrick and I heard Father Fitzpatrick had this group going to the parade, and I couldn't resist. I wish he could have come with us, but he is working. Is your husband marching?"

"No, I'm a widow. My husband died on the way across. My brothers are here, though, and they will all march."

Maria felt awkward. "I'm sorry about your husband." She made the sign of the cross.

The ferry arrived at the dock on the Manhattan side of the East River, and Mary and Maria said their goodbyes. Maria tended to her children and exited the ferry at the bow while Mary joined her brothers with Maggie and Pam at the stern gangplank. They all took off for the Mass at the cathedral.

<hr />

The walk to the cathedral was about a mile. The troupe of Bodkins and Duvals walked along Mott Street, which brought them near to the Five Points, whose rat-infested, disease-ridden tenements lined the Lower Manhattan streets.

The Duval children walked together in the middle of the group as the Bodkin men formed an outside protective ring. They weren't walking alone. The rest of Father Fitzpatrick's parish was either immediately in front of or behind the Bodkins. It was a parade before the parade.

As they walked along Mott Street, they were all jeered by the menacing thugs who lined the sidewalks.

Men and women were drunk on the streets. The sights were astounding. Women with painted faces and nearly exposed breasts; women who looked like men; men who looked like women; fighting, arguing; men with knives. Women were smoking cigars; preachers were preaching from soapboxes; firefighters were fighting with one another. People were screaming about Lincoln, screaming about the draft, screaming about slavery, screaming about the war. Runaway slaves from the South and cowering Chinamen watched in fear from storefronts as the Nativist gang members taunted the new Irish immigrants.

"Go home, scum!"

"You Micks is worse than them black-faced runaways!"

"You does work for five cents the darkies did for ten … We used to get twenty-five cents for the same work! Go back to Ireland, you fookin' Micks."

The Bodkins and the rest of Father Fitzpatrick's parishioners finally arrived at the cathedral and at last were safe.

Maria Drennan was also pleased that she and her children were safe. After the long walk along Mott Street, she was no longer sure she liked city life better than country living.

Maria and her children sat in a pew in the middle of the gospel side. She noticed that her new friend, Mary Duval, was three rows in front of her with what seemed to be the rest of her family.

One of the men with Mary turned around to look at the congregation.

"Dominic!" Maria said out loud.

Mass was over in an hour, and the Bodkins and Maria Teresa Jones Drennan reunited after fourteen years.

They hugged. They kissed. They were amazed by how the years had changed each of them.

Then, the parade began.

The Irish Brigade's 69th Regiment led the way followed by a marching band from one of the firefighting companies.

Then New York City's mayor and councilmen marched—the archbishop, the bishop, and the clergy came next.

The different parishes, civic associations, and hospitals all had banners—stretching the width of the street—held proudly by the marching men.

The policemen, the soldiers, and the firefighters all wore their dress uniforms.

Brian Byrne won accolades for achieving his goals for the 1862 parade—the 100th Saint Patrick's Day Parade was a tremendous success.

Boss Tweed produced at least a temporary truce between the rival gangs, and they encountered no significant problems. In all his glory, Tweed walked both sides of the parade route together with several Nativists, the Bowery Boys, the Dead Rabbits, and, of course, Brian Byrne. This group of leaders all wore stovepipe hats and mismatched plaid trousers and jackets. The show of solidarity helped to encourage the peaceful celebration of Saint Patrick's Day.

The parade was not without some problems, however. Someone reported an attack on two Black men who were watching the parade. One stabbing occurred, and competing fire departments attended fires at two buildings, which resulted in the firemen fighting with each other while the buildings burned to a total loss.

Overall, Brian Byrne, chairman of the Ancient Order of Hibernians, thought it was peaceful in comparison to past years. The large crowd all praised Saint Patrick and their beloved Ireland. Everyone had a grand time at the parade.

After the parade was over, the Bodkins, the Duvals, and the Drennans all walked together back to the ferry. When the boat finally returned to the dock in Brooklyn, Maria said goodbye to everyone as they pledged to be together again.

"In Brooklyn, the next time!"

44

WAR!

THE FRATERNAL LIVING ARRANGEMENT—THE BOYS'
Club—wound down slowly in the same way most shared living
arrangements among brothers ended. Lawrence took a job in
Bushwick and moved out when he married Maggie; John left to
sow his wild oats; Martin married Pamela, and the newlyweds
found a place closer to the Brooklyn Navy Yard, where Martin
was a shipbuilder.

Dominic, still working as a housepainter for Drennan's
Brownstones, found himself as the last remaining member of the
Club, and, in the spring of 1863, for obvious financial reasons, he
was forced to move back into Mary's house.

This will work fine, Dominic mused as he unpacked his belong-
ings in his old room at his sister's home. *I don't want to live alone;
I'm still close to work and the Athenaeum Reading Room; the housekeeper,
Charlotte, is a great cook; and Mary gets the newspaper every day.*

Since his days at Erasmus Hall, Dominic had read every page
of the *Brooklyn Daily Eagle*. He studied the news articles on the
front page and learned about Brooklyn's new baseball team on
the sports page. He perused the obituaries and the society page.

For months and months, the vast majority of the news stories had reported the Civil War, which began in April 1861 when Southern forces fired on the Union garrison at Fort Sumter in South Carolina. The United States' national crisis supplanted local politics in the headlines.

Over the past two years, eleven Southern states had seceded from the Union. The Commonwealth of Virginia—which seceded at the beginning of the war—was itself split in half as the result of the Wheeling Convention, when the northwestern counties of Virginia seceded from the commonwealth to form another state to be known as West Virginia.

At the beginning of the war, most of the battlefields were in the Southern states, but in September 1862, the war moved north into Maryland. The Union Army's success in the battle at Antietam, at least temporarily, thwarted Lee's first march into the North. Antietam would prove to be the site of the bloodiest single-day battle of the war.

Lincoln's Emancipation Proclamation became effective January 1, 1863, and the headlines of the New York newspapers proclaimed what the South had feared:

THE SLAVES ARE FREED!

Editorials questioned what progress Lincoln was making in his war against the South. Newspapers reported on the conflicting attitudes related to slavery and the Emancipation Proclamation that were prevalent in New York City. The editorial pages alternately criticized and then praised President Lincoln. In 1863, increased military activity was taking place as far north as Pennsylvania, which newspaper editors saw as an indication the war could come to New York soon.

In the South, thousands were dying on both sides. Newspapers reported every shot and volley of the battles of Pea Ridge, Shiloh, Seven Pines, Richmond, Bull Run, and Fredericksburg—every gory detail. Coffins were unloaded from troop transport ships late at night on the New York City docks, so citizens would be less likely to become aware of the degree of carnage.

Lincoln's calls for hundreds of thousands of volunteers proved to be inadequate, and as a result, the headlines on March 3, 1863, announced the country's first military draft:

CONGRESS PASSES THE ENROLLMENT ACT
CONSCRIPTION TO BEGIN IN THE NORTH

The *Daily Eagle* reported on the battles of Chancellorsville and Vicksburg. The war headed north again—to Pennsylvania. Nearly 50,000 soldiers were killed in the three-day Battle of Gettysburg.

Despite that they were married men, Lawrence and Martin were of the appropriate age and were selected in the first national draft on July 11, 1863. Dominic was not drafted. John had moved out of the house he shared with his brothers, right after the Saint Patrick's Day Parade in 1862, and had not been seen by the family in more than a year. The family, however, did not see his name on the Consolidated Enrollment List posted on either of the two draft days in July.

The Bodkins, like the rest of New York, were fearful for their loved ones who would be going off to war. Every man and every family had to make their own decision about service in the military. For those drafted, there were choices. The Enrollment Act of 1863 provided two options other than reporting for Civil War duty in the Union Army—commutation or substitution. Under the "commutation" choice, a draftee could pay $300 to buy his way out of service. Under the "substitution" choice, a draftee could furnish a suitable substitute to perform his service for him.

In 1863, the Bodkins—thanks to their individual employment, the residuum of Uncle Laurence's estate, and Mary Duval's still receiving her monthly stipend from the Duval family in Galway— had accumulated enough financial wherewithal to pay the $300 for commutation for any of the brothers who were drafted.

As a child, Martin was the biggest, strongest, and toughest of the Bodkin boys. And now, as a man, he loved his new country and was willing to die to defend it. He was also confident he would be able to kill another human being, and Martin had no issue with the concept of fighting another man for what he thought was right.

On the afternoon of July 12, 1863, Martin read his name on the draft posting. That night, sitting in the parlor of the home he shared with his wife of just a few months, he told Pam he had to go to the war. He said it would only last for a year, and then he would be back to building ships at the Navy Yard. Pam came to him on the sofa and said, "My dearest, this is not what we hoped for—but whatever you want, I also want. Your job will still be here when you return, and then we will start our family. Let us take to our bed so you will be well-rested for the journey in the morning."

On the same night, several Brooklyn streets away, Maggie whined to Lawrence, "Lawrence, you cannot go to war. If you get killed, who will care for me? If you are crippled or maimed, you will not be attractive to me, and we will never have the family I deserve." Lawrence, who always fancied himself an intellectual, and also a man who understood women, said to Maggie, "I will gather the money, Maggie, to pay the price of commutation. I fear that if I leave now for the war, we will never have children. I have no fear of war itself. I am brave, Maggie, but to preserve my business and to create our offspring, I cannot waste my time fighting the Rebels in the South. Anyway, darling, the Southerners appear to be so backward and ignorant, they should lose in short order, without the necessity of me getting involved."

"I agree, my dear," Maggie answered. "Let us retire to our rooms, and you will find to whom you should pay the commutation in the morning."

"Good night, my dear. I will tell you tomorrow when I have paid the fee. Sleep well."

Bitch, Lawrence thought to himself as he walked down the hallway to his bedroom.

⬡⬡⬡ ⬡⬡⬡ ⬡⬡⬡

In the morning, Martin and Pam went to the Enrollment Office in Lower Manhattan. Martin enlisted in the Union Army, and, at evening, in a tearful scene on the dock, he left with hundreds of other recruits on a troop transport ship headed south. Onboard, the new soldiers learned they were going to New Orleans, where they would serve as a controlling force over one of the South's most significant cities, which had fallen to the North in the early phase of the war.

Back in Brooklyn, as soon as Lawrence awoke, he had breakfast, and at the appropriate hour, he went to the Emigrant Savings Bank to withdraw $300. The bank's new president, Liam Finneran, met him at the Emigrant's front door, as he unlocked the bank.

"Good morning, Mr. Bodkin," the banker said.

"Good day to you, Liam!" Bodkin replied, reaching into his pocket for his account ledger.

"What can I do for you on the day after our country's first draft, Mr. Bodkin? Is $300 what you are wanting? Might I be correct?" the bank president inquired.

— 263 —

"It's only to please my wife, I tell you," Lawrence claimed. "She insists I pay the fee for commutation. I, myself, would rather fight Johnny Reb to the death. They deserve death, you know, for the way they have abandoned our Union, and not to mention their history of mistreating the Blacks."

"Well, the bank will have a run on cash this morning, Mr. Bodkin. Many families want husbands and fathers to stay home to tend to their needs and their protection." Finneran counted out the $300.

"How is the family, Mr. Bodkin? You have to bring me your brothers Dominic and Martin to add deposits to their accounts here. That Dominic, he has a great financial future after he opens the medical practice that is his dream. He should find a wife to help him spend all the money he is going to have one day," Finneran said as he handed over the $300. "If not a wife, at least he will need a housekeeper, an office manager, and a coachman to run his home and spend his money. I heard the draft claimed Martin, but as yet, I have not seen him in our bank, or across the street, at George Levinson's bank," Finneran reported.

"He's gone over to Manhattan, Mr. Finneran, gone this morning to enlist in the Union Army. Maggie told me Pam forced him into it. Of course, I mean my sister-in-law Pamela, Mr. Finneran. I suppose there is a good chance I'll never see Martin again—or at least not in one piece as the brother I know."

Lawrence Bodkin walked from the Emigrant Savings Bank to the Brooklyn Enrollment Office to pay his commutation.

Two days later, New York City was on fire. Manhattan's Irish immigrants had had enough. Protests, expressing the working class's displeasure with the right of the wealthy to opt out of military service through commutation or substitution, quickly became draft riots which spread throughout Lower Manhattan.

The hard-working Irish also feared that more and more freed slaves would come to New York and take their jobs. The draft riots became race riots.

Government buildings were burned; Blacks were beaten and lynched; newspaper offices were ransacked; policemen, trying to control the rioters, were attacked.

The military was called in to control the mobs in the streets— and four long days later, peace returned to Manhattan, but not until after more than one hundred and twenty were dead.

On the last day of the riots, Martin was on his transport ship somewhere east of Port Royal Island, South Carolina. The Union Navy blockade protected the boat as it raced past Southern ports. It was August before Martin was on land, in his new army home with two hundred other soldiers, in New Orleans. The bustling port city, with a population of more than one hundred thousand, was left unscathed by the ravages of an attacking army.

Many of Martin's fellow soldiers were Irish boys from New York. The Louisiana heat and humidity were the biggest shocks for them. They had sweated through their heavy blue Union uniforms by the time they were at the bottom of the ship's gang-way. The colors and the fragrances coming from the flowers and trees along the port were like nothing the men had ever seen or smelled. Martin felt as though he had traveled to another country, somewhere in the tropics.

It took several hours to process the men off the transport ship and into their barracks. The barracks were nothing more than a series of large tents.

"Mail call in one hour!" the sergeant yelled. Martin only had an hour, and he had to let Pamela know he had arrived safely. He was able to find a pen and paper in his knapsack and a table in the barracks where he could write.

August 12, 1863
Fort Jackson, Louisiana

My Dearest Pamela,
I only have a few minutes before this week's letter posts are due.
I have arrived safely in New Orleans and should be secure here since the Union has controlled the city for a year and a half. All the Rebels are already in prison camps.
The voyage was at times harrowing because of the fear of Confederate ships and storms in the South Atlantic at this time of year.
My accommodations at the barracks are Spartan, at best, but I will manage. The heat and humidity of this place is a shock to the system. It is nothing like Brooklyn in summer or Briarhill on its warmest day.
I must post this immediately. Please give my regards to the family and tell them I will write if time permits. I love you, my darling. Please address a letter to me at –

Martin R. Bodkin, Cpl.
United States Army Barracks, Fort Jackson
New Orleans, Louisiana

Your husband,
Martin

It was a Saturday afternoon in September by the time the slow-moving United States Postal Service mail carrier, John Walczyk, arrived at the door of what was supposed to be Martin's home. He was met by an older German woman who told the postman, in broken English, that her family had just moved into the house the previous week, and no one named Pamela Bodkin lived at that address anymore.

Luckily, at the beginning of Walczyk's delivery route was the Duval house, and the English-speaking Polish immigrant knew some of the people who lived at that address were named Bodkin. He had already been to the Duvals' house with today's deliveries, so he put the letter addressed to Pamela back in his sack, and made a mental note to bring it with him again on Monday.

Walczyk walked back to the post office and, as usual, was chided by the other men for being the last letter carrier to finish for the day. The Irish and Italian mail sorters teased Walczyk every afternoon for being slow and witless. He didn't like it. Once again, he tried to explain that his route was longer than the other carriers' routes, and it took him longer to finish his deliveries.

He quickly passed through the sorting room and went to the carriers' locker room at the rear of the building. He hung his sack on one of the last available hooks that lined the wall. The bag would hang on the wall, next to all the other identical carrier sacks, until the crew of mail carriers returned to work on Monday morning.

Walczyk left the post office by the back door, so he didn't have to walk into the sorting room again. He'd had enough of being teased for being slow. *Maybe,* Walczyk thought as he walked home, *maybe, I'll just quit this stupid job.*

ABSOLUTION

October 1863

WITH MARTIN SOMEWHERE IN THE SOUTH FIGHTING the Rebels, and after the years of being separated by the Atlantic Ocean from Mary, Dominic decided being apart from one of his siblings was enough, and it was time to find John.

Dominic was a teetotaler, and that made going from tavern to pub, to the next bar, and then to the next pub looking for his brother each night problematic. But after a few weeks, he met a woman in a Brooklyn pub who told him she had been with John in a tavern on Manhattan's east side—Jimmy McCluskey's Tavern.

So, the next evening, Dominic went to Manhattan and found McCluskey's Tavern on the corner of Ann and Nassau Streets. Dominic took a seat on a stool at the end of the bar and ordered a pint. He never tasted the beer. He pushed the glass around the slippery bar for nearly two hours, watching all manner of people come in for a drink.

Many of the men entering the bar had long hair and big mustaches. Some dressed in a very feminine fashion. Their shirts had ruffles, and they were wearing pantaloons in a style Dominic had never seen before. Two men were sitting together dressed as soldiers, one in Union blue and the other wearing Confederate grey. Another man was dressed only in bedclothes and a sleeping cap. Some appeared to be wearing some form of powder on their faces, and many had black liner accentuating their eyes.

The women in McCluskey's all had painted faces, and some wore dresses of a brocade fabric cinched at the waist, squeezing their innards to nothing. Others wore gowns of a light, delicate, translucent material which had a silky quality to it. A strikingly tall, pretty woman was wearing nothing but a bedsheet, wrapped strategically across her well-rounded frame, with sandals on her feet. All of the women had significantly exposed breasts.

The tavern was noisy, with a lot of laughter, merriment, and singing while many toasted with tankards of ale. "Another pint, Timmy?" a bartender called to a man sitting a couple of stools away from Dominic. Then Dominic watched as a sassy waitress— the one with a mischievous smile and long braided hair draped on only one side of her head—squeezed by a crowded table of rowdy men. She playfully smacked one lad in the head and admonished, "You've been here all day, Sean McGinty! Does the missus know where you are?" The tavern was crowded and noisy to Dominic, who thought he might be the only person in the establishment who did not know another.

As the crowd of patrons swelled, a young woman, dressed as oddly as the others, sat on the barstool next to Dominic. She wore a diaphanous gown with a rope belt that seemed to be silver. Her hair was golden and piled upon her head, with tiny flowers entwined in it.

"Hello, luv!" She smiled and batted her big dark eyes at Dominic. "I'm Aphrodite."

She put her hand on his shoulder and turned him a little so she could see his outfit better. "Who might you be playing tonight, my luv?" She tilted his cap a little to one side. "Are you playing the Irish immigrant housepainter? Ha! Ha!" she laughed out loud.

"Very pleased to make your acquaintance, Aphrodite," Dominic innocently answered the woman. "You are correct, I am an Irish immigrant, and yes, I do paint houses. I am originally from Briarhill in County Galway. My name is Dominic Bodkin. Are you familiar with Briarhill?"

"Actually, Luv, I am familiar with—" Aphrodite began to answer, just as a priest, sitting three stools away—dressed in a long, black cassock with a stiff, white Roman collar at his throat—yelled over at Dominic, "Hallelujah, Brother! Are you here to save my soul from this den of hedonism?"

Upon hearing his shout, Dominic and Aphrodite both looked up to see the priest, with long wavy hair and a mustache hanging down on either side of his chin, smiling at them.

"Angel?" Dominic said incredulously.

"Angel?" Aphrodite asked with some confusion in her voice.

The brothers had not seen each other for nearly a year and a half, and they embraced warmly.

"You look well, big brother," John said. "I see you have met Johanna."

"Johanna? You mean Aphrodite?"

"No, Dominic, she's Johanna Crimmons. She is one of the women I live with," John answered. "Several of us live in the Crimmonses' family flat. Let me introduce you to them—almost everyone is here.

"Thimity! Jeremiah! Come here and meet my big brother," John called down the bar.

Thimity Kellahan and Jeremiah Buckly were the two soldiers. The tall, pretty woman in the bedsheet came over, and John introduced her as Bernadette Baiocchi.

John pulled others over to his brother. "This is Daniel Crimmons, and next is Bernadette's sister, Mary Baiocchi. John Herst is wearing those fancy pantaloons—he's standing with the Sullivan brothers, Ronan and Conor."

"John, why is everyone dressed in costumes? Why did Johanna tell me her name was Aphrodite?"

"At night, we are all struggling actors, Dominic. Johanna is playing Aphrodite in a Greek play, *Hippolytus*. Bernadette is playing Phaedra, who is Hippolytus' stepmother. Aren't they beautiful, Dominic?

"I am an actor, too—chasing my dreams, every night. We have to provide our costumes for the productions. I hope you can tell I am playing a priest tonight. I'm still a plumber during the day, but at night we all work at the Winter Garden Theater, right around the corner. When the curtain comes down, and the show is over for the night, we come here for a few pints and a little supper," John continued. "Our theater has a new director, Edwin Booth. It's exciting. Booth is a famous actor, and he has two brothers who are actors as well. Rumor has it, the three brothers will do a special performance of Shakespeare next year to raise money for a statue of 'the Bard' for the middle of the city's new Central Park. I like my life, Dominic. My new friends and I get along very, very well, and please, for God's sake, don't let them hear you call me Angel. They won't understand."

"All right then, Angel. *John* it will be," Dominic allowed. "I've been searching for you for days, weeks actually, John. I have news from the family. The draft selected Martin, and he's gone off to the war. He left the day after the draft, on a transport ship headed south, and Pamela moved to her sister Sarah Jane's house in Hoboken. They drafted Lawrence also, but Maggie made him pay the commutation fee. He says he feels terrible about it. What about you, John? We never saw your name on the Enrollment List.

Does the Enrollment Board know where you are? Why didn't we know where you were? We have been worried about you," Dominic said with a frown.

John drained the rest of his pint and looked at the floor for a moment. Then he looked deep into the eyes of his older brother. "I never saw my name on the Enrollment List either, Dominic … Brother, it's great you found me. I'm happy you did. But I haven't come home because I wasn't sure you would approve of the life I have chosen. Being an actor, I mean, and living with all these friends. I'm not an angel, big brother."

⊗⊗⊗ ⊗⊗⊗ ⊗⊗⊗

The sassy waitress with the mischievous smile was ready to go home to her husband at the end of another busy night, but she made her way through McCluskey's Tavern to be sure everyone heard, "Last call! And none for you, Sean McGinty!"

At the end of the bar Aphrodite loosened her hug on Dominic after crushing her ample breasts into his chest long enough for Dominic to realize what was happening. Her embrace preceded a kiss on his mouth—which she intended he would never forget. "Good night, my luv. I hope to see you again," the actress said with a flirtatious smile designed to make John uncomfortable. She turned to John. "I like your big brother, John. You were right when you told me he was the smarter one. Should I stay awake until you get home, my angel?"

The Angel and Dominic walked arm-in-arm from the tavern, with the Angel leading them in the direction of the ferry back to Brooklyn. The two brothers talked for an hour on the corner of Fulton and South Streets and made plans to get together again. They agreed that John would reunite with the family.

"I think I've had impure thoughts, Father," a young girl whispered with a quivering voice. Kneeling only inches from the priest's left shoulder, she was partially hidden behind the confessional's mesh screen.

"Try thinking of the Virgin Mary at those moments, my dear, and your impure thoughts will disappear. As penance, say three Our Fathers and three Hail Marys." The priest gave her a blessing of absolution with his right hand and slid the solid partition in front of the mesh closed. The elderly priest turned and slid the partition on his right open. This time the screen revealed the obscured outline of a young man's face.

The man made the sign of the cross. "Bless me, Father, for I have sinned." Awkwardly he tried to hush his deep voice but feared his words would be audible to anyone kneeling in the opposite confessional. "It has been a year since my last confession. I …" The man hesitated, realizing he had just lied to a priest.

"Continue, my son. Have no fear. The Lord will forgive your sins and welcome you back into his fold."

"It has been two years since my last confession, Father, and I have committed a mortal sin. The sin has to do with the women with whom I share living quarters." John—formerly known as the Angel—had never before confessed a mortal sin. His heart was thumping, and he could feel perspiration forming on his forehead.

The priest was relieved the man was cleansing himself of the guilt of mortal sin and asking forgiveness. The Angel was on his way to earning absolution, but his confessor needed more information in order to return this lost sheep to his flock.

"How do you know your sin was mortal, my son? Perhaps it was only a venial sin."

"Oh, they were mortal, Father. I'm sure of it."

"You said 'they,' my son. How many sins are we talking about?"

John didn't expect questions from the old priest and was becoming more nervous. He realized he could stand up and leave. *No one will be the wiser*, he thought. *But I'm here and I've made it through the tough part.*

"I don't know how many sins, Father. There are three women who live in our flat. Johanna, Bernadette, and Ma—"

"Stop, son. It is not necessary to tell me their names."

"All right. There are three women, and I have known them all."

"Known them? Do you mean in a carnal way?"

"Yes, Father. I think that is what I mean." His throat felt dry and he thought his voice was getting louder. "We've slept in the same bed, Father." John was sure everyone in the church heard him.

"Another question, son," the priest whispered so low that John could hardly hear him. "You said 'we.' Do you mean you and the three women—all at once?"

"Father, you asked 'How many sins?' Would that count as one sin or three?"

"Let's just go with 'many sins' as an adequate answer to my question, son. Are there any other sins you wish to confess?"

"There are certainly venial sins, Father. I've used bad language, taken the Lord's name in vain, gotten drunk with my friends, been in fights, and listened to dirty jokes. I had impure thoughts, too, as you might well imagine. But maybe, Father, there is another mortal sin."

"What is that, son?"

"Well, Father. I was with my brother a few weeks ago and I didn't tell him the whole truth about my life. I didn't lie to him, but I hid the truth, and now in my heart it feels as though I told him a significant lie, and I'm sorry."

"As you've already proven, son, usually if you think a sin is a mortal sin—it is. Are you sorry for what you have done?"

"I am, Father."

"Try your best to avoid the temptations which result in the failures of which you are guilty. Do you know how to do that, son?"

"I do, Father."

"Say an Act of Contrition, ten Our Fathers, and ten Hail Marys."

The priest gave his blessing of absolution while John made his prayer of contrition.

John was nearly running as he made his way down the front steps of the church. He felt as though the weight of the world had been lifted from his shoulders. Forgiveness. A fresh start. A new life. A new direction. He was going to tell Dominic the real story—with the confidence that Dominic would forgive him, too.

John's youthful experiment was over. Everything he had done for the past year had been an act, and now it was time to return to the reality of life. Maybe not at the "Angel" level, but it was time to settle down. He had one more performance to do, however. Tonight would be his grand finale at the theater, another supper at Jimmy McCluskey's, a final night at the Crimmonses' flat, and then the goodbyes.

46

PAMELA ELIZA
DENSMER BODKIN

November 1863

ON A BLUSTERY DAY IN THE MIDDLE OF NOVEMBER, most of the family was seated around the Duvals' dining table for lunch. The Bodkins were catching up on every aspect of each other's lives. They talked about the war and their worries for Martin. They expressed concerns for Pamela.

"She didn't want to go to Hoboken, Biddy," Mary said as she passed a steaming bowl of buttered cabbage to her sister. "We all knew that, but Pamela didn't want to live alone—without Martin—just thinking about him all of the time, worrying about the war. It seemed to be making her sick to her stomach. She had trouble keeping a meal down."

"But when she left, it seemed so sudden." Biddy shook her head with concern. "I hope Sarah Jane is good company for her. Pamela told me that since Sarah Jane had no children, there would be plenty of room for her in the house."

No one had heard a word from Martin, who left for the war nearly five months ago. When he had left for the war in July, everyone knew it would take a while for the transport ship to get to its destination. They all understood the destination could have been New Orleans, but no one knew for sure.

"I hope we receive something from Martin soon," Dominic said as he placed his hand on John's shoulder. "We need to know where he is, that he's safe. We need an address to write him a letter."

"I agree. We need to know," Lawrence added with a tone designed to mask his feelings of guilt. "Please pass the cabbage, Cate." Everyone understood he was trying to change the subject. "It's a delicious luncheon today, Mary."

Since John was visiting Brooklyn today, all of the others had made an effort to be with him. Lawrence left work and came for the noon meal—Maggie never made an appearance at these get-togethers. Dominic and Biddy were at the house. The family for whom Cate now worked, the Hornblowers, had allowed their cook to watch the children for a few hours so Cate could see her youngest brother.

Danny, Mary's youngest son, saw the Duvals' new postman—Lud Cibelli—walking to the front steps and ran to meet him. Receiving something in the mail was an unusual occurrence, and Danny was excited. He came back into the house and gave a letter, addressed to Pamela, to his mother. It was from Martin, and it had been mailed from Fort Jackson in New Orleans on August 12—nearly three months ago.

"We have to get this to Pamela as soon as possible," Dominic said. "It's been two months since she moved to Hoboken, and we should go to New Jersey and see how she is doing."

"If we leave today, Dominic, I will go with you," John offered. "I have two free days but must be back in Manhattan the day after tomorrow."

"Agreed," Dominic said. "If we have our meal and leave immediately, we will be to Pamela's well before midnight."

The travel went smoothly for Dominic and John, and they arrived at nine o'clock in the evening. Pamela's brother-in-law, James Dewey, answered John's knock on the door as Sarah Jane came into the foyer to see who was visiting so late in the evening.

A few minutes later, Pamela, clearly just roused from sleep, came into the parlor and greeted Dominic and John. Dominic noticed immediately that she had gained some weight and her face was puffy and a little flushed. The Bodkins were shocked by Pamela's news. They were going to be uncles again. Mary Duval's two sons were their nephews, of course, but Pamela and Martin's baby would begin the next generation of Bodkins.

They all sat in the parlor, and Pamela explained the past three months.

"When I told you I was leaving Brooklyn to live with James and Sarah Jane," she began, speaking directly to Dominic, "I thought I was with child, but I was not positive. I hope our baby will not be born without a father, but I have yet to hear from my husband. I do not know if Martin is alive, or even if he arrived at his destination."

Dominic reached into his pocket, and he produced the letter from Martin. Pamela hurriedly opened the envelope and ignored the others as she anxiously read the sentences her husband had written. Tears filled her eyes as she told the others, "He is safe, he says. He is in a barracks in New Orleans. At least he was safe in August when he wrote this letter. It doesn't sound like he is near any fighting with the Rebels.

"I'll write back to him tonight and post it tomorrow."

John said, "Write your letter tonight, and I will post it from the General Post Office in New York. The delivery from the main post office in Manhattan will be much more regulated than it will

Pamela Densmer Bodkin

be from here. Every New Yorker knows our postal services are better than those here in New Jersey."

"Oh, John! Thank you. What a great idea! I'll retire now to write my letter, as well as to get my required sleep. You know the next Bodkin baby will be born in the spring, and I must get my rest," Pamela replied.

Dominic went out on a limb and gave his sister-in-law some advice: "I suggest Martin begin to look for a substitute for his army service so he can come home."

Pamela went to her room and began to write.

November 17, 1863
Hoboken, New Jersey

My Dearest Martin,
I pray you are still well and safe. Just today, Dominic and John delivered your August letter to me.

Martin, I have exciting news. In the spring, you will be a father!

For the past two months, I have been living in New Jersey, with Sarah Jane and James, and they have been taking good care of our unborn child and me. New Jersey is charming, but I miss you.

I hope the security in New Orleans is still as you described it, and the Rebels are still in prison.

Martin, dearest, please come home to me as soon as you can. I pray for your return.

Dominic suggests you begin to search for a substitute. We apparently cannot find one for you here as the man would likely take our money and abscond to places unknown before he ever arrived in New Orleans.

We are all sure we can meet the financial arrangements, but we are concerned that the difficulty will be for you to find a substitute among the Rebel sympathizers in New Orleans.

I think our baby will be born before April is too old, and I have a doctor who believes my calculations—based upon our last night together—may be reasonable.

John lives in New York City, and he will post this to you tomorrow in the main post office.

I hope you are still at Fort Jackson and will receive this before Christmas.

If you have not already heard, President Lincoln has declared that next Thursday, November 26, will be the official Thanksgiving holiday. We have so much to be thankful for, and I do wish we could celebrate the holiday together.

Merry Christmas, my darling! I do love you and miss you.

Love Always,
Your wife,
Pamela

In the morning, Dominic and John bid farewell to Pamela and made arrangements for her to travel with John for Thanksgiving dinner at the Duvals' home.

On the ferry ride to New York, John expressed his excitement to Dominic.

"Starting a new generation of Bodkins, in our wonderful adopted country, makes me invigorated with hope about the future, Dominic. I may be the last Bodkin male born in Ireland, but I won't be the last Bodkin born in our family! I'm looking forward to us all being together for Thanksgiving. Hopefully, Maggie and Lawrence will come also. Maybe over the Thanksgiving holiday, Dominic, we could discuss my moving back to Brooklyn. Do you think Mary would allow me to move back with the family?"

Dominic smiled at John. "I'm sure of it, little brother. I'm sure she will welcome you back. We all will."

47

THANKSGIVING

THE BOOM OF BROOKLYN'S RESIDENTIAL CONSTRUCTION industry provided Dominic with the ability to work for as many hours a week as he wanted, and he was paid well as a painter. Typically, he worked a ten-hour day, Monday through Friday, and reserved the weekends for himself. On Saturday afternoons, he frequently went to the Athenaeum Reading Room. *Uncle Laurence O'Donnell would be proud of his star pupil, and thank you, Headmaster Murtha, for making this all possible,* Dominic often thought. His Sundays centered on morning Mass and then being a leader of his parish's afternoon activities.

The first thing Dominic did each morning in November was stoke the fire to take the chill off the house. During the week, Charlotte, Mary's housekeeper, made everyone's breakfast. Charlotte was a skinny, bony-faced old woman who had been freed by her slave owner before Lincoln's Emancipation Proclamation and had been working for Mary for two years. On weekends, however, her first responsibilities did not begin until the noon meal—because, on Saturdays and Sundays, Dominic liked to make breakfast for everyone.

He rose early on Saturday, November 21, 1863. After Dominic finished his breakfast of scrambled eggs, buttered toast, and orange juice, he went to the parlor, lit one of the kerosene lamps, and sat by the window to read the newspapers from the previous week. He enjoyed the peaceful scene on his lamplit street; Bedford Avenue was quiet before the sun came up.

He read the daily papers in the order each had been received. By the time he finished reading Friday's newspaper, the Saturday edition of the *Brooklyn Daily Eagle* would be at the front door.

As it had been for months and months, the news was the same—political conflicts in New York and war in the South. During the summer, the coverage of the Battle of Gettysburg had dominated the war news. The Brooklyn obituaries listed the names of soldiers killed, and each day during the fall, some of those maimed in the battle returned home.

The headline in Friday's *Eagle* reported President Lincoln's speech to dedicate the Soldiers' National Cemetery at the Pennsylvania battlefield. The president dedicated the massive cemetery to the Union soldiers killed at Gettysburg, and his comments to those gathered for the dedication were brief.

LINCOLN DEDICATES CEMETERY AT GETTYSBURG

Fourscore and seven years ago, our fathers brought forth, on this continent, a new nation, conceived in liberty, and dedicated to the proposition that all men are created equal.

Now we are engaged in a great civil war, testing whether that nation, or any nation so conceived and dedicated, can long endure.

We are met on a great battlefield of that war. We have come to dedicate a portion of that field, as a final resting place for those who here gave their lives that that nation might live. It is altogether fitting and proper that we should do this.

But, in a larger sense, we cannot dedicate, we cannot consecrate—we cannot hallow—this ground. The brave men, living and dead, who struggled here, have consecrated it, far above our poor power to add or detract. The world will little note, nor long remember what we say here, but we can never forget what they did here. It is for us the living, rather, to be dedicated here to the unfinished work which they who fought here have thus far so nobly advanced. It is rather for us to be here dedicated to the great task remaining before us—that from these honored dead we take increased devotion to that cause for which they gave the last full measure of devotion—that we here highly resolve that these dead shall not have died in vain—that this nation, under God, shall have a new birth of freedom—and that government of the people, by the people, for the people, shall not perish from the earth.

The young Irish immigrant painter read Lincoln's words, then again, and then a third time. He put the Friday newspaper on the floor next to his chair and took great comfort in the knowledge that Martin was far from military action in New Orleans. As he had been doing for months, Dominic closed his eyes and said a prayer for his brother's continued safety. Lincoln's Gettysburg Address moved Dominic to a decision he had been contemplating for months. He needed to take action now, to contribute to the war effort. But he knew he was not a fighter. He was not as strong, and unquestionably not as muscular, as Martin. He was not a coward, but he had never even been in a fight. Dominic wanted to help people—not hurt them; he wanted to heal people—not harm them. Sitting in the parlor, the oldest Bodkin brother conceived a plan. It would take time, but he believed the American Civil War was far from over.

The first legally declared Thanksgiving holiday, Thursday, November 26, 1863, was celebrated by the Bodkin family at Mary's home.

Everyone, except Martin, came for the Thanksgiving feast.

By early afternoon John arrived with Pamela. The family was excited to see Martin's wife, and she looked radiant, even after the trip from Hoboken. Mary explained to her teenage sons that they would have a new cousin in the spring. The boys were excited to know they would not be the only young ones at future family reunions.

Mary and Maggie doted over Pam. They asked how she was feeling, when her baby was due, and a dozen other questions. Together, the three women retreated to the kitchen and helped Charlotte prepare the Thanksgiving feast.

In the middle of the afternoon, Biddy came up the front steps with Michael Flanagan, with whom she had been courting for several months. Flanagan seemed to be a nice young man and an acceptable suitor for Biddy.

Cate arrived after Biddy and Michael. She had the afternoon off from caring for the Hornblowers' children.

While Charlotte was making the final preparations for dinner, the family sat in the parlor and joined in serious discussions. They discussed the war, Martin's safety, President Lincoln, the treatment of the freed slaves, the growth of the government at Tammany Hall, and the future of the country. They discussed their views of the liberal pope in Rome, Pope Pius IX.

"He doesn't understand American Catholics," Maggie arrogantly proclaimed.

Dominic had weighty news to discuss with his family, and he had decided a few days ago that this would be a perfect opportunity to let everyone know what his plans for the future involved. As the male leader of this family, when Dominic spoke, everyone listened. Once he began, no one would interrupt his announcement with a question or a comment.

He was sorry Michael Flanagan was with them, but he was. Flanagan was not yet family, but he was present.

"Family," he began, "I have news to share with you. I have been thinking about something for several months, and the dedication of the cemetery last week at the Gettysburg battlefield has cemented my plans and moved me to action."

Everyone in the parlor listened intently. Even the two teenage boys stopped their banter with each other to pay attention.

"Last Friday the newspaper reprinted President Lincoln's 'Gettysburg Address.' His words affected me greatly, and they made me realize I must personally contribute to our efforts to preserve this nation. I cannot sit here—comfortable in Brooklyn—while our brother is at risk in the South; while our friends and neighbors are killed and crippled in battle. I cannot sit here any longer and ask myself, '*Why them and not me?*'

"You all know I am not a fighter. Well, maybe you don't know, Michael Flanagan, or you, my young nephews. But the rest of you know that what Martin is capable of doing, I am not capable of doing. While we hope that Martin has avoided the battlefield by being stationed in New Orleans, the irony of my plan is, it may well put me in harm's way. This week I have been to the Enrollment Office, here in Brooklyn, and discussed with the sergeant in charge of recruiting how I could be of service to the Union Army."

The family emitted a collective gasp, but Dominic went on.

Cate clutched at Biddy's hand, and Mary put her arms around her sons' shoulders.

"I have also talked with Dr. Red Mahoney, who remembered me well. He remembered each of you also, and he sends his regards. Old Red is now long retired from medicine, but he has maintained his connections with the University of the City of New York, his alma mater. This will help me to overcome the first—and most significant—hurdle. Tomorrow morning Dr. Mahoney will propose my name to the university's registrar for admission. Though my medical education will take more than a year, this war is going to continue. When I have achieved certain progress, I will be eligible for enrollment in the army and assigned to a hospital in the fighting zone."

There was fear in the room.

Dominic was going to war.

But when the Civil War was over, he was going to be Dominic George Bodkin, M.D.

AT THE HEAD
OF A HOLLER

January 23, 1902
Saint James Cathedral, Brooklyn

8:45 AM: *God, I loved you, Dominic, I thought you were a good brother to me, to all of us. But I was chilled to the bone waiting for your funeral to begin. Jesus, Mary, and Joseph! Me feet were getting cold. It made sense, though. Everything was frozen in Brooklyn. The stone floors in this old church must've been below zero for a month. It never was that way during me time back in the war. Not in New Orleans—never.*

I remembered one night when we were squatting around the camp-fire outside the barracks and the blue Union Army shirt was stuck to me chest with sweat. The fellows in our platoon were all laughing and joking with each other, and I was talking with one lad I'd gotten to know ...

❦❦❦

Francis Doherty was his name. A fair-haired country boy from West Virginia. Said he lived along a creek at the head of a holler, just a couple of ridges outside a town called Viola. He was a talker. The way he could spin a tale—about almost anything—I'da thought he was Italian, not a Mick. A piece of work Francis Doherty was.

"Do you have children, Martin?" he asked me that night when we was halfway through a bottle of the locals' whiskey.

"No, I don't, Francis. Only been married a few months—but me wife and me loves to try. How about you, lad?"

"My woman," Francis said as he splashed a little more hooch in his cup, "she loves practicing. Practice makin' babies, that is. Mornin', noon, and fookin' night. We've got six young 'uns—four boys, two girls. I hope to get to see them again soon. Her too. Another taste, Martin?" He filled me cup.

"Do you think we'll ever get home, Francis? It's been going on six months now." I spat some tobacco juice into the fire. The gooey gob sizzled a speck.

Francis and me got along pretty well. We worked together in the supply tent, and I taught him how to keep track of the inventory we had of foodstuffs, bullets, gunpowder, medical supplies, shovels, hooch, nails, hammers, axes. We had just about everything.

In exchange for me inventory training, Doherty taught me how to chew tobacco without swallowing the shit, and I could spit with some accuracy—about eight feet. He was a good teacher, but now I could spit better than him, and I could tell he was pissed.

"No, I don't think the war will end soon, Martin. Everybody says Johnny Reb is too dumb to give up." Francis spit a good mouthful toward the fire, but he missed, nearly swallowing his chew. He spat it out, wedged another wad of leaves between his cheek and gum, and chewed.

"You're probably right." I drained me whiskey. Learning how to chew tobacco and drink whiskey at the same time was important. "But, Francis, I'm planning a big family when I do get back. Just as soon as I get home. I've been thinking about it a lot, and we're gonna start right away. I miss Pamela, Francis. Miss her terrible."

"Was it ever this hot in Ireland, Martin?"

I didn't really have to think about the answer—it was always cool in Ireland—but I took a couple of seconds to get some spit ready. I was aiming to get the load to splash off the small round rocks that surrounded the campfire so the juice would just hang there for a few seconds—like it was suspended in the air. We bet money to see how long we could get the tobacco slime to string out before it fell into the dirt.

"Never even close to this hot in Ireland, Francis. The air was always fresh and clean. Breezy. Maybe even windy. We had a lot of rain, though. Always seemed like a cold rain—but it made the meadows nice and green."

Francis rolled his fresh chew around in his mouth and got a good spit to land in the fire. It sizzled. He used the back of his hand to wipe a little residue off his lip and chin, raised one side of his ass, and let out a loud fart. He smiled.

"Nice one, Francis. What's it like living in West Virginia?"

"Well, Martin, I'll tell you ..."

49

ANOTHER BODKIN

ALMOST EVERY DAY THE BUGLER MADE THE CALL SIG-
naling the soldiers to assemble for the distribution of mail.

Since Corporal Martin R. Bodkin's first letter in August, he
had written three other letters to his wife, one to Dominic, and
yet another letter to John. He was worried. He had no responses.
But many of his fellows in the barracks had also written letters
to loved ones at home, and the fact that they had received nothing by return mail calmed his fears—somewhat. The army's
mail system was inadequate. There was no mail call for anyone
in Martin's squad from their August arrival in New Orleans
through the beginning of November. Although many of the soldiers sent letters to cities and towns all over the North, there
were no responses.

It wasn't until the first week of December that Martin finally
heard the postmaster yell "BODKIN" at mail call. Martin opened
his letter and read what Pamela had written: *In the spring, you
will be a father!* He yelled, "YEEEHAAA!" as loud as one of the
Rebel teenagers running through the streets of New Orleans.

Now that Martin had learned his wife's new address in New
Jersey, it made the process of exchanging letters faster than his

initial attempt. Martin and Pamela wrote to each other as often as they could. She wrote to him every week and kept him abreast of how her pregnancy was progressing. He responded with stories of army life and questions about her and their unborn child's well-being. He was excited with anticipation for the birth of a child, but heartbroken he would not be with his wife for the days before and after the baby's birth.

Martin could not get leave from his duties, and he was unable to find a substitute among the Rebel sympathizers in the city of New Orleans. No one in the Crescent City would wear the blue uniform of the Union Army.

He had grown to believe he was wasting his time in the army. He and his fellows guarded a fort—and a city—from Rebels who were all captured and already imprisoned. The Union Army in New Orleans performed endless military drills, but in the twenty months since the North had captured the Crescent City, they had reported no attack from any Southern Rebel. Martin understood that if he and the Union Army left New Orleans, the Rebel fighters, who were within a hundred miles to the north of the city, would return and retake the city which they had surrendered without a fight in the early days of the war.

In the spring, he waited impatiently at the daily mail call for the letter from Pamela that would tell him he was a father, and when the letter finally arrived, the mother of his child sounded eager for his return.

March 17, 1864
General Post Office
Hoboken, New Jersey

My Dearest Martin,
Our baby boy arrived this morning. A little earlier than expected,

but he is a big boy and has a loud voice. Is it acceptable to you that our son will call you "Da"?

As we have agreed, the boy will be named John Stanley. After your return, I promise we will create a baby girl to be called Eleanor to honor your mother.

I pray you are still well and safe. On my knees, I pray for your return every night.

Love always,
Your wife,
Pamela

Most of Martin's brothers and sisters traveled to Hoboken for the baby's christening in April. As the family crossed the East River, Dominic and John reminisced about the Easter morning sixteen years before, when the *Cushlamachree* sailed through these same waters. They talked about how Father Fitzpatrick met the family on the pier, and how Paul Neylon commandeered the customs inspector's launch for the trip from Lower Manhattan to the Brooklyn Navy Yard. They talked about their mother and father. Each remembered his mam and da from a different perspective. John was a young boy of seven when their parents died, and fourteen-year-old Dominic thought of himself as a young man— one of John's protectors.

Pamela and Martin christened their baby John Stanley Bodkin—named for his grandfather and his uncle.

At the ceremony, Dominic commented to John that the baby also shared the name of the notorious Bodkin murderer from Carrobeg, in the 1740s. *"Crom a Boo!* Little Brother, *Crom a Boo!"* Dominic said as he elbowed John in the ribs.

The baby looked exactly like his father. "It's his nose. He has Martin's nose," Cate said, and the Bodkins all agreed.

Pamela's family and the Deweys, on the other hand, agreed that little John Stanley looked like an angel in his linen cap and long white christening gown, and that he resembled his mother. The baby's aunt, Sarah Jane, said, "He has his mother's eyes," and they all agreed.

After the ceremony, where the priest splashed John Stanley with holy water and blessed the baby with the sacred oils, the Deweys hosted a small reception for the families. Everyone wanted to hold the baby and to pinch his rosy cheeks.

Pamela announced to those gathered that the baby would be called Stanley, not John.

"Stanley?" Dominic whispered to Sarah Jane Dewey. "I wonder if Martin knows about this."

"My sister and Martin have expressed themselves in letters on the subject," Sarah Jane explained quietly to Dominic. "At first, Martin was partial to John, but with some prodding, he came around and agreed to Stanley. They may list his name as J. Stanley Bodkin on documents. I believe, if the child had been a girl, she would have been called Eleanor, for your mam."

Hoping to move away from the topic of the baby's name, Sarah Jane asked, "I hear you have begun your medical schooling, Dominic. How do you find the instruction?"

"I am enjoying it very much. My classmates are fine individuals with whom to study and practice, and someday they will be wonderful doctors. Some may even remain in Brooklyn to open their offices. Our instructors are eminently qualified professors, and they tell me that my coursework is satisfactory. I should anticipate meeting the qualifications for medical service in the army before the end of next spring. My time in the war will be brief, hopefully, but it will yield excellent experience in surgery and pharmaceuticals. After I return from the war, I will be required to complete medical school, but I hope my experience in the army will reduce the remaining course load."

Pamela joined the conversation between her sister and brother-in-law, and she added that her correspondence from Martin did not give much hope he would return home this year.

"Our son will be a year old by the time Martin returns," the young mother said.

"It must be difficult for you, Pamela. Your husband has been away for nearly a year, and you have another year to wait for his return. My brothers and sisters share our memories of him frequently and pray for his safety at every mealtime," Dominic said.

50

HEADING SOUTH

1865

"HALLO, LUD. WIE GEHT ES DIR AN DIESEM SCHNEEREICHEN Morgen?" Hello, Lud. How are you on this snowy morning? Dominic said to his postman, as the two men arrived—from opposite directions—at Mary's Bedford Avenue home.

Dominic picked up a good command of his postman's language during the years he worked with a group of German painters, and he usually conversed with Ludwig Cibelli in German to try to improve and maintain his skill. Cibelli's father was Italian but his mother, German. The Cibelli family spoke only German at home.

"Guten morgen, Doktor." Good morning, Doctor.

Dominic had explained to Lud many times that he was not yet a doctor, only a medical student. A year ago, the postman started to call Dominic *"Doktor,"* and he wasn't about to change now.

"Ich Habe einen Brief von der Kriegsabteilung für Sie." Cibelli looked concerned as he presented a letter addressed to Dominic from the Department of War.

"Vielen Dank. Bis morgen, Lud." Thanks. See you tomorrow, Lud.

Lud headed toward the next house on his route, leaving his footprints in three inches of late February snow that had covered the sidewalks.

Dominic stamped the snow from his feet as he entered the front door. He hung his overcoat on a hook in the hallway and looked at the envelope.

"Mary," he called to his sister. "Mary," he called up the stairs again. "My letter from the army is here."

Weeks ago, near the end of his 1865 winter term in medical school, Dominic had renewed his discussions with the army's enrollment officer in Brooklyn, and he coordinated between the university's registrar and the army. He believed he had completed the prerequisite courses to enlist in the army's medical corps, and now he hoped this letter held confirmation.

Mary rushed down the steps.

She stood close behind her brother, a hand on each of his shoulders, and read the letter with him.

UNITED STATES OF AMERICA
Department of War
Washington, D.C.
20 February 1865

Dominic George Bodkin
c/o Duval
Bedford Avenue
Brooklyn, New York

Dear Mr. Bodkin,
Congratulations!
    Your application for enrollment in the United States Army
Medical Corps is hereby accepted.

You have qualified for the rank of Nurse.

Your orders are to provide yourself with the appropriate uniform and report for duty on USS Catawba, Pier 22, NYC, by noon on March 9, 1865.

Regards,
Edwin Stanton
Secretary of War

Since he had not completed medical school, he could not be a surgeon; he would be an army nurse. After all of the successes he had experienced in his life, his title of nurse engendered some disappointment in Dominic, but he did not have any doubts he would be performing the duties of a surgeon.

"You are a brave man, Dominic. Please be careful." Mary fought back the tears as she hugged her brother.

<hr />

The progress of the war during the past few months had been significant. The North's manpower, training, financing, and strategy seemed to be taking its toll on the farmers from the South. Everyone knew the North was winning.

As a result, on March 9, when Dominic prepared to head south, he did not imagine his career in the army would last long. The war would end soon, and he would come home. The "nurse" was looking forward to the experience he would gain as a field surgeon but could not wait to return to complete his education. People in Brooklyn needed a doctor, and he wanted to be their doctor.

John went with Dominic to the *Catawba*'s pier in Lower Manhattan, impressed with Dominic in the Union blue uniform. They embraced, and John told his brother to be careful.

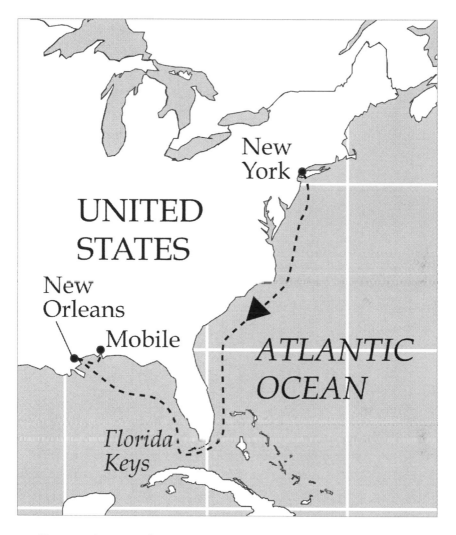

"Let me know where to write you a letter, Dominic, and I'll send a reply immediately."

Dominic made arrangements with John about family matters and told John he would post a letter as soon as the *Catawba* reached her destination.

The two lines of blue-clad Union soldiers trudging up the *Catawba*'s gangway were moving slowly, and Dominic had a moment to relive that Easter afternoon when he and his family disembarked the *Cushlamachree* on a pier a few hundred yards south of the *Catawba*.

The *Catawba* was substantially larger than the *Cushlamachree*. The coal-powered engines of the Union Navy's dual paddle-wheeled troop transport vented through two funnels located amidships. The huge pipes were already spewing dark grey smoke from the coal the crew shoveled into the engines' fires. When the steam power combined with the wind power generated by the ship's four large sails, the *Catawba* would maintain a speed of ten knots. The *Catawba* would sail down the United States coast and around Key West, pass by the Dry Tortugas, head northwest into the Gulf of Mexico toward New Orleans, and then continue to Mobile.

Dominic did not know a single soul of the two hundred and fifty new soldiers heading south from New York Harbor to New Orleans.

"My name is Paddy Maloy." The skinny young private in line next to Dominic extended his hand to greet his new shipmate.

"Dominic Bodkin is my name, Paddy. Glad to meet you."

Paddy explained that only hours ago, he and his family had completed their voyage to America. His family was from Dublin, and when they arrived on the pier in New York, he immediately enlisted in the Union Army in exchange for a blue uniform, a rifle, and the promise of a good meal. He hugged his mother and his sisters, said goodbye, and turned right around to get in line to board the *Catawba*.

The *Catawba*'s horn blasted as she made her way out of New York Harbor. She headed through the Narrows and south along New Jersey's Atlantic coast.

On Dominic's last voyage, in some of these same waters, he and his family worried about disease and storms. The two hundred and fifty Union soldiers on board the *Catawba* were also worried about disease and the elements—but America was at war. In less than two days, the *Catawba* would be in enemy waters, skirting the Confederate gunships and monitors which were prowling the seas between Virginia and Florida. The North's navy had established blockades all along the southern Atlantic coast, blocking ports in Virginia, the Carolinas, and Georgia. The North's blockade ships would attempt to protect the *Catawba* as she traveled south, but the risk of attack would last for days.

Paddy and Dominic shared family histories and watched the Jersey shore while the ship steamed south. The engines were at full throttle, and the ship's sails were catching a stiff breeze.

Paddy said his home in Ireland was on the bank of the River Liffey, in the town of Kilmainham. "It's outside of Dublin, four miles from Trinity College and the city center," Paddy's story went on. "Five years ago my father was taken to Kilmainham Gaol for stealing some bread and sentenced to the penal colony in Australia. We will never see him again. My mother decided that me and my sisters would be better off in America. Now I am probably going to be killed in the war."

"Don't worry that way, Paddy, be positive," Dominic said to the young soldier. "Follow me. I have an idea."

The *Catawba* was a commercial vessel, on lease to the United States Navy. Her captain had been hauling cargo up and down the eastern coast of the United States for years. For the last two years, however, Captain Rob Reiley had been hauling the Northern army's new troops from the docks of New York to Union-controlled ports in the South and sometimes—like this voyage—as far west as New Orleans. His "passengers" on the return voyages to New York were mostly coffins holding the remains of soldiers and the injured or maimed Union soldiers who were lucky enough to be alive.

Dominic and his new friend went up to the bridge, and Dominic asked one of the sailors, "Which way to the captain?"

Dominic felt foolish as the sailor simply pointed to a tall man standing next to the ship's wheel. The tall man was wearing the blue uniform of a captain, with multiple gold stripes on his sleeves and the word "CAPTAIN" emblazoned on his cap. Another sailor, the quartermaster, had both hands on the ship's wheel and was serving as the pilot.

Dominic walked over to the captain and introduced himself.

"Captain, my name is Dominic Bodkin, and this is my new friend, Paddy Maloy. I have a commission as a nurse in this army, and Paddy here will be my medical assistant. I was wondering if you could direct us to the other medical personnel on board."

"Take over for a minute, mate," Reiley said to his engineer as he motioned Dominic and Paddy toward a corner of the bridge, where a pot was keeping the coffee warm.

"My name is Rob Reiley," the captain said as he handed tin mugs of coffee to Dominic and Maloy, "pleased to meet you, gentlemen, and welcome aboard *Catawba*."

Both recruits were standing with a hand on the bridge's bulkhead to secure themselves against the rolling motion of the ship. Dominic had not noticed the effect of the waves only half an hour ago when he and Paddy were on the main deck. Reiley stood with his arms crossed, facing the two men. He seemed oblivious to the motion of the ship, as his large frame swayed right along with the boat.

"Two surgeons are on board," Reiley said after he took a slug of his coffee, "Edward Fox and John Brennan. The medical staff is in an empty officers' cabin, one deck below. You, gentlemen, should join them. It looks like a storm is brewing for tomorrow, and we should be in the middle of it before we get to Cape Hatteras. I suggest you get to your bunks and get some rest. You may be busy tomorrow with soldiers suffering seasickness and such."

"Thank you, Captain. We'll go below and find them." The men shook hands, and Dominic headed off the bridge to find Fox and Brennan.

Paddy, well pleased with his new position on the medical staff, hustled along right behind Dominic. Down below, they found Fox and Brennan and were delighted to see two bunks were available in the officers' cabin. The two doctors were happy to add the nurse and his "assistant" to the medical team.

By morning the two surgeons, Dominic, and Paddy knew the captain was a good weather forecaster and an even better judge of the new soldiers' stomachs. The backs of dozens of the recruits formed a wall of blue uniforms as they retched and puked over the rails on the main deck.

The ocean's swells were getting steeper. The wind coming out of the south—and right into the *Catawba*'s bow—was becoming a gale. The morning sky off the bow was ominous. It was dark, almost black. Cold rain pounded across the ocean in sheets, at times stopping suddenly and after a while beginning again with even more ferocity.

Throughout the day and into the evening, the storm worsened, but the *Catawba* handled it. In this treacherous weather, there was little fear of Southern gunboats or monitors. It seemed the *Catawba* was the only ship on the ocean as she crashed through the monstrous Atlantic waves, making slow progress south.

Near midnight every soul on board hoped the storm had reached its peak, but it had not. Jagged bolts of lightning slashed the sky and illuminated the night clouds. The crack of thunder boomed across the enormous seas.

The *Catawba* rode the ocean's swells up and down. After an hour of the storm's being at its worst, one massive wave was followed quickly by another more giant wave. The second broke the ship's bowsprit loose from its position on the prow, leaving the bowsprit attached only by its rope lines and banging against the ship's hull.

The impact of the second wave also snapped one of the braces holding the boiler in place on the engine room deck. The cry of "fire in the engine room" raised the level of anguish among soldiers and sailors alike. But the fear inspired every man on board to work furiously to extinguish the blaze before flames made it to the hold and the crates of ammunition destined for delivery at the Port of New Orleans.

In the chaos of fighting the boiler room fire, several men received injuries, and the medical team worked together to care for their wounds. Fox and Brennan had medical kits that included a linseed and wax ointment for the treatment of burns, forceps for the extraction of foreign objects, and saws for the inevitable amputations. Dominic's skills and judgment in treating those patients to whom he was assigned won him the confidence of the two surgeons.

The most seriously injured of the soldiers bled to death from his wounds, however. While the surgeons and Dominic tried to save the man's life, Dominic talked to him and learned the soldier was from Seneca County in New York State, but otherwise, no one knew anything else about the man. At the moment the soldier took his last breath, it was immediately evident to Dominic that his efforts had been inadequate. He wondered, *Am I prepared for the tasks I will face? Will I ever be ready?* His sense of failure was short-lived, as Dr. Fox required assistance with another wounded patient.

"Apply a tourniquet to this man's arm, Bodkin. If you put it at the level of his biceps muscle that should slow the flow of blood enough for me to work on his fingers." The soldier's hand had been crushed by falling debris in the boiler room explosion.

By five o'clock in the morning, the fire was out; the storm had subsided; the sky looked as though dawn would break on another beautiful spring day on the North Carolina coast. Off in the distance—east, away from land—Dominic saw the horizon glow. Another, less fortunate vessel was in flames, its passengers and crew destined for death at the hand of the elements, not to be killed by the Southern Rebels or a disease.

After the medical crew treated the final injured soldier, Dominic had some confidence restored when Fox said to him, "Good day's work, Doctor!"

As the afternoon turned into evening, the sky was clear, the air was warmer, and the seas were calm.

The dead soldier's body, together with some scrap pieces of iron, was wrapped in sheets and sewn closed. The men tied the shroud with ropes, to keep the soldier and his grave clothes together when the heavy weights forced his remains to sink into the depths.

All of the Union soldiers, as well as the *Catawba*'s sailors, stood at attention on the main deck for the burial at sea of the man from Seneca County, New York. They wrapped the weighted and tied corpse on a bier, and from the ship's forward cabin, a cortege of soldiers formed and marched past the starboard wheel to carry the man's body to a plank positioned at the stern. At the end of the plank, the cortege came to a halt. A soldier with a fife played a dead march, and the commanding officer read prayers. Many of the men said, "Amen." A few volleys were fired, the end of the plank was raised, and the sea received the remains of a young man who Dominic thought seemed to have been raised by his parents with care and some education.

The soldiers soon dispersed from the funeral party and resumed the usual pastimes of card games and songs. Tonight, the songs were sad songs of both home and war.

51

THE GULF OF MEXICO

IN THE DAYS AFTER THE STORM, CAPTAIN REILEY HAD to use all of his sailing skills to get the *Catawba* from Cape Hatteras to Key West. His ship was damaged. One engine was disabled in the fire, and the hurricane-force winds shredded one of the four sails. On the morning after the burial at sea, the weather was calm, and Reiley's sailors climbed the rigging to make some repairs to the tattered canvas. The damage to the boiler's brace had created a small split in the hull, which was at the waterline. The crack resulted in a leak that required constant pumping and bailing. Sailors and soldiers all participated around the clock with pumps and buckets. Eventually, the men effectuated a repair to the hull and minimized the leaking. They brought the broken bowsprit back on board and strapped it to the deck, near the bow.

With only one functioning engine, the ship's speed was dependent on its sails, as well as the velocity and direction of the wind. Reiley was able to achieve only about five knots at top speed, and he estimated that the thousand miles between Hatteras and the Keys would take nearly two weeks. If he could get to Key West, he knew the navy had facilities to repair the engine and replace the damaged sail. He would then be able to complete the trip and deliver his precious cargo to New Orleans.

Before being damaged, Reiley's ship would have had little chance to outrun a Rebel gunship or a monitor—even at ten knots. Now—only achieving five knots—the *Catawba* was a sitting duck. It seemed miraculous that day after day, the *Catawba* was escorted by Northern blockaders as she sailed past one Southern port after another. Finally, Reiley made it south of Jacksonville and to the relative safety of the Florida coast, which was not heavily patrolled by Rebel gunships and monitors. In the last days of March, the *Catawba* rounded the southern tip of Florida and headed west along the Florida Keys.

The Keys are a string of tropical islands, stretching into the Gulf of Mexico, and Dominic was amazed by the crystal-clear blue water, the warm weather, and the overall beauty of this part of the United States.

The captain told the doctors the ship would dock at Key West for a week for repairs. The soldiers would establish a camp on the island for the duration, and the medical team would stay at a boardinghouse near the dock.

The medical team, including Paddy Maloy, checked into the boardinghouse. While the others went exploring for some liquid refreshment, Dominic went straight to the small, dilapidated post office to write a letter to John.

Key West, Florida
Tuesday Morning–11 O'C
March 28th, 1865

Dear Brother John,
I have arrived safely at the Port of Key West. The passage from
New York to Florida was one of peak danger and was decidedly

unpleasant in the particular—a storm that rose up in the vicinity of Hatteras caused us peak damage, breaking off our bowsprit, destroying the braces of the boiler, opening seams, and causing a leak of nine inches an hour.

Key West is doubtless the most beautiful and pleasant place that I have ever been.

We will be docked at Key West for a week, or more, while our worthy vessel, the Catawba, is repaired.

From here we will go at first to the Dry Tortugas and then on to New Orleans. The medical team with which I am assigned, Fox and Brennan, and our assistant named Maloy, have heard rumors that after our arrival in New Orleans we will be assigned to the Army Medical Hospital, at Fort Gaines, on Dauphin Island in Alabama.

Tell Cate that I have been enquiring for her and that I thank her for my outfit. It is what the commanding officer demanded, and the shirts are admirable.

You will understand, and please excuse me, for not prepaying the postage on this envelope. There is no postal clerk at this post office.

If any letters should come for me at home in Brooklyn, please keep them until you find out my address.

Remember me also to Lucas and Danny and tell them I shall write to them soon.

I must close this letter written under difficulties, as I have to go into the dispensary to see to some prescriptions. Remember me to all. I will write again.

Your fond brother
Dominic

P.S. Love to all, and please send a late newspaper along with several long letters. I hope this will go soon but, without a postal clerk being here, the prospects are not good.

To the chagrin of most of the soldiers and sailors, it only took five days to complete the repairs. The stay on Key West was over. Resupplied with food and other supplies, the *Catawba* was set to sail on the next tide. In the morning, Dominic and Ed Fox stood together on the deck of the *Catawba*, waiting anxiously for Brennan and Paddy Maloy to board. They were late. Dr. Brennan and the young soldier had celebrated late into the evening, as men might on their last night on this island paradise, and they had not returned to their beds in the boardinghouse. Fox looked at Dominic in amazement as the dockhands pulled the gangway back, and the *Catawba* began to move away from the pier.

"Where are they?"

The ship was well out into the harbor when Dominic saw Brennan and Maloy running onto the pier, carrying their kits and haversacks—while at the same time Maloy was trying to tuck his shirttails into his pants. Would they be put on another ship and join them in Alabama? Dominic and Fox asked each other. Or would they be thrown in the brig as deserters? In either event, the medical team had been bolstered at Key West by the addition of six assistant surgeons, to whom the Department of War assigned the dangerous task of tending to the United States Colored Troops regiments on the battlefield, rather than being stationed at the hospital at Fort Gaines. The new doctors—the "Philadelphia Six" Fox called them—were graduates of Philadelphia colleges, and as Dominic noted when he met them one evening in the tavern on the dock, they were "as wild as panthers."

In addition to the six surgeons who joined the ship at Key West, eight prisoners, to be unloaded at Fort Jefferson on Tortuga, were also added. The Union used the fort as a prison for deserters and bond jumpers. It was only seventy miles from Key West to Tortuga, and the day of sailing was beautiful. The waters around Tortuga were shallow for a significant distance from the shore, with submerged coral formations being visible from the ship. Captain Reiley was forced to anchor the *Catawba* more than a mile offshore and signal to the Fort Jefferson guards requesting a dinghy to row out and collect the prisoners. The transfer of the deserters took a few hours, and watching the process gave the soldiers and sailors some entertainment—other than card games and songs—to occupy their time.

When the transfer was complete, Reiley immediately ordered the anchor to be hoisted, and he continued the voyage as the horizon turned to sunset. The captain headed northwest in the Gulf of Mexico, and in two days, the *Catawba* arrived at the mouth of the Mississippi River at Port Eads, Louisiana. It took another day, with the assistance of a river pilot, for Reiley to bring the ship to its berth in the Port of New Orleans. On the way up the Mississippi, halfway between Port Eads and New Orleans, they sailed past Fort Jackson. Dominic knew his brother had been, or perhaps was still, stationed at Fort Jackson, and he looked intently at the activity surrounding the fort, looking for signs of Martin as the *Catawba* steamed past.

The North had captured New Orleans at the beginning of the Civil War without any meaningful battle, and, as a result, the city did not have the scars of battle that were prevalent in many other Southern cities. After the *Catawba* docked, Dominic, together with Fox and several of the surgeons from Philadelphia, took a tour of the "Crescent City" and were delighted to find many beautiful residences on the city's clean and well-manicured avenues and boulevards.

"My brother is stationed at Fort Jackson. He's called it home for nearly two years," Dominic said to Fox as they walked along Saint Joseph Street. "I imagine he has walked these same streets, and he has seen these stately homes. I would have to think that when he walked along here, he would have had the same thoughts I am having now."

"What thoughts are those, Dominic?"

"If this is war, and war is hell, what must heaven be like?" Dominic replied with a chuckle.

The next day, the *Catawba's* quartermaster arranged transportation for the doctors from the *Catawba* to Lake Pontchartrain, where they boarded the USS *James Battle*. The *James Battle* was a small ship, but she was adequate and available to convey the new soldiers and the medical teams to Mobile Bay.

As the steamer skirted the pine forest on the west of Lake Pontchartrain, through Grant's Pass, the signs of the war he and Martin were a part of were everywhere, and the ravages of battle suddenly became clear to Dominic as they passed the ruins of Fort Powell. Fort Powell once guarded the entrance to Lake Pontchartrain for the Rebels, but in 1864 it had been totally destroyed by the North.

In the quiet of his mind, Dominic admonished himself, *Sherman was right, Dominic. "War is hell."*

As they entered the mouth of Mobile Bay, Dauphin Island was off the *James Battle's* port side. They could see Fort Gaines, with its grim breastwork, on the easternmost point of the island. The pentagonal Fort Morgan was to the starboard, on the tip of Mobile Point.

The battle to take Mobile was straight ahead.

BATTLES

THE DECK OF THE FAST, SHALLOW-DRAFT RIVER steamer *James Battle* was crowded. Two hundred and fifty troops were about all she could hold. The ship had been captured from the Confederate Navy in 1863 while attempting to run a blockade and was now used to transport Union troops. The soldiers with their kits and rifles occupied every square foot on the deck. The groan of the ship's engines was numbing as an eerie quiet dominated the men who were alone with their fears. Would they be killed at Spanish Fort, or would they live through Spanish Fort and die in the battle for Fort Blakeley?

Spanish and Blakeley were the heavily fortified eastern and northern defenses for the city of Mobile. Even though Mobile Bay had been under Union control for a year, the city itself was still a Confederate stronghold. The Union's primary goal in the Mobile Campaign was to take control of the city.

Spanish and Blakeley were the first two steps of a three-part battle plan. Taking the city of Mobile was the third.

"Did you hear?" Dr. Bill Day, one of the Philadelphia Six, almost whispered to Dominic and Ed Fox. "General Canby has the XVI and the XIII Corps moving along Mobile Bay, and the attack on Spanish Fort has already begun. They say Canby has forty thousand, maybe even fifty thousand men."

"We're going to be busy, Bill. We better be ready to be fearless bone cutters today," Fox warned the young Philadelphia surgeon. "The Rebs don't have many men left, but I hear they'll fight to the death."

After a day and night of traveling from New Orleans, the *James Battle* docked two miles down the river from Spanish Fort. At dawn, the sight of hundreds of ragged Rebel prisoners filing out of the nearby woods and being herded onto other transport ships berthed nearby erased all of the images Dominic had of the bucolic, tree-lined streets of New Orleans. The Southern prisoners were bloody, bandaged, and dirty. Many looked to be in shock or starving or both.

All members of the medical teams were dispatched to Spanish Fort to tend to the wounded. When they arrived, the ongoing battle was ferocious, and they found the wounded from both sides in heaps, where the assault had been underway for the past week. They helped where they could—for a day, through the night, and another day.

The catastrophic nature and the sheer volume of the injuries were nothing the physicians from New York and Philadelphia had ever dealt with before. Seventy percent of the soldiers' wounds were to their extremities—arms and legs blown apart by cannonballs, or soft lead bullets called "Minié balls." The surgeons' first goal was to save a life—next was to keep a limb. Often, they did not achieve either. They performed amputations with almost nothing to reduce the pain for the soldier, except perhaps some chloroform or a bottle of whiskey. Most of the injured soldiers outside the medical tent bled to death from already having lost an arm or a leg before one of the surgeons was able to attend to the bloody stump. A soldier did not live long with an artery spewing blood into the mud.

"Dominic, help me with this man's leg," Fox instructed the younger Bodkin as he wiped particles of red and grey matter from the bone saw he had used on the last soldier. He wiped the bone saw on an already bloody rag. "I'll cut through the femur at about the middle of the thigh, and you scrape the edges of the bone smooth so that it won't work back through his skin."

"Will do, Doctor. I'll tie the arteries off and close him, too, but the sergeant told me they want us to move on to Fort Blakeley. He said most of the rest here have already bled to death or they will die before anyone gets to them. The injuries at Blakeley are very recent, and we will have a better chance to save them."

The young patient lost consciousness as Fox made incisions in his skin and the muscle, all of the way around his thigh. Fox sawed through the man's thigh bone and tossed the severed leg on a pile with the others.

Enough skin would be left for Dominic to form a flap when he sewed the man's stump closed.

"I'll pack the tools, Dominic, and we will be ready to leave as soon as you have finished with him."

The soldier's leg was closed, and Dominic wrapped it in a sticking plaster and a bandage. Thankfully, the patient was still unconscious.

The Philadelphia Six, plus Dominic and Fox, put their blue uniform jackets back on over blood-soaked white shirts and were directed to a barn where a servant had arranged mules and a guide to lead them along the five-mile trail to Fort Blakeley.

The doctors from the Northern states were in no way confident

Fort Pillow

or comfortable riding on the mules, but they understood it was a matter of necessity for them to proceed at once, and off they went over swamps, through woods, up hills, and down ravines. Dr. Day was scratched off his mule by the branch of a tree. He lost his haversack and some of his food supplies in a fast-moving creek as he tumbled down a steep hill.

The boom of cannon fire from the assault on Blakeley was evident; the crack of shots became louder; the screams of those injured by the shot and shell were terrifying to the doctors, but they pressed on until they could see the thousands engaged on the battlefield.

The Philadelphia Six left Dominic and Fox to join General Steele's five thousand Black troops, who fought with the cry of, "Remember Fort Pillow!" The battle cry was a reference to the massacre of mostly Black troops trying to surrender to the Rebels in a battle months before at Fort Pillow in Tennessee.

Fox and Dominic were welcomed by the surgeons who were already overwhelmed by the injured in Blakeley's surgical tent, and they resumed performing surgeries where they left off at Spanish Fort. The Confederates had almost no medical personnel at the Battle of Fort Blakeley, and the injured in grey uniforms outnumbered the Union's wounded by five to one. The Northern surgeons did not discriminate by blue or grey in deciding which soldier to treat next.

Dominic was dressing the wounds of a Confederate officer, Major Joe Ravenel, from South Carolina. Ravenel told Dominic that his father and four brothers had been killed in the war so far, and Dominic told the Rebel soldier he wasn't going to join them just yet. "You won't see them today, Major." The major shook Dominic's hand, as a friend would, when Dominic told him he was from Brooklyn. Ravenel told Dominic that before the war started, while he was a student at Yale College in Connecticut, he and his college friends spent a pleasant day touring in New York City. After Dominic finished treating Ravenel, guards took the major away and transported him to the prison at Fort Gaines.

That afternoon, April 9, 1865, the few remaining Confederates surrendered, and the Battle of Blakeley ended.

⬥⬥⬥⬥⬥

Dominic and Fox were ordered down the Tenesaw River to Mobile City to await transportation to their original destination—the army hospital at Fort Gaines. Piles of debris from wrecked ships impeded passage on the river, and the men saw unexploded torpedoes floating in the channel.

The doctors watched as a monitor, the *Osage*—a formidable, double-turreted ship—was blown up by a floating torpedo.

Another monitor, whose name they did not know, was sunk when she was within range of enemy guns on the shoreline. They could see five other boats, which had also been transporting Union troops down the river from Blakeley, that had been sunk by Confederate guns still trying to defend the city.

"I believe we were on the first transport to make it from Blakeley," Fox said to Dominic as they disembarked onto the pier at Mobile. "Good thing treating that Confederate major delayed us."

The doctors were surprised to see Mobile was a well-shaded, splendid-looking city with fig trees lining the streets and ornamenting the residences of wealthy families. Roses, of the sweetest fragrances, were in full bloom and untouched by the disaster surrounding the city. The Rebel flag was still flying in the breeze in front of the customs house, and despite that Spanish Fort and Blakeley had fallen, taking the city of Mobile remained as the third part of the Union's battle plan.

Fox hired a carriage to take them along Water Street to the Battle House Hotel. The two surgeons from New York registered at the best hotel in Mobile. The coachman told the doctors a wealthy Mobile family owned the Battle House. It was the same family that previously owned the troop transport, the *James Battle*, on which they sailed from New Orleans to Spanish Fort.

Dominic saw that most of the fine-looking shops along Water Street were closed, but none of the buildings had been destroyed or even damaged by the war. The coachman answered the doctors' question before they asked it. "Mobile will not be recuperated for some time yet, gentlemen. Our city is physically unscathed, but the Union blockade of the Mobile Bay has ruined our economy. Everyone has Confederate notes, but now they are almost worthless, and our shop owners are beseeching the authorities to turn some of their articles of trade into the heretofore despised greenbacks."

The chalkboard in the lobby of the ornate, five-story hotel told the same story:

DAILY ROOM RATES
$250 CONFEDERATE NOTES
— OR —
$5 FEDERAL GREENBACKS

Dominic and Ed Fox were assigned adjacent rooms at the hotel. An army clerk in the hotel lobby issued the doctors new uniforms to replace the blood-stained outfits they were wearing, and for the first time since they had sailed from Key West, the doctors were able to bathe in a tub with heated water and soap. After his bath, Dominic stretched out on his bed and judged what he had done—and seen—on the battlefields. Sleep came quickly. Exhaustion immediately drove his mind into an abyss alternating among fear, guilt, lucidity, and euphoria as he tried to shed the images of dismembered, bloody, and dying soldiers.

Dominic's rhythmic snoring stopped suddenly and his lanky frame tensed. Hidden under his tightly closed eyelids, his eyeballs jolted left and right with fear as images of his little sister invaded his subconscious mind...

... Nellie screamed, "Help me, Mama! Please help me!" as a leprechaun-sized Paddy Maloy worked furiously to stem the bleeding from a gash in her side. The blood gushing from Nellie's wound soaked through her grey Confederate private's uniform from her chest to her muddy boots. "Save her, Paddy. She's my little sister for God's sake!" Dominic begged the

small Irishman. The claw on Maloy's lizard-like appendage dug into Nellie's side and began to extract clumps of tissue and long, bloody sections of her intestine. The three-foot-tall Maloy reached for his bone saw and grinned a devilish grin as he looked over Dominic's shoulder toward a beautiful young woman wearing a diaphanous gown of white and gold silk. The woman floated through cigar smoke in the Battle House's elegant dining room. At the same time a string quartet played the gentle sounds of a romantic melody, and Black waiters attended tables occupied by white soldiers wearing both blue and grey uniforms. She waved flirtatiously toward Dominic as she levitated only inches from his face.

Sudhbh?

Dominic's nightmare flashed images of the violent storm off Hatteras, blue water and coral reefs at Key West, stately homes in New Orleans—and the ferocity of the Mobile battlefields at Spanish Fort and Blakeley. In the hell created by his dream, he saw the juxtaposition of the savagery and the civility of war. The Brooklyn medical student who wanted to be a surgeon—but in his subconscious was only leprechaun Paddy Maloy's nurse—blinked and shook his head in disbelief as he gazed at the beautiful floating woman. "Sadhbh!" Dominic's tried to call to Nellie's fairy friend. He saw her provocative smile. "Sadh—" he tried to yell, over and over, but the word wouldn't come out.

His sleeping mind surveyed the smoke-filled dining room as he studied the waiters—Black men with shackles and chains at their ankles, standing with their backs against the restaurant's walls—wearing black trousers, white collared shirts, and black bow ties. Each had a blood-stained, but neatly folded, white linen napkin draped on his left arm—as he waited for a patron to summon assistance. The head waiter dragged a ball and chain as he greeted Dominic and Fox and escorted them to a table. The waiter filled the doctors' water goblets with a frothing red substance.

"Did you see her, Ed?" Dominic asked Fox. Dr. Fox didn't respond, and Dominic screamed at the top of his lungs, "Can't you see her, Ed? I know her, Ed! That's Nellie's friend Sadhbh! Can you hear me? Ed?" Again, Fox didn't respond.

Dominic's subconscious absorbed his surroundings. Seated around the dining room were the leading men of both the Union and Confederate armies. Both sides in the conflict were staying at the Battle House—half of the patrons flushed with the glory of victory, half stressed with the agony of defeat.

"Ed, I'm pretty sure that's General Canby sitting by the window with Dr. Madie," Dominic whispered, fearful someone would overhear him. Canby and Madie were hairy, bear-like men—the size of giants—who made their dining table and chairs look as though they belonged in a doll's house. Major General Edward Canby was the commander of the Union's XIII and XVI Corps, and Madie was in charge of all medical services related to the Mobile Campaign.

"That looks like Kirby Smith over there," Dominic added, nodding to a baby-sized Confederate general sitting across the room. General Smith's long, dark beard covered his standing collar and half the brass buttons on his miniature double-breasted, grey frock coat. The general's collar displayed three gold stars and a wreath awarded for courage on the battlefield. On his small head, he wore a large slouch hat with a dark feather and a braided gold bullion cord. Smith was significantly smaller than the diminutive Paddy Maloy; as he sat in his chair, the top of his head barely reached the edge of the table.

Dominic watched as Canby excused himself from the table with Dr. Madie. Canby's arms were so extended that his knuckles scraped the floor as he lumbered across the room to where Smith was seated with his Confederate officers.

The miniature Smith climbed from his chair onto the table, straining to look Canby in the eye. The giant and the infant stared at each other.

The two generals nodded and introduced themselves. In the fantasy world in which Dominic found his mind temporarily ensconced, he could hear the two foes' voices as though they were speaking directly to him.

"General Smith, I can assure you that the prisoners we have taken will be treated with the utmost respect," Canby's voice boomed. "Our doctors will tend to your wounded, sir, and we'll bury your dead soldiers. Tell the rest of your men to go home to their families and their farms."

"Thank you, General Canby." Smith had the squeaking voice of a four-year-old child. "The South appreciates your generous gesture of goodwill." Smith attempted to salute the victorious general, but his right arm had been amputated at the elbow. "Following your victories at Spanish Fort and Blakeley," the Confederate general continued, "the documents to surrender the city of Mobile are being prepared at this moment. My sources tell me that General Grant has defeated Lee's army at Appomattox. Everyone believes this war is over, General Canby."

"I hope you are right, General Smith." Canby's hairy, paw-like hand lifted Smith from the table and gently placed the Confederate general back in his chair.

The string quartet reached the crescendo of Handel's Hallelujah Chorus, and the beautiful woman floated through the cigar smoke toward the massive crystal chandelier in the center of the room. In her outstretched arms, she cradled Nellie's lifeless, mutilated corpse as an offering for peace in America.

Dominic woke with a start, his body awash in sweat. The Union cannons on either side of the river roared in celebration, but his mind swirled with dread. He went to the window and watched as stoic Union soldiers lowered the flag of the Rebel states and raised Old Glory over the custom house. Mobile had surrendered. He wept with fear as he tried to make sense of the nightmare he just lived. *Was any of it real?*

An hour later, Dominic and Fox met in the lobby and sat in the Battle House's modest tavern among blue-clad officers who were drinking whiskey, smoking cigars, joking, and laughing.

"The atmosphere in this room makes it feel as though the war is over, Ed. While I was waiting for you to come to dinner, I overheard a couple of our Union colonels talking. They were saying the XVI Corps was chasing the Rebel army to Selma and Montgomery, and the rumor in the Battle House is that the Rebels will not be able to make much of a stand there. Canby's XIII is still in the vicinity of Fort Blakeley but ready to move on. The Union fleet has moved up the Alabama River and is crowding upon the Rebel ironclads *Tennessee* and *Nashville*. Everything is in motion, Ed. The colonels were saying we've got them on the run."

Fox heard what Dominic said this time. "Sounds good, Dominic. We haven't heard much from the North lately, but let's hope Grant, Sherman, and Sheridan are tying the Gordian Knot in Virginia. I pray to God for this war to be over, Dominic. What we've witnessed these past days no man should ever have haunt his memory."

Later that night, Dominic received his orders to report to Fort Gaines on Dauphin Island and wrote to John, relaying stories from New Orleans, the battles of Spanish Fort and Blakeley, and the celebration in Mobile.

Mobile City, Alabama
Monday, April 10, 1865
8 PM

Dear Brother John–
Well, dear Brother, I write to you from my comfortable room at the Battle House Hotel in the splendid city of Mobile, Alabama. In the past several days I have witnessed the savagery of war in the surgery tents at the battles of Spanish Fort and Fort Blakeley. The surrender of the city of Mobile was accomplished earlier this evening.

I have now been assigned to duty at the hospital at Fort Gaines, which is some distance down the river. I shall be on my way there in hours from this time. I will have an excellent chance for practice there, and if I shall live to return, I will have reason to feel benefited by the few months' absence. My time will be much occupied until the wounded and sick are removed.

We must not forget home in our absence from it.

I hope that you succeeded in your effort at the Navy Yard. If so, write me a long letter about matters generally.

I wrote a letter to Mary but was unable to prepay it owing to the scarcity of stamps in this place. It may be that this may overtake my letter to Mary, but the probabilities are that as communications are not regular between this place and New York, it may be long delayed.

Remember me to Lawrence and Maggie. Remember me to Pamela also, and have her tell Martin in a letter that I traveled through many a street in New Orleans, which once must have been familiar to him. I sincerely hope that he found a substitute on easy terms.

Carry out the principles about which we had an understanding before parting. Tell Cate I will write to her in a few days.

Love to all and please send some newspapers with news of Brooklyn.

I will write again soon.

Your fond brother,
Dominic

P.S. Direct mail to:
Dominic G. Bodkin, Acting Assistant Surgeon
U.S. Army General Hospital, Fort Gaines, Alabama

53

BLACK BUNTING

January 23, 1902
Saint James Cathedral, Brooklyn

8:50 AM: *I watched Pamela, standing on the other side of the vestibule, dressed in black, from head to toe, a lace veil covering her beautiful face. Me and her had been through a lot in the forty years we'd been together. Nine children. Eight were grown now.*

I remembered telling her in a letter posted from New Orleans that the war was over, the trip home by train would be faster than sailing to the South on the Atlantic had been. But I was wrong ...

⬚⬚⬚ ⬚⬚⬚ ⬚⬚⬚

The night we heard Lee had surrendered, I thanked God. After two years in New Orleans, the fighting was over, and I had never fired me rifle. I sat around the campfire outside our barracks, drinking some hooch and talking about going home with the fellows in the squad. It was buggy that night, and the mosquitoes and sand flies—we called them no-see-ums—were biting us. The captain told us the war would be over soon and we could catch a train home to New York. He didn't tell us General Sherman had destroyed most of the train tracks in the

South, or that we would have to travel six hundred miles to Saint Louis to find a fookin' train north.

It was raining and still dark, weeks later, the morning we left Fort Jackson and found a barge to cross the Mississippi. We walked until exhaustion, and nightfall converged on a cold but clear night. The men were sleeping on the ground and happy to have blankets in their haversacks. Lying on the ground that first night, me mind filled with thoughts of walking from Briarhill to Galway City with me father. Da was tired when we got to the top of the Bohermore, and the two of us looked ahead into Galway City, but he didn't give up. He had a job to do.

Marching, walking, riverboats—more walking—it took nearly two weeks to get to Memphis, where we crossed the Mississippi for the second time, and most of another week to get to Saint Louis. We were lucky in Saint Louis, where we hopped a boxcar heading east. Three trains later, we arrived at the massive station in Jersey City.

Hundreds of soldiers, wearing the remnants of their faded blue uniforms, crowded the depot's platforms as the steam from a half dozen locomotives swirled at their feet. A crowd of citizens tried to find friends or relatives, and they hailed the rest of us as returning heroes.

"Welcome home, soldier," an older gentleman greeted me. Appreciative of his greeting, I shook his hand. Indeed, it was good to be home. It was early afternoon, but the clock in the great hall read nearly half after seven. I pointed to the clock and asked what hour it was? The man brought a watch on a long silver chain from his pocket. "It's only a quarter after one o'clock, soldier. The clock up there has been frozen at 7:22 for weeks. That was the hour Booth shot President Lincoln." He paused for a moment before he told me the president's funeral train was laid up in the depot's yard last month, while his casket was taken to New York for the procession along Broadway.

Me eyes went back to the clock again, and I noticed black bunting still hanging from the rafters of the massive ceiling.

"I'm traveling to Hoboken, sir. Which way is that city?"

The man put his hand on me shoulder and pointed to an exit. "Through that door and follow Hudson Street. Walk north, along the river. It's only a couple of miles to Hoboken. You're almost home, son."

Almost home ...

HOME AGAIN

LITTLE STANLEY SAT IN HIS HIGHCHAIR AT THE kitchen table, playing with some of the pancakes his mother made for his breakfast. Pamela was encouraging her baby to eat as she enjoyed a cup of tea and opened the morning newspaper.

The headline of the April 10, 1865, *New Jersey Journal* blared the news everyone in the country had hoped for:

THE WAR IS OVER

"Not officially over," the lead article reported, but the fighting had ended, and the South's armies had surrendered.

Pamela read the front-page article—and she reread it. *Soon,* she thought. *Soon.*

Six weeks later, Pamela was smiling and enjoying the sunshine in Hoboken as she pushed fourteen-month-old Stanley's new carriage—a birthday gift for Stanley from his aunt Sarah

Jane—along the path in front of the house. The buds in the trees were turning into leaves, and nature had begun a new cycle as it escaped the stagnation of another cold and dreary winter on the northeast coast of the United States. Pamela felt good about life.

Little Stanley had grown three teeth already, and the boy had been standing on his own for two months. He had recently taken his first steps. He was eating real food and sleeping through the night. The youngster usually took a good nap when Pamela pushed him in his carriage. He was asleep now, and Pamela decided to take advantage of the peace the sleeping child afforded his mother. She pushed the buggy past the Deweys' house and began another loop of her usual route.

Stanley was lying on his back, facing his mother, so she could look at her son while he slept. *He does look a lot like his father,* Pamela thought. The little boy had Martin's nose. *No doubt,* she thought, *it is Martin's nose!* It was Martin's chin also. *No mustache like his father yet,* she thought, laughing to herself.

In his last letter, written weeks ago, Martin wrote that he believed the war was almost over. The men at Fort Jackson were hearing that the North was winning nearly every battle, and the rumor was they would be leaving New Orleans very soon.

Pamela had only one photograph of Martin, and she looked at it many times during every day. It was a picture of Martin in his uniform that he sent from New Orleans with one of his letters. Her husband had medals pinned to his chest. He told her they were for enduring the boredom of army life at Fort Jackson. She hoped he still looked the same, although she would ask him to trim his near-handlebar mustache.

As she pushed the carriage along the path, she took her eyes off Stanley and looked ahead to see a tired and dirty-looking soldier carrying his sack over his shoulder as he shuffled along the walk toward her. The man was looking at the houses as though

Cpl. Martin R. Bodkin

he was lost. He looked down at a paper in his hand and then toward each of the houses he passed. The sight of the soldier in his faded blue uniform reminded her of an older version of the husband she had in the picture.

She became fixated on the man as they walked toward each other. They got closer and closer. *Is it my husband?* she asked herself. *Is it Martin?*

"MARTIN!" she screamed. "MARTIN!"

The soldier shuffled faster toward her. He heard her voice—it was his Pamela.

"PAMELA!" he called as he rushed to embrace her.

The couple's embrace lasted only seconds until he turned his attention to the baby in the carriage. Stanley had been startled from his nap by his parents' shouts. Martin reached to feel his son's face. Pamela's hand met his, and they touched their son together. "A fine-looking boy he is, Pamela. Stanley Bodkin is a perfect name! How do I pick him up?" Pamela lifted Stanley out so her husband could hold the baby in his arms.

"He looks like you, Martin. Everyone says so."

Martin cradled his son in his left arm, and he touched the baby's face with his right hand. Pamela wrapped her arms around them both, and the family was together for the first time.

Although he had joy in his eyes, Pamela also saw the fatigue in her husband's face, and said, "Let's go home, Martin. You need a meal and some rest." Martin carried Stanley like the proud father he was while Pamela shouldered Martin's knapsack and pushed the carriage back to the Deweys' home.

"Sarah Jane!" Pamela shouted as they walked up the sidewalk in front of the house. "Sarah Jane, look who is home!"

Sarah Jane opened the front door, and she rushed down the steps to greet the reunited family. Right behind her was the Angel, who had just arrived to visit for the day. The brothers greeted each other with a strong embrace, and then a handshake, and another embrace, and still another handshake.

"Angel! You look like you've grown."

"Too big to be called Angel, my brother. I'm glad to see you have made it home. And all in one piece!" John said as he grabbed his older brother's shoulders.

Sarah Jane led the others up the front steps. "Come inside. Come inside. We can find something to eat and drink, and a chair for Martin."

For an hour, they discussed Lincoln's assassination, his funeral procession through New York City, and Lee's surrender. They listened to Martin's stories of his time in the South, and Stanley took a few steps to show off for his father's applause.

John announced the reason for his unexpected trip to New Jersey. "I have two more letters from Dominic. He sounds like the old brother we know," John announced as he pulled two envelopes from his pocket. John gave the first letter to Martin.

United States General Hospital
Fort Gaines, Alabama
May 1, 1865

Dear Brother John:
Since my last letter to you, matters are not much changed.

I am yet at Fort Gaines, on Dauphin Island, undisturbed in my duties with splendid practice among the sick and wounded from the campaign which resulted in the capture of Mobile.

I returned yesterday from a tour up the Alabama River some eighty miles, where a part of the 13th Army Corps is stationed. We intended going up to Montgomery City, or as near to it as possible, but our grand expedition was ordered back for the present.

The weather here is changeable—some days agreeably warm, others a little too cool—but the probability is that it will soon be warm enough to dispense with a pine wood fire on the hearth, which we have been burning for the past week.

I heard a few days ago of the assassination of President Lincoln. The news took this place almost by storm; the flag on the fort was set at half-mast and guns fired from sunrise to sunset.

We received little information on how the terrible deed was carried into effect. We also heard by the same mail the fate of Lee's army. This victory, however, had to be celebrated, although the glory was not so much appreciated as if the murder of the president had not been committed.

I have a horse now at my service, and I ride about on the island every other afternoon for a few hours. The island (which is some sixteen miles in circumference) I have pretty well explored by this time, the western portion being a dense wood of pine trees eighty or 100 feet high with a layer of bark compound of little scales to a thickness of four to six inches.

They are noble-looking old trees, straight and clean to the top, where birds of many various sizes, and colors, keep up a wild chorus.

The place, however, is very sickly and since my last letter to you all, my associates here have been unwell at various times. They take huge doses of quinine and whiskey, without much benefit as a preventive, and they wonder not a little at me as to why they have their malaria for so long.

They need not wonder at this as I propose them improving with time, acknowledging in the meantime my indebtedness to the manner of my living, with a due appreciation of the blessings from above.

I have written a number of letters to New York since writing to you. Of course, it is too soon yet to receive answers—especially as people are generally lazy in writing.

Send me some letters with news of various kinds. I have nothing to write about here except sickness, which no one requires to know anything of, or flies, which are now covering everything like a pall and are so tame that I have to sweep them away with my hand in order to write this letter. This, of course, will be a good excuse for the blots!

I hope you have received my letters as there has been no regulation before this in the mails. Remember me to all.

We had "inspection" yesterday afternoon (Sunday) during which I made the acquaintance of Confederate General E. "Kirby" Smith. He visited the hospital to review our treatment of his captured soldiers.

I shall put this in the mail bag immediately and hope for its speedy transmission.

A weekly Herald *once in a while will be acceptable by the way of a change here. I will write soon again.*

Farewell for the present.
Your brother,
Dominic

P.S. I have received two more medals that Martin earned while at Fort Jackson. They will go by this mail.

Martin passed the letter to Pamela to read next.

While she read, John told Martin about Dominic's first letter from Alabama and the one from Key West, with the details about their brother's harrowing voyage south on the *Catawba* and short stay in New Orleans.

Martin took Dominic's second letter from its envelope, carefully unfolded it, and began to read.

United States General Hospital
Fort Gaines, Alabama
May 6, 1865

Dear Brother John:
Since writing to you on the first instant, nothing important has transpired, but having a moment to spare, I think I may as well occupy it with the labor of attempting something by the way of practice.

I made a trip the day before yesterday to Mobile City and remained there five hours. I visited the hospitals, two of which are splendid affairs, one the Marine Hospital and the other operated by the Sisters of Charity.

This last one I spent some time in, and of course let the sisters know how pious a Catholic I was and am at present. The city has a Catholic air and a good member of the faith like me felt much at home.

The citizens, now that they are accustomed to the Union forces, go abroad in the evenings and do not act as they did at first, following the example of New Orleans.

The Southerners generally believed that the Northern soldiers would respect nothing when we came, but of late they are changing their opinions and find that what the newcomers respectfully ask and pay for, the old ones demanded and took without ceremony.

I felt well with my trip and shall revisit it if I can shortly. This island is very unhealthy, there being a great deal of malaria generated from the swamps on the verge of which many of the hospital tents are constructed.

But thank Providence (I would say God if I were in the sisters' hospital) I am enjoying splendid health while every one of my associates has been, and some of them yet are, confined to their bed with intermittent fever and dysentery.

They have yet this great important truth to learn, that temperance, yes, straight-out and total abstinence, is the only preventive and guarantee of good health anywhere but more particularly here on Dauphin Island.

My appetite is of the most enormous character, as the waiter imagines, who brings my meals to the table.

I am attending some of the families of refugees on the island. A couple of years ago they would have been called "reliable authorities," who give me a good idea of the whites of the South. The shapes of their skulls differ from those of people in similar circumstances in the North. I think that the few I have thus far seen are very marked in their lack of intelligent expression.

Thank God the Irish, in their poverty and neglect, never deteriorated in the shape of their skulls no matter how the want of food may diminish their bodies—and if their heads have not been filled with learning rather than left empty, the bad ones just get full of the devil, but this is not the case here. If they are not educated, the brain undergoes some change of fatty degeneration and everything about them bears this character.

I pay an occasional visit to the hospital garden, which grows many things that will make me fit to be landed before returning north.

I hope all friends are well. I have written many letters but not yet received an answer. The time appears long in awaiting them.

Write often and send a paper. If you are rich enough, send me a couple of "three-cent stamps" as I can buy none on the island— and it looks shabby to not prepay letters to strangers.

Your affectionate brother
Dominic
Direct to Dr. D.G.B. U.S.A. Gen Hosp
Fort Gaines, Ala.

P.S. I have realized that I neglected to apprise you concerning the whereabouts of my two shipmates on the Catawba, *Dr. Brennan and our young assistant, Paddy Maloy.*

It seems that after their dalliance at the Port of Key West, the pair was thrown into the brig, whereupon they missed our departure. Charging them with desertion was considered, but after Brennan treated the jailor for an infection the man had on his privates, their reward was to leave Key West on the next transport headed to Louisiana.

The two did not arrive in New Orleans until after the bat- tle at Fort Blakeley, and the war was in fact concluded, but they have since been assigned here at Fort Gaines, and we have worked together well and renewed our old friendship.

D.G.B.

"Our brother certainly doesn't have a high opinion of some of our country's Southern citizens," John added with a laugh after Martin finished reading the letter. "It's amazing you two missed each other in New Orleans."

"Dominic will be home soon, John. We can all be together again. It will take him less than another year to complete his medical education. Maybe we will coax the new doctor into having a pint with us to celebrate our reunion." Martin winked at his brother.

"Brooklyn has grown a lot since you left, Martin. We get a hundred immigrants every day. The churches are full. Families are building new houses to the east of our old neighborhood, and our old friends are moving out there. They say we are becoming over-crowded with immigrants who don't even speak English. The new homes are farther away from the Navy Yard, but they are nice and big enough for a large family. The streets you know well—Lafayette, Hart, Willoughby, DeKalb—are extended more than two miles to the east. They run all the way out to Bedford and Nostrand Avenues, and farther—all the way to Lewis. The *Brooklyn Daily Eagle* says they will keep building until they have brownstones on the farms out on Long Island, and they'll build churches, and shops, and schools. Will you move back with us?"

"I don't know, John. Pamela seems to like Hoboken. In her letters, she told me it is a fine place to raise children, and her sister is here. I was a shipbuilder before the war, but while I was at Fort Jackson, I learned to be a store clerk. Every store needs a clerk, so finding a position in Hoboken won't be difficult. We'll have to see how it works out, John. We will have to see. Pamela and I agree that our children need to have a better life than we have had, John. It's all about the children, little brother. It's all about the children."

CALL HIM DOCTOR

June 1866

OF COURSE, IT WAS THE WARMEST DAY OF THE YOUNG summer—Wednesday, June 27, 1866—and the temperature rose to ninety-two degrees in Brooklyn.

Days were never like this in County Galway, Cate thought as she finished buttoning the last button on her beautiful brocade dress. For the first time in their lives Cate, Mary, Biddy, and Pamela needed to wear fancy dresses.

"How will I ever be able to sit in this thing?" she said out loud as she looked at herself in the mirror and thought, *Dominic, you better appreciate what I am doing for you!* She looked pretty. Her brocade dress was multiple shades of blue, and Cate thought it accentuated her azure eyes.

Maggie had experience with fancy clothing and a month ago helped her sisters-in-law shop for what they needed. Pam came over from Hoboken, and together the ladies perused all of the best shops in Brooklyn, window-shopping, touching the material, trying dresses on for each other, and, eventually, each buying a dress for the big evening.

The Bodkins weren't poor anymore, but they weren't wealthy either. They knew this day would arrive, and they had all saved as much money as they could. Mary's stipend from the Duvals continued to arrive from Galway each month, and she covered any shortages that arose from her sisters' purchases of the dresses and other required items of clothing.

The men would all wear jackets, vests, and cravats.

John was accustomed to costumes from his days as an actor, and Lawrence, like Maggie, frequently dressed for a grand evening in the city. Martin, however, felt silly as he adjusted his hat in the mirror and looked at himself wearing a black jacket that came nearly to his knees, a waistcoat of a different color, and a cravat tied into a bow.

Mary had arranged for several carriages to take them all to the Fulton Ferry, and once they crossed the East River, they would ride the horse-drawn trolley to New York's Academy of Music, on Irving Place at 14th Street. The academy could seat three thousand, and it would be the most massive crowd any of the Bodkins had ever been in.

It was a large and festive family group. Dominic was graduating from medical school tonight.

The medical school had only seventy-nine graduates this year, but when combined with several hundred graduates from the university's other schools, the faculty, and guests, the Academy of Music would be bursting at its seams.

As all of the graduates marched in procession to take seats on the stage, it was easy to discern which group of men was the new doctors. For the first time, the medical school graduates of the University of the City of New York were allowed to wear the full-length white coat that was the privileged attire of a doctor. When Dominic was handed his knee-length, white laboratory coat before the ceremony, he looked with pride, and with some amazement, at the black scripted embroidery above the pocket of his lab coat:

Dominic G. Bodkin, M.D.

The candidates for degrees sat on the stage, facing the guests in the audience, and Dominic scanned the crowd looking for his family. The light in the large theater was not designed for performers to look at the theater's patrons, and since he was sitting in the performers' vantage point, it took Dominic a long time to find his family out in the crowd. The family's attention was all on Dominic, and when he found them, he made eye contact with Cate and waved to her. All eight of his adult guests waved back at the same time.

The speeches and the introduction of the graduates from the university's other colleges dragged on for more than two hours before, finally, the president of the Medical Department of the university, John William Drapper, M.D., L.L.D., took the podium.

Drapper began his speech, "Gentlemen"—the graduates were all men—"we are here today ..." He proceeded eloquently for nearly an hour before he began to award the diplomas.

"Herman R. Ainsworth,
James Henry Anderson,
Ferdinand Axt,
Milton Julius Baker."

Each man walked across the stage, shook Drapper's hand, and accepted his diploma.

"Henry Balser, Jr.,
Robert W. Beers,

Charles William Bernacki,
Dominick George Bodkin."

With the pronouncement of Dominic's name, Martin let out a Rebel yell—YEEEHAAA—that would have made the boys in New Orleans proud and could have raised the South from its ashes. The Bodkins in the gallery hugged and kissed and slapped each other on the back.

Martin said to John, "If we had paid more attention to Uncle Laurence and his strange stories, or if we had asked more questions, it might be you or me standing there." John barely remembered Uncle Laurence, but he agreed wholeheartedly, and he beamed with pride when his brother walked across the stage.

President Drapper went on ... and each of the graduates followed Dominic across the stage.

"Jessie P. Brown,
James Brown Burnett,
Aaron Y. Hanson,
and finally,
Emil August Wettengel."

After the president's presentation of diplomas, all seventy-nine graduates became new doctors. Some were from New York City, some from Brooklyn and farther east on Long Island. Most were from other parts of the United States, including several from the Southern states. A few were from other countries.

Sitting by herself in the middle of the audience was Cate's friend, and Dominic's ninth guest, Mary McCann. Mary was a nurse.

New York Academy of Music

Mary and Cate met years ago while Cate worked at Gramercy Park with the Massey children, and the two women had maintained a friendship for all of the years since. Months after Cate moved to Brooklyn to work for the Hornblowers, Mary left the doctor's office where she worked in Manhattan and took a job at Saint Mary's Maternity Hospital in Brooklyn.

Cate had introduced Mary to Dominic when he first began medical school. Mary judged Dominic to be a man who was committed to his beliefs. He was a little strange and extremely intelligent, but most of all, she thought he was caring.

A month ago, she had agreed to leave her job at Saint Mary's Maternity to become Dominic's nurse and office attendant. Mary knew she was taking a chance on Dominic.

As she sat by herself, alone with her thoughts among the invited guests, the talented young nurse wondered if she might be a little infatuated with this strange, gawky man—or if she might be a bit crazy. She had relinquished an excellent position at Saint Mary's Maternity. Still, she had a sense of confidence that the medical office of Dominic G. Bodkin, M.D., at the corner of Cumberland Street and Greene Avenue in Brooklyn—opening on Monday morning—would run like a well-oiled machine.

56

A WELL-OILED MACHINE

DR. BODKIN'S FIRST OFFICE OPENED ON MONDAY, July 2, 1866, and by the following Wednesday morning, Mary had answered at least one of her ponderings.

No, she was not infatuated with him. It only took two days for her to understand that.

She loved people, patients, especially; she loved medicine, making people better; she loved organization, a place for everything and everything in its place.

But no, she was definitely not infatuated with him.

The months flew by for Mary, and after five years at the Cumberland and Green location, Dominic's practice had grown substantially. He needed a new office—more examining rooms, more seats in the waiting room. Dominic was too busy with patients to look for a larger place, so Mary did the searching and eventually found a big home for sale on the corner of Jay and Sands Streets that would fit their needs. Dominic went with her one evening to look at it. He said, "Yes," and they moved.

Six years later, the office at Jay and Sands seemed as though it had always been home to Mary. Patients were comfortable in the examining rooms, plenty of storage for extra supplies and patient charts, and the doctor was happy. There was a place for everything, and everything was in its place. But both Mary and Dominic agreed he was wasting too much time traveling in Brooklyn's traffic. Horse-drawn delivery carts and large passenger carriages were double- and triple-parked on the streets in front of shops and businesses, making it nearly impossible for John Alpers' two-horse, four-wheeled carriage to pass. It seemed to Mary that every other day Dominic would return to the office from the hospital, only to be sent back into the congested traffic immediately to see a very sick patient at her home in another part of Brooklyn. Too much time in the carriage. Too much wasted time. Mary knew she had to fix this.

Bobby Emmett was only ten years old, but he could run like the wind. He ran through the streets of Brooklyn every day after school. The weather didn't matter to Bobby—rain or snow, he ran. In the winter, like all the other boys his age, he wore a tweed paperboy's cap and a heavy cloth jacket to keep warm. His family lived on Myrtle Avenue, only a few doors away from Mary McCann's roominghouse. Mary had seen Bobby running up and down Myrtle, but she had also seen him running blocks away, over by Dr. Bodkin's office at Sands and Jay Streets. One day Mary saw Bobby running toward her, and she waved at him to stop.

"Hello, Bobby! You surely are a good young runner."

"Hi, Miss McCann. Thank you. Running is fun, and I can run farther than any of the other boys—faster, too. But my mum tells me I'm too hard on my shoes." The pride in his voice was evident, and Mary noticed Bobby wasn't even winded while he talked to her. Mary had an idea. She looked at his well-worn leather shoes and realized she'd have to talk to Bobby's mother first.

The temperature was in the forties on New Year's Eve, December 31, 1877—but it was going to drop to twenty-five degrees by morning, and New Yorkers were expecting snow in the middle of the night. Having lived thirty-nine winters in Brooklyn, Alpers understood winters could be nasty.

Alpers stood on the sidewalk next to Dominic's brand-new hansom cab. He expected the doctor to burst through the door of Saint Mary's Maternity Hospital at any second, and he watched as a young lad came running up St. Mark's Avenue and stopped next to his cab.

"Are you Mr. Alpers?" It had taken only fifteen minutes for Bobby to run from the doctor's office to the side door of the hospital.

"Indeed, I am. What can I do for you, son?"

"I have a message from Miss Mary McCann. It's for you and Dr. Bodkin. Miss McCann says the doctor is needed at Patricia Felton's house as soon as possible. She says the doctor must go to her house straightaway, before he comes back to the office."

The side door of the hospital flew open, and Dominic ran down the steps to his hansom.

Alpers grabbed his medical bag. "Doctor, Mary says we have to go immediately to Patricia Felton's house. She sent this boy, a runner, with the message."

"Mary sent you, lad? What's your name?"

"Yes, sir. Bobby Emmett, sir. Are you Dr. Bodkin?" Bobby looked at Dominic and saw an intensity, combined with kindness, in his eyes.

"All right, John. Let's get the lead out! Felton lives over on Schermerhorn, near Hoyt."

Dominic reached in his pocket for a couple of coins and gave them to the boy. "The Feltons' house is back in the direction of the office, Bobby. Will you ride back with me? It's going to be dark soon."

"Thank you, sir. I will. I've never been in a cab before, sir." Bobby put the coins in his pocket. They jingled with the fifty-cent piece Mary had given him.

Alpers helped Dominic close the folding doors at the front of the cab. Bobby was already in the other seat. The hansom's front doors theoretically protected passengers from stones and mud sent flying from the horse's hoofs, as well as the other equine matter that could splash on a passenger. Each door had a glass window on top, so passengers could see where they were going. The front doors and side windows totally enclosed Dominic's new hansom cab, and, with his overcoat, hat, and a blanket he kept in the cab, the doctor would be warm on the coldest nights.

Alpers climbed to the rear of the cab and into his elevated seat. He turned up the collar of his woolen greatcoat and wrapped a scarf around his neck to cover his mouth and chin. He always turned the wide brim of his squashy, brown hat down.

With one flick of Alpers' long horsewhip, the two tall wheels of the hansom rolled forward. Pulled by a single horse, the two-wheeled cab was light and quick on the road. With its low center of gravity, it maneuvered easily for Alpers through Brooklyn's congested streets. Back at the coach house at 290 Clinton, Alpers still maintained the old, four-passenger carriage for Dominic. The doctor only used the larger carriage on infrequent outings with Lawrence and Maggie, or when he was transporting a couple of priests from the diocese. But, traveling from his office to a hospital, or a patient's home—it was always the hansom.

Alpers had worked for Dominic for twenty years, and he never had any regrets about it. His schedule was never his own, and the days were long—and sometimes cold or too hot—but he loved working for the doctor. The man who had become the most preeminent doctor in Brooklyn treated his coachman with respect and dignity, and Alpers reciprocated. Sometimes, Dominic called Alpers "John," sometimes he called him "Mr. Alpers." John never called Dominic anything but "Dr. Bodkin," but he felt he was part of the doctor's family.

Alpers knew the streets of Brooklyn like the back of his hand. He knew where the pharmacies were if the doctor needed to restock something, where the grocers and restaurants were to get Dominic another mug of coffee. The coachman even knew the streets on "the other side of the tracks," where the doctor might make a house call to a patient's run-down tenement. In 1877, there were still Irish immigrant "haters" in Brooklyn, and at six foot, three inches tall and one hundred and ninety pounds, Alpers often provided some security for Dominic. He would carry the doctor's black leather medical bag from the hansom to the hospital's door or to a patient's front porch.

He drove slowly when Dominic had been awake too long and was taking a nap in the cab, but on the way to the Felton home on Schermerhorn, Alpers could hear Dominic talking to Bobby Emmett, so he knew the doctor wasn't sleeping, and he could drive quickly to Felton's. After Felton's house, it would be back to the office, then back to Saint Mary's, and last, back home to 290 Clinton.

Some sleep would be required—later.

DA BUM COULDN'T
THROW A STRIKE

January 23, 1902
Saint James Cathedral, Brooklyn

8:55 AM: *Me sons and me nephews were all grown men, and they would use the brass handles on the coffin to lift Dominic to their shoulders. They had their instructions from the undertaker and were just awaiting the signal to begin.*

As the cousins stood along the sides of me brother's mahogany casket, I saw that Stanley was the biggest of them all. He was thirty-eight years old now—with muscles bigger than mine ever were. The lad began working for me at the ironmongery more than twenty years ago—while he was still in secondary school—and the first time I knew he was as strong as an Irish cob was the day I watched him lift a keg of nails into the back of a cart.

Stanley and I had a relationship that was different than I had with me other sons. He was the oldest and I had missed the whole first year of his life, and that probably impacted how I felt about him. But working together every day, we had become real friends. We talked about things a father and son didn't always talk about. The other lads had taken off in their own directions, and I became closer to Stanley than I was with the others.

In the beginning he was my delivery boy. After a year he moved up to stocking the shelves in the shop, and later he was dealing with our suppliers and customers. In the years he'd been with me, Stanley learned more about the ironmongery business than I'd ever known. He could tell a builder or a homeowner the best hammer to buy or the correct nails to use for a particular job. A homeowner was always asking how to affix new brass shutter hinges, or the drawer pulls his wife had selected for their fancy brownstone, and Stanley always had the answer.

We worked six days a week at the shop, from eight in the morning until six—except for the afternoons when we went to Atlantics baseball game. At home, after Pamela fixed our dinner, we'd drink some whiskey while we worked on the inventory and tallied up the cash receipts to do our banking. Stanley was good with the numbers and he had a fine eye for quality hardware. The lad had a real imagination for a new product, and insight into what our customers would want to buy.

Two of me other sons were doctors. They were smart, but Stanley knew his trade and had a way with people that would get him through.

I knew me days were numbered and, thankfully, Stanley did the lion's share of the work at the shop. Most of the responsibilities of the business were his now, and I'd been thinking I should change the name of the shop. BODKIN & SON—RETAIL & WHOLESALE IRONMONGERY would look good in me front window.

We'd worked hard together and we both loved baseball. A memory of a Brooklyn Atlantics game flashed through me mind as the lads worked as a team and hoisted Dominic's coffin to their shoulders ...

<hr />

"STRIKE ONE!"

"You're fookin' blind, ump! The ball was high!" I remembered how Stanley cupped his hands around his mouth when he hollered at the umpire who was calling balls and strikes. A chorus of catcalls and boos

from the other Brooklyn fans made the umpire glare into the grandstand and signal that the pitch was at the batter's waist. "IT WAS RIGHT DOWN THE MIDDLE!" he shouted back to no one in particular.

With two outs in the bottom of the sixth inning, the Brooklyn Atlantics trailed 6–2 and it looked like our rivals—the New York Metropolitans—would win again. I had hoped we might pull off the upset against the Metropolitans after Brooklyn's Charlie Householder and Tug Wilson hit back-to-back four-baggers to start off the fifth to give us the lead. But the Atlantics' 2–1 advantage quickly vanished. Leading off the top of the sixth, our pitcher, Sam Kimber, was tagged for a pair of doubles by the Metropolitans' third baseman, Dasher Troy, and their big catcher, Henry Oxley. Then Kimber was plagued by his frequent control issues and had to give up the mound to Jimmy Conway. I went to take a piss while they changed pitchers.

"Da bum couldn't throw a strike, Stanley," I complained when I got back to my seat. "Want something to eat?"

"One of each, Billy!" I called to the guy hawking bags of peanuts and popcorn. The men sitting next to us passed the bags down the row of fans, and I sent a quarter back to Billy. As usual, Stanley took the peanuts and I ate the popcorn.

The Atlantics mounted a furious rally in the ninth inning but fell short again. This time we lost 9–6. The 1884 season had become a disaster for the Brooklyn team.

We left the grandstands at Washington Ball Park and walked up Fourth Avenue toward Flatbush on our way home. "Wait till next year, Stanley." He had his big hand on me shoulder as we walked home.

"Don't worry, Da. We'll be better next year ..."

58

OCTOBER 1890

MORE THAN 100 YEARS HAD PASSED SINCE THE THIR-
teen American colonies declared independence from the British.
The multiple wars fought, on both land and sea, by the Americans during this period were punctuated by brief outbreaks
of peace. It was a century of change throughout the world, but
especially in Brooklyn—a city still in its historical infancy. It
was a time of strife and anxiety, but it was also a time of inno-
vation and growth.

Seventeen seventy-six had been a momentous year, marking
the beginning of the American Revolution and the birth of a new
country. France was a crucial American ally in the Revolutionary War against the British. Still, twenty years later, America and
France were at war with each other, as naval battles were fought
in the Atlantic and in the Caribbean, over unpaid American
debts. In the early 1800s, the Americans fought the Barbary Wars
against Muslim corsairs in Morocco, Algiers, Tunis, and Tripoli.

For generations, the United States fought with Native Americans. The colonial Americans fought the Indians all over the
newly defined United States map.

For five years in the 1860s, Americans fought with each other over the issues surrounding slavery in the American Civil War. The North battled the South, while brother fought brother.

Winning wars allowed the United States to expand its modest beginnings on the shores of the Atlantic across the North American continent to the Pacific, and from Canada in the north to Mexico in the south. Expanding in both population and landmass, America benefited from the height of the Industrial Revolution, which saw the transition from hand production methods to machines. The American standard of living improved because of the enhanced efficiency of manufacturing, as well as the availability of new products that resulted from mechanized production.

In the last half of the nineteenth century, each month saw the arrival of thousands of immigrants from European countries, resulting in a population growth that fed the manpower needs of the factories and farms and increased the demand for products. The new immigrants fulfilled both sides of the "supply and demand" equation.

By 1890 Dr. Dominic Bodkin had worked incessantly at his medical practice for a quarter of a century. He spent more time at his office, or the hospital with his patients—or with John Alpers in his carriage—than he ever spent at home. Frequently Dominic's only sleep came in his hansom cab as he traveled throughout Brooklyn to a patient's home or Saint Mary's Maternity Hospital. Often, his sustenance was only another cup of black coffee. He was a general practitioner and a surgeon, but his specialty had become obstetrics. The European immigrants were producing offspring at an incredible rate, and Dominic was delivering three or four babies a day, seven days a week.

In addition to his medical practice, Dominic filled his days with hours of service to the New York Physicians' Mutual Aid Society, the Catholic Benevolent Legion, the Knights of Columbus, the Diocese of Brooklyn, and Saint Cecelia's Parish. His list of charity patients was long. He offered the same ministrations to a depraved outcast or a poor beggar that he gave to a wealthy aristocrat. The indigent never received a bill. Many of the priests of the parishes in Brooklyn were his patients. A priest never received a bill for Dominic's services. He cared for the nuns who worked at the orphanages, the hospitals, and the schools. The doctor never billed the good sisters.

Dominic worked so much that his family and friends were concerned about his health. They encouraged him to take some time off, to relax a little, to rest a little. Dominic listened to their pleas but ignored them for months, or more likely, years. His patients needed him. His nephew Marty would be joining his practice in a few years—after graduating with the class of 1894—and sharing his patients with Marty would significantly reduce his daily workload. Dominic decided he would hold out for Marty before he took a vacation. It would be less than four years.

Among Dominic's patients was the Right Reverend John Loughlin, the bishop of the Diocese of Brooklyn. He was Dominic's good friend as well. The bishop was the one priest to whom Mary McCann sent bills for Dominic's services. "He can afford our services, Mary. Go ahead and send him an invoice," Dominic instructed Mary years ago.

Monsignor Ed McGoldrick, Dominic's pastor and also his patient, had asked Dominic to take a lead role in the preparations for Bishop Loughlin's golden jubilee celebration. Dominic obliged, but the planning consumed much of his time for months and had increased the doctor's physical manifestations of fatigue. The doctor was wearing down.

The weekend-long event was to be one of the most impressive civic and religious demonstrations ever witnessed in any city in the United States.

It began with a public reception on the evening of Friday, October 17, 1890, at the Brooklyn Ice Skating Rink. On Saturday morning, Bishop Loughlin celebrated pontifical Mass at Saint James Cathedral on Jay Street.

Dominic was the keynote speaker at the Saturday afternoon banquet at the Brooklyn Academy of Music, where he was seated on the dais next to Monsignor McGoldrick. The head table included Bishop Loughlin; James Cardinal Gibbons; three archbishops: Michael Corrigan, John Ireland, and Henry Elder; and several other bishops. Hugh Grant, the mayor of New York City, came over from Manhattan for the banquet. Loughlin was a baseball fan, and McGoldrick had arranged for the Brooklyn Bridegrooms' manager, Billy McGunnigle, to sit at the head table between the mayor and James McMahon, a shipping magnate and prominent benefactor of the diocese. Dominic's speech was delivered eloquently. He spoke of his friend's accomplishments and his dedication to his beliefs. "This man from County Down," Dominic said of Bishop Loughlin, "has a willingness and the ability to work tirelessly for the poor."

At the conclusion of Dominic's remarks, the crowd stood, cheered, and applauded for Bishop Loughlin for several minutes. After the closing blessing, a gaggle of newspaper reporters and well-wishers pressed in front of the dais. All were trying to get the attention of Bishop Loughlin.

Monsignor McGoldrick found Dominic and led him away from the crowd by the arm. McGoldrick said, "Thank you for all your help and your well-delivered speech tonight. I'm sure Bishop Loughlin appreciated your words. Dominic, I know you are the doctor, and I am the patient, but let me tell you, my friend, in my opinion, you do not look well. You look exhausted. Take some time off to rest. Will you do that for me, Dominic? For your family? Please, for your patients?"

Later that night, Dominic was among the dignitaries who led a massive torchlight parade of men from all of Brooklyn's parishes as they walked through the streets of Brooklyn and past Bishop Loughlin's villa-style residence. Dominic was tired when he arrived at the bishop's residence and remembered what McGoldrick had said.

The three-day celebration concluded with yet another parade on Sunday, for which the organizers were planning for twenty thousand Catholic school children to march in the bishop's honor along Brooklyn's streets, lined with maple and oak trees at the height of their fall colors.

The events of the weekend transpired precisely according to the plan. Even the late October weather was warm and dry.

59

MAGGIE

December 20, 1894
290 Clinton

ANNIE CAME BACK INTO THE DINING ROOM AND
poured Maggie and Father Kevin McCann each a last glass from
the second bottle of Bordeaux. The visiting priest from County
Galway enjoyed his wine, and Maggie was pleased that the Bordeaux had paired beautifully with the roasted lamb.

If he was anything, McCann was persistent, and Maggie had
not answered his question. "As I said before, Maggie, I only knew
your husband as a young, skinny boy from Briarhill. When did
you and Lawrence meet?"

"Lawrence loved his time in Briarhill, Father. When we were
younger, he used to tell me about his childhood." Maggie looked
wistful as she ran a finger around the rim of her crystal glass.

Even though she had just met McCann a few hours ago, there
was something about the Irish priest that inspired Maggie to
expose her soul to him—to tell him the truth.

"Lawrence and I rarely ever speak to each other anymore,
Father. Not real conversations, anyway. We go places and we are
seen out in public together, but it's just a façade. Actually, we've

had a terrible relationship since the first year of our marriage, when we had trouble conceiving a child, and then I lost two babies during pregnancy. Nothing was right between us after that."

Kevin saw the forlorn look in Maggie's eyes as she continued. "But my husband had many fond memories of Briarhill, and when we first met, he loved to tell me stories about playing games with his brothers, running through the green meadows close to their home. He remembered Briarhill as a magical place.

"Never did I think he was too skinny. Lawrence said he never had much of an appetite as a boy, and he didn't eat much. Part of that may have had to do with having older siblings fighting over every lumper and scrap of stirabout his parents could put on the table. Of course, the trip across the Atlantic was difficult for him. He told me that every once in a while, on the voyage, Cate or his mam would sneak him some Berwick cockles they had secreted away. Those little candied treats probably helped him survive the ordeal. Anyhow, when I first knew him, he was tall and lean. Shirley Neylon, the lady the children lived with after Mam and Da died, must have fed him well."

Father McCann had been through similar conversations with parishioners, but he was taken aback by this woman he didn't know. "Sometimes, Maggie, it's helpful to think of the better times—the good days. When did you two meet each other?" Kevin persisted with his question, but this time it was an attempt to redirect the conversation.

"Let's see." She thought for a moment as she placed her index finger under her eye to make sure a tear didn't escape and run down her cheek. "My family came across in 1850, when I was nine. We had been here for a few years when Lawrence and I first met. We were young teenagers playing in the streets near our homes. We played 'hide and seek' and 'tag.' We all played together. So, I might have been thirteen when we met, and, I guess … that would make him fifteen. Life was simpler, then, Father," Maggie mused as she took a sip of wine.

McCann saw Maggie's expression change as she moved on with her story. "The Bodkins moved into their sister Mary's house at about that same time. You probably knew Mary back in Galway. Bishop Laurence married her and Dan the year before the rest of the family left Ireland. Anyway, Mary left Galway a few years later with Dan and their two boys."

Kevin remembered Mary and Dan, and he told Maggie about the Diocese of Galway's buying their house for his rectory.

"Poor Mary." Maggie rolled her eyes and swirled the last of her wine around her glass.

"Anyway, she missed her family terribly, and after her mam and da passed away, she insisted that she and Dan move to America. She was pregnant with her second child when she learned of her parents' deaths and wanted to wait until the baby was strong enough to make the trip. They waited more than a year before they left Galway. Her husband died on the voyage. The ship was only two weeks out of Liverpool. It was the fever, I assume—what a shame. Bishop O'Donnell expected to travel to America with them, but his health had taken a turn, and he never made the trip. He died shortly after that. In 1855, wasn't it, Father?"

"Yes. Bishop Laurence died in '55. I knew he would never be able to make it across to America. He spent much of his time working with the poor and visiting the sick, exposed continuously to their diseases and infestations. The bishop eventually caught the fever. I was on the altar at his funeral."

As Annie began clearing the dinner table, Maggie continued telling of the Bodkin children's fates once they landed in Brooklyn. She paid particular attention to Nellie, who took her parents' deaths so hard.

"Being her pastor, I got to know Nellie well over the years, Maggie. She was quite a legend in our part of County Galway."

"Please, Father, tell me about her. All I ever heard was that she was 'surviving' after she returned to Galway. But living alone. Lawrence told me Nellie always had a friend, an imaginary friend—a fairy—she was always talking to."

"Well, it all starts with Bishop O'Donnell's will," McCann answered. "When the bishop passed away, his estate held several parcels of real estate and, as it turned out, none of his nieces or nephews wanted any of the properties. So, they were all put up for sale. Most sold quickly—and for good prices I might add—but no one had an interest in the Briarhill cottage."

"That is the same cottage where the Bodkins lived before they came across, isn't it?" Maggie asked.

"Yes, it is. Anyway, the diocese wanted Bishop O'Donnell's estate finalized so that they could distribute checks to his heirs. So, the diocese bought the Briarhill cottage and told me to look after the place. It made sense since I was closer to the property than anyone in Galway City.

"After Nellie came back to Galway, she was living with Dan's parents, and I met her when they all came to the ceremony to finally set the monument on Bishop O'Donnell's grave. The little cemetery on the Claddagh is beautiful, by the way.

"Nellie and I got to talking, and I told her about the family cottage in Briarhill. I told her the diocese owned it, and it was empty. That did it. She wanted to know all about the place and three weeks later was living in the family cottage. All by herself, mind you. She cleaned the old place up, fixed the thatched roof in a couple of places, painted the whole cottage herself, and put some stones back where they had fallen off the walls around the property. She had the place looking wonderful."

"It sounds like a lonely life to me, Father. How did she get around?"

Georgie

"In his will Bishop Laurence left me a horse, but I didn't need another old horse, Maggie. I still had my Irish cob, Georgie, you know. So, since the cottage came with a small two-wheeled cart, I gave Nellie the extra horse. So now Nellie had a cottage, a cart, and a cob."

Kevin knew all about Sadhbh, but a conversation in the confessional was sacred. He went on, "I don't know anything about her imaginary friend, Maggie, but Nellie became a legend in the townlands around Castlegar. She had the time to help anyone with anything. She could cook. She could clean. She could care for children. Somehow, she knew how to do everything. She even learned how to midwife and how to care for the sick. Amazing, she was! For years she helped everyone—for years and years. She was indeed a legend. Nellie loved the children. Especially the little ones. She would gather four or five small children around and tell them stories. The children would be spellbound. '*Fadó* ... ,' she would begin each tale. *A long time ago* ... The children would be mesmerized while she told stories about ancient Irish kings and goddesses. I guess they were all stories about fairies, but they were all good fairies. She was a storyteller who inspired many children, Maggie.

"Nellie was at Mass every morning. She cleaned the church. Cleaned the rectory. Even laundered the altar cloths for me each week. When Dominic arrived at Saint Columba's a couple of weeks ago, I rode him out to Nellie's grave. He was glad to see her final resting place."

Kevin finished his glass of wine. "She was an artist, too, Maggie. Did you know that? As Nellie went around Briarhill and Castlegar, she was always known to have a sketching pad and her charcoals. She would draw the children, and the cottages in the townland, and sketched the landscapes and the walls. There are a lot of walls in Galway, Maggie. She sketched Saint Columba's and even did a beautiful charcoal of my old cob, Georgie. She was very talented."

"We knew Nellie died, Father, but how?"

"I'm not sure, Maggie, but she didn't come to Mass one morning, and that was so unusual I became worried. I rode Georgie out to the cottage and found her inside. She was sitting, peacefully, in her favorite chair. Dead. Probably her heart gave out. It was a shame. Everybody loved her. She helped so many of my parishioners. They all came to her funeral, and a dozen carts full of families came out to the cottage for the burial. We buried her right on the edge of the family property, out in Briarhill. Right along one of the walls. Her da might have built the wall himself. Maybe he did, Maggie. Maybe he did."

"What a shame, Father. At least it sounds like she was happy at the end."

"I believe so, Maggie. It was so sad. She loved life, and she never gave up." The priest made the sign of the cross. "You were telling me about the other children back here in Brooklyn."

"I was. Let me see." Maggie collected her thoughts for a second.

"Before Mary arrived, Dominic was still living in the rectory with Father Fitzpatrick. God bless good old B.J.'s soul. He had a difficult death. Something—consumption or something—was killing him from the inside. Máire, his housekeeper, nursed him through until the end. He was a good priest."

She went on to talk about the impact the priest had on Dominic's life and about the siblings' moving in with Mary. "The timing of Mary's arrival couldn't have been better for poor Shirley Neylon. Shirley was getting old, and she had buried her husband months before. She was raising Lawrence and John as a grandmother would. What a saint she was! Biddy still lived with Shirley, and she was a help in the evenings, but by now, Biddy was working somewhere, as a maid, I think, during the day. Biddy's real name was Adelia. Did you know that? Anyway, Shirley herself passed on a few years after her husband. Paul was his name. They were a good family to the Bodkins."

Father Kevin could see Maggie was reaching way back into her memory for the rest of the story from all those years ago, and the last glass of Bordeaux seemed to have given Maggie a second wind. The wine didn't seem to be helping her recall ... but it did loosen her tongue.

The bells at the top of the front door jingled to announce Dominic's return from the hospital.

Annie Corliss scurried down the hall to get the doctor's coat while Mr. Alpers put the hansom away for the night.

"You two seem to be getting along well." Dominic smiled as he looked at Maggie, Father McCann, and the empty wine bottle.

"Ah, Dominic!" Kevin was happy to welcome the doctor home. He still had not learned much about Lawrence's successful career from Maggie.

"Glad you made it back. Maggie has been filling me in on the years after you all arrived in Brooklyn. Did you deliver twins, Dominic?"

"Yes, twin boys. Giuseppe and Antonio Caputo!"

Annie brought Dr. Bodkin a small plate of leftovers and a steaming cup of black coffee. She knew to serve the doctor a late dinner.

"You and Lawrence must be great friends. Living here together with his family for all these years," Kevin said to Dominic, in an attempt to find out more about Lawrence.

"We are, Kevin. We are."

"Lawrence and I are great friends. All four of us brothers were. They called us 'the Bodkin Boys.' John and Lawrence did a lot together, especially after John got over his youthful experimentations. John was an actor for a while. Did you know that?" Dominic responded, thinking he had told the seventy-three-year-old priest everything while they were together on the *Gallia*. *Maybe,* Dominic thought, *the wine is making the old priest a little forgetful.*

"There were a few years where they worked together at the coal yard. People would pay good money to keep warm in the winter. Coal, that's where Lawrence made all his money. Well, most of it anyway. A few of his real estate deals worked out pretty well, too. He loves to buy and sell buildings. That is what occupies most of his time these days. He is very successful. Saved every nickel he ever made. Let me phrase a little differently ... Lawrence never spent a nickel of his own money. Ha! Ha! He and Maggie have a beach house in Sea Girt down on the New Jersey shore. They spend most of the summer at the shore."

Dominic went on. "I was never much of a real estate deal maker myself, but I do have a few properties. Several, I guess. Cate is staying in the one over on High Street. Daisy lives in my house next door. Did she come over for dinner? Daisy is Biddy's daughter.

"Martin lives in my building on DeKalb—number 999 DeKalb. It's a big house, but he needed it with all those children."

"How many children did you tell me he had?" Kevin asked.

"Six boys and three girls. They lost a daughter in her first year. Five of them still live in the DeKalb house.

"Martin's my hero. Did I tell you that, Kevin? He teased the hell out of Lawrence when we were younger, but always with good intentions. He's brave and strong, and a survivor. We were all afraid that Stanley would grow up fatherless, but Martin came home. Came home from the war, like he said he would, and he made something from nothing. I teased him sometimes and called him 'the progenitor.'

"His son Marty covered my patients while I was in Ireland. Marty is a fine young man and will be a good doctor. Did I tell you that another of Martin's sons, George, is just about to begin medical school? George will be excellent in his practice.

"I've always been happy that I've been able to put these buildings to good use—provide homes for the family. I have a few empty lots here and there, too. Brooklyn is growing, you know. The building lots will be worth something someday. I've never sold any real estate. Just bought it. I've worked most of the time, Kevin. I love what I do. Delivering babies takes a lot of hours, but my office attendant, Mary McCann, keeps me on a schedule. You'll meet Mary, too. She's been with me since the beginning. Right, Maggie?" Dominic tried to bring Maggie back into the conversation while he ate his dinner.

"We brothers stayed closer with each other than we did with our sisters. Cate was off working from the first moment the *Cushlamachree* docked. Mary was like another mother to us when she eventually arrived with her family. Nellie had her problems after Da and Mam passed. Poor girl. And Biddy was always great, but after she married Mickey Flanagan, we didn't see much of her. Funerals and weddings were about it."

Dominic's tone got a little nostalgic. "We were all lucky to have each other, though. It could have gone bad in the early, difficult years without the help and the guidance of Father Fitzpatrick and the bishop. Sometimes we struggled to keep our large family fed and clothed. We all worked as much as we could. After school and in the summers. Painters, plumbers, office work. In the beginning, Lawrence was a stair builder. We did it all. Old B.J. Fitzpatrick, and the people from his parish, were terrific to us.

"It's difficult for me, Father, to see so many of my family already gone. We indeed came a long way from Briarhill, and I have no complaints about my life, but to know my parents never enjoyed a breath of the freedom—or the prosperity—the rest of us have enjoyed in America is a fact that haunts me. Now I'm losing my brothers and sisters. Biddy has been dead for more than three years and losing John a few months ago made me realize it's time to be looking at saying goodbyes rather than hellos."

Dominic decided not to eat his last bite of potato and wiped his mouth with the napkin. "John's death was very difficult for me. As his doctor, I feel like I failed him. I know that's not accurate—with some diseases, Father, a physician can do nothing, but it hurts so much when a doctor loses a patient. When the patient is your brother, it hurts even more. Not that losing Biddy didn't hurt, but after she married Mickey, it was as though she left us then. Visiting with Nellie at her grave two weeks ago helped me to know her a little better. She was still a child when she went back to Galway. She was only seventeen, you know. I never knew her as an adult, but seeing her grave, and our cottage—her cottage, I should say—helped me to understand her and what her life had been about. We both deal with death a good bit in our professions, Father. You prepare my patient to meet his Maker while counseling the grieving family with images of the glorious meeting between God and His newest angel. I, on the other hand, try my best to prevent you from having to do your job while always knowing I will eventually fail. I imagine that's why I have made obstetrics my life's work, Father. I know I will usually succeed in helping a child take the first breath."

Dominic yawned. He was tired. He would go to his office in the morning to see patients and tell the expectant mothers how many weeks it would be before their babies arrived.

Maggie was nodding off with sleep. Too much talk. Too many stories she knew too well—too much wine.

Father Kevin was exhausted himself, but he was anxious to meet Lawrence tomorrow evening.

60

LAWRENCE

December 21, 1894

"YOUR MARTINI, MR. BODKIN, WITH TWO OLIVES AS you requested, sir. And for you, Mr. Lynch, a scotch on the rocks. It's a blend, a fine blend. I hope it's acceptable. Gentlemen. Let me know when you are ready to order lunch."

Tommaso Donzella worked as the parlor car waiter on the Montauk Division of the Long Island Rail Road. He was average in height with broad shoulders and black hair slicked back, revealing his receding hairline. His waiter's uniform was a spotless white jacket worn over a white shirt, a long white apron, and black trousers. His shoes were highly polished, and his red bow tie perfectly shaped.

"Thank you, Tommaso," Lawrence said. "We'll let you know when we are ready."

Donzella nodded to the two executives and moved on to another table. The twelve passengers in the parlor car were sitting at tables for six, set with sterling silverware on white linen tablecloths. This afternoon's trip was from Patchogue to the Long Island Rail Road's Flatbush Terminal in Brooklyn.

As the train rattled along through Sayville and Oakdale, Lawrence said to his attorney, Thomas Lynch, "It was a beautiful piece of property in Patchogue, Tom. If I don't buy it, I hope someone in the family does so that I can visit for the summer holidays."

Lynch loved putting real estate deals together. He believed there was a degree of "art" to making a real estate deal, and another client of his owned almost a mile of property on both sides of the Patchogue River, including the sandspit that hooked out into Great South Bay. It was the first day of winter 1894, and Lynch had encouraged this three-day trip in the hope Lawrence would be interested in buying the entire mile of Patchogue property. He understood selling the property—nothing more than a beach and sand dunes—would be difficult with the temperature at the freezing mark and snow flurries blowing around the grey skies. But as any attorney would, Lynch would charge both of his clients if he could have them reach an agreement on at least part of the undeveloped property.

"It has potential, Lawrence. Maybe you and Dominic should buy it, as partners, and hold it for Martin's sons. His boys will surely be successful in their medical practices. One of them will want to buy if from you when he can afford it. Let's face it, Lawrence, these young men aren't going to work as hard as Dominic has. Dominic doesn't have a wife and children—he's married to medicine. Your nephews will get married to women, and their wives will want to get out of Brooklyn in the summers. Just like Maggie does."

Lawrence knew Dominic should have returned from his trip to Ireland the previous night, and he made a mental note to discuss the possibilities with him in the next day or two.

"I wouldn't wait too long, Lawrence. Pristine waterfront property like this on Long Island won't stay on the market very long," Lynch prodded his friend.

"Let's order lunch, Tom."

Lynch caught Donzella's eye, and the waiter came back over to the table.

"Ready for lunch, gentlemen? We loaded last night's catch from Montauk on board in Patchogue. Our specials today are either fluke or striped bass, both prepared almondine and served with broccoli."

The two men ordered lunch and another round of cocktails.

As they waited for their meals, Lawrence watched the scenery as the train passed the more populated Long Island towns of Amityville, Massapequa, Wantagh, and Merrick, stopping for two minutes at each town's small station.

Tom could be correct, Lawrence thought, as he noticed the relative congestion in these communities closer to Brooklyn. *Dominic and I better not wait too long,* he decided.

The trip from Patchogue to Brooklyn took every bit of four hours. The train stopped at twenty stations, including a more extended stop at the Richmond Hill station in the Jamaica section of Queens, where many passengers rushed to change trains. It was half past three in the afternoon when the conductor finally announced the Flatbush Avenue station. A cold wind caught the passengers by surprise as they stepped onto the platform. Lawrence pulled his hat low to keep it from blowing off, and the two men walked toward the waiting carriages.

"Tom, I'll talk to Dominic tonight and get back to you right away. Thanks for spending the time with me for the last few days. Merry Christmas, my friend."

The two men shook hands, and each climbed into a waiting carriage for the trip to his home.

Lawrence closed the carriage door and said, "290 Clinton, Billy." He had developed a habit that was common among a particular class in Brooklyn. Anyone in a servant's position—like a coachman, a train porter, or a hawker at a Brooklyn Bridegrooms baseball game—could be called "Billy" if you didn't know his real name.

After the short trip, Billy hustled Lawrence's suitcase up the steps, and Lawrence heard the familiar jingle as he let himself in the front door.

Three miles away from the Flatbush station, Dominic was in a meeting at Saint Mary's Maternity Hospital with his nephew Marty and his good friend Dr. John Griffin. Dominic had covered Dr. Griffin's patients in the past when Griffin was taking time off, and, for the last two months, Griffin had returned the favor by overseeing Marty as the young doctor managed Dominic's patients during his trip to Ireland.

The three doctors were reviewing patient charts and discussing Marty's performance. The plan had been for Marty and Dr. Griffin to split Dominic's cases while he was away, but as it turned out, Marty was able to cover much more than half the load, and, according to Griffin, the young doctor had performed well.

"It certainly looks like you received a good medical education at Columbia, Marty," Dominic was happy to say as he looked over the charts stacked on his desk. "I think you and I should continue to work together, adding George when he graduates. A lot can happen in four years, but I'll be ready to retire by then. I enjoyed my trip to Ireland, and I plan to be doing more traveling."

Marty smiled at the praise and confidence. "It's hard work, Uncle Dominic, but I enjoyed it, and I'm looking forward to working with you as a partner—junior partner, I should say."

"Marty, I'm going to head home to enjoy dinner with Father McCann and your aunt Maggie. Lawrence will be home tonight, also. Stop off and meet Father McCann later, if you are in the neighborhood."

Dominic headed to the hospital's St. Mark's Avenue exit, where John Alpers was waiting for him.

"If I may be so bold, Dr. Bodkin," Alpers responded to Dominic's fatigued appearance, "you look poorly, sir, and you could use a couple of days of rest, to recuperate from your voyage."

The ride home took only fifteen minutes, and Dominic spent most of the time mulling what Alpers said, and also remembering what Monsignor McGoldrick told him four years earlier at Bishop Loughlin's banquet.

Alpers and McGoldrick were two people who knew Dominic well, and they were both right. Dominic was afraid it would take him another four years to adjust his work schedule, and by then, it could well be too late.

<hr />

The bells above the front door jingled, and Lawrence greeted his brother in the hallway.

"Hello, Dominic, you look no worse for wear after your trip," Lawrence lied. "Welcome home!

"Will you join us for a cocktail, Dominic? Did Father McCann teach you to have a drink on your travels?" Lawrence joked with the teetotaler as they walked down the hall to the parlor.

Annie Corliss knew better and smiled as she handed Dominic a cup of black coffee. "Dinner will be ready in a few minutes, Dr. Bodkin. It's a glazed ham with scalloped potatoes and creamed spinach, and I've baked an apple pie for dessert."

"As always, it sounds wonderful, Annie. We'll be right in.

"It is good to be home, Lawrence. My trip was exhausting but filled with fun and memories. It's amazing we all lived in that tiny cottage. The rolling meadows are still beautiful, and we had more room to run across the fields in Briarhill than we would have had here in Brooklyn. As expected, the weather was cold and damp." Dominic took a sip of his coffee. "Most of the old friends we knew in County Galway are all gone now. The Flynns and Mickey Bellew are dead. The Duvals are all gone. I couldn't find any O'Donnells, but Father Kevin brought me by Uncle Laurence's grave. His monument is quite impressive. Nellie's grave is lovely too, Lawrence. I wished you were with me to see it. She's buried out behind the cottage. Right next to a wall Da probably built himself." Dominic ushered Lawrence into the dining room. "Ireland is as green as we remember, Brother. Our old friend Bruce Boehmcke was the captain on our voyage home on the *Gallia*. He and Father Kevin got along well. How was your trip to Long Island? Patchogue, was it?"

"It was Patchogue, Dominic, and from the train, I got to see the rest of the towns along the south shore of Long Island. There is growth out east. Merrick and Wantagh are booming. Many from Brooklyn seem to be moving there. They are starting to build in Patchogue. It's a vibrant community with more than a few shops in the town. The train station is busy, and the beach on Great South Bay was beautiful, albeit cold and windy yesterday. A lot of potential as I see it. I can imagine it being delightful on a summer day. The train service was a little long but comfortable. Tom Lynch was pushing me hard to buy a piece of property on the waterfront. I have some ideas about that. We can hash them out after dinner."

As the brothers walked arm-in-arm into the dining room, followed by Father McCann and Maggie, Lawrence said to Dominic, "Glad you are home, Brother. Do the Galwegians at least remember the Bodkins? We are still one of the 'Tribes' after all!

"Dinner smells great, Annie. Let's eat, everybody."

61

THE 4:47

February 1895

"DOCTOR, WE WILL HAVE TO LEAVE VERY SOON IF WE are going to catch the 4:47 train out of Flatbush." The tone of John Alpers' voice was telling everyone to leave the house and get into the carriage.

"Lawrence! Father Kevin!" Dominic shouted. "John says we have to leave this minute if we are to catch the train."

"I'm ready," Kevin McCann shouted back from the top of the steps with his suitcase. "Come along, Lawrence. It sounds like they are serious." Kevin was looking forward to this trip. Lawrence and Maggie had taken him into Manhattan several times and down to the Jersey shore—all the way to Cape May—but this would be his first trip out onto Long Island. He was returning to Ireland next week.

Maggie was pushing Lawrence out the bedroom door with his suitcase. "Now, Lawrence, please be careful you don't have too many drinks on the train before you eat dinner. You know how badly you sometimes behave, when the gin gets to your brain before dinner gets to your stomach. You don't want to embarrass your brother."

The three men rushed out and into Alpers' waiting carriage.

Chaos! Dominic thought. *How can three grown men have so much trouble leaving on an overnight trip? Helping a woman to deliver triplets isn't this chaotic.*

"I told Lynch and Hamilton we would meet them in the parlor car," Lawrence informed the others. "Hamilton will be there, no doubt, but Lynch is a different story. He's a little scatterbrained."

The trio rushed out of the carriage and into the station at 4:40. "Plenty of time to spare," Lawrence chided his brother. "Is it time for a cocktail, Kevin?" Lawrence prompted the Irish priest.

To nobody's real surprise, Lynch and Jack Hamilton were already sitting comfortably at a table, and Tommaso Donzella was serving them two scotches.

"Hello, Lawrence! Dominic!" Lynch greeted the Bodkin brothers.

Dominic had previously introduced Father McCann to Lawrence's banker, Jack Hamilton, during a fundraising event at church. Dominic effectively knew everyone in Brooklyn, and everyone knew "the Doctor." Jack's mother-in-law was the Bodkin family's old friend Maria Teresa Drennan. McCann and Hamilton greeted one another, and Lawrence introduced the priest to his attorney, Tom Lynch.

"Hello again, Mr. Bodkin. Welcome back," Tommaso said to Lawrence. "Martini, sir?"

The sun had already set as they passed the Richmond Hill station, and Kevin turned his attention from the darkness outside the train's windows to the meal Tommaso was serving, and then to the men with whom he was traveling. The conversation rambled from politics and the economy to baseball. The breadth of knowledge all of the men showed on this variety of topics impressed Kevin. His four companions varied greatly in age and education. Jack was the youngest at forty, and Lynch the oldest, around sixty. Educationally, only Lawrence did not have a degree to compare with the doctor, the lawyer, the priest, and the banker.

The seventy-three-year-old Irish priest knew nothing about baseball or local politics, but Father Kevin had learned during his visit to America that the economy was booming along the eastern coast of the United States. As they rode along Long Island, he listened to the others' conversations and participated in each round of cocktails served by Tommaso.

Kevin was asleep in his chair when the locomotive's huge iron wheels screeched to a halt at the Patchogue train station.

It was well after ten o'clock when the carriage brought them to the front entrance of Hamann's Sandspit Inn. Looking into the darkness, Dominic could see they were right on the water. As they walked to the front door of the inn, Dominic caught the smell of the saltwater bay. As he did more and more as he got older, he once again thought of that morning fifty years ago when he stood on the deck of the *Cushlamachree* as the family enjoyed its first view of the American shore. Lynch had reserved all five bedrooms in the inn for the night, and Mrs. Hamann was relieved when her boarders finally arrived. The attractive innkeeper greeted the men at the door, and she welcomed them to Patchogue.

"The bedrooms are all on the second floor, gentlemen, and you'll find the bath at the end of the hall. I'll have breakfast ready at seven o'clock."

Dominic's room had a window that faced Great South Bay. The light from the moon reflected off the bay's small waves as Dominic looked across the inn's grassy yard and small beach. He knew then that he and Lawrence would buy some of this beachfront property. The doctor wondered only how much they would buy. The trip here was for the benefit of their banker, and, of course, he wanted Father McCann to see Long Island.

Mrs. Hamann served a hearty breakfast the next morning in the dining room that faced south to the bay. It was a bright February morning, and the sun made the water sparkle.

At breakfast, Lynch explained the plan for the day was to take a walking tour of the waterfront property and then a carriage ride from the inn through the village of Patchogue, and finally back to the railroad station.

The morning was unseasonably warm, and the men were comfortable as they set out for the short walk from the inn toward Maiden Lane. The side roads in Patchogue were little more than dirt paths, and Maiden Lane was simply two wagon tracks that were about seventy-five yards parallel to the bay. Lynch and Dominic walked together as they led the others.

Lynch was surprised when Dominic asked, "Don't the Younglings live somewhere on Maiden Lane?"

"They do, Dominic. It's the house on the left. Do you know the Younglings?"

"I've known them for years. From work, you know. George Youngling is a doctor in Manhattan. The Caranicus family lives on this lane too, don't they, Tom?"

"Here on the right, Dominic. You know them also?"

"More work, Tom."

Maiden Lane reminded Dominic of the boreen that ran by the cottage in Briarhill. The only thing missing was a stone wall.

After walking about fifty yards, they came to the prime property Lynch wanted to show the brothers and Hamilton. The empty waterfront lot was on the right, and it extended the short distance from Maiden Lane down to the water's edge. Perpendicular to the property, from the left, was a narrow walking path called Furman Lane. It was only about fifteen feet wide, and Lynch said there were a couple of houses which were several hundred yards down toward the end of the path.

The group made a right off Maiden into the waterfront property and toward the bay. They trudged through the brush and sand, and after only a couple of minutes, they were at the water's edge. Looking east, they could see a large hotel less than a quarter of a mile away. Lynch, a good salesman, pointed to the building and explained it was called the Clifton House. "A fine resort, and a sign of the desirability of the Patchogue waterfront." They continued walking along the water in the direction of the Clifton House and made their way back onto Maiden Lane before backtracking to the inn.

Mrs. Hamann had more coffee ready for the men, and they sat back down in the breakfast room to enjoy the view.

"I'm sold, Tom," Dominic said. "How much should we buy, Lawrence?"

"Definitely the waterfront lot, Dominic, and we should get as much of the available property as we can from Maiden up along Furman. In years to come, Martin's boys and their families can all split it up." Lawrence knew his brother well, and he was confident Dominic would accept his plan.

"I agree, Lawrence. Jack and Tom can work out the details. Let's get our bags, see the town, and catch an early train. I've got some patients to see."

THE DOCTOR'S HOUSE

1898

DOMINIC AND MARY MCCANN HAD WORKED TOGETHER for thirty-two years.

The original office in 1866—at Cumberland and Green—was a distant memory for Mary. She couldn't even remember the name of the first patient who walked through the door when they set up his practice on the Monday after he graduated from medical school. She did remember, though, that when the man said he was sick and needed help—but had no money—Dominic didn't bat an eye. He simply put his hand on the man's shoulder and said, "Let's take a look and see what we have here."

Their current office, on Sands and Jay Streets, had become known throughout Brooklyn as "the Doctor's House."

For three decades, Mary had also been part of Dominic's family and spent as much time at 290 Clinton as she did at her boardinghouse room on Myrtle Avenue. She had dinner almost every evening with Maggie and Lawrence and after dinner helped Annie with the dishes while she waited for Dominic to return from the hospital. When he did eventually come home, they would review the day's activity at the hospital and plan his schedule for the next morning. John Alpers would always give Mary a carriage ride home before he fed and groomed his horse for the night. Her only real friends, outside of the Bodkin family, were Annie and Alpers. Her life was her work, and she loved her life.

When Lawrence died suddenly in February of 1896, Maggie was devastated and struggled to hold herself together. Mary stepped in. She helped Maggie with selecting a cemetery plot, planning for the wake, and Lawrence's funeral Mass. In the months after his death, Maggie was withdrawn and suffered from his loss—so Mary and Annie ran Dominic's household.

Without question, the office routine had been different for the last four years. The addition of Dr. Martin Bodkin, M.D., as a partner in 1894 made a significant difference to Mary McCann's daily routine.

Before the doctors arrived each morning, however, Mary's schedule was the same. At seven every morning, she greeted and made her way past six to eight patients who were waiting on the porch. She unlocked the front door, let the patients into the house, and directed them to the waiting room.

Next, she went through the medical area, past the examining rooms to the kitchen, where the coffee pot was sitting on the stove. After the coffee was brewing, she organized the patient charts for those who were in the waiting room. Mary had done this for years, but now she allocated the files between two stacks. One stack for Dr. Dominic and one for Dr. Marty.

She still had a difficult time addressing Marty as Dr. Bodkin, but she was doing better. Having watched him grow from a boy to a man, he would always be Marty to her, and in her heart, there was only one Dr. Bodkin.

After organizing the patient charts, her next task was to take an inventory of the medical supplies in each of the four examining rooms to make sure everything was in its proper place. A cleaning woman came to the office in the evenings and made sure the examining rooms were spotless. Mary, however, always restocked the medical supplies herself in the morning, before the doctors arrived.

Dominic usually went to Saint Mary's Maternity Hospital at an early hour to see how yesterday's babies were doing, so Marty was generally at the Doctor's House first to see the group of waiting patients. Marty was a great doctor, well-educated, personable, and precise. He could find the medical cause of a symptom almost as well as Dominic. Mary thought Marty's surgical skills were better than Dominic's, but she could tell he had slightly less interest in obstetrics than his uncle.

"It's a beautiful morning, Mary," Marty would always greet her.

"Good morning, Doctor. We have eight in the waiting room this morning, and two of them are pretty sick; you have to see them before the others." Mary was not much for small talk with Dr. Marty when patients were waiting to see him. "Your uncle should be in shortly. Only two mothers delivered yesterday."

Marty didn't drink coffee, so he went straight to his office as Mary guided the sickest patient to the first examining room.

By the time Marty was seeing the first patient, Mary was directing the second into another examining room and getting the charts for four new patients who had arrived. The waiting room, and the porch, would be full for the rest of the day, but Mary only organized the charts for those who made it into the waiting room.

When Dominic finished his rounds at the hospital, Alpers would drop him off at the back door of the Doctor's House, so he would not have to spend time with each of the patients on the front porch and in the waiting room. "As much as I love to talk to my patients, there are only so many hours in the day, John," Dominic explained to Alpers years ago, when he made the decision not to go in the front door anymore.

"Good morning," Dominic called as he headed for the coffee pot. Mary gathered a stack of patient charts and met him at the door to his office.

"George is coming in today to spend the day with us, Mary. He's completed his two-week rotation at Sloane Maternity Hospital under Dr. Vorhees, and he has a couple of days off. Please be a dear and see if you can find the spare stethoscope for him. It's only going to be a little more than a year until he is with us every day. Let's be sure to introduce him to any of the patients he doesn't already know."

Mary would never tell anyone, but she could hear the excitement in Dominic's voice. She believed George was his favorite nephew.

Mary had known the brothers since the boys were children. They were different. They were both smart men and had a passion for medicine. Each loved the idea of having a life, as well as the risk of death, in his hands, and she knew they would be able to handle the responsibility.

Marty was big and athletic looking. And, like his father, he had an aggressive edge to his personality. His father always seemed to Mary like someone you might not want to cross.

George, on the other hand, was tall, thin, and awkward. He was quiet. His personality was subtle. He would enjoy being able to cajole another man, dominate him mentally, rather than physically.

Mary loved both of the boys as family, but, as was common with any change, the transition from "the Doctor's House" being Dominic's domain to eventually being "Marty and George's Office" would be difficult for her. She wasn't sure if she would make it through to the inevitable conclusion.

"I know right where the extra stethoscope is, Dr. Bodkin," Mary said, going straight for the equipment cupboard. "What time do you expect him?"

"George should be here within the hour, Mary, and when I go to the hospital this afternoon, he will come with me. Two more women should be delivering today. It will be a good experience for him. I'll get to see what old Dr. Vorhees taught him about delivering babies at Sloane Maternity. George seems to have a strong interest in maternity. The nurses over at Saint Mary's will love him. He'll tease them, and they'll flirt with him."

Mary guided Dominic's first case into the examining room, and she went out to the waiting room to find the next patient waiting to see Dr. Bodkin.

❊❊❊

Dominic's decades-long commitment to the medical profession, combined with his altruism, had left him with little time for a personal life—and no wife or children. When Martin told him twenty-two years ago that he and Pamela were naming their new son Dominick George, the bearded physician was overwhelmed with pride, even though they planned to call him George. Of all Martin and Pamela's children, George *was* his favorite. George and his uncle Dominic had become good friends, and now that George was about to graduate and join his uncle and his brother in practice, Dominic wanted everything to be perfect as his favorite nephew began his career. He even wanted to make sure George found a wife, and finding a wife for George among the nurses at Saint Mary's Maternity would not be an easy task for Dominic.

Most of the nurses at Saint Mary's were nuns, and Dominic knew the sight of a group of Sisters of Charity in the hospital's hallway presented an intimidating image that would usually not engender feelings of immediate attraction in a young male. The sisters wore all white habits, scapulars, and veils. The veil covered a headdress that was about four inches tall and flat across the top of a sister's head, coming to a point on both sides. A small wimple covered a sister's ears.

Dominic and George—the doctor and medical student—walked through the doors at the end of the Maternity Ward.

"Let's face it, Uncle, I'm pretty sure I know more about young women than you do, at least young women who aren't pregnant yet. In our practice of medicine, you are the teacher and I am the student, but when it comes to picking girlfriends for me, Uncle Dominic, I'll—"

"But, George, Nurse Fisher is attractive." The grey-haired, sixty-four-year-old physician tried to keep his voice low as he spoke. "She comes from a nice family, and the other nurses say she is a fantastic cook." George shook his head and kept walking across the Maternity Ward toward the nurses' station to collect their patients' charts.

The young nurse working the station at the end of the third-floor ward was definitely not one of the Sisters of Charity, and Madeline Fisher appeared to have smiled at the tall, good-looking medical student. George thought she was quite attractive, but he noticed she had heard some of his uncle's words, and, in embarrassment, she had returned her gaze to the medical charts on her desk.

The hospital's third floor had two identical wards: the Maternity Ward and the Labor Ward. Each was a large, rectangular room with tall ceilings and six large windows on either side. Each of the twelve beds was under a window, and the abundance of sunlight gave a feeling of warmth to the otherwise sterile rooms. A nurse's station was at either end of each ward, and a crucifix hung in the middle of one wall.

Saint Mary's was always a busy place. A mother and her baby usually stayed for a week in the hospital. After their discharge, a new mother and baby occupied the bed and bassinet within hours.

As usual, the Maternity Ward was busy.

"We have four women to see here today, George, and two to visit over on the Labor Ward. Then we'll go over to Saint Catherine's Hospital and help out with some of the charity cases," Dominic said, handing him the medical charts. "Let's see Mrs. Hurlihey first." They stopped at the foot of a bed with a nameplate which read: "MRS. KATHLEEN HURLIHEY AND BABY SHEILA."

"Hello, Mrs. Hurlihey. My name is George Bodkin. I'm in my last year of medical school, and I'll be working with Dr. Bodkin this morning. How are you feeling today?"

Dominic smiled at Mrs. Hurlihey and nodded his approval of George's words—a smile generated by pride in his favorite nephew. "Good morning, Kathleen. You are looking better today."

He turned to George. "Mrs. Hurlihey delivered two days ago, and the little redheaded bundle in her arms is Sheila. Sheila arrived in this world at seven pounds and nine ounces."

George put his right index finger under the baby's chin. "Nice to meet you, little Sheila. She's a pretty girl, Mrs. Hurlihey. Isn't she now?" Sheila smiled at George. "Let's have a look at what we have here."

George put his fingers on the baby's belly and gently probed around for any signs of unusual firmness or tenderness. The infant didn't squirm or react with any sign of discomfort. "She has good color and moves her arms and legs symmetrically," George said out loud as he went through a mental checklist. "She's breathing all right, without any signs of effort." He examined her eyes for clarity and then looked in her tiny ears with a scope that allowed him a view into the canal and to the eardrum.

"Are her bowel and bladder functions all right, Sister?" George asked Sister Frances Imelda, the nun who was attending the men on their rounds.

"Everything is working fine, Mr. Bodkin," the nun replied. "And Mrs. Hurlihey is producing plenty of mother's milk for Sheila."

George put his stethoscope in his ears and said, "Let's listen to the baby's heart and lungs." He moved the stethoscope to several places on Sheila's chest and turned the little one over to listen to her lungs. Her heartbeat was strong and her lungs clear.

"Everything sounds fine, Doctor," George said to his uncle. "Will you take a listen and confirm my findings?"

Dominic repeated the examination and nodded his concurrence.

"Has Mrs. Hurlihey's bleeding ceased, Sister?" George resumed his questioning.

"Yes, Mr. Bodkin. She is doing very well. Kathleen has been sitting up in bed and has been able to eat her meals since this morning."

"May I examine your belly, Mrs. Hurlihey?"

Mrs. Hurlihey handed little Sheila to Sister Frances.

George put his hand under the bedsheet to protect the new mother's privacy. He pressed her abdomen carefully with his right index and middle fingers, searching for any lumpiness or tenderness, and then felt to ensure her uterus had contracted back to its normal position.

"It all seems good, Mrs. Hurlihey. Do you feel any pain?"

"No pain, Mr. Bodkin, and my soreness is going away."

"Doctor?" George said to his uncle, again asking for concurrence.

Dominic repeated the physical examination of Mrs. Hurlihey's belly.

"Everything looks good, Kathleen. Continue your bed rest, and I'll be back tomorrow." Dominic patted his patient on her shoulder.

"Thank you, Doctor. Thank you, Mr. Bodkin, it was nice meeting you."

"Very nice to meet you too, Mrs. Hurlihey. Good luck to you."

Dominic and George moved to the patient in the bed directly across the room from Mrs. Hurlihey. Her nameplate read: "CONCETTA LEONE AND BABY ANTHONY."

"Mrs. Leone should be ready to go home tomorrow, Doctor," Sister Frances indicated to Dominic as George introduced himself to the new patient.

The doctor and his student repeated the routine for Mrs. Leone and her baby, Anthony, and then a third time as they moved down the ward to Patricia Burkhart. Finally, they finished with their fourth patient, Lara Boddorff.

"George, we have two ladies on the Labor Ward to see. They should both deliver sometime later tonight."

The men hurried to the Labor Ward on the other side of the third floor. Physically, the Labor Ward was the same in dimensions and floorplan as the Maternity Ward. Still, the evidence of fear and anxiety among the expectant mothers—being fed by the moans and screams of pain from the few women in the latter stages of labor—made the Labor Ward a different place than the cheery and happy Maternity Ward.

"Women are afraid of the pain during childbirth, George, terrified. Our profession is doing a better job for them, but it's not good enough."

"Their fear is understandable, Uncle Dominic. Dr. Vorhees tells our class about advancements in many areas of medicine. It seems we get information every day about new forms of pain medication. Ether is being used in most surgeries as well as in childbirth. New anesthesia products make a patient think she is asleep and not remember the pain associated with the delivery. Scientists are trying to perfect dosage standards."

Dominic introduced George to his two patients on the Labor Ward, and the doctor and student discussed the women's progress with Sister Frances Imelda.

"I'll come back later tonight, Sister. Thank you for your assistance today. There's nothing we can do here now, George. Let's move on."

They went down the back steps of the hospital to the St. Mark's Avenue entrance, where John Alpers was waiting for them. Alpers had a message from Mary McCann. "Mrs. Colleen Delaney is at the office with her six-week-old son, and you need to see the boy. Mary says to hurry back."

"We're going to stop at Saint Catherine's for a few minutes, Mr. Alpers, and then it's directly back to the office. Let's hurry."

Dominic and George climbed into the carriage, and Alpers took off along St. Mark's with his horse at an urgent pace.

"You've learned a lot at Sloane, George. I'm sure you will be able to hit the ground running once you've graduated. What you and Marty have learned in medical school is so much more advanced than what I learned on the battlefield."

George continued to tell his uncle about new products, tools, and instruments that could be sterilized and reused on patient after patient, with reduced risk of infection. "Soon, forceps will be available in different sizes and shapes to fit a woman's body. Dr. Vorhees says the new forceps will reduce the chance of lacerating a woman while at the same time decreasing spinal cord injuries and head traumas for the babies."

Over the past thirty years, Dominic had played a significant role in the advancement of maternity care in New York. His work in Brooklyn had established standards that were accepted in maternity hospitals throughout the United States. But as he listened carefully to his nephew, he visualized Dr. Fox in the surgery tent at Spanish Fort, wiping his bone saw on a bloody rag before moving on to the next soldier. Dominic feared that he wasn't keeping up with the latest improvements his profession was making.

"I'm glad you and your brother are ready to take over for me, George," Dominic said as he let his thoughts drift into the future a little before returning to the problems at hand.

"We have two patients to see over at Saint Catherine's, George. Probably unwed mothers. Many of our charity cases are unwed mothers, and they deserve our care as much as the rich man or the politician's wife. Don't ever forget that, son."

Son? Dominic realized his slip of the tongue, but he didn't think George had heard it.

"Pick up the pace, John," Dominic called to Alpers. "We've got to be back at the house soon."

63

THE PROGENITOR

June 1899

THE SMALL, THATCHED-ROOF COTTAGE IN COUNTY
Galway was a distant memory for Dominic and Martin, as was
the degradation endured at the hands of the British monarchy
by every person the two old men knew when they were boys
growing up in Briarhill. They had forgotten the names of neighbors who had starved to death or walked through the gates of
the Galway Workhouse: *Adults this way and children that way.* The
voyage on the *Cushlamachree* lasted thirty-six days, yet somehow—
fifty years later—they remembered every terrible day and
were still proud their brothers and sisters withstood the ordeal.
They had survived their teenage years in Saint Patrick's Parish—with the help of Father Fitzpatrick and the Neylons—and
were always amazed that each sibling had lived to adulthood.
Then, as young men, Martin and Dominic had witnessed the
destruction of a war that threatened the very fabric of American
society. To the brothers, the fact that their family had traveled
this path over the past fifty years was like a miracle. The family
had made a journey not only from Briarhill to Brooklyn, but it

seemed they had wended their way to a life of prosperity—after so often being close to destitution and death.

Life had taken many twists and turns for sixty-two-year-old Martin. Oppression in Ireland … fear on the Atlantic Ocean … poverty in Saint Patrick's Parish … war in New Orleans … peace in New Jersey … prosperity in Brooklyn. His mother and father had been dead for half a century and Martin's time serving in the war left another void in his life that he couldn't fill. He had missed the entire first year of his son's life. It seemed everything changed for him after returning from the South in the spring of 1865 and finally meeting young Stanley for the first time. Martin's training as a clerk in the army had served him well, and his financial well-being advanced nicely after he returned from Fort Jackson in New Orleans. Martin first worked as a clerk and later as an ironmonger with his own shop.

The American economy thrived after the war, and he and Pamela managed to raise and educate eight children. They didn't have Uncle Laurence to tutor the children, but the school systems in New Jersey, and later in Brooklyn, did their parts, and the children received an adequate education.

⬦⬦⬦ ⬦⬦⬦ ⬦⬦⬦

Today is another chapter in our family's success story, Crom a Boo! Dominic thought with pride as they rode in a carriage from Martin's home in Brooklyn. John Alpers drove Dominic's old four-wheeled carriage and it had plenty of room for Dominic, Martin, and Pamela. The trip would take them across the Brooklyn Bridge, up Broadway to Amsterdam, all the way to Columbia University's new Morningside Heights campus on the Upper West Side of Manhattan.

Even though they had been back and forth across the mile-long

Brooklyn Bridge many times, each trip was still a thrill. Today was a clear day, and they were able to see the Statue of Liberty.

The two brothers reminisced and laughed about the days when the trip to Manhattan required a ride on the Fulton Ferry—and the potential of getting splashed by the wake from another boat. They watched the activity in the bustling city, as Alpers made his way up Broadway.

As Alpers maneuvered his team of horses through traffic on the ride along the cobblestones on Amsterdam, Dominic allowed himself to think back on their lives. He continued to be amazed that just a little more than fifty years ago they were children—penniless orphans—living in random homes throughout a Catholic parish of immigrants in a brand-new city. Now they were riding in a fancy black carriage to a third medical school graduation. His own was the first, at the University of the City of New York; next was his nephew Marty's, at the College of Physicians and Surgeons at Columbia University; and now, Columbia again—another nephew, George. *Sweet Jesus,* Dominic thought, *somebody's been looking out for us.*

The carriage arrived at the ornate iron gates which framed the university's Amsterdam Avenue entrance. The 1899 graduation for Columbia University was in the school's new gymnasium, and most of the family was already seated. Martin took a seat between his brother and Marty, "the doctors."

"Did I ever tell you, Dominic, what I said to the Angel years ago at *your* graduation?" Martin said with a voice that told of years of smoking and whiskey.

"No, Martin. What in God's name did you say?" Dominic answered with a skeptical smile.

"I said to the Angel, 'Little brother, if we had paid more attention to Uncle Laurence, and his strange stories—if we had asked more questions—it might be you or me standing on that stage.'"

Dominic laughed, "You did fine, Martin, just fine. Eight wonderful sons and daughters, and now two doctors." He grasped Martin by his shrunken shoulders and kissed the top of his brother's hairless head. "You did well, Martin. We all did, by God. We *all* did."

⬦⬦⬦⬦⬦ ⬦⬦⬦⬦⬦ ⬦⬦⬦⬦⬦

The graduation ceremony began with the procession of faculty and graduates to which the brothers had become accustomed. The orchestra played the usual march. The faculty wore robes and colorful caps, associated with their respective colleges and universities—the Columbia graduates' baby-blue-colored robes combined with distinctive colors in their caps signifying individual degrees. Columbia was awarding degrees to new lawyers, engineers, scientists of all kinds, philosophers, teachers, and finally, the doctors.

The university's president, Seth Low, made a familiar long speech and awarded the diplomas, shaking hands with each graduate.

The Bodkin family stood and cheered when they heard the name DOMINICK GEORGE BODKIN. Dominic knew that it might be Martin's last chance to yell like a Rebel and to everyone's enjoyment, he did. "YEEEHAAA!" Martin shouted. Dominic grinned. *The boys at Fort Jackson would be proud.*

Alpers drove the Bodkins back to Brooklyn, where the family held a party for friends and neighbors.

The coffee Dominic drank so often had harmed his stomach to an extent from which he would not recover. At times the burn, the pain, was almost unbearable. Hopefully, he thought, he could continue to work for a few more months while he acclimated young George to the real world of being a physician and a surgeon.

Dominic wasn't feeling well and excused himself early. Alpers drove him home.

64

REQUIEM

January 23, 1902
Saint James Cathedral, Brooklyn

8:59 AM: *Me and Cate stood together, now off to the side of the vestibule, supporting each other, so we would not feel alone. On January 23, 1902, we were the only two left, and I waited to escort Cate down the center aisle of Saint James Cathedral.*

The last mourners entered through the main doors of the church, and some shook me hand—some just nodded. Others fixed their eyes straight ahead.

A young lady, whom I didn't know, hugged Cate. I was always amazed by me sister and how many friends she had. Cate never married, and at the age of seventy-four, it seemed her life's work of caring for other people's children introduced her to half of Brooklyn's families. She spoke softly with her friend and tenderly wiped a tear from the young woman's cheek.

The vestibule was quiet, except the undertaker was too loud giving more instructions to the family. I'd been able to block the man's *voice out of me own mind and allowed thoughts to meander through the grey images which consumed me memory. The memories were good. Fifty-four years after the* Cushlamachree *sat at anchor in the Narrows, life had been excellent for many of us. For some, it had been exceptional—just as Da told me it would be. Better than it ever could have been in County Galway. For most of the brothers and sisters, though, life was over.*

But the undertaker got to the part where I needed to clear me thoughts of the past and pay attention. I had been in churches like this one too many times before. Biddy, Lawrence, Mary, Nellie, and the Angel were all gone. Now ... Dominic.

Cate gave me arm a firm squeeze and said, "It's time, Martin." She was stoic, standing straight and tall next to me, as we began to move.

Tommy Corrigan led the procession. The skinny eleven-year-old altar boy wore a black cassock and a white surplice his mother ironed just before he left home. Tommy's father told me yesterday that his son was afraid he would not be strong enough to hold the six-foot metal crucifix high above his head.

Tommy was followed by the clergy, walking two by two. Father Robert Foley, the pastor of Our Lady of Mercy parish, walked next to Father Patrick Fahey, from Saint Benedict's. Father John Donlon and Monsignor Edward McGoldrick, from Saint Cecelia's, were next. The bishop of Brooklyn, Charles McDonnell, walked alone, directly in front of Dominic's casket.

The family followed.

Me and Cate were last, and as we walked down the aisle, every head turned to watch. The eyes of Dominic's colleagues from the medical society, his nurses, friends from the Knights of Columbus, and his patients—Brooklynites from all walks of life—all looked at us. Jack Hamilton and his wife, Mamie, were there, sitting with her mother, Maria Teresa Drennan. Tom Lynch was in the pew with them. Mary McCann was weeping. John Alpers and Annie Corliss sat with Patt O'Donnell and Nora Jones, directly behind the rows reserved for immediate family.

The cathedral was full. Every seat, in every pew, was taken. People holding their coats and hats stood along the side aisle—against the doors of the confessionals, and underneath plaster images depicting the Stations of the Cross.

Saint James was the oldest church in Brooklyn. Erected in 1823, it was only the third Catholic church in New York City and the first church on the other side of the East River. Thirty years later, it became the cathedral, and the seat of Brooklyn's first bishop, John Loughlin. In disrepair, it was scheduled to be torn down and replaced by a new cathedral within months. But that day, I saw the altar cloths were perfectly laundered and on either side of the tabernacle, the flames on the white candles flickered—left and right. It was a cold winter day, and the decaying, old church was being warmed from below by the coals glowing in its furnace.

The congregation watched me and Cate take our seats with Pamela in the front pew.

⬧⬧⬧ ⬧⬧⬧ ⬧⬧⬧

The footfalls of two men from the funeral parlor broke the silence in the cathedral. The sound of their steps echoed throughout the church, and I found myself counting the clicks of their leather heels as they walked up the center aisle. Together the men covered Dominic's casket with a white pall. One man carefully placed a silver crucifix on top of the cloth.

Monsignor Edward McGoldrick, the pastor of Dominic's home parish of Saint Cecelia's, was the celebrant for the Mass, and he began the liturgy with the usual prayers at the foot of the altar. Father Donlon stepped into the pulpit and read the epistle. One of the other priests *read the gospel, and then Monsignor McGoldrick came down the six marble steps in front of the altar and walked through the open gate in the communion rail. The monsignor acknowledged Cate and me, and reverently bowed to Bishop McDonnell, who was seated in the sanctuary. McGoldrick positioned himself between the communion rail and the foot of Dominic's casket. He addressed the congregation.*

"We are assembled here this morning to pay the last tribute of respect to one whom we all loved and honored in life. We loved him for his many lovable and admirable qualities, and we honored him because of his magnificent personality."

McGoldrick's voice was loud and powerful, and it reverberated throughout the cavernous church. The mourners were silent as the monsignor continued the eulogy of his friend and physician.

"Within that casket lie two feet that never wearied of responding to the call of duty. There, too, repose two hands that have performed countless acts of kindness and whose firm grasp made us feel we were in the presence of a man; a tongue that will speak no more; and a heart, forever stilled, that beat with loving sympathy for suffering humanity, whether it was a depraved outcast, a venerable servant of God, or an aristocrat surrounded by all the luxuries that money could procure.

"'DOCTOR BODKIN IS DEAD.' The daily newspapers made the announcement, and we, the citizens of Brooklyn, felt that we had lost one of our dearest friends, aye, one of our household. For is not the doctor, in a most particular manner, a member of the home into which his ministrations call him?"

Nodding in agreement, I wiped at a teary eye. Cate put a hankie under her nose.

McGoldrick continued to speak as he paced left and right in front of the congregation.

"The doctor was born near Galway, Ireland, in the year 1834.

"He comes from one of the most distinguished families in the western part of Ireland. The Bodkins and the Burkes, or de Burgos, are names found in connection with every effort made by our forefathers for God or their native land. The Bodkins were recognized leaders among their countrymen.

"The doctor's first preceptor was his distinguished uncle, Bishop Laurence O'Donnell, then bishop of Galway, under whom he studied until his fourteenth year. This fact may no doubt answer the question many of you have so often asked: How comes it that Dr. Bodkin had such a mastery of the English language? How comes it that this man whom we considered self-educated, who claimed no preparatory college as his alma mater, should manifest from time to time such an intimate knowledge of the classics?

"It was within the last few weeks that I learned what I now narrate.

"Standing by his bedside one morning, I remarked at the wonderful depth and clearness of his voice and said, 'Doctor, that voice gives no indication of weakness.'

"His answer was, '*Vox et praeterea nihil ...*'"

McGoldrick seemed to whisper the English translation directly to me.

"... a voice and nothing else.

"This little phrase so appropriately uttered caused us to speak of the classics, and then it was that he told me that at the age of six, he began the study of Greek and Latin under his uncle the bishop of Galway."

The congregation sat with rapt attention—no one making a sound, no one moving—as they listened to McGoldrick tell a story, unknown to most of them, about the life of me brother. A man they thought they knew well.

"When the deceased reached his fourteenth year, the family came to this country. A few weeks after their arrival, a fever carried off both parents. An orphan at fourteen, friendless, penniless, he carved out a path for himself. How well he succeeded, this large and representative audience gives but eloquent testimony.

"When the rebellion broke out, the orphan boy had grown to manhood, and we found him near the cherished goal of his ambition. He had by dint of brawn and brain, and magnificent willpower, reached the graduating class of the New York University Medical College. In a few months, he would have been in possession of his diploma.

"But then, like a thunderbolt from a clear sky comes the awful news that Fort Sumter had been fired upon, the South had seceded, the Union was in danger—the call for volunteers. This news stirred every fiber in every true man's heart and found no more responsive, nor generous, answer anywhere than in the great Celtic heart of Dominic Bodkin."

Pamela gently squeezed me hand in a knowing, thoughtful gesture to acknowledge me own time in New Orleans, as Monsignor McGoldrick narrated that Dominic had interrupted his medical education to qualify in the army for duty as a nurse.

"He remained in the army until the cause for which he had sacrificed so much had triumphed and then modestly returned to continue his studies. He received his degrees from the New York University Medical College in 1866.

"Since that time, his career has been an open book, on every page of which may be discerned, not with the eye of the body, but with the eye of the spirit, the most beautiful illuminations. The subject matter is there glowing with life and pathos, and it needs but the soul of an artist to bring it forth to life and light. Who was ever more devoted to duty?

"What doctor of the present day or generation had such a practice? He was a general practitioner, yet in one branch, obstetrics, his annual returns to the Health Board were, for eight or ten years, more than 1,000 cases each year. Never did he refuse his service when called on, no matter how great the distance, no matter how cold the night or warm the day, or poor the patient. He was, of a truth, a Napoleon in the practice of medicine, knowing no distraction by day or night and sleeping only when forced to do so—often in his carriage, in going from one call to another.

"During these years, his only vacations were practically forced upon him when he was sent abroad by his brother physicians to represent them at the medical conventions of London, Paris, Berlin, and Saint Petersburg.

"In obstetrics, his career will be spoken of in years to come as fabulous and inconceivable. In the eyes of the physicians of the future, his life will appear as extraordinary as does the life of a saint to the ordinary Christian.

"Besides being a great physician, we recognize in the doctor a ripe and profound echo, a charming conversationalist, and an orator of wonderful ability, and a linguist. He spoke Irish, French, and German, and was conversant with Greek and Latin, as we have already intimated. He was a credit to his race and a shining light to his profession.

"When we consider the surroundings of this life just brought to a close, we have to stand in admiration at the great and glorious fight he has fought. Think of that bright and ambitious Irish boy of fourteen in New York some fifty years ago, when our race and creed were despised and ridiculed; when every avenue to preferment was closed; when the only obstacle to obtain even an inferior position was the misfortune of being Irish; when those advertising for help boldly announced: 'NO IRISH NEED APPLY.'

"Now, dear doctor and friend, in the name of the thousands of children you ushered into life, some of whom without your skill might never have been washed in the regenerating waters of baptism, some of whom are here in this church, representatives of every walk of life, aye, even of the priesthood, medicine, and law, I say in their name, 'Thanks and farewell!'

"In the name of the poor, who have lost a friend and a benefactor, I say, 'Thanks and farewell!'

"In the name of all those whom you have assisted by your medical skill, I say, 'Thanks and farewell!'

"In the name of your brother physicians, whoever looked up to you as a model of all that was best, noblest, and most honored, I say, 'Thanks and farewell!'

"In the name of the bereaved family, the tenderest chords of whose hearts vibrated with the purest love for their dear departed, and who looked up to him as does the mariner toward the polar star, I say, 'Farewell, Brother; farewell, Uncle!'"

McGoldrick finished his eulogy where he began, at the foot of Dominic's casket. He placed his right hand on the coffin, closed his eyes, and prayed silently for a moment.

He walked the few steps to the front pew and shared private words with me, Cate, and Pamela before returning to the celebrant's chair on the epistle side of the altar. The monsignor sat motionless for two more minutes, again in silent reflection, before resuming the Mass with the profession of faith and the liturgy of the Eucharist.

At the Communion, two priests distributed the sacred Hosts on the tongues of the Catholic congregation as they knelt at the marble rail between the first pew and the altar. A tenor—an Irish cop from Bushwick—sang "Ave Maria" in Latin.

At the end of the Mass, McGoldrick and his altar boy returned to the casket for final prayers and blessings. Tommy Corrigan carried the sterling silver holy water bucket and the thurible, already smoking with incense. McGoldrick circled the coffin twice, first shaking the thurible over Dominic's remains and then, a second time, sprinkling holy water on the pall.

Corrigan's final responsibility was to lead the clergy, the pallbearers, and the family as we reversed our path to the vestibule of Saint James.

The organist keyed the first few deep notes of the recessional, and Tommy held the crucifix as high as his arms would reach. Monsignor McGoldrick led what sounded to be a thousand resonant voices as they sang:

"Ho-ly God, We Praise Thy Name ...
Lord of All, We Bow Before Thee ..."

Cate and Pamela each grasped one of me arms as we followed Dominic's casket up the aisle. Both women were sobbing. It seemed every solemn eye in the congregation was fixed on us again. Me lip quivered, uncontrollably.

"... Ho-ly, ho-ly, ho-ly, Lord."

Tommy was beyond the rear doors of the church and into the vestibule as the congregation finished the verse.

The family filed out of the church and onto the street, where the pallbearers transferred me brother's body into the shiny black funeral wagon for his final carriage ride—to Calvary Cemetery. We all clung together, sharing embraces and tears.

I saw George and Marty standing next to each other, and I watched as George put his arm around his brother's shoulder. He squeezed Marty's shoulder and quietly said, "Crom a Boo! Big brother, Crom a Boo!"

EPILOGUE

AFTER DAYS OF FULL SPEED AHEAD ON THE ATLANTIC, "Mighty Mo" slowed to a crawl as she triumphantly entered New York Harbor. The tanned, smiling faces of the soldiers and sailors crowded on her decks belied the horrors of the battles just ended. The war in the Pacific had been over for seven weeks. On September 2, 1945, the military leaders of the world had signed the Japanese surrender agreement a few yards from where Jack Bodkin was now relaxing with his friends on the deck of the massive battleship USS *Missouri*.

Jack began his career working for the Associated Press after he graduated from Georgetown University, but World War II resulted in a leave of absence from the AP for duty in the navy. In 1943 an undergraduate degree in business administration, combined with the early experience he had with the AP, earned him a commission as a lieutenant in the navy and a tour of duty as a public information officer on the USS *Marts*. For nearly two years, Jack sailed on the destroyer as it patrolled the mid-Atlantic, providing escort services for other navy ships and searching for German U-boats. Jack's time on the *Marts* brought him to the ports of Bermuda, Trinidad, Recife, and Gibraltar.

In anticipation of an Allied victory over the Germans, the navy reassigned Jack to the Pacific island of Guam—CINCPAC, Commander in Chief Pacific Fleet Headquarters—and assigned him to the Still Picture Pool.

Lt. John S. Bodkin

He arrived on Guam on February 14, 1945.

Five days later, the American invasion of the tiny but strategic island of Iwo Jima began, and only days later, Jack had a photo editor's opportunity of a lifetime.

On February 24, when he selected Joe Rosenthal's iconic Iwo Jima flag-raising picture for distribution to the newspapers of the world, he announced to the navy crew working in the Still Picture Pool, "Men, we can stop making pictures right now. Here is the one for all time."

Seven months later, the war was over, when general of the army Douglas MacArthur, together with high-ranking military officials from Great Britain, China, Russia, Australia, France, the Netherlands, and New Zealand, officially accepted the Japanese surrender. The ceremony took place on the deck of the *Missouri*, as she sat anchored in Tokyo Bay.

"Can you see your house from here, Lieutenant?" Chief Petty Officer Louis Costanzo asked his friend Lieutenant Jack Bodkin.

"Remember, Chief, the war is over, and I asked you to call me Jack. And no, I can't see my house from here."

It was October 23, 1945, and the two navy men were sitting

on the foredeck of the USS *Missouri*. The crisp autumn air temperature, combined with sunny skies, made for a comfortable day as they sat under one of the battleship's giant 16-inch gun turrets. Bodkin and Costanzo were among the lucky few sailors who boarded the *Missouri* at the Port of Guam, only days after the battleship departed Tokyo.

As part of Operation Magic Carpet, the *Missouri* was completing her mission from Tokyo to Guam, then to Hawaii, through the Panama Canal, past Cuba, and back to New York City. For more than a month the *Missouri* had been "home" for several thousand of America's war heroes from the Pacific Theater. The sailors' journey was almost over. The Iowa-class battleship was being guided by four New York Harbor tugboats as she passed through the Narrows.

"What you can see now, Chief," Jack said, as he pointed to the shore, off Mighty Mo's starboard, "is all part of Brooklyn. We just passed Coney Island. You can see the Parachute Jump from miles away. Old Fort Hamilton is at the top of that hill."

The leaves on the oak and maple trees at Fort Hamilton had reached their autumn peak, and Costanzo admired the different shades of red, orange, and gold. Brooklyn was beautiful.

"On our port side is Staten Island, and farther to the west is New Jersey," Jack said, as he acted as a tour guide for the chief petty officer from Wheeling, West Virginia. Costanzo had initially shipped out from the navy base at Norfolk, Virginia, and had never been to New York City.

"How will you get back to your home, Chief?"

"They're going to detach us from our units in a few days," Costanzo answered, "and I'll get a Greyhound to Pittsburgh. In Pittsburgh, I can catch a local bus to Wheeling. What about you, Lieutenant?"

"My house, I mean my in-laws' house," Jack clarified, "is only a couple of miles from the Navy Yard. Hopefully, Dorothy will be on the pier to meet me, but if not, I'll just get a taxi home."

After Jack and Dorothy Hamilton's wedding, two and a half years earlier—on March 13, 1943—Jack had been assigned to the USS *Marts* and then sent on to Guam.

The *Marts*, Guam, and Rosenthal's Iwo Jima flag-raising picture were only memories to Jack now, as Mighty Mo sailed past the Statue of Liberty and the tall office buildings that create the canyons of Wall Street. They passed the Fulton Fish Market at the South Street Seaport, where decades ago, thousands of immigrants first stepped on American soil.

The harbor pilots guided the *Missouri* under the Brooklyn Bridge, and finally to her berth at the Brooklyn Navy Yard. The shouts and cheers from the thousands of sailors, marines, and soldiers on board the *Missouri* were deafening. They were answered by "HOORAY" and "WELCOME HOME" from the massive crowd of parents, wives, children, and friends gathered in the Navy Yard to greet the returning heroes.

As Jack and Lou headed down the gangway and onto the dock, Jack quickly found Dorothy in the crowd on the pier. "She's the redhead, holding the baby, Chief." Jack waved furiously toward his wife. "She sees me, Lou. She's waving now, Chief! I can't wait to meet my daughter. She's already two months and eleven days old." He shouted, "DOROTHY! ... DOROTHY!"

Five years later, on a Saturday morning, as he was backing his Buick out of the driveway of 17 Juniper Avenue, Merrick, New York, forty-year-old Jack Bodkin believed he was the luckiest man in the world.

He had a beautiful wife and family. He had a new house. He had a good job. He loved photography, and his job was buying and selling photographs to newspapers and magazines around the world. The Associated Press paid him to do his hobby!

When he returned to New York after the war, he was promoted to be the foreign photo editor of the AP's New York Bureau. He also stayed in the navy—the Navy Reserve—and today he was Lieutenant Commander John Stanley Bodkin, USNR.

Jack was a newspaperman, and once the family moved from Brooklyn to Merrick, he was now also a "commuter." He was getting used to his weekday travel on the Long Island Rail Road from Merrick to his Associated Press desk at Rockefeller Center in Manhattan. He called it "riding on the LIRR."

But Jack's *coup de grâce*, for every guy he knew, was the beautiful redhead sitting next to him in the car.

Dorothy Hamilton was eight years younger than Jack, and she loved to fish. She was beautiful and bright, caring and funny, and she was photogenic. Jack knew he would have to work on her "love" of sailing.

Jack and Dorothy grew up in Brooklyn, in childhood homes that were less than a ten-minute walk apart. He lived at 897 Lafayette Avenue and Dorothy at 799 Willoughby Avenue. They met at Saint John the Baptist Church, right after Dorothy graduated from Saint Joseph's College for Women in Brooklyn. Their eight-year age difference had undoubtedly kept them from ever being in the same place during school.

A few weeks before the war in the Pacific ended, Dorothy gave birth to the couple's first child. They named her Dorothy and called her "Dotsie."

The new mother and daughter lived with Dotsie's grandparents, Pappy and Frankie Hamilton, in the house where Dorothy grew up across the street from Saint John's. After Jack got home from the Pacific, the new family shared the top floor of the Hamiltons' brownstone.

When the couple's second child, a son, was born, the family moved to an apartment in the Clinton Hill neighborhood of Brooklyn. The address was Apartment #12B, at 325 Clinton Avenue. It was nice, but it proved too small for the family of four. They lived in the twelfth-floor apartment for only two years before the Bodkins moved to Merrick, a town on the railroad's Babylon branch that ran along the south shore of Long Island.

Dorothy Hamilton Bodkin

After he had cleared the driveway and backed across the street, Jack depressed and then eased up on the clutch as he lowered the gear lever on the steering column from reverse down into first gear. The car lurched forward, and Jack turned the steering wheel to the left. The Buick was a big car for the young family of four, but Jack and Dorothy Bodkin were planning to have a big family. The four-year-old black 1946 Buick was the couple's first automobile. They bought it used, two weeks after they moved to Merrick.

Dotsie stood in the middle of the front seat of the Buick, and her little brother, Jackie, sat on his mother's lap. The two-year-old boy could see out the window, and he looked at all of the new houses on Juniper Avenue as they drove down the street. His parents had prepared him for the long drive to his grandparents' summer home in Patchogue with tales of splashing in Great South Bay, and maybe even trying to catch a fish or sailing on a boat. The children were already wearing their bathing suits.

Juniper Avenue was one of the six streets in a small development called Merrick Lee, one of the dozens of post-war communities springing up on Long Island. It seemed everyone was moving out of Brooklyn. Everyone was moving to the suburbs, and Jack and Dorothy weren't going to be left behind. The Bodkins had called the house at 17 Juniper Avenue home for about six months.

"Good morning, Mrs. Alexander!" Dorothy waved out the car window as she said hello to her neighbors Harry and Anne Alexander.

"Hi, Mr. Alexander."

Dorothy loved living in Merrick. Their new house had a large, grassy backyard where the kids could play. The families in the new neighborhood were just like those who had lived in Brooklyn— Irish, Jews, and Italians, older couples and young families with children to play with Dotsie and Jackie. The shops in town were close enough for a daily walk to Bohack's grocery store and Ed's Deli. Dorothy didn't drive, so having the shops in walking distance had been one of her house-buying prerequisites.

Jack estimated the thirty-five-mile drive from Merrick to his parents' summer home could take a couple of hours, but with the Southern State Parkway having just opened to the Bay Shore exit, it might be a little faster. He was excited to see his parents for the weekend and spend Saturday night at their beachfront house on Great South Bay. Their large summer home was on Maiden Lane, in the sleepy Long Island town of Patchogue.

I'm loving life, Jack thought, as he drove past the parkway's exit for the town of Babylon, and he smiled at his wife and two children. *I'll get some good photos of Dorothy and the kids on the beach. Then I'll go for a sail with my brothers.* He was glad he remembered to bring some cigars to smoke with his brothers on the front porch after dinner tonight.

The kids were happy to be going to Grandma and Grandpa's house, too. So much had happened over the last six months for Jack and Dorothy's family that the kids had only seen their grandparents a couple of times in Brooklyn. Spending the weekend in Patchogue was going to be fun for everyone.

As Jack drove along Southern State Parkway, he accelerated the Buick to about forty miles per hour, and the breeze felt good coming through the rolled-down car windows. Dorothy directed the breeze a little by opening the small, triangular vent window to a position that deflected the airflow. She didn't want her long red hair to be too much of a mess when she arrived at her in-laws' house.

Two-year-old Jackie was getting restless, squirming on his mother's lap. Dorothy reached into her bag and produced the season's first box of Mallomars. Dotsie became a beneficiary of Jackie's restlessness.

"I can't wait to see everyone," Dorothy said to Jack, as she tried to avoid Jackie's chocolate-covered fingers. "I talked to Marie on the telephone yesterday and she said the whole family would be at the house today. Betty and Marian were afraid it might be too hot on the beach for their little ones, but they could always go up on the porch to stay out of the sun."

Dotsie and Jackie asked for two more of the tasty chocolate, graham cracker, and marshmallow treats—and got them.

"The girls and I were so close when we all lived in Brooklyn," Dorothy continued. "I haven't seen them for months since we moved. Marie told me your sister would be there, too. Maddie will be in Patchogue for another week until school starts."

Maddie was a New York City school teacher who lived in Patchogue during the summer and worked as a lifeguard and swimming instructor at the town pool. Jack's brother Fran was married to Betty, George to Marian, and Dick to Marie.

"It's going to be a great weekend, Dot. The kids are going to have fun with their cousins, and I can't wait to see everyone."

In the last six years the Bodkin tribe had expanded—eight boys and four girls in the combined families, ranging in age from six years to six months.

Jack's parents, George and Madeline, were both seventy-four years old, and the patriarch was still working at his medical practice. Following what seemed to be the Bodkin family tradition, two of his sons, George and Dick, were also doctors.

George and Dick had offices in Brooklyn and physician's privileges at a few Brooklyn hospitals. The brothers spent time during the summer with their families at neighboring Patchogue houses—only a hundred yards from the beach—on Furman Lane.

Fran was a dentist. He and Betty still lived in Brooklyn but packed their four boys into the car and came to the Maiden Lane house every weekend.

⬥⬥⬥ ⬥⬥⬥ ⬥⬥⬥

A large orange and white construction barricade announced the end of the Southern State Parkway, and arrows pointed the way to Sunrise Highway. The kids were getting restless, and Jack hoped the traffic wasn't too slow on Sunrise.

Jack was happy to see they had only been on the road for an hour and a half when he turned off Sunrise and followed Ocean Avenue down to Laurel Street and took Laurel to Cedar Avenue.

He turned left off Cedar onto Maiden Lane, and fifty yards later made a right turn into his parents' driveway.

As Jack parked the Buick in front of his father's five-car garage, he noticed the hedge on either side of the driveway was taller than he remembered from his last visit. Everyone climbed out of the car, and the kids raced toward the bay.

"Please, Daddy, can we go play with the other kids?" Dotsie and Jackie took off, running along the sand to the water's edge.

Dorothy ran after them as the children splashed in the bay with their cousins. She hugged Betty, Maddie, Marian, and Marie, who were supervising the children from the three-foot-high seawall in front of the Bodkin family's Patchogue home.

Jack walked up to the porch and greeted his parents. His mother's housekeeper, Matilda, met him on the porch and offered a Coke.

George, Dick, and Fran were down at the dock, getting Dick's thirty-foot sloop, *Cormorant,* ready to go out for a sail. The gaff-rigged sloop sported a cranberry-colored jib and a white mainsail. They called out to Jack to hurry and join them. The Bodkin boys were going sailing.

CROM A BOO!

BODKIN

CROM A BOO!

AUTHOR'S NOTE

WHEN I WAS A CHILD, MY FATHER, JOHN STANLEY BOD-
kin, reminded my siblings and me—many times—that our family
was Irish, but being children, we didn't listen to the details of the
stories he told. Let's face it, "Bodkin" doesn't sound Irish. People
often suppose my heritage to be a variety of different nationali-
ties or religions. Russian is a common guess, and some suppose
we're Jewish, especially if they think it's spelled "Botkin," but not
many guess Irish. A good friend of mine told me a few years ago
he had it on good authority that I was Polish. Polish? Jesus, Mary,
and Joseph!!

In all honesty, the Bodkin name is not to be found in Ireland
until well after the time of Christ, but historians report that after
the invasion of the Emerald Isle by Strongbow and the Normans,
a name morphed from Baudekin, and the appearance of Irish
families named Bodkin nearly a thousand years ago is not an
unreasonable estimate.

In 1997, my mother, Dorothy Hamilton Bodkin, taught my
son, Dr. John Stanley Bodkin III, how to make a corned beef and
cabbage dinner for his Greek and Italian roommates. It was Saint
Patrick's Day, and the group of medical students needed a celebration. Before my son's dinner party, he asked me to explain
the who, what, where, and when of our family's Irish ancestry. I
realized I could not even tell him in what Irish county our family
had lived before migrating to Brooklyn.

Several years later, I started to work on a family tree, and to do some ancestry research. It was a few more years before I progressed far enough to be convinced our Bodkin family was from County Galway, and I went to Ireland to further my research. When I checked in at the Park House Hotel, in Galway City, I gave the desk clerk my credit card and passport, and the nice young man looked at me, smiling, and said, "So, Mr. Bodkin, you've come all the way to Galway to claim what's rightfully yours, have you?"

Recently, I met a woman named Mary O'Connor, from the Nun's Island section of Galway, whose mother was a Bodkin, but from what I have learned there are no Bodkins left in Galway. The Bodkin banner, however, still flies proudly in Eyre Square, along with the banners of the other thirteen Tribes of Galway. In Galway's Forthill Cemetery a grave marker has an inscription: "We earnestly beg, dear Christians, to say one Ave Maria for the soul of John Bodkin, of Anagh, his wife, Megg, of Ardfry, and their posterity." I have not been able to connect a line of descent to the late John and Megg Bodkin.

However, Laurence O'Donnell, my great-great-grandmother's brother, was the second bishop of the Catholic Diocese of Galway from 1844 until his death in 1855. He is buried in an area of Galway called the Claddagh. The Claddagh was an ancient fishing village on the western shore of the River Corrib, where the river meets Galway Bay. It's a beautiful location, especially at sunrise. A significant monument marks his grave in a nicely maintained cemetery behind the Dominican friary at the Church of Saint Mary on the Hill.

A seemingly reliable family document indicates that my great-great-grandparents John and Eleanor Bodkin actually had eleven children between 1818 and 1839. Their second child, Catherine, died in 1824 when she was two. Another daughter, an infant named Anne, died in 1830, and twenty-five-year-old Celia died in 1847, only five months before the family left Galway on the

Cushlamachree. One can only imagine that it was "the fever" that killed Celia and spurred her parents' decision to leave Ireland.

In the years before the Bodkins left Ireland, John and Eleanor lived in a cottage a few miles outside of Galway City—a townland called Briarhill—with their surviving children: Mary, Cate, Biddy, Dominic, Martin, John, Lawrence, and Nellie.

The area surrounding Briarhill is beautiful, rolling countryside with property lines marked by the stone walls which are so common in and around Galway. Stone laid upon stone, by generation after generation, over the course of centuries. There are some old houses in Briarhill, but none I saw would I estimate to have been standing in the 1840s. Saint Columba's Church is down the road, in the townland of Castlegar. This was the Bodkin family's church. The church still has the baptismal records for Martin Bodkin and five of his brothers and sisters, showing their baptisms between 1829 and 1839, listing the children's parents' and godparents' names. Additionally, the church has the marriage record of Mary Bodkin to Daniel Devilly, on May 5, 1846. Apparently, when Mary arrived in New York in the 1850s her name was changed to Duval by the customs official registering new immigrants. For simplicity, throughout *Briarhill to Brooklyn* I have called Mary and her in-laws Duval.

Also, I have seen some documents that conflict as to Nellie's age and placement in the line of children. I chose to make her the youngest.

It was likely in March of 1848 that the Bodkin family left Galway, bound for New York on a ship named *Cushlamachree.* The captain's manifest lists the Bodkin family as passengers traveling in steerage, and it shows the ship docked in New York on Easter Sunday, April 23, 1848. *Briarhill to Brooklyn* relates what I have imagined about the Bodkins' lives between 1848 and 1902, sewn together with places, names, and dates I have found to be factual.

There is an alternative theory that some or all of the children returned to Ireland for a period of years after their parents died. Very little, if any, documentation exists about the Bodkin children's lives between 1848 and the middle of the 1850s, and in *Briarhill to Brooklyn* I chose to have them all remain in Brooklyn.

Many of the chapters of this story revolve around Dominic, the oldest son of John and Eleanor. This apparently brilliant, industrious, fearless boy grew to become a successful and very necessary Brooklyn doctor serving the incessantly procreating immigrant community from 1866 to 1902. In several chapters of *Briarhill to Brooklyn*, I used excerpts from actual letters written by Dominic to his youngest brother, John. These letters give tremendous insight into the young medical student's thoughts, feelings, and experiences. In the Civil War chapters, I novelized other pages of his correspondence with John, as he traveled from New York to Mobile, Alabama. It was just outside of Mobile where he participated as a surgeon in the medical tents supporting the nearly fifty thousand troops at the battles of Spanish Fort and Fort Blakeley. As it so happened, the battle at Fort Blakeley was the final major battle of the Civil War, ending just hours after Lee surrendered to Grant at Appomattox Court House.

Though many, if not most, of the scenes, thoughts, words, and images in this historical novel relate to Dominic, I did not write *Briarhill to Brooklyn* because of Dominic. It was written because of one of Dominic's brothers, Martin—the clerk and ironmonger—who lived in New Jersey after the Civil War before returning to Brooklyn and sending two sons to medical school. As you saw, Martin—my great-grandfather—is the *sine qua non* for those of us descended from John and Eleanor O'Donnell Bodkin.

—JACK BODKIN
February 2021

ACKNOWLEDGMENTS

FIRST OF ALL, I THANK MY PARENTS FOR THE MOST important gift—the gift of life—and for molding and educating me as they did.

In addition to my parents, there are many people I want to acknowledge and thank.

I'll begin with my wife, Christine. She was the first to read the original manuscript—she read the first chapter, then read it again, and again, and again; then the first five chapters and the next ten. They read nothing as they do now, but she rallied me every day and allowed our living room to become my office. *Briarhill to Brooklyn* would not be finished without her patience. Thank you, Christine.

Thank you to my daughter, Kate Plemich, for her constructive critiques of the manuscript from the beginning, her uplifting comments when they were appropriate, and the confidence to say "terrible" when it was necessary.

My son, John, joined me on my first trip to Galway. He has encouraged me every step of the way. From one John Stanley Bodkin to another—thank you for your inspiration.

Thank you to the many friends and acquaintances whose names I have used in *Briarhill to Brooklyn*. Their names come from all phases of my life—grade school, high school, college, as well as my business and personal life. B.J. Fitzpatrick and Gene Murtha— you are long gone, my friends, but you will never be forgotten.

Early on, Lou and Jane Costanzo both read the whole book twice. Their input was important on so many different levels.

Other friends who read my book—Tom Lynch, Ginnie Riggs, April Stolfer, Bill Parsons, Dr. Brendan O'Hara, and Jim Poisson—gave me insights and suggestions from a variety of perspectives. The amount of time, thought, and energy they put into *Briarhill to Brooklyn* was amazing, and I can't thank them enough.

Jocelyn Carlson, Max Dobson, and Aja Pollock were my editors at different levels and different stages of *Briarhill to Brooklyn*. Thank you all for not only your knowledge and professionalism, but also for being supportive and encouraging to a first-time author.

Domini Dragoone was the designer and producer of *Briarhill to Brooklyn*. Thank you, Domini, for the beautiful cover and interior design, and for getting me through the technical aspects of publishing my novel.

Diane Rose Dunnigan, PhD, earned her doctorate from National University of Ireland, Maynooth, Department of History, after submitting her dissertation titled *Irish Return Migration from America at the Turn of the Nineteenth Century*. Without a doubt, finding her thesis online, and reading the pages she dedicated to Dominic and his family, was the original inspiration for this book.

Another source of inspiration for me was a 1931 book written by Agnes King, detailing the history of Saint Cecelia's Parish in Brooklyn. In one chapter of *The Story of a Rare Parish* she included the eulogy delivered by Monsignor Edward J. McGoldrick at the funeral of Dominic G. Bodkin, M.D., in 1902. The final chapter of *Briarhill to Brooklyn* includes an abridged, and slightly edited, version of McGoldrick's eulogy.

I first met Kitty Carr in Galway, at the Park House Hotel in August 2016. She demonstrated a real interest in the Bodkins of Galway and encouraged me to learn what I could about our family's history. I give a special thank-you to Kitty for reserving Table

#33 in the Park House dining room for me every day—on several visits—and for taking an interest in my story. On our last visit to Galway, she introduced Christine and me to Peadar Ó Dówd— archaeologist, Galway City historian, and author. Thank you to Peadar for sharing his knowledge and encouragement.

Kitty also introduced me to Ciarán Ó Moráin, a young man from Galway who has served as my English-to-Irish translator. For the reader's convenience, a glossary at the end of *Briarhill to Brooklyn* provides translations of Irish phrases and conversation, as well as my attempt at the pronunciation of Irish words and names. Thank you, Ciarán.

Thank you to Rodney Charman, an amazing English artist, for allowing me to use his painting *Below Deck*, a dramatic image of emigrants huddled in the steerage compartment of an Irish Famine Ship, and for his beautiful painting *Opportunity*, of the *Cushlamachree* on the Galway quay.

On my first visit to Galway in 2016, Rev. Michael Reilly and Olive Stewart put up with three more American tourists searching for their Irish roots at Saint Columba's Church, Castlegar, County Galway. Their patience resulted in locating the children's baptismal records.

Thank you to the Diocese of Galway for their permission to use the image of Bishop Laurence O'Donnell, to Alan Gilliland for his maps, to Dan Buchwach for his illustrations, and to Terry Gurley for his voice, insight, and encouragement.

I moved from Long Island nearly fifty years ago and have had only occasional contact with my Bodkin cousins since. However, the Civil War letters written by my great-great-uncle Dominic to his brother John were provided by my cousins George, Martin, and Marian. Thank you all.

The portrait of Pamela Densmer Bodkin was provided by a distant cousin, Donnette Donley. Thank you, Donnette.

The letter from Patrick Drennan to Maria Teresa Jones was given to me by a cousin on my mother's side of the family, Jessica Drennan. Thank you, Jessica.

In chapter 11 of *Briarhill to Brooklyn*, seven-year-old Nellie is inspired to draw the sights she is seeing on the quay in Galway before the Bodkins board the *Cushlamachree*. Nellie is frightened, but she is calmed by her fairy friend, Sadhbh, and together they produce a beautiful drawing of a young steerage passenger for her mam. Thank you very much to my granddaughter, Sally Plemich, for creating Nellie's sketch *Galway Girl*.

GLOSSARY

IRISH TO ENGLISH
PRONUNCIATIONS / TRANSLATIONS

Meiriceá: America

John, do todhchaí ár bpáistí, ní mór dúinn dul go Meiriceá:
John, for the future of our children, we have to go to America.

Lumper: a potato

Prattie: [PRAY-tee], a potato

An Gorta Mór: The Great Famine

Claddagh: [KLAAD-duh]

Cushlamachree: [Cuish-la-MA-cree]

Séamus: [SHAY-mus]

Siobhán: [Shi-VAUN]

Dúisigh, mo stór. Tá sé ina mhaidin: Wake up, my treasure. It is morning.

Dúisigh, Honora beag: Wake up, little Honora.

Tá sé am chun dul, mo stór: It's time to go, my dear.

Maidin mhaith, Dhaidí. An lá an taistil atá inniu ann?:
Good morning, Daddy. Is today the day of our voyage?

Sea, mo stór. Is é inniu an lá: Yes, my treasure. Today is the day.

Curragh: [CUR-ra-ch], small framed boat with an animal-hide hull

Stróc: stroke

A stór: [ah-STORE], treasure, sweet, lovely

Mo stór: [mu-STORE], my treasure, my sweet, my lovely

Cad is ainm duit, a cailín óg?: What is your name, little girl?

Bhuel anois. Tá sé iontach bualadh le cailín chomh deas leatsa, a Nora bheag: Well now. It's nice to meet a girl as nice as you, little Nora.

Cad as a tháinig do bhád, a Nora?: Where did your boat sail from, Nora?

Cén aois atá tú, a Nora?: How old are you, Nora?

Tá mé trí bliana d'aois!: I am three years old!

LÁ FHÉILE PÁDRAIG FAOI SHONA!: HAPPY SAINT PAT-RICK'S DAY!

Búachaill: [WOO-(ch)ul], boy

Stop na capaill, John!: Stop the horses, John!

Na daoine maithe: the good people, the fairies

Sadhbh: [SIVE]

Coinne ort, a chapall: Come on, horse.

Fadó: [FAH-doe], a long time ago, once upon a time

Clachán: [klaxn], a small village

Boreen: unpaved path

Gaeltacht: Irish speaking

Poitín: [pah-CHEEN], illicit whiskey

Cailín: [KAY-lynn], girl

Stirabout: a porridge of corn, rice, and water

Crom a Boo: Our Family Forever (or Our Castle, Our House)

Go n-eirí leat i Meiriceá: Good luck in America

Agus go n-eirí linn, mo dheartháir: And good luck to us, my brother.

Go sabhála Dia ár dteaghlach: May God save our family.

Táimse ag déanamh go maith: I'm doing well.

Dia dhuit: [JEE-uh-ggwich], hello

Tar isteach: come in, come inside

Gaol: jail

Púcán: [POOH-kawn], a Galway hooker, a boat

Gleoiteog: a small Galway hooker, a small boat

Bád mórs: a large Galway hooker, a big boat

Slán go fóill: Goodbye for now.

Sláinte: [SLAWN-cheh], health, a toast

Eejit: idiot

Ailis: [AY-lish]

Máthair: mother

Athair: father

Quay: [key], pier

Giorraíonn beirt bóthar: Two travelers shorten the road

Máire!: [MAH-ree], Mary

Tá mé fágáil don bhád farantóireachta: I'm leaving for the ferry.

An t-Athair Fitzpatrick: Father Fitzpatrick

Go han-mhaith, Athair: Very well, Father.

Bí cúramach os a chionn, Athair: Please be careful over there, Father.

Beidh mé ar ais ag an am dinnéar, Máire. Geallaim: I'll be back by dinnertime, Máire. I promise.

Fáilte go Brooklyn: Welcome to Brooklyn

Dia dhuit, **Eugene!** *Bhí sé ró-fhada, mo chara!:* Hello, Eugene. It has been too long, my friend!

ABOUT THE AUTHOR

JACK BODKIN IS A RETIRED CERTIFIED PUBLIC accountant. *Briarhill to Brooklyn* is his first book.

He was born in Brooklyn in 1947, and for the first two years of his life his family lived at 325 Clinton Avenue, about a hundred yards from his great-great-uncle Dominic's home at 290 Clinton.

In 1950 the family moved to the post–World War II community of Merrick, Long Island.

After graduating from Chaminade High School and Wheeling College, he returned to Long Island in 1969 and worked in New York City until 1977. He lives in Wheeling, West Virginia, with his wife, Christine, and their Yorkie, Lilly.

Made in the USA
Middletown, DE
16 January 2022

58812145R00260